THE WARLOCK

THE SECRETS OF THE IMMORTAL NICHOLAS FLAMEL

MICHAEL SCOTT

DOUBLEDAY

THE WARLOCK
A DOUBLEDAY BOOK 978 0 857 53026 4

Published in the US by Delacorte Press,
an imprint of Random House Children's Books
a division of Random House, Inc.

First published in Great Britain by Doubleday,
an imprint of Random House Children's Books
A Random House Group Company

Delacorte Press edition published 2011
This edition published 2011

1 3 5 7 9 10 8 6 4 2

The Random House Group Limited supports the Forest Stewardship Council (FSC),
the leading international forest certification organization. All our titles that are printed on
Greenpeace-approved FSC-certified paper carry the FSC logo. Our paper procurement
policy can be found at www.randomhouse.co.uk/environment.

Mixed Sources
Product group from well-managed
forests and other controlled sources
www.fsc.org Cert no. TT-COC-2139
© 1996 Forest Stewardship Council

FSC

Set in Galliard

RANDOM HOUSE CHILDREN'S BOOKS
61–63 Uxbridge Road, London W5 5SA

www.**kids**at**random**house.co.uk
www.**totallyrandom**books.co.uk
www.**random**house.co.uk

Addresses for companies within The Random House Group Limited
can be found at: www.randomhouse.co.uk/offices.htm

THE RANDOM HOUSE GROUP Limited Reg. No. 954009

A CIP catalogue record for this book is available from the British Library.

Printed in the UK by CPI Mackays, Chatham, ME5 8TD

THE
WARLOCK

THE SECRETS of the IMMORTAL
NICHOLAS FLAMEL

www.kidsatrandomhouse.co.uk

ALSO BY MICHAEL SCOTT

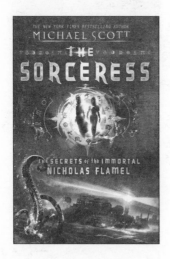

This is for Anna,
sapientia et eloquentia.

Nicholas Flamel is dying.

This is the time I have feared for so long; this is the night when I might finally become a widow.

My poor brave Nicholas. Even though he's aged, weakened and utterly exhausted, he sat with Prometheus and me and poured the last of his strength into the crystal skull so we could track Josh into the heart of San Francisco, deep into Dr. John Dee's lair.

We watched in horror as Dee turned the boy into a necromancer, a summoner of the dead, and urged him to call forth Coatlicue, the hideous Archon known as the Mother of all the Gods. We tried to warn Josh, but Dee was too strong and cut the boy off from us. And when Aoife, Niten and Sophie arrived, Josh sided with Dee and his deadly companion, Virginia Dare. I cannot help wondering if he did so voluntarily.

Watching Josh—our last hope, our final chance to defeat the Dark Elders and protect the world—leave with the enemy was too much for my husband, and he collapsed into unconsciousness. He has not awakened, and I no longer have the strength to revive him. What little power remains within me I must conserve for what is to come.

One by one, we have lost those who might have fought alongside us: Aoife is gone, trapped in a Shadowrealm, forever locked in combat with the Archon Coatlicue. Scathach and Joan are in the distant past, there has been no communication from Saint-Germain, and we have now lost contact with Palamedes and Shakespeare. Even Prometheus is so weakened now after using the skull that he no longer has the strength to hold his Shadowrealm together, and it is beginning to disintegrate around him.

Only Sophie remains, and she is completely distraught by her brother's betrayal. She is somewhere in San Francisco, I don't know where, but at least she has Niten to protect her. I must find her—there is much she needs to know.

So it comes down to me, as I have always known it would.

When I was a child, more than six hundred and eighty years ago, my grandmother introduced me to a hooded man with a hook in place of his left hand. He told me my future, and the future of the world. And then he swore me to secrecy. I have been waiting for this day my entire life.

Now that the end is almost upon us, I know what I have to do.

From the Day Booke of Nicholas Flamel, Alchemyst
Writ this day, Wednesday, 6th June, by
Perenelle Flamel, Sorceress,
in the Shadowrealm of the Elder Prometheus,
adjoining San Francisco, my adopted city

WEDNESDAY, 6th June

CHAPTER ONE

*T*he anpu appeared first, tall jackal-headed warriors with solid red eyes and saber-teeth, wearing highly polished black glass armor. They poured out of a smoking cave mouth and spread around Xibalba, some taking up positions in front of each of the nine gates that opened into the enormous cave, others sweeping through the primitive Shadowrealm, ensuring that it was empty. As always, they moved in complete silence; they were mute until the final moments before they charged into battle, and then their screams were terrifying.

Only when the anpu were satisfied that Xibalba was deserted did the couple appear.

Like the anpu, they were wearing glass and ceramic armor, though theirs was ornate rather than practical, and in a style that had last been seen in the Old Kingdom of ancient Egypt.

Minutes earlier, the couple had left an almost perfect facsimile of Danu Talis to travel across a dozen linked Shadowrealms, some remarkably similar to earth, some completely alien. And although the couple were both by nature intensely curious about the myriad worlds they ruled, they did not linger. They raced through a complex network of leygates that would lead them to the place known as the Crossroads.

There was so little time left.

Nine gates opened out into Xibalba, each one little more than a roughly carved opening in the black rock wall. Avoiding the bubbling pits of lava that spat sticky strings of molten rock across their path, the couple traversed the width of the Shadowrealm from the ninth gate to the third, the Gate of Tears. Even the anpu, which were by nature fearless, refused to approach this cave. Ancient memories rooted deep in their DNA warned them that this was the place where their race had almost been exterminated after they'd fled the world of the humani.

As the couple neared the circular cave mouth, the crude and blocky glyphs carved over the opening began to glow with a faint white light. It reflected off their mirrored armor, illuminating the interior of the cave, painting the couple in stark black and white and, in that instant—briefly—they were beautiful.

Without a backward glance, the couple stepped into the dark cave mouth . . .

. . . and less than a heartbeat later, a couple dressed identically in white jeans and T-shirts winked into existence on the circular stone known as Point Zero before Notre Dame Cathedral in Paris, France. The man took the woman's hand in his and together they set off at a brisk pace, picking their way through the debris of stones and broken statues that still littered the square where Sophie and Josh Newman had used Elemental Magic to defeat the cathedral's animated stone gargoyles.

And because this was Paris, no one looked twice at a couple wearing sunglasses at night.

CHAPTER TWO

*F*ire raged through the building. Dozens of alarms howled and shrieked and the air was filled with choking black smoke, thick with the reek of burning rubber and melting plastic.

"Out, out, now!" Dr. John Dee used the short sword in his right hand to rip apart a heavy steel and wooden door, carving through it as if it were paper. "Down the stairs," he ordered.

Virginia Dare leapt into the opening without hesitation, sparks hissing in her long dark hair.

"Follow me," Dee commanded Josh, and ducked through the shredded door. Tendrils of the doctor's yellow aura visibly streamed from his flesh, its rotten-egg stench hitting Josh Newman in the face as he hurried close behind.

Josh was feeling sick to his stomach, and not just from the foul sulfurous cloud leaking from Dee. His head was pounding and tiny dots of color pulsed before his eyes. He was dazed, still shaking after his encounter with the beautiful Archon Coatlicue. And try as he might, he still couldn't make any sense of the events of the past few minutes. He only had the vaguest idea how he'd ended up in this place. He remembered driving down country roads . . . on the freeway . . . and into the city. But he'd had no idea where he was going. All he'd known was that he was supposed to be somewhere.

Josh tried to focus on the sequence of events that had brought him to the burning building, but the more he concentrated, the hazier those events became.

And then Sophie had appeared. Foremost in Josh's mind was the terrible change that had overtaken his twin. When Sophie had stepped into the doctor's apartment moments earlier, Josh had been thrilled . . . but confused. Why was she there? How had she found him? The Flamels must have sent her, he realized. But it didn't matter; she was with him and she could help him bring Coatlicue into this world. That was the most important thing.

His happiness had been short-lived, though. It had quickly turned to fear, disgust and even anger at his sister's actions. Sophie hadn't come to help him, she'd . . . well, Josh didn't know *what* she wanted. He'd watched, stunned, as her aura hardened to a sinister-looking silver armor around her body, and then she'd callously used a whip on the beautiful and defenseless Archon. Coatlicue's agonized cries had been heartbreaking, and when she'd turned to Josh and stretched out her hand, the look of pain and betrayal in her huge eyes had been too much to bear. He was the one who'd called her from her Shadowrealm; he was responsible for her pain. And he was unable to help her.

Aoife had leapt onto Coatlicue's back and held her while Sophie beat her again and again with the terrible whip. And then Aoife dragged the wounded Archon back into her Shadowrealm. When Coatlicue disappeared, Josh had felt a moment of horrible loss. He had been close, so close to doing something remarkable. If Coatlicue had been allowed to return to this world, she would have . . . Josh swallowed a great mouthful of rubbery-tasting smoke and coughed, eyes watering. He wasn't sure what she would have done.

Two steps below, Dee turned to look back up at him, gray eyes wide and wild in the gloom. "Stay close," he snarled. He raised his chin back toward the burning room. "You see? They did what they always do! Death and destruction follow the Flamels and their minions."

Josh coughed again, struggling to get fresh air into his lungs. It wasn't the first time he'd heard the accusation. "Scathach said that."

"The Shadow's mistake was choosing the wrong side." Dee's smile was ugly. "A mistake you too almost made."

"What happened up there?" Josh asked. "It was all so fast, and Sophie—"

"This is hardly the time for explanations."

"Tell me," Josh demanded angrily, and the foul air was now touched with the odor of oranges.

Dee stopped. His aura was so bright his eyes and teeth appeared yellow. "Josh, you were moments away from changing the world forever. We were about to begin a process that would have turned this earth into a paradise. And you would have been the instrument of that change." The doctor's face transformed into a hard mask of anger. "Today the Flamels thwarted me. And do you know why? Because they—and the others like them—do not want the world to be a better place. The Flamels thrive in the shadows, they exist on the outskirts of society, living secret lives, living lies. They grow strong on the pain, the needs of others. They know that in my new world, there would be no shadows for them to hide in, no suffering for them to exploit. They do not want me—and the others like me—to succeed. You helped us to get perhaps closer than we have ever been."

Josh frowned, trying to make sense of what the doctor was saying. Was Dee lying? He had to be . . . though Josh couldn't push away the feeling that there was an element of truth in what the immortal was saying. What did that make the Flamels?

"Tell me this," Dee said. "You saw Coatlicue?"

Josh nodded. "I saw her."

"And was she beautiful?"

"Yes." He blinked, remembering. She was so beautiful, like no one he'd ever seen before.

"I too have seen her true form," Dee said softly. "She was one of the most powerful of the Archons, an ancient race, perhaps even an alien race, who ruled this world in the Time Before Time. She was a scientist using tech-nology so advanced it was indistinguishable from magic. She could manipulate pure matter." Dee eyed Josh carefully and continued slowly. "Coatlicue could have remade this world today, repaired it, restored it. But you saw what Aoife did to her?"

Josh swallowed hard. He'd watched Aoife leap onto the Archon and drag her back toward the gaping entrance to her Shadowrealm. He nodded once more.

"And you saw what your sister did to her?"

"Yes."

"Sophie whipped her—and that was no ordinary whip, either. I'll wager it was Perenelle's tool, woven from snakes pulled from the hair of Medusa. The merest touch of it is agony." Dee reached out and placed his hand on the boy's shoulder and Josh felt heat flow down his arm. "Josh, Sophie is lost to you now. She is deep under the Flamels' spell. She is their puppet, their slave. They will use her up, as they have used so many in the past."

Josh nodded for the third time. He knew there had been other twins before them, and knew also that they had not survived.

"Do you trust me, Josh Newman?" Dee suddenly demanded.

Josh looked at the Magician, opened his mouth to respond, but said nothing.

"Ah." Dee smiled. "A good answer."

"I didn't answer."

"Sometimes no answer is an answer," the immortal said. "Let me rephrase the question: do you trust me more than you trust the Flamels?"

"Yes," Josh said instantly. Of that he had no doubt.

"And what do you want?"

"To save my sister."

Dee nodded. "Of course you do," he said, unable to keep a touch of scorn from his voice. "You are humani."

"She's under a spell, isn't she? How do I break that spell?" Josh demanded.

Dee's gray eyes turned to yellow stone. "There is only one way: you have to kill whoever controls her—either Nicholas or Perenelle Flamel. Or both."

"I don't know how. . . ."

"I can teach you," Dee promised. "All you have to do is trust me."

Glass exploded deep in the building, tiny, tinkling, almost musical sounds, and then the door above them burst open with the heat and a blast of air flowed down the stairwell. A series of rattling explosions shook the building, and cracks spiderwebbed the plasterwork. The metal handrail was suddenly too hot to touch.

"What are you storing up there?" Virginia Dare yelled from the stairwell below. The immortal was outlined with a translucent green aura that lifted her fine black hair off her back and shoulders like a cloak.

"Just a few small alchemical experiments . . . ," Dee began.

A thunderous explosion dropped the trio to their knees. Bits of plaster rained down from the ceiling and a heavy smell of sewage filled the stairwell.

"And one or two big ones," he added.

"We need to get out of here. The entire building is going to collapse," Dare said. She turned and continued down the stairs, Dee and Josh close on her heels.

Josh breathed deeply. "Am I smelling burning bread?" he asked, surprised.

Dare glanced back up at Dee. "I don't even want to know what that smell is coming from."

"No, you don't," the doctor agreed.

When they reached the bottom of the stairs, Virginia flung herself against the double doors but bounced off them. They were padlocked, a thick chain woven through their handles.

"I'm sure that breaches a fire code," Dee murmured.

Virginia Dare spoke in a language that had not been used on the American continent for centuries, then quickly shifted back to English. "Could this day get any worse?" she muttered.

There was a click and then a hiss, and the sprinklers built into the ceiling spun to life, spraying water on the trio, laying an acrid-scented blanket over everything.

"I guess it could," she said. She poked her index finger into Dee's chest. "You are more like the Flamels than you care to admit, Doctor: death and destruction follow you, too."

"I'm nothing like them." Dee wrapped his hand around the padlock and squeezed. His aura flared yellow around his fingers, dripping to the floor in long sticky streamers.

"I thought you didn't want to use your aura," Dare said quickly.

"I guess it doesn't really matter who knows where I am

at this point," the doctor said, ripping the padlock down the center as if it were made of cardboard and tossing it aside.

"Now everyone knows where you are," Josh said.

"They'll come for me," Dee agreed. He pushed open the doors and stood back to allow his fellow immortal and Josh to precede him outside. Then, with a glance at the flames burning despite the sprinklers, he darted through the doors . . . straight into Josh and Dare, who had stopped just over the threshold.

"I think they might already be here," Josh muttered.

CHAPTER THREE

"Mars Ultor."

He had been imprisoned for so long now that he had lost the ability to tell whether he was dreaming or remembering. Were these images and thoughts swirling around inside his head really his, or had they been implanted by Clarent? When he recalled the past, was he remembering his own history, that of the sword, or the histories of those who had carried the sword before him? Or was it a confused mixture of all three? What was the truth?

And while there was so much Mars Ultor was unsure of, there were a few memories he clung to. Memories that were an essential part of him. These were the memories that made him.

He remembered his sons, Romulus and Remus. Those memories never left him. But no matter how hard he tried, he could not remember his wife's face.

"Mars."

He could recall certain battles in exquisite detail. He knew the name of every king and peasant he had fought, every hero he had slain and every coward who had run from him. He remembered the voyages of discovery, when he and Prometheus had traveled across the unknown world and even out into the newly created Shadowrealms.

"Lord Mars."

He had witnessed wonders and horrors. He had fought Elders and Archons, Ancients, even the scattered remnants of the legendary Earthlords themselves. In those days he had been worshipped as a hero, the savior of the humani.

"Mars. Wake up."

He did not like to wake, because that brought the pain, but worse than the pain was the realization that he was a prisoner, and would remain one until the end of time. And when he was awake, his punishment, his pain, reminded him of the times when the humani had come to fear and loathe him.

"Wake up."

"Mars . . . Mars . . . Mars . . ."

The voice—or was it voices?—was insistent, irritating and vaguely familiar.

"Wake up!"

In his prison of bone, deep in the catacombs far below Paris, the Elder opened his eyes. They were bright blue for a single instant before they burned red. "What now?" he snarled, voice echoing inside the helmet that never left his head.

Directly in front of him were what looked like a humani

couple. They were tall and slender, their deeply tanned skin stark against pristine white T-shirts, white jeans and white sneakers. The woman wore her dark hair short against her skull, whereas the man's head was smooth shaven. The couple's eyes were hidden behind matching wraparound sunglasses.

Simultaneously, they took off their glasses. Their eyes were bright, brilliant blue, the pupils tiny black dots. Even through the pain of his perpetually burning and hardening aura, Mars Ultor remembered them. These were no humani: they were Elders. "Isis?" he rasped in the ancient language of Danu Talis.

"It is good to see you, old friend," the woman said.

"Osiris?"

"We have been searching for you for a very long time," the man added. "And now we've found you."

"But look at what she has done to you," Isis breathed, obviously distressed.

The Witch of Endor had trapped Mars in this prison cell, which she had created from the skull of a creature that had never roamed the earth. But imprisoning him had not been enough for her: she had created an extra torment for her prisoner. The Witch had caused Mars's aura to continually burn, then harden on the surface of his skin, like lava bubbling from the earth's core, leaving him trapped in the skull cell and in constant agony beneath a leaden crust.

Mars Ultor laughed and the sound came out like an echoing growl. "For millennia I see no one, and now it seems I am popular again."

16

Isis and Osiris separated and moved to either side of what looked like an enormous gray statue forever frozen in the act of trying to rise. The lower half of Mars's body, from the waist down, was sunk deeply into the ground, which Dee had turned to liquid bone and then frozen solid again, trapping him. The Elder's outstretched left arm dripped stalactites of ivory, and clinging to his back were the petrified shapes of the hideous satyrs Phobos and Deimos, their jaws gaping. Behind the Elder was a long rectangular stone plinth, where he'd lain undisturbed for thousands of years. Now the thick slab was cracked in two.

"We know Dee was here," Isis said.

"Yes. He found me. I am surprised he told you where I was," Mars rasped. "We fought. He is the one who trapped me here in the ground."

"Dee told us nothing," Osiris said. He was standing behind Mars, examining in almost minute detail the statues of the satyrs. "He betrayed you. He betrayed us all."

Mars hissed in pain. "I should never have trusted him. He asked me to Awaken a boy, a Gold."

"And then he used the Gold to summon Coatlicue to this Shadowrealm," Isis whispered.

Red-black smoke curled from Mars Ultor's eyes. A spasm wracked his body and huge chunks of hardened aura fell off, only to instantly re-form. The dry air stank of burnt meat. "Coatlicue: I fought the Archon the last time she ravaged the Shadowrealms," he gasped through the pain of his burning aura. "I lost many good friends."

The woman in white nodded. "We all lost friends and

family to her. The doctor somehow discovered her location and summoned her."

"But why?" Mars rumbled. "There are not enough Elders in this earth Shadowrealm to satisfy her appetite?"

Osiris rapped on the Elder's back with his knuckle, as if testing its strength. "We believe he wanted to loose her into the Shadowrealms. We have declared Dee *utlaga* for his many failures. Now he wants revenge, and there is a danger that his vengeance will destroy all the Shadowrealms and ultimately this world. He seeks to end us all."

Isis and Osiris had walked full circle around the Elder and now stood facing him again. "But by following his stink, we were able to track him here . . . to you," Isis said.

"Free me," Mars pleaded. "Let me hunt the doctor."

The couple shook their heads in unison. "We cannot," Isis said sadly. "Zephaniah bound you using Archon lore and Earthlord spells that are unknown to us. Something Abraham taught her, no doubt."

"Then why are you here?" Mars growled. "What brings you from your island Shadowrealm?"

A shape moved in the doorway. "I asked them here."

An elderly-looking woman in a neat gray blouse and skirt stepped into the cave. She was short and round, and her blue-tinged hair was tightly permed. Overlarge black glasses covered much of her face, and she held a white cane in her right hand. Tapping her cane before her, she stepped up to the trapped Elder, stopping when the white stick struck stone.

"Who are you?" Mars demanded.

"Do you not recognize me?" Wisps of brown aura rose

from the old woman's flesh, and the air was touched with the bittersweet odor of woodsmoke.

Mars drew in a deep shuddering breath as long-forgotten memories came flooding back. "Zephaniah!"

"Husband," the Witch of Endor said very softly.

Mars's eyes flickered red to blue to red again, and smoke poured from beneath his helmet. His stone-hard skin ran with countless burning cracks and began to fall away in stinking sheets. The trapped Elder managed to inch forward before his new skin hardened once more. The Elder howled and screamed until the cave stank of his rage and fear, a fetid mixture that reeked of burnt meat and seared bone. Finally, when he was exhausted, he looked at the woman who had been his wife, the woman he had loved above all others and the woman who had bound him to this eternity of suffering. "What do you want, Zephaniah?" he asked in a ragged whisper. "Have you come to mock me?"

"Why, husband," the old woman said with a gap-toothed smile. "I have come to free you. It is time: this world needs a warlock again."

CHAPTER FOUR

$\mathcal{T}$wo San Francisco police officers stopped as the odd trio—a woman, followed by a teenage boy and then an older man—burst through a set of side doors into the ruined glass and marble foyer of the burning building.

"Anyone else in the buil—" one of the officers began, and then saw that the man facing him was holding a short sword in his hand and had a second sword shoved into his belt. Even as the officer was reaching for his gun he saw that the boy also had two short swords in his belt, one on each hip. Bizarrely, the long-haired woman was carrying what looked like a wooden flute.

"Hold it right there," the second officer ordered. "Drop those weapons." Both policemen raised their guns.

"Gentlemen, thank goodness you're here." The small gray-haired man stepped forward.

"Stay where you are."

"I am Dr. John Dee, and I am the owner of this company, Enoch Enterprises."

"Put the swords on the ground, sir."

"I don't think so. These are priceless antiques from my personal collection." The Magician took another step forward.

"Stay there! I don't know you," one of the officers said, "but I do know I don't want anyone coming close to me holding a sword. Put the weapons on the ground and then move over here. And quickly," he added, as a curl of foul smoke leaked out from between the lobby elevator's closed doors.

The last words the policemen heard came from the woman: "John, why don't you do what the officer says?" Even as she was speaking, she was bringing her wooden flute to her lips. The two men only heard a single note before they dropped to the ground, unconscious. "And stop wasting time," Virginia Dare snapped. She stepped over the bodies of the men, through a gaping hole where the main door to the building should have been and out into the street. "Let's go."

"We'll take the car." Dee started toward Telegraph Hill but paused midstride, realizing that Josh had remained behind. The boy was standing over the two unconscious police officers in the foyer. "Come on, we have no time!"

"You're just going to leave them here?" Josh asked, clearly upset.

Dee looked at Dare and then back at Josh. The two immortals nodded in unison.

Josh shook his head. "I'm not leaving them. This whole building is about to collapse on top of them."

"We don't have time for this . . . ," Dare began.

"Josh." Dee's aura crackled around his body—his anger was palpable.

"No." Josh's left hand fell onto the leather-wrapped hilt of the sword tucked into his belt. Immediately the rich citrus odor of oranges filled the ruined foyer and the stone blade pulsed with a slow steady heartbeat of dull crimson. Josh felt the shudder of heat flow up his left arm and across his shoulders and settle into the base of his neck. His fingers tightened around the familiar hilt: this was Clarent, the ancient weapon known as the Coward's Blade.

Memories gathered. . . .

Dee, in the clothing of another era, running through a burning city, clutching a handful of books.

London, 1666.

Josh's other hand dropped to the sword on his right hip. A chill seeped into his flesh and instantly he knew its name. This was Durendal, the Sword of Air, once carried by some of the finest knights the world had ever seen.

New memories flickered and blossomed. . . .

Two knights in shining silver and gold armor standing on either side of a fallen warrior, protecting him from the ravening beasts that circled in the shadows.

A raw burning rage settled into the pit of his stomach. "Carry them outside," Josh commanded. "I won't leave them here to die."

For a moment it looked as if the English doctor was about to challenge him, but then he nodded and his lips curled into

22

a smile that didn't reach his eyes. "Of course. You're right. We could not leave them, could we, Virginia?"

"I could," she said.

Dee glared at her. "Well, I could not." He shoved his sword into his belt and went back into the building. "You have a conscience, Josh," he said, bending to grab one of the officers under the arms. "Be careful of it: I've seen good men die because of their scruples."

Josh easily pulled the second officer across the marble floor and outside. "My father taught me and Sophie that we had to follow our hearts and do what we knew was right."

"He sounds like a good man." Dee grunted. He was breathless with the effort of dragging the officer across the road. They laid out both men behind their police cruiser.

"Maybe you'll meet him someday," Josh said.

"I doubt it."

Virginia Dare had climbed into the limousine that was still parked on the street. The roof of the car was now dusted with cinders and ash, glittering beneath a fine coating of broken glass. "We need to get out of here—now!"

Dee slid into the rear of the car next to Dare, and Josh pulled both swords from his belt and laid them on the floor in front of the passenger seat before climbing into the driver's seat. "Where to?" he asked.

Virginia Dare leaned forward. "Just get off the Hill first." Even as she was speaking, a plume of green-tinged smoke erupted from the roof of the building. Immediately, all three of their auras flickered—yellow, pale green and gold. "We need to get out of this city. That will have alerted everything on the West Coast of America. Everything is coming."

The morning air came alive with the sounds of approaching sirens.

"And I wasn't including the police," she added.

CHAPTER FIVE

*T*he world was ending.

A dirty white 1963 Jeep Wagoneer raced across a landscape that was rapidly losing every vestige of color. Prometheus sat in the driver's seat, huge hands locked onto the steering wheel, holding it tightly enough to crack the plastic and metal. Perenelle Flamel sat behind him, with Nicholas stretched out beside her, his head in her lap.

Prometheus's Shadowrealm was collapsing. The robin's-egg-blue sky had paled to chalk; clouds had taken on the appearance of curled tissue and faded to monochromatic smudges. In the space of a single heartbeat, the sea had stopped moving. Waves had peaked and frozen, blue-green dissolving to white before turning to cascades of gray dust, while the golden sands and polished pebbles had taken on the appearance of burnt paper and charred lumps of coal. A ghost wind scattered the ashes, spiraling them up into the air. They fell on trees and grasses already losing form and definition, turning them the color of parchment; anything that grew was fading to the yellow of brittle bone before finally dissipating into chalky gray powder.

And when all traces of color had vanished, the shades of gray started to fade, and the horizon fractured into a million sparkling dust motes that fell like a dirty snow, leaving nothing but a solid impenetrable blackness behind it.

The Wagoneer bounced along a narrow coast road, engine howling, tires spinning to find purchase on the rapidly fading roadway. The interior of the car stank of anise and the Elder's aura glowed around him, bright red and hot enough to scorch the seats and melt the roof over his head. He was desperately attempting to hold his Shadowrealm together long enough to get the car back into the earth Shadowrealm at Point Reyes. But it was a losing battle; the world he had created millennia ago was dying, returning to its Unmade state.

The events of the previous hours had exhausted Prometheus, and using the vampire-like crystal skull to help the Flamels track Josh into San Francisco had sapped his energy. He had known how dangerous the skull was—his sister, Zephaniah, had warned him about it often enough—but he'd chosen to help the Alchemyst and his wife. Prometheus had always sided with the humani.

And so he had laid his hands on the ancient object and used its powers . . . and in return the skull had drunk his memories and feasted off his aura. He was weakened now, desperately weakened, and he knew he was dangerously close to being overwhelmed by his own aura, reduced to flame and ashes. In a matter of a few hours, the Elder's once-red hair had turned snow-white, and even his brilliantly green eyes had paled.

He was close, so close to the edge of his world . . . but even as the thought was forming, an opaque gray mist abruptly enveloped the car.

Prometheus's startled reaction almost sent the car off the narrow road. For a moment he thought the dissolution of the Shadowrealm had caught up with him; then he breathed in cold air and the odor of salt and realized the mist was only the natural sea fog that regularly rolled into Point Reyes in the earth Shadowrealm. Occasionally it leaked from one world into the other. It was another sign that he was close to the edge of his Shadowrealm.

Vaguely human shapes suddenly appeared out of the fog, shadows in the gloom lining the last stretch of roadway. "My children," the Elder breathed. These were the remnants of the First People. In a distant age, in the Nameless City on the edge of the world, the Elder's blazing aura had injected a spark into inert clay and brought it to shambling life. The clay folk had become the First People: monstrous in appearance, but not monsters—unlike anything the world had ever seen. Created from mud, ill-shaped, with bald heads too large for narrow necks and blank unfinished faces with just the vaguest impressions where a mouth or eyes would normally be, they had trailed Prometheus across the Shadowrealms, inspiring myths, legends and terror in their wake. They had survived millennia. Now only a handful of the creatures remained, roaming Prometheus's Shadowrealm in search of the life and the light of auras. The sound of the car's engine had drawn them, and now, like flowers tracking the sun, their faces turned toward the rich stew of auras in the car—especially the familiar odor of aniseed, the source of their life eternal.

But without the Elder's tremendous will keeping the world and its inhabitants alive, their mud skin cracked and chunks began to break away, disintegrating to dust before hitting the ground. Watching the last of the First People dissolving into nothingness, Prometheus wept, bloodred tears leaking from the corners of his eyes. "Forgive me," he whispered in the ancient language of Danu Talis.

One of the mud creatures stepped onto the road directly behind the car and raised an unnaturally long arm in what might have been a salute or a farewell. The Elder tilted the rearview mirror to watch the figure. He had never given them names, but he knew this one by the scarred pattern across his chest. This was one of the first creatures his aura had brought to life in the desolate Earthlord city. Black nothingness blossomed behind the figure, and brown mud turned the color of salt as the creature spilled away into oblivion. "Forgive me," Prometheus begged once more, but by then the last of the First Race, the race he had brought to unnatural life, were gone, all traces of their existence wiped away.

The interior of the car blossomed with the Elder's aura,

and tiny sparking flames danced across every metal surface. His burning fingertips left deep impressions in the rearview mirror as he tilted it down to look at the two figures in the back of the car. "Scathach was right," he snarled. "She always said that death and destruction followed Nicholas Flamel."

CHAPTER SIX

"Walk—don't run," Niten commanded. Iron-hard fingers bit into Sophie's shoulder and pulled her to a halt.

She shook herself free. "We've got to—"

"We have to avoid attracting attention," the slender Japanese man said evenly. "Hide the whip under your coat."

Sophie Newman hadn't realized she was still holding Perenelle's silver and black leather whip in her right hand. Coiling it tightly, she shoved it under her left arm.

"Look around you," Niten continued. "What do you see?"

Sophie turned. They were standing at the bottom of Telegraph Hill. An oily black plume of smoke, shot through with dancing flames, rose high into the heavens. Sirens and car horns blared while all around them people struggled to look at the fire blazing through one of the elegant buildings just below Coit Tower.

"I see fire . . . smoke. . . ."

There was a dull thump from inside the building and shards of glass and pieces of masonry cascaded across the red and white Volkswagen Microbus parked outside. All the windows on the right side of the van shattered to powder. A shadow of dismay flickered over Niten's normally impassive face. "Look at the people," he said. "A warrior needs to be aware of her surroundings."

Sophie studied the faces. "Everyone is looking at the fire," she said quietly.

"Just so," Niten agreed. "And so must we, if we are to blend in. Turn and look."

"But Josh . . ."

"Josh is gone."

Sophie started to shake her head.

"Turn and look," Niten insisted. "If you are arrested, then you will be in no position to assist your brother."

The girl turned and glanced back toward the fire. Niten was right, but standing still and not chasing after her twin felt *wrong*. Every second they delayed meant that Josh was slipping further and further away from her. The image of the burning building fragmented and disappeared as her eyes filled with tears. Blinking hard, she rubbed them away with the heels of her hands, leaving sooty black streaks across her cheeks. The smell of burning rubber and the acrid tang of oil and scorched metal mingled with other noxious odors and drifted over the gathering crowd, making everyone back away. Niten and Sophie flowed with them.

Josh is gone.

31

Sophie tried to make sense of the words but it was almost impossible. He had left her. Minutes ago he had been close enough to touch, and yet when she'd tried to help him, he'd turned away from her with a look of horror and disgust on his face and followed Dee and Virginia Dare.

Josh is gone.

A feeling of absolute despair washed over her; her stomach churned and her throat ached. Her twin, her little brother, had done what he had sworn he would never do: he had left her. The tears came then, deep wracking sobs that shuddered through her body, leaving her breathless.

"You will attract attention," Niten said softly. He stepped closer to Sophie and gently rested the fingers of his left hand on her right forearm. Instantly the girl was enveloped in the spicy, woody odor of rich green tea, and a sense of calm washed over her. "I need you to be courageous, Sophie. The strong survive, but the courageous triumph."

The girl drew in a deep breath and looked into Niten's brown eyes. She was suddenly and shockingly aware that they were swimming with unshed tears. The Swordsman blinked and the blue-tinged liquid rolled down his cheeks.

"You are not the only one who lost someone you loved today," Niten continued softly. "I've known Aoife for over four hundred years. She was . . ." He paused and his face softened. "She was infuriating and outrageous, demanding, selfish and arrogant . . . and very, very dear to me." Blue-green smoke twisted from the burning building and swirled through the crowd.

Sophie watched the spectators turn away from the smoke,

coughing as it caught in their throats. Most people started to cry as the smoke and ash stung their eyes. Niten's tears went unnoticed.

"You loved her," Sophie whispered.

His head moved in the tiniest nod. "And in her fashion, she loved me, though she would never admit it." The Swordsman's fingers tightened on the girl's arm, and when he spoke, it was in the precise and elegant Japanese of his youth. "But she is not dead," he said fiercely. "Even the Archon will find it impossible to kill Aoife of the Shadows. Two centuries ago, she single-handedly fought her way through the Jigoku Shadowrealm when I was kidnapped by servants of the Shinigami, the Death God. She found me. I will find her." He paused and added, "Just as you will find and rescue your brother."

Sophie nodded. She would find Josh, and she would rescue him, no matter what. "Yes, yes I will. What do I have to do?" she asked, unaware that she had replied in perfect Japanese.

"Follow me," Niten said, and eased through the rapidly dispersing crowd, hurrying down Telegraph Hill Boulevard toward Lombard Street.

Sophie ran after him, staying as close behind as she could. She didn't want to lose him in the crowd. Niten moved effortlessly around the tourists and onlookers, not even touching them. "Where are we going?" She had to shout to be heard above the noise of the converging fire trucks and police sirens.

"To see Tsagaglalal."

"Tsagaglalal," the girl repeated, the name triggering the Witch of Endor's memories. "She Who Watches."

CHAPTER SEVEN

"*R*eserve your anger for those who deserve it," Perenelle
Flamel snapped. "This is not my husband's fault."

"He is the catalyst," Prometheus said.

"That has always been his role." Perenelle was sitting in
the backseat of the car, Nicholas stretched out beside her. She
was stroking her husband's forehead. The Alchemyst was unconscious, his skin ashen, cheeks speckled with broken veins
and purple threads. The bags beneath his eyes were bruised
purple, and each time her hand ventured over his skull, strands
of his short hair came away beneath her fingers. Nicholas was
unmoving, his breathing so shallow it was barely perceptible.
The only way the Sorceress could tell that he was still alive
was by pressing her fingertips lightly against his throat to feel
the weak pulse.

Nicholas was dying and she felt . . .

She *felt* . . .

34

Perenelle shook her head; she wasn't sure how she felt. She had met and fallen in love with this man in the middle of the fourteenth century, in Paris. They had married on the eighteenth of August in 1350, and she could probably count on the fingers of one hand the number of months they'd been apart over the following centuries. She was ten years older than Nicholas and he was not her first husband, though they had been married for a century before she'd told him she was a widow.

She'd loved him from the moment she'd met him and she loved him still, so surely she should feel more . . . surely she should be more upset . . . angry . . . saddened that he was now dying?

But she didn't.

She felt . . . *relieved*.

Unconsciously, she nodded. She was relieved that it was coming to an end.

The bookseller who had become an alchemist—almost by accident—had taught her wonders and shown her marvels. They had traveled all across this world and into the adjacent Shadowrealms. Together they had fought monsters and creatures that should not have existed outside of nightmares. And although they had made many friends—humani and immortal, some Elders and even a few Next Generation—bitter experience had taught them that they could only depend on one another. They could only fully trust one another. Perenelle's fingers gently traced the lines of her husband's cheekbones and the shape of his jaw. If he was to die now, he would die in her arms, and it was some consolation that she would not survive very much longer, because she did not think that after more than six hundred years living with him, she could bear to live without him. But he couldn't die yet—she would not allow it; she would do everything she could to keep him alive.

"I apologize," Prometheus said suddenly.

"You have nothing to apologize for," Perenelle said. "Scathach was correct: death and destruction have followed us through the centuries. People have died because of us— died saving us, protecting us, died because they knew us." Her face suddenly creased in pain. Over the years she had created a shell around herself to keep her from feeling all the death and suffering, but there were times—like now—when the shell cracked and she felt responsible for every single loss.

"But you saved many, Perenelle, so very many."

"I know that," the Sorceress agreed, her eyes on Nicholas's face. "We kept the Dark Elders at bay, we frustrated Dee and Machiavelli and the others like them for centuries." She twisted in the seat to watch the roiling nothingness race ever closer to the car. "And we are not done yet. Prometheus, you cannot allow us to die here."

"I'm driving as fast as I can." A light sheen of blood-colored sweat covered the Elder's face. "If I can only hold the world together for just a few moments longer . . ." Outside, the salty-smelling clouds thickened, wrapping the car in a damp cocoon, and Prometheus turned on the wipers, clearing the windshield. "We're nearly there," he said, and then, as they left the Shadowrealm and returned to Point Reyes, the fog lifted and the world exploded into colors so bright they were almost painful to look upon. The Elder slammed on the brakes and the heavy Wagoneer skidded to a halt on the dirt road. He turned off the engine and climbed out of the car. Standing with one arm on the roof, he turned to look back at the fog banks, watching as they swirled and shifted, paling to gossamer threads.

He had spent an eternity creating this world, shaping it. It was part of him. But now his own Shadowrealm was collapsing into nothing, and his aura was so depleted, his memories stripped and ravaged by the crystal skull, that he knew he would never be able to re-create it. There was a moment when the fog twisted away, giving him a last image of his beautiful and serene Shadowrealm. . . .

It was gone.

Prometheus climbed back into the car and swiveled around to look at Perenelle and Nicholas. "So the end is upon us? Abraham spoke of this time."

"Soon," Perenelle said, "but not yet. There is one thing more we must do."

"You have always known it would end this way," Prometheus said.

"Always," she said confidently.

The Elder sighed. "You have the Sight."

"Yes," Perenelle agreed, "but more than that. Some of this I was told about." She looked at Prometheus, her green eyes glowing in the shadows. "My poor Nicholas. He never really had a chance: his destiny was shaped the moment the one-handed man sold him the Codex. The book changed the course of his life—of both our lives—and together we changed the course of human history. When I was still a child, and before Nicholas was even born, the same man who would eventually sell him the book let me see my future and the future of the world. Not an absolute future, but a possible future, one of many possibilities. And over the years, I've watched many of those possibilities come true. The one-handed man told me what must happen—what I had to do, what my future husband would have to do—if the human race was to survive. He has been the puppeteer down through the millennia, nudging, shifting, moving us—all of us—toward this point. Even you, Prometheus."

The Elder shook his head. "I don't think so."

"Even you. Who do you think encouraged your friend Saint-Germain to steal fire from you; who do you think taught him its secrets?"

The Elder opened his mouth to speak but closed it again without saying a word.

"The hook-handed man told me he was there at the be-ginning and said that he would be there at the end." Peren-elle leaned forward. "You were there, Prometheus; you were on Danu Talis for the Final Battle. He claimed he was there—you must have seen him."

Prometheus slowly shook his huge head. "I cannot recall him." He smiled ruefully. "The crystal skull fed off my oldest and earliest recollections. I am sorry, Sorceress, but I have no memory of the hook-handed man." His smile faded, turning bitter. "But there is so much about that day that was lost or confused to me even before the skull took my memories."

"Have you no recollection of him—bright blue eyes, a silver hook replacing his left hand?"

38

Prometheus shook his head again. "I'm sorry. I remember the faces of the good friends I lost, though I no longer recall their names. I remember those who stood against me, and those whom I slew." He frowned and his voice grew soft and distant. "I remember the screams and shouts, the sounds of battle, the clash of metal, the stink of ancient magic. I remember there was fire in heaven . . . and then the world was split asunder and the sea roared in."

"He was there."

"This was the Final Battle, Sorceress. *Everyone* was there."

Perenelle sat back into the seat. "When I first met him, I was little more than a child. I asked his name. He said he was called Marethyu," she said softly.

"It is not a name. It is a title: it means Death. But it can also mean 'man,'" the Elder said, translating the ancient word.

"I thought he was an Elder. . . ."

Prometheus frowned, sudden fragments of memories catching him by surprise. His fingers tightened on the back of the seat. "Marethyu," he murmured, nodding. "Death."

"You remember him?"

He shook his head. "Shadows of memories. Marethyu was not one of us. He was neither Elder nor Next Generation, neither Archon nor Ancient. He was—and is—something more and less than all of us. I believe he is humani." Prometheus swiveled around and rested his huge hands on the steering wheel. "Where do you want to go, Sorceress?"

"Take me to Tsagaglalal."

39

CHAPTER EIGHT

"*O*h man, it stinks down here." Billy the Kid sneezed loudly. "I mean *really* stinks." He pressed the heels of his hands against his watering eyes and sneezed again.

"Actually, it's not too bad. I've smelled worse," Niccolò Machiavelli said softly.

The two men were standing in a tunnel deep beneath Alcatraz prison. Water dripped from the low ceiling and small waves lapped around their ankles. The air reeked of rotting fish and fetid seaweed, mingled with the pungent tang of bird droppings and the acid odor of bat guano. The only light came from the opening high above their heads, a startling square of blue against the blackness.

The tall elegant man in the dust-stained suit breathed deeply. "Actually, it reminds me of home."

"Home?" Billy coughed. He pulled a patterned red bandana out of the back pocket of his jeans and tied it over his nose and mouth. "Does your home usually smell like a wild animal's bathroom?"

Machiavelli's teeth flashed in a quick smile. "Well, Rome and Venice—ah, sweet Venice—in the fifteenth and sixteenth centuries were smelly . . . though not as bad as Paris in the eighteenth century or London in the middle of the nineteenth. I was there in 1858; the air was so foul it was virtually unbreathable. It was called the Great Stink."

"Can't say I'd like that," Billy said. "I like fresh air, and lots of it." He snapped his fingers and the rancid air was filled with the exotic odor of red pepper. A wispy curl of deep reddish-purple smoke wrapped around his fingertips, and then a globe of translucent red fire rose from his hands to bob at head height. It bounced and floated like a soap bubble as it was pulled by the salty sea air that whistled down the tunnel. "An Apache medicine man taught me that," Billy said proudly. "Not bad, eh?"

"Not bad at all." Machiavelli brought his hands together and the scent of Billy's aura was swept away with the stench of serpent. A blaze of stark white light lit up the tunnel in sharp relief. The red bubble popped and burst. "My master, Aten, taught me that," Machiavelli said.

Billy the Kid quickly rubbed his hands together, tendrils of his purple-red aura dripping into the water at his ankles. "Nice," he admitted, his voice muffled behind the bandana.

Machiavelli glanced sidelong at the younger man. "You look like a bandit, wearing that bandana."

"I think it suits me."

The two men, one in a ruined suit and expensive Italian shoes, the other in jeans and beat-up boots, splashed down the corridor. The white light kept pace with them, sending red-eyed rats skittering into the darkness.

"I hate rats," Billy muttered.

"They have their uses," Machiavelli said softly. "They make excellent spies."

"Spies?" Billy the Kid stopped. He sounded confused. "Spies?"

The Italian had walked on but stopped as well to look back at Billy. "Have you never looked through an animal's eyes?"

"No. I had a Navajo medicine woman tell me she could look through an eagle's eyes, but I wasn't entirely sure I believed her until she was able to tell me that thirty miles away, a lawman was putting together a posse to hunt me. She said it would take them two days to find me. And sure enough, two days later, they did."

"Projecting your will into an animal—or a human, for that matter—is fairly simple. Did your master teach you nothing?"

Billy tilted his head to one side. "Guess not." Then he added quietly, almost shyly, "Do you think you could teach me?"

The Italian immortal looked at the American in surprise. "Teach you?"

Billy shrugged uncomfortably. "Well, you've been around

for a long time. You're . . . well, you're *medieval*. That's really old."

"Thanks."

"And you Europeans have all been trained by your ancient masters. . . ."

"Your own master, Quetza . . . Quezza . . ."

"Quetzalcoatl," Billy finished.

"He is as ancient as my master. Quetaz . . . Quezta . . ."

"Call him Kukulkan."

"Kukulkan is an immensely powerful Elder. You heard him: he was on Danu Talis when it fell. He could teach you wonders. More, much, much more than I ever could."

Billy shoved his hands in the back pockets of his jeans and suddenly looked far younger than his years. "Well, to be perfectly honest, he's never really taught me anything. I saved his life and he made me immortal as a reward. And then I don't think I saw him for another fifty years or so. Anything I learned about the Elders and my own immortality, I found out for myself, discovering things here and there."

Machiavelli nodded. "My own path was not dissimilar. My master left me to my own devices for half a century. Surely your research led you to other immortals?"

"Not many, and not for a long time." Billy grinned. "I didn't even realize I was immortal until the day I fell off my horse on a trail on the Sierra Madre and rolled into a canyon. I could hear my bones breaking on the way down. I lay in the bottom of that ravine and watched this purple-red smoke rise off my skin, and I could feel my bones crunch and slot back together again. I saw my cuts heal and the skin mend, leaving not so much as a scar behind. The only evidence I had that I'd fallen down a mountainside was that my clothes were ripped to shreds."

"Your aura healed you."

"I had no name for it then." Billy held up his hand and wisps of his purple-red aura curled off his fingertips. "But once that happened, I started to see the auras around people. It got so I could tell good from bad, powerful from weak, healthy from sick, just by looking at the colors around their bodies."

"I believe all humans once had this ability."

"And then one day I was in Deadwood, South Dakota, when I saw this amazingly powerful aura—steel-gray—wrapped around a man climbing onto a train. I had no idea who he was, but I actually ran up to the train and rapped on the window. And when he looked out at me, I saw his eyes—the same gray as his aura—widen and I instantly knew that he could see the color around me. I knew then that I was not alone, that there were other immortals like me."

"Did you ever find out who the man was?"

"A century later I met him again: it was Daniel Boone."

Machiavelli nodded. "I have heard his name among the list of American immortals."

"Is my name on that list?"

"It is not," Machiavelli said.

"I'm not sure whether I should be insulted or grateful."

"There is an old Celtic saying I am particularly fond of: 'It is better to exist unknown to the law.'"

Billy nodded. "I like that!"

"However, it is a master's duty to train his servant," Machiavelli continued. "Kukulkan should have trained you."

Billy shrugged again. "Well, it's not entirely his fault. I've always had a bit of a problem with authority. Got me into trouble when I was a youngster, kept me in trouble all my life. Never really got over it. Black Hawk trained me—when he wasn't trying to kill me, that is. He taught me the little I know." Billy paused and added, "There is so much I've only heard about or read about. So much I want to see." He paused again and then said softly, "I want to see all the Shadowrealms."

"There are some you do not want to go to," Machiavelli said automatically.

"But there are many more I'd like to see."

"Some are wonderful," the Italian agreed.

"I could learn a lot from you," Billy said. "And maybe even teach you a bit in return."

"Possibly. However," Machiavelli added, "I haven't taken a student in a long time."

"Why not?"

"Trust me," Machiavelli said, "you really do not want to know. . . ." He stopped, tilting his head back, long thin nose testing the air. "Billy," he said quickly, "I will take you as a student and teach you all that I know—on one condition," he added.

"What's the condition?" Billy asked warily.

"That you keep your mouth shut for the next ten minutes."

45

Even as he was speaking, the fetid reek of dead fish and rotting seaweed rolled down the tunnel.

And a monster appeared out of the shadows.

Billy the Kid took an involuntary step backward. "Oh man, you are one ugly—"

"Billy!"

CHAPTER NINE

"The Isle of Danu Talis," Marethyu said softly, wrapping his long cloak tightly around his body. "One of the lost wonders of the world."

Scathach, Joan of Arc, Saint-Germain, Palamedes and William Shakespeare were on a hill looking down over a huge golden city-island that stretched as far as the eye could see. The city had been laid out in a circular maze, with sparkling blue waterways surrounding and weaving through it. Sunlight glinted silver on the water, reflecting blindingly off the golden buildings. Some places were almost too bright to look at.

Saint-Germain sat on the brilliant green grass and Joan lowered herself to sit beside him. "Danu Talis is no more," he said evenly. "I seem to remember reading that it sank."

"We have stepped back ten thousand years," the hooded man explained. A warm wind tugged at the hem of his cloak, pulling it back and revealing the flat metal hook that took the place of his left hand. "This is Danu Talis, just before the Fall."

"Before the Fall," Scathach whispered. The Warrior walked to a knoll and shaded her eyes with her hands. She did not want the others to see that they were bright with tears. Taking a deep breath, she tried—and failed—to keep her voice from trembling. "My parents and brother are down there?"

"Everyone is there," Marethyu said. "All the Elders are on the island—they have not yet scattered throughout the Shadowrealms. Some—like Prometheus and Zephaniah—you have encountered in your own time, but here they are still young. They will not know you, of course, because they have not yet met you. You will know your parents, Warrior, but they will not recognize you, because you have not been born to them."

"But I could see them again," Scathach whispered, bloodred tears rolling down her face.

"You could. Though there may not be time."

"Why not?" Saint-Germain asked quickly.

"Danu Talis is doomed. It could happen in a day, or two days, or maybe three. I do not know. What I do know is that it must sink soon."

"And if doesn't?" Saint-Germain asked. He brushed his long hair back off his face. "What if the island survives and thrives?"

"Then the world you know will cease to exist," Marethyu said passionately. "The island must be rent asunder and the

48

Elders spread out across the globe. The magic needed to destroy Danu Talis must poison the soil of the earth, the very air itself, the waters of the sea and the fire from the volcanoes, so that the children born to the Elders after the destruction of Danu Talis, the Next Generation, will be as different from their parents as their parents were from the Ancients who came before them." The hook-handed man turned back to Scathach. "If the island does not fall, then neither you nor your sister will ever have existed."

Scathach shook her head. "But I am here, and therefore the island must have sunk."

"In that strand of time certainly—" Marethyu began, but Shakespeare interrupted him.

"Tell me about the strands of time," the bard said.

The hook-handed man drew his cloak about him and turned to face the group. "There are many strands of time. Chronos the Elder can move back and forth through these various threads, though only as an observer. He never interferes. A single change would affect that entire strand of time and all the strands that flow from it."

"My master, Tammuz, could move through time," Palamedes said.

Marethyu nodded. "But he could only go back and see what had been. Chronos can go forward and see what might be."

Saint-Germain looked up at Marethyu. "I have dealt with that foul creature Chronos before. He is not to be trusted."

Marethyu's blue eyes crinkled as he smiled. "He has no

love for you, that is true. And let us hope you do not meet one another."

"So what makes *this* strand of time so special?" Saint-Germain asked quietly.

Marethyu turned back to look at the golden island. "Every great event creates multiple time streams, various possibilities and what-ifs." He waved his hand. "You can imagine that the destruction of this place created an extraordinary number of different time streams."

"Yes . . . and?" Saint-Germain said sharply.

"We jumped through the thirteen Shadowrealm gates to get here. Chronos sequenced them for me so that we were moving not only back through time, but across the time streams. Here, *now*, we are in the primary time stream before the world sank and the time streams split."

"But why?" Will asked. "If we do nothing, then surely the world sinks and everything goes on as it always has?"

"Ah, but the Elders, under the leadership of Osiris and Isis, have been working on a plan that will change everything. They intend to ensure that Danu Talis never sank."

Saint-Germain nodded. "I'd do the same if I were in their position, and I presume they have had millennia to perfect this plan."

"What happens if they succeed?" Joan asked.

"Then everything you know simply ceases to exist," Marethyu repeated. "Not only in this world, but in all the myriad Shadowrealms. Billions of lives, tens of billions, will be lost. But you—all of you here—have the power to prevent that."

Sitting on the low hill, gazing across the island, Joan of Arc reached out and caught her husband's hand in hers. The Comte de Saint-Germain took her hand in both of his and she squeezed his fingers tightly. Leaning over, he kissed her cheek. "Think of it as just another adventure," he whispered. "We've had so many."

"None like this," she murmured in French.

Shakespeare moved closer to Palamedes, the Saracen Knight. "I wish I were still writing," he murmured. "What a tale this would make."

"It's how this tale ends that worries me," Palamedes rumbled. "I've never wanted anything more than a quiet life. And yet I always end up in the middle of wars and battles." He shook his head.

"How old is the city?" Saint-Germain wondered aloud. He squinted down at the maze of streets and waterways. "It reminds me a little of Venice."

Marethyu shrugged. "The city is younger than the island, and the island is younger than the earth. It is said that the Great Elders raised the island in a single day by combining all the Elemental Magics. It was considered the greatest feat of magic the world had ever seen."

"Has it a library?" Shakespeare asked.

"It has, Bard. One of the most remarkable in the world. The Great Library of Danu Talis is in a vast chamber hewn out of the bedrock at the base of that pyramid. You could spend the rest of your life exploring just one shelf. And there are hundreds of miles of shelves. The island is relatively modern, but the civilization of Danu Talis is older, much, much older. The Great Elders ruled before the Elders, and there is a King List carved into the steps of the pyramid that stretches back hundreds of thousands of years. And before the Great Elders there were other races: the Archons, the Ancients and, in the very distant past, the Earthlords. One civilization building upon the ruins of the other." Marethyu pointed with his hook to a huge stepped pyramid. "That is the Pyramid of the Sun, the very heart of not only the island but the empire. The Final Battle will be won or lost there."

"And you know all that because it has already happened," Scathach said.

"In one strand of time, yes."

"And what happens in the other strands?"

Marethyu shrugged. "There are many strands, many possibilities, but we have come back to the point before those strands split apart, where our actions can shape the future."

"How do you know this to be true?" Scathach demanded.

"Because Abraham the Mage told me."

"I think we should go and see this Abra—" Scatty stopped suddenly and whirled around, eyes flaring.

The still morning air was filled with a low humming, the sound of distant bees.

"Down . . . ," Marethyu began, and then choked and staggered as a flickering blue-white electrical discharge rippled across his chest, sparking and snapping into his hook. He collapsed to the ground, pale smoke rising from his body, white sparks crawling across the runes etched into his hook.

Joan went to move to Marethyu's side, but Saint-Germain

caught her arm and held her back. He shook his head slightly. "No. Wait."

Shakespeare and Palamedes immediately moved apart, the bard taking up a position behind and to the left of his friend. If there was a battle, Will would guard his friend's back.

"Vimanas coming," Scathach snarled. She crouched but made no move to reach for the matched swords on her back. "Remain still, touch no metal."

"What are vim . . . ," Joan began; then she followed Scathach's finger. It was pointing straight up.

The warm air trembled and turned chill and suddenly three large spinning discs dropped out of the clear sky and hovered just above their heads, buzzing and vibrating gently. Everyone looked up. On the undersides of the metal discs was etched a map of Danu Talis.

"Vimanas," Scathach explained. "Flying discs. A few survived the Fall of Danu Talis and made it to the Earth Shadowrealm. My father had one . . . until Aoife crashed it. She blamed me," she added bitterly.

The largest disc—which was at least twelve feet across—dropped lower but did not settle on the ground, and a thin sheen of ice appeared on the grass beneath it. Under a crystal dome on top of the disc, two black jackal-headed creatures with solid red eyes glared out at them.

"I hate these guys," Saint-Germain muttered.

"Anpu," Scathach whispered. "I think we're in trouble. Big trouble."

CHAPTER TEN

"Turn here." Dr. John Dee leaned forward and pointed to the right. "Take the Barbary Coast Trail and continue around to the Embarcadero. Then follow the signs for the Oakland Bay Bridge."

Josh nodded, mouth clamped tightly shut, unwilling to speak and trying hard not to breathe too deeply. The Magician's breath was foul with the stink of rotten eggs.

"Where are we going?" Virginia Dare asked from the shadows.

"Away from here," Dee spat. "The streets will be swarming with police and firefighters."

Josh adjusted the mirror so that he could see into the back of the car. Dee was sitting almost directly behind him, outlined in the faintest tracery of yellow, while the young-looking woman sat on the right, as far away from the Magician as possible. She was tapping the wooden flute against her bottom lip.

Josh focused on driving, keeping the heavy car under control and within the speed limit. He tried not to think about what had just happened and, more importantly, what had happened with his sister. She'd turned against him—or rather, the Flamels had turned her against him. But where was she now . . . and how was he going to tell his parents that he had lost her? He was supposed to look after her, protect her. And he'd failed.

"What was the name of the comedian," Virginia Dare asked suddenly, "part of a double act, who said, 'Here's another nice mess you've gotten me into'?"

"Stan Laurel," Dee said.

"Oliver Hardy," Josh corrected him. His father loved Laurel and Hardy. Even though Josh preferred the anarchic humor of the Marx Brothers, one of his earliest memories was of sitting on his father's lap, feeling his entire body shake as he laughed uproariously at Laurel and Hardy's antics.

"Oliver Hardy," Virginia Dare repeated, nodding in agreement. "I met them once, a long time ago, when I first came out to Hollywood."

"Were you in movies?" Josh asked, glancing at her in the mirror. She was certainly beautiful enough.

Dare's white teeth flashed a quick smile in the gloom. "Before there was sound," she said, then turned to the English Magician. "Well, here's another nice mess you've gotten me into."

"Not now, Virginia," Dee said tiredly.

"You've gotten me in trouble before, John, but nothing like this. I knew I should never have joined with you."

"It did not take much to convince you," Dee reminded her.

"You promised me a world . . . ," she began, and then Dee's hand shot out and touched her arm, his eyes darting toward Josh. The pause in her sentence was so brief it was barely noticeable. ". . . free of all pain and suffering," she finished, unable to keep the note of sarcasm out of her voice.

Josh turned right off Bay Street onto the Embarcadero.

"All is not lost yet," Dee said. "Not while we still have this." Opening his stained and torn coat, he pulled out a small book bound in tarnished green copper. The book was about six inches across by nine inches long and was older than humanity. The doctor ran his fingers across the metal surface and yellow particles danced and crackled beneath his flesh. The air immediately turned sour as their three auras—orange, sage and sulfur—mingled. Sparks danced across every metal surface inside the car. The interior lights flashed on and off, then died, and the satellite navigation system's LCD screen bubbled with warped rainbow-colored streamers. The radio turned itself on and ran through a dozen stations before dying in a squawk of static. Every indicator on the dashboard lit up with red warning lights. The heavy car jerked and stalled.

"Close it," Josh called from the front. "It's going to destroy the electronics in the car." Dee snapped the book shut and shoved it back under his coat and Josh turned the ignition to restart the car. The engine coughed, then caught, and Josh floored the accelerator.

"Nicely done," Virginia Dare said.

"The Codex is the key," Dee continued, as if nothing had happened. "I am sure of that. All I have to do is figure out how to use it." He leaned forward and tapped Josh on the shoulder. "If only someone hadn't torn out the last two pages."

Josh kept his mouth shut. Concentrating on the drive had, curiously, allowed him to think more clearly again. Beneath his red 49ers Faithful T-shirt he was carrying the two pages he'd torn from the Codex in a cloth bag around his neck. Although he had come to trust the English Magician—or to distrust him less than Flamel, anyway—for some reason he didn't quite understand, Josh was still reluctant to let Dee know that he had the pages.

"Everything is coming," Virginia Dare said quietly. "And I mean *everything*. Those cucubuths we encountered in London are nothing compared to what's heading toward this city." She twisted in her seat to look out the rear window. A tall column of smoke was rising into the sky over San Francisco. "The humani authorities will start investigating. First your company causes chaos in Ojai and now your head office burns down." Even as she was speaking a rumbling explosion rippled through the air, sounding like distant thunder. "And this is not just any ordinary fire. I'm sure they'll discover that you were storing illegal substances in the building."

"A few chemicals I needed for my experiments," Dee said dismissively.

"*Dangerous* chemicals," Dare continued. "Also, you attacked two police officers. The authorities are going to be

57

looking very closely at you, Dr. Dee. How vulnerable are you to that type of investigation?"

Dee shrugged uncomfortably. "If they dig deep enough I'm sure they will find something. Nothing can remain truly secret in this digital age."

Virginia blew gently across the top of her flute. The sound was harsh, discordant. "The SFPD will bring in the FBI; they will talk to Scotland Yard in London, and if they link it to the recent devastation in Paris, they will get in touch with the French Sûreté. Once the police start to look for you on their surveillance cameras, they'll find you. Then they will start asking questions. I am sure they will want to know how you got from Ojai to Paris with no record of your travel, and then managed to get back to San Francisco without boarding a commercial or private jet."

"You don't have to sound quite so pleased about it," Dee muttered.

"And let us not forget the Elders. I would imagine even now, Elders, Next Generation and assorted creatures are making their way here, following the stink of magic. No doubt a phenomenal reward has been offered for you dead or alive."

"Alive," Dee said miserably, "they want me alive."

"How do you know?"

"Machiavelli told me."

"Machiavelli!" Virginia and Josh said simultaneously.

"No friend of yours, John," Virginia said, "unless you've had an extraordinary change of heart in the last few hundred years."

"Not my friend, but not exactly my enemy, either. He too has failed his Elder master." He jerked his thumb behind him. "Do you know, he's only a couple of miles away? He's on Alcatraz with Billy the Kid."

"Billy the Kid?" Josh said quickly. "*The* Billy the Kid? The outlaw?"

"Yes, yes," Dee snapped. "The immortal Billy the Kid."

"What are they doing there?" Josh asked, confused.

"Mischief," Dee said with a smile.

"How can they get onto the island? I thought it was closed to the public."

"It is," Dee said. "My company, Enoch Enterprises, owns it. We bought it from the state. We told them we were going to turn it into a living history museum."

Josh slowed as the traffic lights ahead of him turned red. "I'm guessing that was a lie," he said.

"Dr. John Dee is incapable of telling the truth," Virginia Dare muttered.

The immortal ignored her. "My masters instructed me to gather a menagerie of beasts and monsters in a secure location as close to the city as possible. The island prison was the perfect location. And it had ready-made cells to house them."

The woman sat forward. "What sort of monsters?" she asked. "The usual kind, or did you find something interesting?"

"The worst kind," Dee said. "The nightmares, the savages, the abominations."

59

"Why?"

"When the time is right, they want to release them onto the city."

"Why?" she asked again.

"To distract the humani and allow the Elders to return to this Shadowrealm. The creatures will ravage through the city, and even the most modern army, with all its weapons and firepower, will be unable to stop them. When the city is on the very edge of collapse, the Elders will appear and defeat them. The Elders will become the saviors of the humani and be worshipped again as gods."

"But why do that?" Josh asked.

"Once they come back, they can start to repair the earth."

"I know that. But why can't they just return? Why do you have to destroy the city?"

"Not the entire city . . . ," Dee began.

"You know what I mean!"

"The Elders will destroy the beasts and repair the city. It will happen in the full glare of the media and be a spectacular demonstration of their powers. Josh, remember, the Elders' powers are nothing short of miraculous. Well, they can tell people about those powers or they can simply show the humani just what they can do. And a picture is worth a thousand words."

Dare nodded. "And when is all this due to happen?"

"At the Time of Litha."

"But that's two weeks away. What are Machiavelli and the Kid doing on the island now?"

"The plan must have changed," Dee said shortly.

60

"But Machiavelli won't release the monsters into the city, will he?" Josh asked quickly. He had no difficulty imagining Dee loosing creatures into San Francisco, but he'd thought Machiavelli had a little more humanity.

"Who knows what the Italian will do?" Dee snapped. "This is a man who made plans that took decades to mature. The last I heard from him, he said he was trapped on the island—"

"Hang on a second," Josh said quickly. "If Enoch Enterprises owns Alcatraz . . ."

". . . and the police are looking into Enoch Enterprises," Virginia Dare continued, "then they will visit the island as soon as they have a warrant."

"That will end badly for them," Dee said.

Virginia Dare laughed. "Why, Dr. Dee, it seems there is no place for you to hide in San Francisco. And once the FBI become involved, your face and name will be known across America. Where will you go then? What will you do?"

"Survive," the immortal answered. "As I have always done."

Josh was driving across Green Street when he spotted a young man with a heavy-looking backpack standing under the arch of Pier 15 to his left. There was something about the way the man was holding himself—something awkward and unnatural. Josh squinted his eyes and focused—and instantly spotted the wisps of a dull green aura streaming from the figure. He watched the figure's pale face turn to follow them, and then the man raised a phone to his mouth. "We've been spotted," he said instantly.

61

The doctor pressed himself against the dark window and looked across the road. "Bogeyman," he said shortly.

Virginia Dare leaned across the seat to look out. "Actually, it's a Sack Man," she said, "and we have definitely been spotted. The Sack Men are mostly harmless, but they act as lookouts for far more dangerous creatures."

Josh could make out three more of the Sack Men standing beneath the archway of Pier 9. He was expecting them to look like . . . well, he wasn't exactly sure what he was expecting, but they looked like normal teenagers, wearing jeans, T-shirts and scuffed sneakers and carrying bulging and battered backpacks on their shoulders.

"I see them," Dee said miserably.

The Sack Men's pale faces turned to follow the car as it passed. Together they raised cell phones to their mouths. One dropped a skateboard to the pavement and pushed off after the car, weaving through the crowd.

"I'll wager they're laying a trap," Virginia said quietly.

The lights changed and Josh shot across Broadway. There was another huddled group of teenagers around Pier 5, and yet another farther down the road outside the Port of San Francisco at Pier 1. An identically dressed trio hopped onto modified bicycles, pedaled furiously across the road, dodging oncoming traffic, and set off after the car.

"I've never seen so many of them in one place. They are expensive spies; I wonder who they are reporting to."

One of the cyclists caught up with the car and kept pace with it. He looked like any other bicycle courier—a brightly colored T-shirt, helmet, black wraparound glasses—except for the bag on his back. Josh adjusted the side mirror to watch the man. "What's he got in the bag?" he asked.

Dare's laughter was bitter. "Trust me, you do not want to know."

John Dee sat back in the car as the cyclist tried to take pictures with his cell phone.

Josh tightened his grip on the steering wheel, terrified that he was going to hit the weaving cyclist and send him spinning across the street.

"They don't even care that you know they've found you," Dare said. "They must be very confident of capturing you." She pressed the flute to her lips and the air vibrated as a sound almost too high for human hearing trembled on the air.

The front and rear tires of the bicycle next to them exploded into black shreds and the cyclist shot over the handlebars, skidding across the road. The bicycle smashed into one of the palm trees lining the center island with enough force to reduce it to a twist of metal.

Virginia Dare sat back into the leather seat and laughed. "You have become the hunted, Doctor. Hunted, and with nowhere either in this realm or any other Shadowrealm to hide. What are you going to do now?"

Dr. John Dee remained silent for a long time and then he started to laugh, a low rasping wheeze that shook his entire body and left him breathless. "Why, become the hunter again."

"And whom will you hunt, Dr. Dee?"

"The Elders."

"You tried that with Coatlicue and it failed," Dare reminded him.

The back of the car turned foul with the stink of sulfur. "Do you know which is the most dangerous animal of all?" he asked suddenly.

Taken aback by the odd question, Josh shrugged and said, "A polar bear? A wolverine?"

"Rhino?" Virginia suggested.

"It's any trapped animal," Dee answered simply. "It's the one with nothing to lose."

The woman sighed. "I have an idea I'm not going to like where this is going."

"Oh, I think you will like it very much," Dee said softly. "Virginia, I promised you a world . . . but I am about to better my offer. Stand with me, fight with me, lend me your powers, and I will offer you your pick of all the Shadowrealms in existence. I will give you any one you desire."

"I believe that is what you already offered me."

"Think of it, Virginia," he said quickly, "not one world, but two or three or more. You can have your own empire. You've always wanted that, haven't you?"

Dare's eyes found Josh's in the mirror. "The stress has driven him mad," she said sadly.

"And you, Josh. Side with me, give me the power of your golden aura, and I will give you this earth, this Shadowrealm, to rule. And I swear to you that I will give you the powers to do whatever you wish with it. You—you, Josh Newman—can become the savior of this earth."

The idea was so outrageous, it almost took Josh's breath away. And yet . . . a week ago, he would have said it was ridiculous, but now . . . He could feel the pages of the Codex getting hotter and hotter against his skin, and suddenly the idea didn't seem so improbable. To rule the world. He laughed shakily. "I think Miss Dare is right: you *have* gone crazy."

"No, not crazy. Sane. For the first time in my long life I am beginning to see things clearly, so very clearly. I have been the servant all my life, a servant to queen and country, to Elders and Next Generation. I have done the bidding of men and immortals. Now it is time for me to become the master."

Josh stared straight ahead and stayed quiet. He drove past the Ferry Building. The clock tower showed eleven-thirty. Finally he broke the silence. "What are you going to do?" he asked, his stomach suddenly queasy. Even as he was asking the question, the pages of the Codex pulsed warmly against his flesh again, beating like a heart.

"I'm going to use the power of the Codex to destroy the Elders."

"Destroy them?" Josh felt his stomach lurch. "But you said we needed them."

"We needed their powers," Dee said quickly, "to repair and restore this world. But what if *we* had those powers? What if *we* could do everything they did? We would not need them. We would become like gods."

"You're talking about destroying the Elders," Virginia said quietly, eyes fixed on Dee's face.

"Yes."

"All of them?" she asked incredulously.

"All of them."

The woman laughed, delighted. "And how do you intend to do that, Doctor? They are scattered across a thousand Shadowrealms."

Dee's aura bloomed around him like yellow fungus. "Now they are. But there was a time when they were all in one place, and not as powerful as they are today."

Dare shook her head, confused. "When? Where?"

Josh suddenly knew the answer.

"Ten thousand years ago," he said very softly, "on Danu Talis."

CHAPTER ELEVEN

The one-eyed Elder walked across a metal world. He knew that there was life in this Shadowrealm, but none of it was recognizable.

Gritty black sand swirled and formed arcane patterns beneath his feet, and huge unnaturally regular boulders shook, shifted and inched toward him as he strode past. Bubbles of mercury rose to the surface of shining silver lakes, and when they burst, tiny globules bounced toward the solitary figure. There was no sky, only a distant metal roof covered in varicolored lights. There had once been an energy source in the center of the roof, but it had long since burned out.

Odin did not know who had created this metal Shadowrealm. He believed that it had once been a thriving world, and he knew it must have been important—the effort of creating it was unimaginable, beyond his limited powers. Yet now it did not even have a name.

The Elder crested a low mound of glittering black silica and turned to look back across the landscape. A series of dark undulating sand dunes punctuated by slabs of metal disappeared on the horizon. The air was still, but his long gray and black hooded cloak shifted on his back. Millennia ago, one of his human servants had slain a hideous Archon dragon beast and presented him with a cloak made from the skin of the creature. Its natural color was blue, but it changed with its surroundings, and at times of danger the scales grew rigid.

The cloak had turned hard as iron and hung heavy about his shoulders.

"Who's there?" Odin called. The metallic landscape sent his voice echoing across the sands, bouncing it off the ceiling and the irregular wedges of metallic rock. The gnarled fingers of the Elder's left hand tightened around the staff he carried, a remnant of the original Yggdrasill, which had grown in the heart of Danu Talis.

Odin brought the staff to his left eye. His right eye was covered by a faded leather patch; he had sacrificed it a long time ago to the Archon Mimer in return for eldritch knowledge, and he'd never regretted the bargain. A chunk of bloodred amber was embedded in the top of his staff, held in place by a tracery of delicate silver wires. Trapped within the amber were creatures that had become extinct even before the Earthlords lived, tiny delicate beings of crystal and bone, ceramic and chitin.

Odin gazed through the amber and allowed the merest hint of his aura to flow into the Yggdrasill staff. A wisp of gray smoke curled off the wood, and the oily-smelling metallic air was suffused with the clean sharp odor of ozone.

The world shifted, colors flowed and—for a brief instant—Odin saw the Shadowrealm as it had once been: a soaring metropolis of alloy and glass, where sentient metal shaped and reshaped the landscape, creating architecture of extraordinary beauty. The Elder's solitary eye blinked and the image faded to reveal the world as it was now . . . and the creature stalking him.

It crawled on its hands and feet. Short and squat, it looked like a woman. Long greasy black hair fell in two thick braids on either side of her head, and the flesh of her face and bare arms appeared diseased, speckled with black and white patches. Raising her head, she sniffed the air like a beast.

"I can see you," Odin said.

The creature stood, dusted herself off and staggered toward the Elder in a peculiar stiff-legged walk. She had been beautiful once, but no longer. Her features were almost canine, with two thick fangs jutting from beneath her upper lip. Her eyes, sunk deep in her skull, perpetually leaked a foul-smelling black liquid down her face. Now and then her overlong tongue would dart out to lick the ichor. For as long as he had known her, she had dressed the same way: gray leather tunic, matching leather trousers and high boots with thick stacked heels and soles.

Odin noticed that while the sand about his feet formed smooth circles and spirals, the ground beneath the creature was patterned with jagged lightning bolts. The sand seemed to be flowing toward him but away from this creature. "What do you want?" he called.

The creature's mouth moved, but it took her a moment to form words, as if she was unused to speech. "I want what you want," she mumbled. She staggered forward and almost fell on the shifting black sands.

Odin shook his head. "No."

The creature attempted to climb the mound of sand, but her knees would not bend and she fell forward. Odin knew that the same terrible curse that had robbed her of her beauty had taken the flesh and muscle off her legs, and now they were little more than bare bones, fragile, hardly able to support her weight. Crawling again, painfully slowly, she inched up the hill toward the Elder. "I want what you want," she repeated. "Justice for the death of my world. Revenge for the dead."

Odin shook his head again. "No."

The creature lay on the sand and raised her head to look up. "He destroyed our Shadowrealms. He attempted to loose Coatlicue," she said, panting. "There are others hunting him. When Isis and Osiris declared Dee *utlaga,* they offered a huge reward for him. Shadowrealms. Immortality. Incalculable wealth and knowledge to the person who brings him in alive." The creature attempted to clamber to her feet, but her stiff legs betrayed her and she fell back. "But you and I do not want to bring him back for trial and judgment. Our argument with this immortal humani is personal. He killed those we loved . . . and we will have our revenge."

Odin took pity on the creature and stretched out his staff. She caught hold of it, fingers with broken black nails wrapping around the ancient wood. Her aura flared bloodred, and for a single heartbeat Odin caught a glimpse of the woman she had once been: tall, elegant and very, very beautiful, with eyes the color of a morning sky and hair like storm clouds. Then the image faded, leaving the stunted, mottled creature before him. Odin raised her up and set her down beside him. Even with the stacked heels, she barely came to his chest.

"Isis and Osiris came to me—both of them—and offered me my beauty if I would lead them to him."

"Why did they ask you?"

"They knew I had sent the *Torbalan*—the Sack Men— after him."

"What did you tell them?"

"I said I did not exactly know where he was."

"A lie?" he asked.

"Not the whole truth," she said. "I did not want them to find him first."

"Because he would be taken for judgment."

The creature nodded. "Just so. Once they have him, he would be beyond my grasp."

"It seems we are both in search of revenge."

"I prefer to call it justice."

"Justice. What an odd word to hear coming from you." Odin put his hand under the creature's chin and tilted it up. "How are you, Hel?"

"Angry, Uncle. And you?"

"Angry," he agreed.

"I can help you," Hel said.

"How?"

The creature produced a cell phone from a pouch on her belt and turned it toward the Elder. The screen showed a photograph of a black car. Dr. John Dee's face was dimly visible through the darkened glass. "I know where Dr. Dee is right now. I can take you there."

CHAPTER TWELVE

"*I* don't want you to say anything that is going to upset my aunt," Sophie said as they drew near the corner of Sacramento Street in Pacific Heights—Aunt Agnes's house.

"I will say nothing," Niten promised.

"If I can slip inside and get a change of clothes without seeing her, then that would be great, but she's usually in the living room in the front of the house watching TV or staring out at the street," she continued. She was red-faced and a little breathless from the walk from Coit Tower. "So I'll probably have to introduce you to her. If she remembers you from yesterday, I'll say you're a friend."

"Thank you," Niten murmured, his features expressionless.

"Then, while you talk to her, I'll slip upstairs and get a change of clothes. I'll grab some things from Josh's closet for you, though they may be a little big on you."

"I would be grateful," Niten said. He brought the sleeve of his ruined black suit to his nose and sniffed cautiously. "I stink of smoke and old magic. You too, miss," he added. "You might think about taking a shower."

Sophie's cheeks bloomed red. "Are you saying I smell?"

"I'm afraid so." Closing his eyes, he tilted his head back and breathed deeply. "But that's not the only odor in the air. Tell me, what can you smell?" he asked.

Sophie drew in a deep lungful of air. "I can smell the smoke in my clothes," she said. "Salt in the air . . . car exhaust . . . ," she continued, and then stopped. "There's something else." She breathed deeply again and looked around at the gardens surrounding the homes they passed. "It's like roses."

"Not roses," Niten said.

"And it's really familiar," she said. "What is it?"

"Jasmine."

"Yes, that's it—jasmine. Why does it smell like jasmine?"

"It is the odor of ancient power. Tsagaglalal has awakened."

Unconsciously the girl shivered. Wrapping her arms around her body, she turned to look at Niten. "Who is she? *What* is she? Every time I try to access the Witch's memories, nothing will come . . . not even fragments."

"Tsagaglalal is a mystery," Niten admitted. "She is neither Elder nor Next Generation, not immortal and not entirely human, but as old as Gilgamesh the King. Aoife once told me that Tsagaglalal knows everything and has been on this Shadowrealm from the beginning, watching, waiting."

"Watching what, waiting for what?" Sophie pressed. She

74

tried again to call up the Witch's memories of Tsagaglalal. But she got nothing.

Niten shrugged. "It is impossible to tell. These are creatures who do not think like humans. Tsagaglalal and others who have been on this earth for millennia have seen entire civilizations rise and fall. So why should they care for individual human lives? We—humani—mean nothing to them."

They continued in silence down Scott Street and then Sophie breathed the air again. The smell of jasmine seemed to have grown even stronger.

"Immortality changes the way people think," Niten said suddenly, and the girl abruptly realized that he rarely instigated a conversation. "Not only about themselves, but about the world around them. I know what it is like to live for hundreds of years, I have observed the effect it has had on me . . . and I cannot help wondering what effect it must have on those who live a thousand, two thousand, ten thousand years."

"My brother and I met Gilgamesh the King in London. Nicholas said he was the oldest humani on the planet." She felt a sudden wash of emotion just remembering the King. She had never felt so sorry for anyone in her life.

Niten glanced sidelong at the girl, a rare flicker of emotion on his face. "You met the Ancient of Days? That is a rare honor. We fought together once. He was an extraordinary warrior."

"He was lost and lonely," Sophie said, her eyes filling with tears.

"Yes, that too."

"You are immortal, Niten. Do you regret it?"

Niten looked away, his face impassive.

"I'm sorry," Sophie said quickly, "I didn't mean to pry."

"There is no need to apologize. I was considering your question. It is something I think about every day of my life," he admitted with a brief sad smile. "It is true that I regret what immortality has cost me: the opportunity for family, for friends, even for a country. It has made me a loner, an outcast, a wanderer—though in truth, I was all of those before I became immortal. But that same longevity has shown me wonders," he added, and for the first time, Sophie saw the Swordsman become animated. "I have seen marvels and endured so much. The humani lifespan is not long enough to experience a fraction of what this world alone has to offer. I have visited every corner of every continent on this planet and explored Shadowrealms both terrifying and awe-inspiring. And I have learned so much. Immortality is a gift beyond imagining. If you are offered it: take it. The benefits far outweigh the disadvantages." He stopped suddenly. It was probably the longest speech Sophie had ever heard him make.

"Scathach told me that immortality was a curse."

"Immortality is what you make of it," Niten said. "A curse or a blessing—yes, it can be both. But if you are brave and curious, then there is no greater gift."

"I'll remember that if someone offers it to me," she said.

"And of course, it all depends on who is doing the offering!"

Sophie took a deep breath when she saw her aunt's white wooden house appear on the corner. What was she going to say to Aunt Agnes? First she had gone missing; now she was back, but her brother was gone. Agnes might be old, but she was no fool: she knew the twins were always together. Finding one without the other was very rare. Sophie knew she'd have to be careful. Everything she told Aunt Agnes would go straight back to their mother and father. And how was she going to begin to explain what had happened to Josh? She didn't even know where he was. The last time she'd seen him, he hadn't been the brother she'd grown up with. He'd looked like Josh, but his eyes, which had always been the mirror of hers, had looked like those of a stranger.

She swallowed hard and blinked away more tears. She would find him. She *had* to find him.

Sophie saw the white net curtains twitch as she approached the steps and knew her aunt was watching her. She glanced back at Niten and he nodded slightly. He too had seen the movement. "Whatever you say, keep it simple," he advised.

The door opened and Aunt Agnes appeared, a tiny frail figure, slight and bony, with knobby knees and swollen arthritic fingers. Her face was all angles and planes, with a sharp chin and straight cheekbones that left her eyes deeply sunk. Steel-gray hair was combed straight back off her face and held in a tight bun at the back of her head. It pulled the skin on her face taut.

"Sophie," the woman said very softly. She leaned forward and squinted short-sightedly. "And where is your brother?"

"Oh, he's coming, Auntie," Sophie said, mounting the steps to the front door. When she reached the top she leaned in and kissed her aunt on the cheek. "How have you been?"

"Waiting for you to come back to me," the old woman said, sounding tired.

Sophie felt a pang of guilt. Although the twins' aunt drove them insane, they both knew that she had a good heart. "Auntie, I would like you to meet a friend of mine. This is—"

"Miyamoto Musashi," Aunt Agnes said very quietly, a subtle change altering her voice, deepening it, making it powerful, commanding. "We meet again, Swordsman."

Sophie had stepped past her aunt into the darkened hallway, but at the woman's strange words she stopped and spun around. Her aunt had just spoken in Japanese! And she somehow knew Niten's name—his real name. Sophie hadn't even introduced him! The girl blinked: the faintest wisp of white smoke was curling off the old woman. And suddenly the smell of jasmine was very strong.

Jasmine . . .

Memories gathered.

Dark and dangerous memories: of fire and flood, of a sky the color of soot and a sea thick with wreckage.

"And where is the redoubtable Aoife of the Shadows?" Agnes continued, slipping from Japanese back into English.

Memories of a crystal tower, lashed by a boiling sea. Long ragged cracks raced across the surface of the tower, only to instantly heal again. Lightning wrapped around the tower in huge spirals. And a woman, running, running, running up an endless flight of stairs.

Sophie felt the world shift and spin about her. She reached out to touch the wall and was aware that her silver aura was beginning to sparkle on her flesh.

Jasmine . . .

Memories of a woman kneeling before a golden statue, clutching a small metal-bound book, while behind her the world shattered into glass and flame.

Niten stepped up to Agnes and bowed deeply. "Gone into a Shadowrealm with the Archon Coatlicue, mistress," he said.

"I pity the Archon," Aunt Agnes said quietly.

And Sophie suddenly remembered why the jasmine was so familiar. It was Aunt Agnes's favorite perfume. And the scent of Tsagaglalal, She Who Watches.

And then the world spun around her and turned black.

CHAPTER THIRTEEN

*O*n the wild northeast shores of Danu Talis, an impossibly tall, incredibly slender twisting glass spire rose directly out of the sea off the city of Murias. The city was ancient, but the spire predated it by millennia. When the Great Elders had created the Isle of Danu Talis by raising the seabed in an extraordinary act of Elemental creation, the glass spire and the remnants of an Earthlord city had also been wrenched up from the seafloor. Much of the ancient city was fused to enormous globes of melted glass shot through with threads of solid gold, evidence of the terrible battles the Earthlords had fought with the Archons and Great Elders in the Time Before Time.

But the crystal spire was pristine and gleaming, untouched or unaffected by the incredible heat that had melted the surrounding buildings. It occupied a rocky spur of land that became an island at every high tide. The tower of unbroken white quartzlike crystal changed color with the weather and tides, from chill gray to icy blue, to alabaster white, to an arctic green. When the high tides lashed against the smooth walls, the salt water hissed and boiled, so that the tower was perpetually wreathed in steam even though the stones themselves were cool. At night, the spire glowed with a pale phosphorescence the color of sour milk, throbbing to a slow regular rhythm like a great heart, sending pulsing streaks of color—reds and purples—up the length of the needle. During the winter months, when bitter hailstorms sleeted in from the Great Ice at the Top of the World and sheathed the city of Murias in thick snow and solid ice, the tower remained untouched.

The Elder and Great Elder inhabitants of Murias regarded the tower with a mixture of awe and terror. No strangers to wonders, they were masters of Elemental Magic, and there was little that was beyond their powers. They knew that they inhabited an old world, an ancient world, and that remnants of its primeval past still lurked in the shadows. For generations, the Great Elders and the Elders who had come after them had fought the Archons and defeated them, and had even swept away the last of the hideous Earthlords. The Elders' powers—a mixture of science fueled by auric energy—rendered them almost invulnerable. But even they feared the tower's solitary occupant. Legend had named the island the Tor Ri. In the ancient language of Danu Talis it meant "The King's Tower"—but no king lived there.

The crystal spire was the home of Abraham the Mage.

The tall redheaded warrior in shimmering crimson armor staggered through the narrow doorway and leaned forward, hands on thighs, breathing heavily. "Abraham, those stairs will be the death of me," he panted. "They seem to go on forever and always leave me breathless. One of these days I'm going to count them."

"Two hundred and forty-eight," the tall, angular man standing in the center of the room said absently. He was concentrating on a blue and white globe rotating in front of him in midair.

"I thought there were more. Always feel like I'm climbing for ages."

Abraham half turned, light from the spinning globe spilling over the right side of his face, lending his chalk-colored skin an unhealthy blue glow. "You have stepped in and out of at least a dozen Shadowrealms on the way up here, Prometheus, old friend. Why do you think I've told you never to linger on the stairs?" he added with a sly smile. "You have news for me?" Abraham the Mage turned to fully face the tall warrior.

Prometheus straightened, his warrior's discipline ensuring that when he looked at the Mage, his face was impassive. Before he could speak, the blue globe drifted down and floated directly in front of him, hanging in the air between the two men.

"What do you see, old friend?"

Prometheus blinked and focused on the ball. "The world . . . ," he began, then frowned. "But there is something wrong with it. There's too much water," he said slowly, watching the globe revolve. Realization struck home when

82

he began to make out the shapes of some of the continents. "Danu Talis is gone."

Abraham raised a metal-gloved hand and stuck his forefinger into the sphere: it burst like a bubble. "Danu Talis is gone," he agreed. "This is the world not as it will be, but as it could be."

"How soon?" Prometheus asked.

"Soon."

Prometheus found himself looking directly at Abraham the Mage. Even before he'd first met him, the Elder had heard the legends of the mysterious wandering teacher, a figure who was rumored to be neither Elder nor Archon but older than either, older even than the Earthlords. It was said that he was from the Time Before Time, but Abraham never discussed his age. Prometheus's sister, Zephaniah, had told him that the history of every race mentioned a teacher, a wise seer, who had brought knowledge and wisdom to the natives in the distant past. There were very few descriptions of the scholar . . . but many stories mentioned a figure who might have been Abraham the Mage.

The Mage's pale blond hair, gray eyes and ashen skin suggested that he was from one of the distant northlands, but he was much taller than the Northern Folk, and his features were finer, with high prominent cheekbones and slightly uptilted eyes. He also had an extra finger on each hand.

Over the last few decades, the Change had started to overtake Abraham.

Prometheus knew that there were accounts that it happened to all the Great Elders—so perhaps Abraham was of that race—but since so few of them survived and none ever appeared in public, no one knew the truth. Zephaniah had explained to him that when extreme old age overtook the Great Elders, what might have been a disease or mutation, or perhaps even a regeneration, began to work on their DNA.

The Great Elders Changed. And each Change was different.

Some of them transformed completely into monsters, sprouting fur and fangs; others became hybrid creatures, growing wings or fins on their bodies. Some shrank, while others grew monstrously tall. Many went mad.

Abraham was slowly turning into a beautiful statue. His gold aura no longer glowed over and above his skin. It had actually settled onto the surface of his flesh, coating it, turning it metallic. The left side of his face from forehead to chin and from nose to ear was a solid gold mask. Only his eye remained untouched, although the white had turned a pale saffron with threads of gold twisted through the gray iris. The upper and lower teeth on the left side of his face were solid gold, and his left hand was covered in what looked like a golden glove, though Prometheus knew it was actually his flesh.

Prometheus suddenly realized that Abraham was staring at him. A curl of a smile appeared on his thin lips. "You saw me yesterday," the Mage said gently. "I've not changed since then."

The Elder nodded, his cheeks turning the same color as his fiery hair.

The transformation was both horrible and beautiful. And

although Abraham never spoke of it, both he and Prometheus knew that it could only end one way: the Change would turn the Mage into a living statue, incapable of speech or movement, though his mind would remain alert and curious. He had never asked, but Prometheus suspected that Abraham knew exactly how much time he had left.

"Tell me the news," Abraham said.

"It's not good," Prometheus warned him. He saw the look of pain cross the fleshy part of the Mage's face but pressed on quickly. "The strangers appeared—as you said they would—on the hills south of the city. But the anpu were waiting for them. They were captured and were taken away in the vimanas. I've no idea where they are now, but I'm guessing they're in the dungeons below the imperial court."

"Then they are lost to us and we are doomed." Abraham turned away. He raised both hands and the blue-green globe once again appeared in the air. Wisps of white cloud spun around the sphere, floating over the green and brown landmasses. And in the center of the globe was the Isle of Danu Talis.

"What happens now?" Prometheus asked.

Abraham brought both hands—metal and flesh—together, enclosing the floating world. Then he squeezed. Grains of blue and white, green and brown, dribbled like sand between his fingers. He turned to the Elder, light flowing off the metallic side of his face. "Now the world ends."

CHAPTER FOURTEEN

"This is Nereus," Niccolò Machiavelli said quickly to Billy the Kid. His left hand was resting lightly on the young man's shoulder, but his fingers were locked over the nerve in the side of his neck. Every time Billy opened his mouth to say something, Machiavelli squeezed, silencing him. "Billy, this is the Old Man of the Sea, one of the most powerful of all the Elders." He released the pressure on the American immortal's neck for an instant.

"Pleased to meet you, I'm sure," Billy squawked.

The harsh white light Machiavelli had created still lit up the tunnel. It revealed a short broad man with a head of thick shoulder-length hair and a tightly curled beard. An ugly burn marred his deeply tanned forehead, and there was a smattering of similar burns across his chest and shoulders. A sleeveless jerkin of overlapping kelp leaves held together with seaweed covered his chest, and he held a spiked stone trident in his left hand. He moved forward and the white light dipped and illuminated the lower half of his body. Machiavelli felt Billy draw in a shocked breath, and once more his fingers tightened on the nerve in the American's neck to prevent him from commenting. The Old Man of the Sea was only human from the waist up; overlong octopus legs twisted and writhed beneath him.

"It is an honor to meet you," Machiavelli offered.

"And you are the immortal human the Italian." Nereus's voice was a liquid bubbling. "The one they call the King Maker."

Machiavelli bowed. "That is a title I have not heard in a long time."

"That is what your master called you," the Old Man of the Sea continued.

"My master is very generous," the immortal said smoothly.

"Your master is very dangerous. And not very pleased with you. However, that is not my concern. I have been instructed to assist you, King Maker. What do you want?"

"I was sent here to loose the creatures in the cells into San Francisco. My instructions are to start with the amphibious creatures and release them into the bay. I was told that you or your daughters would guide them toward the city."

Nereus's voice was wet and sticky. "You have the words to awaken the creatures?"

Machiavelli held up a high-resolution color photograph. "My master sent this to me. It is from the Pyramid of Unas."

Nereus nodded. Three of his legs rose into the air and waved in front of the Italian. "Let me see."

Machiavelli took a step back from the Elder's grasping tentacles.

"Do you not trust me, Immortal?" Nereus snapped.

Machiavelli turned the photograph to face the creature. "I do not want to get the images wet," he explained. "I printed this on an ink-jet printer. If it gets wet, the ink will run. And I most certainly do not want to disappoint my master any further."

"Hold it up. Let me see." Nereus leaned forward and squinted. Then, reluctantly, he reached into a pocket on his jerkin and removed a plastic Ziploc bag. Inside the bag was an eyeglasses case. Opening it, Nereus popped a pair of rimless half glasses on his nose and looked at the image again. "Old Kingdom," he muttered, then nodded. "These are the Utterances. Be careful, Italian: there is great power in them. What do you want to release first?"

Machiavelli let go of Billy and reached into his pocket for a scrap of paper. "My master also gave me instructions," he said, unfolding the page to reveal a series of dots and dashes.

"Do we have a kraken?" Billy asked quickly. "Could we unleash a kraken?" Nereus and Machiavelli turned to look at the young American immortal. "What?" he asked, looking from one to the other. He turned to Machiavelli. "What?"

The Italian's gray eyes blazed a warning.

"We do not have a kraken," Nereus said. "Besides, even if I did have a kraken, they're only about this big." He spread his thumb and forefinger roughly an inch apart.

"I thought they were bigger."

"Mariners' tales. And you know sailors are terrible liars."

"What do you have?" Machiavelli asked. "I need something dramatic. I thought we would start with something theatrical, something that will make an impact on the city, something to focus their attention."

Nereus considered for a moment and then he smiled, revealing his hideous teeth. "I do have the Lotan."

Machiavelli and Billy looked at him blankly.

"*The* Lotan," Nereus said.

The two immortals shook their heads. "I have no idea what that is," Machiavelli admitted.

"Doesn't sound scary to me," Billy said.

"It's a seven-headed sea dragon."

Machiavelli nodded. "That might work."

"It'll certainly get their attention," Billy muttered.

CHAPTER FIFTEEN

"We're being followed," Josh said.

John Dee and Virginia Dare turned in their seats to look out the rear window. Five cyclists were pedaling furiously after them, weaving smoothly in and out of the traffic on the lower deck of the Oakland Bay Bridge. Car horns blared, echoing off the metal struts and the steel upper deck. "I didn't think bicycles were allowed on the bridge," Dee said, reaching for the swords at his feet.

"Why don't you get out and tell them," Virginia Dare suggested.

"There are two motorcycles coming up fast, left and right," Josh said. At any other time he might have been frightened, but the last week had changed him. Made him strong and confident. And he could defend himself, he thought, glancing down at the stone swords on the floor beside him.

"Might be nothing . . . ," Dee began.

"They're wearing backpacks," Josh added.

"Sack Men," Dare said confidently.

Josh glanced in both side mirrors and his heart sped up. Black-helmeted motorcyclists were visible on each side. "They're right behind us."

"You concentrate on driving," Dee said. "Virginia and I will take care of this."

"Traffic is at a standstill ahead," Josh said evenly, watching brake lights flare farther down the bridge. His voice was calm, controlled.

Dee leaned forward between the seats. Then he pointed to the left. "Take the Treasure Island exit. Don't signal, just do it."

Josh turned the wheel and the heavy car squealed across two lanes of traffic. The motorcyclist on the left hit his brakes and his back tire locked, leaving a long smoking trail behind him. The bike wobbled and fell over, sending the rider tumbling to the ground. Cars screeched to a halt.

"Nicely done," Virginia said. "Been driving long?"

"Not that long"—Josh grinned—"but I've had a lot of practice over the past week." The road curved to the left, and Josh's eyes watered as he came out from beneath the shadowed lower deck of the bridge into brilliant sunshine. Then, suddenly, the expanse of San Francisco Bay and the city beyond opened up. In the distance, directly ahead of him in the middle of the bay, was the island of Alcatraz.

"Virginia. The rider's coming up on your side!" Josh called.

The woman hit the button that rolled down the electric

window. The remaining motorcyclist had drawn up alongside the speeding limo and was in the process of trying to reach into his backpack with his right hand while controlling the bike with his left. "Hi," she said. The gloomy interior of the car lit up with a warm green glow and the scent of sage filled the air. Virginia rubbed her forefinger and thumb together, and in the mirror, Josh saw a tiny ball of green energy appear. She flicked the ball at the motorcyclist.

"You missed!" Dee snapped. "Here, let me. . . ."

"Patience, Doctor, patience," Virginia said.

The rubber on the bike's front tire abruptly crumbled to black powder. Spokes collapsed, the wheel buckled and the bike careered across the road, the front forks scraping a shower of sparks from the concrete. Then the bike hit the low restraining wall on the bay side of the road and the rider was catapulted over it, disappearing without a sound.

"Subtle, as always, Virginia," Dee said.

Josh put his foot down and roared up Treasure Island Road. Traffic had stopped behind them as cars were abandoned and drivers rushed to help the motorcyclist. Josh slowed as the road dipped toward the island. He could see a small marina on the right. He caught a flicker of movement from the corner of his eye as he was passing Macalla Road and, without thinking, pushed his foot flat to the floor. The car shot forward, jerking Virginia and Dee back in their seats. "The bike riders are back," Josh said. Although his heart was racing, he wasn't afraid. He found himself automatically preparing strategies and working out escape routes. He did a quick count. "There's lots of them."

The cyclists had appeared from the side road and were pedaling furiously after the car. All eight wore mirrored cycling glasses and aerodynamic helmets that gave them a vaguely insectile appearance.

"This is getting tedious," Dee muttered. "Drive on. Turn right into the yacht club. I have an idea." He looked at Virginia. "Can you stop them?" He jerked his thumb at the cyclists.

Virginia Dare gave him a withering look. "I have stopped armies. Or have you forgotten?"

"I doubt you'll ever let me," he sighed. Then he stuck his fingers in his ears.

Rolling her window halfway down, Virginia placed her flute on the edge of the glass, took a deep breath, closed her eyes and blew gently.

The sound was appalling.

Josh felt it deep in his bones. It was like a dentist's drill . . . only worse, much worse. His teeth and cheekbones ached, and he could actually feel the sound behind his right ear. His golden aura flared protectively around his head, and for an instant his skull was encased in an archaic warrior's helmet. The noise immediately faded and Josh opened and closed his mouth, relaxing tense jaw muscles. The speed with which his armor had formed over his body had been astonishing, and he had no conscious memory of having called it up. He flexed his gloved fingers. Did that mean it was getting easier to shape and control his aura?

A seagull appeared. It flew in from the water, straight for the windshield, and for a heartbeat, Josh thought it was going to smash into the glass. At the last moment, it sailed up and over the car . . . and landed on the head of the first cyclist. The bike wobbled furiously as the cyclist attempted to brush the bird off his head.

A second and a third seagull dropped out of the sky, and suddenly the air was full of the huge white birds. They descended onto the cyclists, flapping and cawing, spattering them with their white droppings, pecking at them. The first bicyclist crashed to the ground and the second smashed into him. A third and then a fourth piled into them. The remaining cyclists skidded to a halt, threw down their bikes and backed away, waving their hands ineffectually at the screaming, circling birds.

Virginia sat back with the flute on her lap and rolled up the window. "Satisfied?" she asked Dee.

Dee took his fingers out of his ears. "Simple and effective, with a flair for the dramatic, as always."

In the rearview mirror, Josh watched the enormous flock of seagulls dart and soar over the tumbled mess of bodies and bicycles on the road. The birds pecked at the fallen riders. One grabbed a helmet and flew away with it, another ripped the saddle off a bicycle, and every rider was covered from head to foot in white bird droppings. All traffic on Treasure Island Road had come to a halt, and most of the drivers had cell phones or digital cameras in their hands, recording the extraordinary scene.

"I bet that's going up on YouTube right now," Josh muttered. "What's in those backpacks?" he asked again.

"I've already told you." Virginia smiled. "You really do not want to know!"

94

"I do, actually," Josh protested.

"Turn here," Dee commanded, pointing to the right. "Find a parking spot."

Josh swung onto Clipper Cove Way and pulled the car into an empty spot between two expensive sports cars. He put the car in park and spun around in the seat to look back at the two immortals. "Now what?"

Dee opened the door and climbed out. Then he reached back into the car to retrieve the two stone swords. He shoved both into his belt. "Let's go," he said.

Neither Josh nor Virginia moved. "I'm not moving until I know what we're doing here," Virginia spat.

The Magician put his head back into the car. "As you so rightly pointed out, we're trapped in San Francisco. And now we are also trapped on Treasure Island. There is only one road on and off the island, and we know it's being watched." He turned to look at the heaving mass of seagulls still clustered around the fallen cyclists. "We need a strategy. . . ."

"A boat," Josh said immediately.

Dee looked at him in surprise. "Yes, exactly. We'll hire a boat if we can, steal it if we have to. By the time anyone gets here, we'll be long gone."

"Gone where?" Virginia asked.

Dee rubbed his hands together gleefully. "To the last place they will look for us."

"Alcatraz," Josh said.

CHAPTER SIXTEEN

$\mathcal{I}$t had been a dream.

Nothing more than a particularly vivid dream. And what a dream it had been!

Sophie Newman lay back in her bed and stared up at the familiar ceiling. A long time ago someone—maybe her mother, who was an extraordinarily accomplished artist—had painted the ceiling a deep rich blue. Silver stars formed the constellations of Sirius and Orion, and a huge luminous half-moon took up the corner directly opposite her bed. The moon had been painted in phosphorescent paint, and its glow lulled her to sleep every night she slept at her aunt's house. Josh's room, next door, was in complete contrast: it was a pale eggshell blue with a huge golden sun in the center of the ceiling. Sophie loved nothing more than falling asleep looking up at this ceiling, tracking the patterns of the constellations. Often she would imagine herself falling *up* into the stars, and then she would dream of flying. She particularly loved those dreams.

Sophie stretched and wondered what the time was. The room was dull, which usually meant that it was just before dawn, but the air didn't feel still, the way it always did before the city came alive. Her eyes moved down from the ceiling: there was no trace of morning light on the walls. In fact, the room was gloomy, which suggested that it was early afternoon. Had she slept that late? She'd had such crazy dreams. She couldn't wait to tell Josh about them.

Sophie rolled over . . . and found Aunt Agnes and Perenelle Flamel sitting on the side of the bed, watching her. And suddenly she felt sick to her stomach: it hadn't been a dream.

"You're awake," Aunt Agnes said.

Sophie squinted at her aunt. She looked exactly the same as always, and yet the girl now knew that this was no ordinary human being.

"We were worried about you," Agnes said. "Get up, have a shower and get dressed. We'll be waiting for you in the kitchen."

"We have a lot to talk about," Perenelle Flamel added.

"Josh . . . ," Sophie began.

"I know," Perry said gently. "But we will get him back. I promise you."

Sophie sat up in bed, drew her knees to her chin and buried her head in her hands. "There was a second there when I thought it had been a dream." She drew in a deep shuddering breath. "And I was going to tell Josh and he was going to laugh at me, and then we'd try and figure out where all the different parts of the dream had come from, and then . . ." The tears came, and huge wracking sobs that spilled silver drops onto the sheets. "This isn't a dream. This is a nightmare."

Showered, dressed in fresh clean clothes and feeling slightly better, Sophie was leaving her room to make her way down to the kitchen when she heard the voices coming from her aunt's bedroom at the end of the hall.

Her aunt.

The words stopped her cold.

For as long as she could remember, the family had been visiting Aunt Agnes. The twins had their own rooms in the house, and the front bedroom was always set aside for their parents. Sophie and Josh knew Agnes wasn't really related to them by blood, though she was somehow connected to their grandmother's sister or a cousin. But they'd always called her aunt: even her mother and father called the old woman Aunt Agnes.

Who was she? *What* was she?

Sophie had seen the white of her aura, smelled the jasmine, heard her speak in Japanese to Niten and address him by his real name. Agnes was Tsagaglalal, who was not an Elder, but was older than the Next Generation. Even Zephaniah, the Witch of Endor, knew very little about her.

Memories suddenly bled into and out of her consciousness.

A shining crystal tower, lashed by huge waves that dissolved into steam when they struck it.

A golden mask.

The Codex.

As quickly as they had arrived, though, the memories faded, leaving her with more questions than answers. All she knew for certain was that the woman she had grown up believing to be her aunt Agnes was Tsagaglalal, She Who Watches. But the chilling questions remained: Who had she been watching? And why?

Sophie walked down the corridor toward Agnes's bedroom. It took her a moment to recognize the voices coming from behind the closed door. Two men speaking together, slipping easily from Japanese to English and back again: Prometheus and Niten. She was so numbed by events that she wasn't even surprised that the Master of Fire was there. Sophie knew instinctively that both men were aware that she was in the hallway. Pressing the palm of her hand flat against the white door, she was about to push, but instead she rapped gently.

"Can I come in?"

"Please do," Prometheus said softly.

Sophie pushed open the door and stepped into the room.

Although she'd been visiting this house for more than a decade, Sophie had never seen the inside of her aunt's bedroom. Both she and her brother had always been intensely curious about it. The door was always locked, and she remembered once trying to peer through the keyhole, only to discover that something had been hung on the back of the door, blocking the opening. Josh had even tried climbing the tree in the garden to peer through the windows, but a branch had snapped off beneath him. Luckily, Aunt Agnes's rosebushes had broken his fall, though he was scratched from head to foot. Agnes had said nothing as she cleaned his wounds with a foul-smelling blue liquid that stank and stung, though the twins both knew that she guessed what they'd been attempting to do. The following day new lace curtains had appeared in her windows.

Sophie had always expected that it would look like something out of the Victorian Age, filled with heavy dark furniture, an ornate large-faced clock on the mantel, the wall crowded with pictures in wooden frames, and a huge four-poster bed, complete with lacy pillows, frilly bedcovers and a hideous quilt.

She was shocked to discover that it was plain almost to the point of austerity. A single bed was positioned in the center of the white-painted room. There were no pictures, only a small rough-hewn and highly polished wooden cabinet against one wall that held a small collection of ancient artifacts Sophie assumed were gifts from her parents to Agnes: spearheads, coins, trinkets, beads and a green stone pendant in the shape of a scarab beetle. The only splash of color in the room besides the scarab was a spectacular dream catcher hung in the window over the head of the bed. Within a delicate circle of turquoise, two hexagons were set one inside the other, held in place by a tracery of gold wire. Each one was beautifully worked in black onyx and gold, and in the center of the inner hexagon was an emerald-green maze. Sophie guessed that when the sun rose in the morning, the light would illuminate the dream catcher and the white room would come alive with iridescent color.

The room was in shadow now.

Niten and Prometheus stood on either side of Agnes's narrow bed. Lying motionless on the white sheets was Nicholas Flamel.

Sophie felt her heart lurch. Her hands flew to her mouth. "He's not . . ."

Prometheus shook his huge head and the girl suddenly noticed that his red hair had turned white in the few hours since she'd last seen him. Tears magnified his green eyes, making them huge in his face. "No, he's not. Not yet."

"But soon," Niten whispered. He reached out and pressed his hand gently against the Alchemyst's forehead. "Nicholas Flamel is dying. He will not survive the day."

CHAPTER SEVENTEEN

*A*rm in arm, looking like any other ordinary couple enjoying a nighttime stroll, Isis and Osiris walked along the Quai de Montebello on the banks of the river Seine in Paris. To the left, lit up in warm golden spotlights, was their destination, the Cathedral of Notre Dame.

"Pretty," Isis said, using a language that had been ancient before the pharaohs ruled Egypt.

"Very pretty." Osiris nodded, the amber light running liquid across his shaven skull. He had taken off his black sunglasses and they were folded onto the neck of his white T-shirt. Isis still wore hers, and two miniature cathedrals were reflected in the black glass.

Although it was close to ten o'clock at night, there were still plenty of tourists milling around the famous landmark—possibly even more than normally would be. The destruction of the gargoyles earlier in the week had attracted worldwide media attention. Some reports claimed it was an act of terrorism or vandalism, others suggested it was the result of global warming and acid erosion, but most newspapers were beginning to report the story as simple stone fatigue. The gargoyles had been carved onto the building more than six hundred years previously. It was only a matter of time before some broke off.

"I like this Shadowrealm," Isis said suddenly. "It was always my favorite. It will please me to regain control of it again."

"Soon," Osiris agreed. "Everything is falling into place."

Isis squeezed her husband's hand for emphasis. "Do you remember when we made this world?"

"We?" he teased.

"Well, you, really. But I did help," she added.

"You did."

"This wasn't our first world, was it?" she asked, her perfectly smooth brow creasing in a frown as she tried to recall.

"No. Don't you remember . . . we did make a couple of . . . well, shall we call them mistakes?"

Isis nodded. "There were some trials and errors."

"Mostly errors. When Danu Talis fell, we didn't know about the poisonous wild magic in the air. It took some time before we realized that it tainted everything we had created and we should have waited a few centuries before we started to build the world." He shrugged. "But how were we to know?" He stopped, suddenly spotting the old woman with the white stick sitting on a metal bench at the edge of the pavement. She sat with her back to the cathedral, facing up the river. "How did she get here before us?" he breathed. "She was still in the catacombs with Mars Ultor when we left."

The old woman raised her left hand and, without moving her head, beckoned them over.

"How does she know we're here?" Isis whispered. "She can't see us, can she?"

"Who knows what she can do," Osiris murmured. "My lady Zephaniah," he said loudly, approaching the bench.

"Sit with me." Zephaniah, the Witch of Endor, turned the simple sentence into a command.

Isis and Osiris exchanged a quick look before parting to sit on either side of the old woman.

"Will your husband be joining us, madam?" Osiris asked, glancing around.

"He is busy at the moment. He is . . . catching up on the world," she said with a wry smile. "It has changed somewhat since he last walked this earth."

"And how is he?" Isis asked.

"Well, considering his ordeal, he is in remarkably good shape. Angry, of course. And when all of this . . ." She waved her hand vaguely in the air and the Parisian night was touched with the scent of woodsmoke. "When all of this *excitement* is over, I think that he and I will have a somewhat difficult conversation. If we survive, of course." The Witch fell silent and continued to stare straight ahead, face hidden behind her overlarge dark glasses. Both hands were resting atop her white stick, which she'd planted on the pavement directly in front of her.

"Why did you summon us?" Osiris asked slowly. "You do not speak to us for millennia; you either side with the humani or block us at every turn for centuries. And suddenly you want—no, *demand*—to see us."

"Well, this is nice," Zephaniah said, reverting to the ancient language of Danu Talis and ignoring the question. "How long has it been since we sat and chatted together?"

"We never chatted," Osiris said with a smile that showed brilliantly white teeth. "You always commanded, demanded and ordered."

"You treated us like children," Isis added, a hint of anger in her voice.

"You *were* children. Abraham was right. You were spoiled, petulant children." Zephaniah drew in a deep breath. "But I suppose I should have been . . ." She stopped, hunting for the word.

"Kinder?" Isis suggested.

"More understanding?" Osiris added.

"I was going to say firmer." She turned her face toward the woman with the short black hair. "Some things haven't changed, it seems."

"And some things have, Zephaniah," Isis said. "You've gotten old, whereas we are still young and vibrant."

"Old?" The Witch smiled. "Looks can be deceptive." For the merest instant, almost too fast to see, a transformation flickered across the Witch of Endor's entire body, her skin suddenly white, then black, yellow, green and brown. The woman sitting on the seat became tall, short, broad, incredibly thin, old, then young, then middle-aged. "I am—as I have always been—many things. Whereas you two," she added, voice hardening, "have always been upstarts."

"And you were always a tyrant who—" Isis began.

"Enough," Osiris snapped. "All of that is in the past. A long time in the past."

The Witch nodded. "A long time in the past. And what's done is done and cannot be undone." Her swollen knuckles tightened on the head of her white cane. "Except you *are* trying to undo the past."

Isis opened her mouth to speak, but Osiris shook his head.

"Don't try to deny it," Zephaniah said. "I've known about your plan for millennia." She reached up and touched the dark glasses, moving them down her nose, then turned to look at each of them in turn. The Witch of Endor had no eyes; nestled in the empty sockets were two ovals of mirrored glass. "Oh, the things I've seen," she said. "The myriad futures, the possible pasts, the incalculable presents."

"What do you want, Zephaniah?" Isis asked coldly.

Once again the Witch ignored the question. "At first I was opposed to your plan and did everything in my power to thwart it. I wanted this Shadowrealm left in peace. So I chose not to get involved when your agents fought with the Next Generation. I deliberately didn't retaliate when your people started earthquakes or raised floods because I knew that in the end, it would all balance out. You would win some battles, your enemies would win some and the old order would remain."

"As it did for millennia," Osiris said.

The Witch nodded in agreement. "Until you found Dr. John Dee."

"A wonderful agent. Cunning, knowledgeable, ambitious, curious and so very, very powerful," Isis said immediately.

"And now completely out of control. And all of those attributes—his cunning, knowledge, ambition, curiosity and power—are turned against you."

"We have taken steps to neutralize him," Isis said confidently. "He will not escape."

"He has escaped thus far," Zephaniah answered. "You should have acted the moment you learned that he intended to raise the Archon Coatlicue."

Isis started to shake her head, but Osiris said, "You are right, of course. We should have. There *was* some talk of having Machiavelli neutralize him."

"Now his actions threaten not only this world, but every Shadowrealm." Zephaniah stood up suddenly and Isis and Osiris came to their feet alongside her. "Walk with me," she said.

Folding her white cane and tucking it into her pocket, she slipped an arm through each of theirs. "Don't be frightened," she said lightly, patting Osiris's strongly muscled arm.

"You do not frighten me, old woman," Isis snapped.

"Well, I should, dearie. I really should. Walk me toward

the cathedral and let me tell you about a future I saw, a future in which Coatlicue roamed free, a future in which the Archon rampaged through the Shadowrealms, leaving nothing but cinders in her wake. A future in which we were no more. There were no more Elders, none of the Next Generation, either. And when we were all gone, she started on the humani. Oh, and both of you were amongst the first to die—and you died horribly," she added.

"And where was Dee in this future of yours?" Osiris asked.

"Safe," Zephaniah said. "He had sealed this world off from the Shadowrealms, using the Swords of Power to destroy the doorways to Xibalba. He ruled the Shadowrealm as an emperor."

"And Dare, the killer, was she by his side?" Isis asked.

"In this future, she was dead. Betrayed by Dee, fed to the Archon."

"And is this a possible future or a probable future?" Osiris asked carefully.

"Neither. Events have moved on. The strands of time have already shifted and twisted into a new pattern. Dee has a new plan, something on a much grander scale." The Witch pulled the couple to a halt. "Wait a moment."

The trio stopped before the great Gothic cathedral and Zephaniah raised her head, almost as if she could see the building. "Hmm, this is where they fought. . . ." Her face moved left and right as she sniffed the air. "You can still smell the magic."

"Vanilla," Isis said.

"Orange," Osiris added.

"And the mint of Flamel," Zephaniah murmured, "and the stink of Dee and Machiavelli."

A harassed-looking security guard was moving through the tourists who stopped to photograph the building's ruined façade, trying to direct them away from the building in case any more stone came tumbling down. He marched straight up to the odd trio, who were standing far too close to the front of the building. Just as the security guard reached him, the bald man turned and smiled and the guard visibly blanched, as if he had just seen a ghost. He stumbled away and did not look back.

"Take me back to my seat," Zephaniah commanded.

Isis and Osiris turned and walked the Witch back toward the metal bench. "You never liked Abraham the Mage, did you?" Zephaniah asked them.

"No," Isis said quickly.

Osiris took a few moments before answering. "I think we all feared him," he said eventually.

"I worked with him for a long time and I think I came to understand him better than most, but even I am not sure what he was. An Ancient, perhaps; maybe even an Archon. And certainly there was some Great Elder blood in him. Prometheus and I were with him when the Change started to overtake his body. I watched as he worked day and night, without stopping, to create the Codex." She laughed, and the sound was deeply bitter and sad. "Do you know why he created the Book?"

"As a repository of the world's knowledge?" Osiris offered.

"The book was created for a sole purpose. Abraham knew that this time would come."

"What time?" Isis asked.

"When you abandoned Dee, when you declared him *ut-laga,* you created a dangerous enemy. He intends to destroy us all."

"How?" Osiris demanded. "Dee is powerful, but not *that* powerful."

"He is now. He has the Codex. It is filled with all the knowledge in the world. And he has the Golden Twin to translate it for him. He has access to some of the oldest, deadliest magic in the world. Dee intends to go back in time and destroy the Elders on Danu Talis." She grunted a laugh. "He's going to ensure that we all died that day when the island sank."

Isis started to laugh, the sound high and pure on the night air. Tourists turned to look, smiling at the sound, but her husband remained stone-faced, eyes wide with shock. Finally Isis's laughter died away to silence. Osiris nodded. "Yes . . . yes, he could do that. And more importantly, he *would* do it."

"How do we stop him?" Isis asked.

"So at last you decide to ask me for advice?"

"Please, Zephaniah," Osiris begged.

The old woman reached over and patted Osiris's hand. "Why do you think I released my husband from his curse?" Zephaniah said carefully. "Why do you think I put him under a spell in the first place? I needed to keep him safe and well for this day."

"You knew this would happen?" Isis asked incredulously.

"I knew it *might* happen." She lowered her glasses to reveal the mirrors in her face. "I gave my eyes for this."

"Where is Mars Ultor now?" Osiris asked.

"Gone to San Francisco to kill Dr. John Dee."

CHAPTER EIGHTEEN

"This is so not like driving a car." Josh gritted his teeth and gripped the wheel as the small powerboat Dee had hired at the Treasure Island Marina hit another wave with enough force to rattle his teeth. He actually bounced off the hard vinyl seat.

"Faster, faster!" Virginia Dare urged, ignoring Josh's complaint. She was sitting in the copilot's chair beside him, her long hair streaming out behind her, speckled with water droplets. When she turned to Josh, her gray eyes bright with excitement, he was surprised—she looked so young he could almost imagine seeing her at his high school.

"No," John Dee croaked from the back of the boat. The English Magician was leaning over the stern, pale and sweating. He'd been seasick almost from the moment Josh had gingerly maneuvered the boat from the shelter of the marina and into the choppy waters of the bay. "Slower, slower," he said miserably.

Josh had to admit he found just the littlest bit of pleasure in having the upper hand. He looked at Virginia and they grinned; then Dare nodded toward the throttle. Josh nudged it forward and the two powerful outboard engines howled, churning the water to froth just beside Dee's head. They heard the Magician's strangled squawk, and when they turned to look at him again they found him glaring at them, and soaked to the skin.

"Not funny. Not funny at all. I blame you, Virginia," Dee growled.

"I thought a little splash of water would wake you up." She looked at Josh. "He has always been a terrible sailor. It was one of the reasons he missed the Spanish Armada. And he's always had a queasy stomach," she added, "which makes the scent he chose for himself all the more surprising."

"I like the smell of sulfur," Dee muttered from the back of the boat.

"Wait." Josh forgot the sick Magician for a moment. "You get to choose your aura scent?" It was the first he'd heard anything about this. He wondered if he could change his to something more dramatic. "You can pick any smell?"

"Of course. Well, except for those with gold or silver auras. They have no choice: since time immemorial, apparently, they have always smelled the same." She turned back to Dee, hair whipping around her face and gathering at the corner of her mouth as she spoke. "How did you manage to acquire this boat?"

"I asked nicely," he mumbled. "I can be very persuasive when I want to be." He twisted around to look back at the Treasure Island Marina, where an elderly man in a white baseball cap was sitting on the jetty, looking blankly into the water. Then, shaking his head, the man stood up and wandered back toward the yacht club.

"We didn't steal this boat, did we?" Josh asked, vaguely uncomfortable with the thought.

"We borrowed it." Dee smirked. "He voluntarily gave me the keys."

"You didn't use any of your aura again, did you?" Virginia said in alarm. "That would alert everything—"

"Don't take me for a fool!" Dee interrupted angrily, but then had to lean over the boat as another bout of nausea gripped him.

Virginia grinned and winked at Josh. "It's hard to sound masterful when you're throwing up, isn't it?"

"I hate you, Virginia Dare," Dee mumbled.

"I know you don't really mean that," she said lightly.

"I do," he croaked.

Virginia tapped Josh on the shoulder and pointed to the shoreline on the left. "Stay close to Treasure Island. We'll follow it all the way around to the northern tip; then we should be able to see Alcatraz across the bay."

Before Josh could answer, an enormous pier, like a wall of concrete, appeared directly in front of them and he turned the wheel to the right. He overcompensated and the boat lurched at a sharp angle, almost pitching Dee over the side. Water sloshed in and the Magician scrambled to hold on, only to slip and land sitting in a puddle of oily water.

Virginia howled with laughter.

"You forget I have no sense of humor," Dee snapped.

"But I do," Virginia said. She turned back to Josh and pointed directly ahead. "Keep right and go around the pier, then swing back to the left again and stay close to the beach. But not too close," she added. "Some rocks may have come loose from the shore. This is an artificial island, and it's always in danger of falling apart. I watched it being built in the 1930s, and back then it was higher than it is today. The entire island is slowly sinking. The next big earthquake will probably shake it to pieces."

Josh glanced at the rocky shoreline. Most of the buildings seemed to be industrial, and many looked run-down. "It looks deserted. Does anyone live here anymore?"

"Yes. As a matter of fact, I actually have some friends who live on the other side of the island."

"I didn't think you had any friends," Dee grumbled.

"Unlike you, Doctor, I am a *good* friend," Dare said without turning around, then continued, "The island was a naval base until it closed in the late nineties. After that a bunch of movies and a few TV series were shot on it."

"Why is it called Treasure Island?" Josh asked. "Was there ever any treasure?" There was a time when he'd have laughed at the idea, but right now he was prepared to believe almost anything.

Virginia's laughter was infectious, and Josh found himself

liking her more and more. "No. It was called Treasure Island after the book of the same name written by Robert Louis Stevenson. Stevenson lived in San Francisco for a year or so before he wrote the book." As they rounded the top of the island, Virginia stood to look back at it. "I'm sure it was named as a joke—here's an island built on scraps and junk called Treasure Island." She turned and pointed straight ahead to a surprisingly small speck of rock in the middle of the bay. "And there's Alcatraz. Just keep the nose pointed straight for it."

Josh grunted as the boat hit another wave. It rose and fell back with a bone-shaking bang. "It's farther away than I thought it would be. I've never been this far out from shore before. I've never even driven a boat before."

"One should always embrace new experiences," Virginia said.

"I'm a little nervous," he admitted.

"Why?" Virginia asked curiously. She sat back in the vinyl-covered chair and looked at him.

The young man suddenly felt uncomfortable under her intense scrutiny. "Well," he said eventually, "anything might happen. The boat could sink, or the engine could break down, or . . ."

"Or what?" she asked. "Do you know, in my experience, humani waste too much time worrying about things that will never happen. Yes, the boat could sink . . . but it probably will not. The engine might stall . . . but I doubt it. We could also be hit by lightning, or—"

Dr. John Dee suddenly scrambled up from the back of

the boat. "Or eaten by mermaids," he said urgently. "I just remembered. The island is surrounded by a protective ring of Nereids." He coughed in embarrassment. "And I gave them instructions not to allow anything to get within fifty feet of it."

Virginia spun around. "There are mermaids around the island?"

"The Old Man of the Sea is on Alcatraz, and he brought the wild Nereids with him," Dee said. "I need to get hold of Machiavelli! He needs to tell Nereus that we're coming." He pulled out his cell phone, but when he flipped it open, water poured from it. Without pausing, Dee pulled his phone apart, popped out the battery and wiped it on his grubby shirt.

Josh looked at Virginia. "I have no idea what he just said."

"Nereus, the Old Man of the Sea, is a particularly foul Elder," Virginia explained. "He's human-looking as far as his waist, and then he becomes octopus. He claims the lower part of the oceans as his domain. The largest of his watery Shadowrealms touches this earth around the place known as the Bermuda Triangle."

"Where all the ships disappear?" Josh asked.

"Right there. The walls between his world and this are worn thin, and occasionally ships or planes from this world slip into his, or some foul sea monster from his world slinks through into the Earth Shadowrealm. The Nereids are his daughters." Virginia smiled. "Do not allow yourself to be tempted too close to the water by their smiles or songs. They are flesh eaters."

Dee hurriedly reassembled his phone and powered it on.

Then he flung it away in disgust. "Nothing. I have no way of getting in touch with Machiavelli."

Virginia produced her wooden flute and spun it in her fingers. "I don't know why you're so worried, Doctor. I can easily lull them to sleep with—"

Before she could finish her sentence a green-skinned, green-haired, fish-tailed woman had leapt straight up out of the sea, snatched the flute from Virginia's fingers and splashed back into the water on the opposite side of the boat, leaving her empty-handed.

Virginia Dare's scream was hideous. Flinging off her smoke-stained jacket and pulling off her shoes, she launched herself over the side of the boat and disappeared beneath the waves without a trace.

"Doctor!" Josh yelled over the noise of the motor. He raised his left arm to point, and he was pleased that his fingers didn't shake too badly.

Dee hurried forward and leaned over the prow of the boat.

The sea ahead of them was dotted with women's heads, green hair spread out about them like seaweed. As one, they opened their mouths to reveal piranha-like teeth. And then they launched themselves toward the boat, dipping in and out of the water like dolphins.

"Now we're in trouble," Dee said. "Deep, deep trouble."

CHAPTER NINETEEN

Sophie Newman stood in the kitchen and looked out on the small paved patio where Perenelle Flamel and Tsagaglalal sat together. To any casual observer, they looked like two elderly ladies, one tall and thin but strong, the other short and frail, sitting under a large candy-striped umbrella drinking iced tea and nibbling chocolate chip cookies. But these were no ordinary ladies: one was almost seven hundred years old, and the other . . . well, Sophie doubted if the other was even human.

Both women turned to look at her, and although they were beneath the dark shade of the umbrella, their eyes were glowing—green and gray—giving their faces an alien appearance.

Tsagaglalal beckoned Sophie out of the house. "Come here, child. Sit with us. We have been waiting for you." She had not spoken English, but Sophie understood her and recognized the ancient language of Danu Talis. When she went to stand by the old woman, Tsagaglalal caught her hand. "Have you no kiss for your favorite auntie?" she asked, reverting to English.

Sophie jerked her hand away. She had no idea what this woman was—or even if she *was* a woman—but she was definitely no relative of hers. "You're not my aunt," she said coldly.

"Not by blood, but you are family to me. Always have been," Tsagaglalal said, almost sadly, "always will be. I have watched over you and your brother from the moment of your birth."

Sophie swallowed the sudden lump in her throat but sat down without kissing the old woman's proffered cheek. There was a glass of iced tea and chocolate chip cookies already set out on a plate for her. She picked up the tea but then noticed the slice of orange floating in the drink. The scent reminded her of Josh, and she felt her stomach lurch. She put it down untasted and pushed the plate of cookies away. A sudden wave of absolute despair washed over her. In the last week, she had lost everything, including her brother. Even the touchstones of her past—like her aunt—had disappeared. She felt lost and utterly alone.

"Are you not hungry?" Tsagaglalal asked.

"How can you even ask me that question?" Sophie's anger was palpable. "No, I'm not hungry. I'm sick to my stomach. Josh is gone—and he hates me. I saw it in his eyes."

The two women looked at one another.

Sophie rounded on Perenelle. "And Nicholas is dying upstairs. Why aren't you up there with him?"

"I will go to him when it is time," the Sorceress whispered.

Sophie shook her head and suddenly there were furious tears in her eyes. "What are you?" she demanded of Tsagaglalal. "You're not . . . you're not even human. And you," she accused Perenelle, "you're just *in*human! I hate you. All of you. I hate what you've done to Josh and me. I hate this world you've dragged us into. I hate these powers, and knowing stuff I shouldn't know, and having my thoughts invaded. . . ." Huge tears rolled down her face, but she didn't want them to see her cry. Gripping the edge of the table, she tried to push her chair back, but suddenly Tsagaglalal and Perenelle both reached out and placed their hands on hers. Sophie's aura blazed for a moment, but it fizzled and died, and the girl's vanilla odor was swamped by the scent of jasmine. Perenelle's aura had no scent.

"Stay," Perenelle said coldly, and it was not an invitation. Sophie couldn't move. It was as if she had suddenly slipped into a dream. She was awake and alert, but there was no feeling in her body.

"Listen to the Sorceress," Tsagaglalal said gently. "The fate not only of this world but of all worlds now hangs in the balance, and both you and your brother have the power to tip it one way or another. All the time lines have converged, as was prophesied ten thousand years ago. Circumstances have conspired to confirm that you are indeed the twins of legend." Her gray eyes filled with tears. "I wish it were otherwise, for your sakes. This is a hard road you must follow. Josh is with Dee, and this too, believe it or not, was foretold millennia ago. What was not foreseen—what could not be foretold—was Dee's insanity and what he proposes to do."

"Sophie," Perenelle Flamel said quietly, "you have to believe me when I tell you that I wish none of this had happened to you or Josh. Do you believe that?"

Sophie wasn't sure what to believe anymore. She wanted to trust the Sorceress, and yet . . . something prevented her. The woman had lied to her, but the Flamels had been living a lie for centuries. Sophie guessed that they lied only to protect themselves and those around them. Still, Josh hadn't wanted to trust the Flamels. Maybe he'd been right. Maybe going with Dee had been the correct decision. The sudden thought chilled her: what if she was on the wrong side in this age-old battle?

The truth—the cold, bitter truth—was that she simply did not know. Right and wrong, good and bad, had become twisted and confused. She couldn't even distinguish friends from enemies anymore.

Tsagaglalal and Perenelle lifted their hands off Sophie's at the same time, and the feeling flowed back into her body. Her silver aura flared and crackled protectively around her, steaming in the early-afternoon sunlight. She drew in a great heaving breath but made no move to leave the table.

"Sophie, what will you do to help Josh, to save him, to bring him back?" Tsagaglalal asked.

"Anything. Everything."

Perenelle leaned forward to place both forearms on the table. Her hands were tightly locked together, knuckles white with tension. "And Sophie, what do you think I will do to help my husband?"

"Anything," Sophie said again. "Everything."

"We will do anything—everything—to help those we love. That is what separates the humani from the Next Generation or the Elders or those who came before them. That is what makes us human. That is why the race thrives; it is why the race will always survive."

"But that type of love requires sacrifice," Tsagaglalal said slowly. "Sometimes extraordinary sacrifices . . ." The old woman's gray eyes suddenly swam with huge tears.

And Sophie had a flickering memory of a woman—younger, so much younger, but with the same high cheekbones and gray eyes of Tsagaglalal—turning away from a tall golden statue. The woman stopped and looked back, and Sophie discovered that the statue's bright gray eyes were alive and were following the woman. Then Tsagaglalal turned and raced down endless glass stairs. She was clutching a book in both hands: the Codex. And her tears dripped onto the metal surface.

"Sophie," Perenelle continued, "more than ten thousand years ago, Abraham the Mage foresaw all this, and he began to put in place a plan to help save the world. You and your twin were chosen for these roles long before you were born. You were spoken about in a prophecy that predates the Fall of Danu Talis and the Flood."

"'The two that are one, the one that is all. One to save the world, one to destroy it,'" Tsagaglalal quoted. "This is your destiny. And no one can escape their destiny."

"My father says that all the time."

"Your father is correct."

"Are you saying that my brother and I are just puppets?" Sophie began, but her mouth was dry and she took a long swallow of the cold drink in front of her. "We don't have free will?"

"Of course you do," Perenelle said. "Josh made a choice, and all choices are made out of love or hate. He decided to go with Dee—not because he liked him, but because, when he saw you attack the Archon, he hated you. He saw Coatlicue as a beautiful young woman and not as the hideous creature that she really is. And you . . . well, now you need to decide what you are going to do."

Perenelle's words stung. *Josh hated her.* And yet Sophie knew it was true. She'd seen it in his eyes. But it didn't matter what he thought of her—it didn't change what she knew in her own heart and how she felt about him. "I'm going after Josh."

"Even though he abandoned you?" Tsagaglalal asked gently.

"You said that all choices are made out of love or hate. He's my brother. I'm going after him. That's my choice."

"And where will you go?" Perenelle asked.

Sophie looked at her blankly. She had no idea. "I'll find him," she said with a confidence she didn't feel. "When . . . when he's in trouble, or pain, I can usually feel it. Sometimes I even get flashes of what he's seeing."

124

"Can you feel him now?" Tsagaglalal asked, clearly curious.

Sophie shook her head. "But I have the Witch of Endor's knowledge within me. Maybe I can draw on that."

"I doubt the Witch foresaw this latest turn of events," Tsagaglalal said. "I have known her throughout my long life, and while she was able to determine the grand sweeps of history, the movements of individuals always escaped her. Unlike her brother, Prometheus, or her husband, Mars Ultor, she never really understood the humani."

"You could make another choice," Perenelle said quietly. "You could choose to help us save the world. We need you," she added urgently. "Right now, Machiavelli is on Alcatraz. We know he intends to release monstrous creatures into San Francisco. How do you think a modern city like this will react when the air fills with dragons and nightmares crawl up out of the sewers and down the streets?"

Sophie shook her head. The very idea was incomprehensible.

"How many will die?" Perenelle continued. "How many will be injured? How many more will be utterly traumatized by the experience?"

Numb with shock, Sophie shook her head again.

"And if you knew someone who could help—someone who had the power to fight these monsters—would you want them to stand and fight and protect tens of thousands, or would you want them to run away to help one person?"

Sophie was about to reply, when she realized she'd been cleverly maneuvered into a trap.

"We need you to fight with us, Sophie," Tsagaglalal continued. "You remember Hekate, the Goddess with Three Faces?"

"Who lived in the Yggdrasill and Awakened me. How could I forget?" she said sarcastically.

"She was immeasurably powerful: maiden in the morning, matron in the afternoon and ancient in the evening. She represented the entire scope of woman's knowledge and power." Tsagaglalal leaned forward, her lined face inches from Sophie's. "You are the maiden, Perenelle is the matron and I am the ancient crone. Together we have extraordinary knowledge and remarkable power. Together the three of us can stand and defend this city."

"Will you stand with us, Sophie Newman?" Perenelle Flamel asked.

A window above their heads suddenly opened and Niten appeared. He did not speak a word, but the look on his face was enough.

"It is time to decide," Perenelle said. "Time to choose a side."

Sophie stood and watched the Sorceress help Tsagaglalal out of her seat and into the house. She wanted to run through the house and out into the street . . . and then what? Where would she go? She wanted to find Josh. But she had no idea how she was going to do that. And what would happen when the creatures invaded the city? Her aura and the Elemental Magics she'd learned would protect her . . . but who would protect everyone else?

It was indeed time to choose a side.

But which side?

In the distance a ship's horn sounded, and it made Sophie think of Alcatraz. There were beasts on the island—creatures of nightmare. And Perenelle was right: if they were released on the city, there would be death and massive destruction . . . and no right-thinking person wanted that. No right-thinking person would deliberately bring that sort of chaos to a city.

But that was what Machiavelli, Dee and Dare—and Josh—were about to do.

Unconsciously, Sophie nodded, and suddenly the choice became very simple. She could work with the Sorceress and Tsagaglalal to prevent that from happening. Afterward, she would go in search of her brother.

The girl followed the two older women back into the house, through the kitchen and up the stairs.

Prometheus was waiting for them at the bedroom door. He stood back and allowed them to file into the room and gather around the bed holding Nicholas Flamel. The Alchemyst looked shrunken and frail, his skin the same color as the white sheets. Only the tiniest movement in his chest indicated that he was still breathing. "His time has come," Prometheus whispered.

And Perenelle buried her face in her hands and wept.

CHAPTER TWENTY

"Flying saucers?" William Shakespeare asked. He pushed his glasses up onto his nose and grinned delightedly. "Flying saucers." He nudged Palamedes with his elbow. "I told you they were real. I told you there were more things in—"

"Vimanas," Scathach corrected. "The legendary flying ships of Danu Talis." Tilting her head back and shielding her eyes, she watched as another six spinning silver craft swept out of the clear blue sky to hover in the air above them. Four of the craft descended to settle just above the ground, bobbing gently, like boats on the surface of a river. There was the faintest trembling in the air, and the grass beneath the vehicles developed a thin sheen of ice.

The glass domes on top of each vimana opened and the anpu appeared. Tall and muscular, dressed in black armor etched with silver and gold threads and armed with curved metal sickle-swords—the lethal kopesh—the jackal-headed warriors took Marethyu first. The hooded man had not regained consciousness and remained on the ground, continuing to twitch and shake as blue-white sparks crackled off his hook and arced into the green grass. Three of the anpu bundled him into the largest of the ships, which instantly hummed away.

Scathach turned to track its progress across the mazelike city, the silver disc reflected in the canals while simultaneously casting shadows across the streets below. She saw it fly over the huge pyramid at the heart of the city and then dip down to settle into the courtyard of a vast glittering silver and gold palace spread out behind it.

Scathach turned back to the gathered anpu. She'd encountered the anpu in a score of Shadowrealms, and though she had never fought them, she knew their fearsome reputation. They were deadly warriors . . . but the Shadow was deadlier. The Warrior readied herself to fight. Rubbing the palms of her hands against her legs, she twisted her head from side to side, working the stiffness from her neck. The anpu had made a cardinal mistake: they had not disarmed their enemy yet. Scathach still had her swords, knives and nunchaku. Lifetimes of combat had honed her fighting instincts: she would take the nearest anpu first, using her weapon to sweep its legs out from under it. She'd catch it as it fell and spin its body into those of its two companions, taking them down. The distraction would be enough for Joan and Palamedes to join in, at which point she'd toss swords to Saint-Germain and Shakespeare. It would all be over in a matter of minutes. Then they'd commandeer a vimana and . . .

Scathach caught Palamedes looking over at her. "It would be a mistake," the knight murmured in the ancient language of his homeland. He turned away and shielded his eyes, looking at the city as he continued to speak to her. "There is none better than you, Warrior, but the anpu will not fall so easily. There will be casualties. Saint-Germain perhaps, Joan possibly, Will certainly. These are unacceptable losses. Besides, if the anpu's masters had wanted us dead, they could have killed us from the sky."

Scathach's vampire teeth bit into her lip. Palamedes was correct. If even one of them was killed or injured, then the price of escape was too high. The Warrior's head had moved almost imperceptibly, but she knew the Saracen Knight had seen her. "There will be another time," she said.

"Always," he agreed.

The anpu moved among them, collecting their weapons, and then divided them into groups. The bulky Palamedes was pushed toward one craft, while the smaller Saint-Germain and Shakespeare were urged toward a second. Scathach and Joan were escorted to a silver vimana by three heavily armed anpu. Scathach climbed aboard first, the craft dipping slightly with her weight. The interior of the craft was practically bare, empty except for four long narrow seats that were designed for canine anatomy. One of the anpu, shorter and broader than the others, with the faintest tracery of white scars across its snout, wordlessly pointed at the seats, then gestured at the two women. Scathach tried sitting but almost slid off the seat before she discovered that lying down was more comfortable.

Joan followed her example, and the anpu fixed three metal bands around each of them, locking them down.

"How much trouble are we in?" Joan asked lightly in French.

The scarred anpu glared at her, its long canine mouth opening to reveal a maw of teeth. It pressed a claw to its lips to signal silence. Joan ignored it.

"On a scale of one to ten," Scathach said, "we're heading toward twelve."

The scarred anpu leaned over the Warrior, huge black eyes locked on hers. Ropey saliva dripped off its teeth.

"Do they not talk?" Joan asked.

"Only when they charge into battle," Scatty said. "And then their screams are bone-chilling. It often shocks their prey motionless."

"What are they?"

"I believe they are kin in some way to the Torc clans. Another Elder experiment gone wrong."

Finally, after realizing that the women were not going to obey, the scarred anpu swung away in disgust.

"Are they friend or foe?" the Frenchwoman asked.

"Hard to say," Scathach admitted. "Even I don't know who's who anymore." She was looking straight up through the opening of the roof at the blue sky. The vimana dipped as the two large anpu warriors climbed inside, and then a glass dome slid over the top, sealing off all outside sound. Scathach noticed that the dome was speckled and smeared with crushed flies.

131

"They knew who Marethyu was, though," Joan said.

"It seems everyone but us knows who he is. And it's clear he is the puppet master behind all this. I really hate the idea that we have all been manipulated," Scatty said grimly. "I promise you that the hook-handed man and I will meet again. And then I'll ask him some hard questions."

There was a sensation deep in their bones, a quivering vibration, and then it was as if they fell upward into the white wispy clouds. The craft dipped, the clouds spun and then darted by—the only indication that they were moving.

"And what if Marethyu chooses not to answer you?" Joan asked quietly. "You will note that our doggy friends were careful to render him unconscious from a distance. Obviously they fear him and his powers."

"He'll answer me," Scathach said confidently. "I can be very persuasive."

"I know you can." Joan of Arc closed her eyes and drew in a deep breath. She laughed quietly, ignoring the anpu's glares. "I was just thinking: we've not had a real adventure in such a long time." She sighed. "It'll be just like the old days."

Scathach grunted a laugh. She was sure that this would be like no other adventure. She and Joan had fought—either singly or together—to save kingdoms and even empires, to restore princes and prevent wars, but now the stakes were so much higher. If they believed Marethyu, then they were fighting for the future of not only the human race, but all the races in all the various and myriad Shadowrealms.

Joan squirmed on the seat, trying to get comfortable.

"When Francis and I were in India last year, we saw pictures of these flying craft in ancient manuscripts and carved into temples. Francis told me that there were many stories of flying ships in the ancient Indian epics."

"It's true," Scathach said. "And they also turn up in Babylonian and Egyptian legends. The handful of vimanas that were not on Danu Talis when it sank escaped the destruction. My parents had one," she continued, "though it was nothing like this. By the time I was old enough to fly it, our machine was incredibly old and had been repaired and patched so often it no longer resembled its original state. It could barely get off the ground." She shook her head, smiling at the memory. "My father once told me that he had watched the skies darken with fighting vimanas when the fleet went to fight the last of the Earthlords. . . ."

Scathach's voice trailed away. She rarely spoke of her parents, and never voluntarily. She considered herself a loner, and she had been an outcast for such a long time. But she had family—a sister in the Earth Shadowrealm she never saw, and her parents and brother lived in a distant Shadowrealm that was modeled after the lost world of Danu Talis. Now she had gone back ten thousand years, and it was odd to think that—at this very moment—her parents were alive and living in the city directly below her. The thought struck her an almost physical blow that took her breath away.

And she suddenly found that she would like to see them. No, more than that. She needed to know what they had been like before she and her sister had been born. Scathach and

Aoife's parents had been made bitter and angry by the destruction of their world. They had grown up in a time where they were the undisputed masters. All of that had ended when the island sank. It had been immediately apparent even in the hours just following the destruction of Danu Talis that there would no longer be masters and servants, Great Elders and Elders. There would simply be survivors.

Growing up, Scathach and her sister had quickly realized that their parents resented them, since they had been born after the sinking of the island. The twin girls were the first of what would later be called the Next Generation. Later, much, much later, Aoife and Scathach had come to believe that their parents were ashamed of them. The girls had been brought up knowing that their elder brother, with his ashen skin and bright red hair, born on Danu Talis, was their parents' favorite. Unlike the twins, he was an Elder.

Scathach felt her stomach lurch as the craft dipped, falling toward the city.

She wanted to see them. Even if only for a moment. She wanted to stand and watch her mother, father and brother as they had been before the island sank. Because in all the millennia she had known them, she had never once seen them laugh or smile, and when they spoke of others—even Elders—it was always with bitterness. That anger had manifested itself on their bodies, turning them hunched, twisted and ugly. Just for a single instant, Scathach wanted to see them when they were young and beautiful. She needed to know if they had ever been happy.

Abruptly it grew dark. Scathach and Joan watched jagged

black mountains appear overhead and stretch tall as the sky shrank to an irregular circle of blue.

"We're falling into something . . . ," Scathach began, and then she caught a hint of sulfur. She breathed deeply, trying to isolate the odor from the unwashed-dog scent of the anpu and the tart metallic tang of the vimana.

"I can smell it too," Joan said. She laughed shakily. "Sulfur—reminds me of Dee."

The flying disc came to a rocking halt and the scarred anpu appeared over Scathach. It waved a curved metal kopesh in front of her face as it carefully undid the straps holding her down with its left hand. Scathach's green eyes narrowed as she looked at the weapon. It brought back bitter memories: a lifetime ago she had trained the boy-king Tutankhamen how to fight with two of the lethal sickle-swords. Years later, she'd discovered that he had been buried with the matched blades she'd given him.

"Scatty . . . ," Joan began, the tiniest thread of panic in her voice. She twisted her head to watch the Warrior come to her feet. "Where are we?"

"Prison." Scatty turned and smiled. "And you do know that there's not a prison in the world that can hold me," she said in rapid French.

The top of the vimana popped up and retracted and the stench of sulfur was so strong it took their breath away. A blast of heat seared their skin and they were enveloped in a rumbling, grinding, roaring noise.

"I've got a feeling this is not your average prison," Joan called as Scatty was urged up to the edge of the craft.

135

The anpu prodded her in the back and the Shadow turned and snarled, her mouth suddenly full of her vampire teeth. The anpu scrambled back. Just before she stepped off the craft, Scathach looked down, and when she turned back to her friend, tiny dots of reflected fire danced in her eyes. "You could say that—we're in the mouth of an active volcano."

CHAPTER TWENTY-ONE

*H*ands close to their sides, the Nereids dived in and out of the water like a school of dolphins.

"What's the problem?" Josh demanded. "I can use my aura and just . . ."

". . . just reveal our location to everyone," Dee snapped. "No, I forbid it."

"Well, if you have a genius plan, now's the time to reveal it," Josh said nervously. The Nereids were closer now, long green hair streaming behind them. Some looked like astonishingly beautiful young women, but others had fins and claws and were more fish or crab than human. Their mouths were all full of ragged needle-pointed teeth. They reminded him of piranhas.

"Drive through them," Dee snapped. "Full speed."

"That's the plan?" Josh asked.

"Do you have a better one?" Dee's English accent had

become pronounced, and the small man's hands were clenching and unclenching into fists.

Josh pushed the throttle; the engine roared and the heavy powerboat surged forward, nose tilting upward. He turned the wheel and the boat plowed straight into the school of Nereids . . . who simply parted smoothly around it, then reached out to try and catch hold of the boat. Claws scraped along the sides, and two actually grabbed the low metal railing and attempted to pull themselves aboard.

"More power!" Dee snarled. He grabbed a length of rope and used it to whip the sea creatures off the side of the craft. They fell back into the water with high-pitched, almost delicate squeals that sounded like children's laughter. There was a thump as one of them suddenly leapt from the water and landed in the back of the boat, savage mouth snapping closed inches from Dee's ankle. The doctor hopped back out of range, caught the Nereid by the tail and flung it overboard again. He rubbed his hands on the legs of his trousers, leaving a scattering of shining scales on the dark cloth. "I hate Nereids," he muttered.

"Doctor . . . ," Josh shouted. "Hang on!" A Nereid had leapt onto the prow directly in front of him and was wriggling toward him, two-inch-long razor-sharp fingernails digging into the fiberglass hull. Josh jerked the wheel to one side and the speedboat tilted to almost a forty-five-degree angle. The creature shrieked and started to slide off the boat, claws leaving long ragged gouges in the hull. It clung on for a moment, then splashed into the bay.

"Faster!" Dee shouted.

"It doesn't go any faster," Josh said. The boat was bouncing up and down, slamming into waves with enough force to jar him out of his seat. His jaw ached and his head throbbed, salt water stung his eyes and crusted on his lips, and although he didn't normally suffer from seasickness, he knew he was going to throw up at any moment.

Suddenly the boat gave a lurch and slowed as if it had hit a sandbank. The engine screamed and howled, but the craft barely moved. Josh risked a glance over his shoulder. Dozens of Nereids were clustered around the boat, clinging to the sides, holding on to it, dragging it down into the sea. Waves slopped over the edges and water pooled in the bottom of the craft. And looking at the hungry eyes and needle teeth of the Nereids, Josh knew that neither he nor Dee would survive for more than a minute in the water.

Dee stood behind Josh, lashing out with the coil of rope, but the Nereids were too fast for him, and not one blow landed on the creatures. He struck out at one as she leapt out of the water. She balanced on her tail and bit at the rope as it lashed past her face, neatly severing it in two.

"Use your aura or we're dead!" Josh screamed.

"If I use my aura, then we *are* dead!"

"And if you don't use your aura, we're going to be fish food in a few minutes." The young man gritted his teeth in frustration. "We need to do something. . . ."

"A *strategy*," Dee said, gently emphasizing the word.

Josh nodded. "A strategy," he began, but even as he was saying the words, he caught a flickering image that was almost a memory, but not *his* memory . . .

139

. . . of an army in the lacquered armor of Japan, trapped, surrounded and outnumbered . . .

. . . of a warrior in leather and chain mail, head encased in a metal helmet, alone on a bridge facing off against an army that had never been human . . .

. . . of a trio of lightly armed sailing ships surrounded by a huge fleet . . .

And in every case the underdog had triumphed because . . . because they had a strategy.

"The spare fuel tanks," Josh yelled. "Is there gas in them?"

Dee lashed out with the rope whip at a Nereid with two pincers instead of hands. Her claws snapped and another chunk of rope fell away as she dropped back into the water. The Magician grabbed a plastic fuel tank and shook it. Liquid sloshed inside. "Half full. Maybe more." He shook a second container. "This one's full."

"Hang on," Josh said. "We're turning." Hauling the wheel to starboard, he aimed the boat away from the fast-approaching island and began to make a huge circle in the water. The confused Nereids were briefly left behind. "Empty them overboard," Josh commanded. "But not all at once. Spill it out slowly."

Without comment, the doctor pulled the cap off the first can and flung it away. The stink of diesel fuel was overpowering, and he coughed, eyes watering. Then he rested the can against the side of the boat and allowed the gas to spill onto the surface of the bay.

Josh was abruptly conscious that he seemed to be seeing everything in slow motion. He saw the Nereids move through the water and knew how they were going to position themselves. He watched a wave break against the bow of the boat and he was able to count the individual water droplets as they spun past his face.

A spectacularly ugly Nereid—more fish than human—reared up in front of him. He saw her ridged stomach muscles flatten and knew that beneath the water, her enormous fish tail would be twitching furiously, readying to propel her up into the air. She was going to land on the prow of the boat and then leap for his throat. Josh spun the wheel at the precise moment that the Nereid launched herself into the air. She missed the boat by inches and sank wordlessly back beneath the waves.

"Done," Dee shouted.

"Light the end of the rope," Josh commanded.

"With what?" Dee asked.

"You don't have matches?"

"Never needed them." Dee wiggled his fingers. "Always had my aura."

Josh's mind was spinning, instantly creating and rejecting a dozen scenarios. "Take the wheel," he instructed. "Keep us turning." And even before the English Magician had grabbed the wheel, Josh had ducked belowdecks to the tiny cabin. He was looking for something. . . . He saw it immediately.

A first-aid box was pinned to a wall, and directly beneath it, in a glass-fronted box, hung a red plastic flare gun, designed to shoot a bright flare high into the sky to attract attention if the boat was in trouble.

Josh pulled open the box and wrenched the gun off the

wall. He'd seen his father use flare guns like this before, and he knew how they worked, though he'd never been allowed to fire one himself. He darted back on deck. If he'd had matches, he would have soaked the end of the rope in gas, then lit it and dropped it in the water. With the gun he would only have one chance to drop the blazing flare onto the thin film of gas on the surface.

The Nereids were closing in. They were gathered around the boat, mouths opening and closing, teeth clicking and rasping together, and the rancid odor of fish was almost over-powering.

Josh grabbed one of the fuel cans and shook it. Liquid sloshed. Catching the can by the handle, he swung it as if he were tossing a baseball and pitched it out to where he could see a thin oily rainbow film of gas on the water. The can splashed directly into the middle of the stain.

The boat dipped as a crab-clawed Nereid snipped a chunk out of the side of the hull.

Holding the red plastic flare pistol in both hands, Josh instinctively aimed a little above the floating gas can. He was acutely conscious of the direction of the wind, and he knew that the flare would arc out and then fall.

Just like an arrow.

Thumbing back the hammer, he fired. A cherry-red flare sizzled from the barrel, arced through the air, fell . . . and struck the gas can, which instantly erupted into streamers of yellow and orange flames. The flames danced across the sur-face of the water, leaping from wave to wave, curling around to encircle the boat in a ring of fire.

142

For a brief moment, the air hummed with the incredibly beautiful song of the Nereids, and then, without a word, they slipped beneath the waves and vanished. A heartbeat later the blue-flamed fire sizzled out.

Dr. John Dee looked around the battered and scratched boat. Then he nodded to Josh. "Very impressive, young man."

Josh was suddenly exhausted. The world had returned to its normal speed, and with that had come a leaden fatigue. He felt as if he'd just completed two back-to-back football games.

"Where did that idea come from?" Dee asked, watching Josh closely.

Josh shook his head. "Memories," he muttered.

. . . *of an army in the lacquered armor of Japan, trapped, surrounded and outnumbered, creating a maze of burning reeds and grasses to divide and trap the enemy.*

. . . *of a warrior in leather and chain mail, head encased in a metal helmet, alone on a bridge, facing off against an army that had never been human, setting fire to the bridge to ensure that the monsters could only come at him single file.*

. . . *of a trio of lightly armed sailing ships surrounded by a huge fleet. One of the ships was loaded with black powder, the ship's timbers soaked in fish oil. It was set alight and sailed into the tightly packed enemy fleet, where it exploded, causing chaos.*

Josh knew they weren't his own memories, and he didn't think they had anything to do with Clarent. The memories he experienced while holding the Coward's Blade always left him feeling slightly sick. These memories, these thoughts, were different. They were exciting, exhilarating, and in those few moments when everything had slowed down, when every problem had a solution and nothing was beyond him, he had felt truly alive. Once the memories that were not his memories had washed over him and the world had slowed to a crawl, there had never been a single moment when he doubted they would escape. He'd been planning two or three steps in advance. If the flare had failed to ignite the gas, he knew that another dozen scenarios would have presented themselves.

"How do you feel?" Dee asked. He'd turned the boat toward Alcatraz, but his eyes were fixed on Josh.

"Tired." He licked salt-dried lips as he looked out across the waves. "I was hoping Virginia would have reappeared by now. . . ."

Dee cast a cursory glance over the surrounding water. "She'll turn up. She always does," he grumbled.

The Magician spun the boat in a huge circle, and Josh leaned over the side, looking for the immortal, but there was no sign of her. "Maybe the Nereids got her?"

"I doubt it. They'll leave her alone if they know what's good for them."

"They're gone too."

"But they'll be back," Dee said. He stepped aside to allow Josh to take the wheel again. Alcatraz Island loomed before them. "Let us watch our Italian friend set the monsters free."

CHAPTER TWENTY-TWO

"It is time." Perenelle took her hands away from her face. Her eyes were huge with milk-colored tears. More tears streaked her cheeks. "Prometheus," she said quietly, "Niten. Would you give us some privacy, please?"

The Elder and the immortal looked at one another, and then both nodded and left without saying a word, leaving Perenelle, Tsagaglalal and Sophie standing around the bed.

Sophie looked at Nicholas. The Alchemyst seemed peaceful, composed, and although the last few days had etched deep lines into his face, some of those lines had smoothed out and she caught a glimpse of the handsome man he'd once been. She swallowed hard. She'd always liked him, and she knew that in the weeks Josh had worked with him in the bookstore, the two had become close. Perhaps because their parents were away so often, Josh had always drifted toward authority figures like teachers and coaches. Sophie knew her brother had really looked up to Nicholas Flamel.

Perenelle moved to stand at the top of the bed. The ornate blue and gold dream catcher behind her haloed her head, ringing it in silver-blue light. "Tsagaglalal, Sophie, I know I have no right to ask this of you." The immortal's French accent was pronounced and her green eyes were shimmering with liquid. "But I need your help."

Tsagaglalal bowed her head. "Anything you need," she said immediately.

Sophie took a moment before answering. She didn't know what Perenelle wanted, but she was guessing it had something to do with a dead body. She'd never seen a dead body before, and the thought of touching it made her squirm. She looked up to find the two women staring at her.

"I can't . . . I mean . . . what do you want me to do? I'll help, of course. But I can't do anything like preparing a body. I don't think I could even touch it. Him," she amended hastily.

"No, it is nothing like that," Perenelle said. Her fingers moved across her husband's short hair, gently stroking his head. Silver strands came away in her fingers. She smiled. "And, besides, Nicholas is not dead. Not yet."

Shocked, Sophie looked at the Alchemyst again. She'd assumed he'd passed away quietly in his sleep. But now, looking closely, she could see the tiniest movement of the pulse in his throat, an irregular beat. She squeezed her eyes shut and focused her Awakened hearing. Listening intently, she could actually hear the slow—very slow—thumping of his

146

heart. The Alchemyst was alive—but for how much longer? She opened her eyes and looked at the Sorceress. "What do you need me to do?" she asked urgently.

Perenelle nodded gratefully. Spreading her fingers wide, she placed them on both sides of her husband's head. "When I was a little girl," she said, her gaze distant and dreamy, "I met a blue-eyed, hooded man with a metal hook in place of his left hand."

Tsagaglalal drew in a sharp breath. "You met Death! I did not know that."

Perenelle's smile was sad, wistful. "You knew him?"

The old woman nodded very slowly. "I met him on Danu Talis before it fell . . . and then again, at the end. Abraham knew him."

Sophie slowly turned to look at Tsagaglalal. Had her aunt just said that she was on Danu Talis? How old was she? Fragments of images and memories winked in and out of her mind . . .

. . . *of a beautiful young gray-eyed woman clutching a metal book, running up the endless steps of an impossibly tall pyramid. Figures raced past her, human and nonhuman, monsters and beasts, fleeing the ragged streaks of wild magic dancing above them. A shadowed figure appeared at the top of the pyramid, a man with a glowing hook in place of his left hand that leaked a pale blue fire. . . .*

Perenelle's voice cut through the memories and brought Sophie back to the present. "I was six when my grandmother brought me to see the hooded man." Wisps of Perenelle's ice-white aura drifted off her flesh and wreathed around her,

147

dressing her in a white robe. "In a crystal-studded cave on the shores of the Bay of Douarnenez, he told me my future. And he told me about a world, an indescribable world, a magical world, full of dreams and wonders."

"A Shadowrealm?" Sophie whispered.

"For a long time I believed so, but now I know he was describing this modern world." Perenelle shook her head and her language changed, slipping first into French and then into the ancient Breton tongue of her long-lost childhood. "The hook-handed man told me that I would meet the love of my life and become immortal."

"Nicholas Flamel," Sophie said, looking again at the still body on the bed.

"I was very young," Perenelle continued, as if Sophie had not spoken. "And although this was an age when we believed in magic—remember, this was early in the fourteenth century—even I knew that people did not live forever. I thought the man was mad or a simpleton . . . but we respected such people in those days and listened to them, paid attention to their prophecies. Centuries later, I learned the hook-handed man's name: Marethyu."

"Death," Tsagaglalal said again.

"He predicted that I would marry when I was not much more than a child. . . ."

"Nicholas," Sophie murmured.

"No." Perenelle shook her head, surprising her. "Nicholas was not my first husband. There was another man, older than me, a minor lord and a landowner. He died shortly after we wed, leaving me a wealthy widow. I could have had my pick of husbands—but I went to Paris and fell in love with a penniless scrivener ten years my junior. The first time I saw Nicholas I remembered that Marethyu had said that my life would be filled with books and writing. So I knew that his prophecy was coming true."

The temperature in the room had fallen, becoming cool and then cold. Sophie's breath plumed before her face, and she resisted the temptation to rub her hands together to warm them. The Sorceress's aura was streaming off her body, gathering behind her and billowing out like two huge white wings. Sophie felt her own aura crackle and crawl across her skin, and when she looked over at Tsagaglalal, she found that the old woman's features were becoming indistinct behind the pale gauze of hers. Like the Sorceress, she was wrapped in a white robe, and when Sophie looked down, she was startled to see that she was sheathed in a long silver robe that covered her from neck to ankles. Her hands were lost in its long billowing sleeves.

"Marethyu—I had almost forgotten the man existed until he turned up in our shop one day," Perenelle continued. She held both of her palms pressed to her husband's head as she spoke, and gossamer threads of his green aura spun from his flesh, rising into the air to burst like bubbles. "It was a Wednesday—I can recall it as clearly as if it happened yesterday—because that was the one day of the week I was not with Nicholas in the shop. I have no doubts that Marethyu deliberately chose that day to catch my husband alone. I came home to find the shop closed even though it was early in the afternoon and there was still light left in the west. Nicholas was in the back room. The place was ablaze with light—there were candles of all sizes on every surface. He'd arranged a dozen of them on a table, surrounding a small rectangular metal object. It was the Codex, the Book of Abraham the Mage, and the first time I saw it, light was reflecting off its cover as if it were a miniature sun. Even before Nicholas opened his mouth to name it, I knew what it was. I had never seen it before, but I knew what it would look like."

"Marethyu," Tsagaglalal said, nodding. Tears rolled down her lined cheeks. "He had it."

"How do you know?" Sophie whispered, though even as she was asking the question, the answer was forming. . . .

"Because I gave it to him," Tsagaglalal said, and her aura flared briefly.

And the memory struck Sophie like a blow.

The skies erupting with lightning, the ground belching fire, huge slabs of the pyramid shaking themselves apart . . . and the gray-eyed young woman thrusting a metal-bound book at the one-handed man . . .

Sophie staggered away from the table and the images faded.

The room was icy cold and everything was beginning to take on the sparkling patina of frost. Some of Perenelle's aura had now washed across the floor, billowing like mist, while the rest pulsed like enormous white wings over her shoulders. Some of the strands curled down her hands and wrapped around her fingers before crawling across Nicholas's skull like wriggling worms.

"I was a child when Marethyu told me that my husband

150

and I would become the guardians of a metal-bound book. We would be the last in a long line of humans to protect this precious object. He said that the book contained the entire knowledge of the world . . . but when I first saw it, I knew that could not be the truth. There were so few pages in it. How could the entire knowledge of the world be contained in twenty-one pages? It was much later before Nicholas and I began to discover the secrets of the Codex and its ever-changing text."

"You couldn't read it?" Sophie asked, and was not even shocked when she realized she'd spoken in the same language Perenelle was using.

"No. That understanding came more than two decades later." Perenelle's skin was glowing with an ice-white light. A tracery of pink veins was visible on the back of her hands, and the light had gathered in her green eyes, robbing them of color, making her look blind. "Eventually, everything Marethyu had told us came true. . . ." Her breath plumed a huge white sigh in the icy air. "Finally, only one prophecy remained."

"Tell us, Sorceress," Tsagaglalal said. Her own aura now sheathed her body, wrapping it in a vaguely Egyptian-looking gown, and beneath her wrinkled skin, Sophie caught a glimpse of the beautiful young woman she had once been.

"Marethyu told me that there would come a day—in a distant future, in an as-yet-unnamed land—when both my husband and I would be close to death." Perenelle's voice was soft, and emotionless, but there were tears on her cheeks. "Nicholas would die first, and then, two days later, I too would die."

Sophie blinked and silver tears ran down her cheeks. She couldn't imagine what it must be like to live with the knowledge of your own death. Would it be terrifying, or completely liberating?

"Marethyu asked me what I would do if I could keep my husband alive for one day more. And I told him. . . ."

"Anything. Everything," Sophie whispered, unaware that she had spoken the words aloud.

"Anything. Everything," Perenelle agreed. "Without the immortality potion, I have perhaps two days of life left." Her aura grew brighter, the wings fuller, the tips brushing the ceiling. "Marethyu said that I could not save my dear Nicholas, but I could grant him one extra day of life if . . . I gave him one of mine."

Sophie gasped.

"You would do the same for your twin," Perenelle said without hesitation.

Sophie shivered as something cold slithered along the length of her spine. The price of love was anything . . . and everything.

The Sorceress looked from Sophie to Tsagaglalal and then back at the girl again. "I need you both to help me transfer a portion of my aura into Nicholas."

"How?" Sophie breathed.

"I need you to give me your auras."

CHAPTER TWENTY-THREE

$\mathcal{S}$ome of Scathach's proudest boasts were that no prison could hold her and that no friend of hers would ever be imprisoned against their will. But she was beginning to discover that the Danu Talis prison was different. "I'm thinking," Scatty said, "that we might be in trouble. Real trouble."

The Warrior was standing at the entrance of a crude cave cut into the walls of the mouth of an active volcano. The cave was her cell.

Over the course of her long life, Scathach had been imprisoned dozens of times. But never like this. The Warrior had been hunted and trapped in lethal Shadowrealms, abandoned on desert islands and left to fend for herself in some of the most isolated and dangerous places on earth. She had broken out of the dreaded Elmina Castle in Ghana and had tricked her way off the Chateau d'If in the Mediterranean.

Scatty looked around. The towering walls of the volcano were dotted with hundreds of caves. More than half of them held captives, and others were filled with nothing but moldering bones and scraps of cloth.

She watched the vimana move upward, its metallic smell briefly dispelling the stink of sulfur. It stopped before another cave mouth and she watched Joan hop from the craft and into the cave. A second craft dropped down into the volcano's mouth and came to a halt almost directly across from her. The top opened and Saint-Germain was pushed into a cave. The immortal dusted himself off, then spotted her and Joan. He waved and Scatty waved back. Saint-Germain cupped his hands around his mouth and shouted, but the rumbling roar from below covered whatever he'd tried to say. He shrugged with an elegant roll of his shoulders and disappeared into his cave . . . reappearing a moment later, shaking his head.

Scathach ducked into her own cave to examine it. Her cell—and she was guessing the others would be identical—was more an alcove than a cave. It was barely high enough to stand up in and was narrow enough that she could touch both walls at the same time. She almost laughed at the thought of Palamedes in such a cell. Unless the cells came in a bigger size, he was going to be very uncomfortable. There was no door, nor was there any need for one: directly below the cave entrance—a long way down—was the bubbling red-black lava, and from the back wall of the cave to the sheer drop into the pit was about three short steps. Only Joan, the smallest

154

of the group, would be able to lie down. What little light there was came from the flickering reflections from below. The smell and the heat were indescribable.

The Shadow folded her arms across her chest and looked around. There were no stairs, ladders or bridges; the only way to access the caves was to use the vimanas. And she'd just watched the last of the silver crafts spiral up and out of the volcano.

She looked over at Saint-Germain and then to where William Shakespeare leaned almost casually against the wall of his cell, looking down at her. Directly across from him she spotted Palamedes sitting in a cave mouth, feet dangling over the edge, and when she glanced up, Joan was leaning over the edge of her cave mouth looking down at her. She waved and the Shadow waved back. They were all looking at her. And Scathach knew why.

Whenever her friends had been in trouble, Scathach had freed them. She'd rescued Nicholas from Lubyanka prison in Moscow hours before his execution, and had liberated Saint-Germain—even though she didn't really like him—from the notorious Devil's Island prison. When Perenelle had been locked up in the Tower of London, Scathach had fought her way through a hundred heavily armed guards and mercenaries who'd been lying in wait, expecting her. It had taken the Warrior Maid less than thirty minutes to free the Sorceress. And of course, she had ridden into the heart of Rouen to free Joan from certain death at the stake.

Lying flat on her stomach, Scathach examined the rock

walls, looking for footholds or handholds, but they were glass-smooth. Rolling over on her back, she examined the rock above her head. It too looked as if it had been polished. Sitting up, she folded her legs into a lotus position and rested her hands in her lap. "This could be tricky," she muttered.

Often, even the threat of the Shadow was enough to secure the release of a prisoner. When Hel had captured Joan and dragged her into her Shadowrealm, Scathach had let it be known that she would be standing on The Bridge of Gjallarbrú at the entrance to Hel's kingdom at exactly midnight. If Joan was not released unharmed, Scathach promised that she would continue over the golden bridge into the Shadowrealm. When she was finished, she vowed, the entire world would be nothing more than dust. At exactly one minute to midnight, Hel herself had escorted Joan to the bridge to hand her over into the Warrior's care.

A pebble dropped on her head and she looked up. Joan was peering over the edge of a cave about ten feet over her head. "So, on a scale of one to ten," the French immortal shouted down, "how much trouble are we in *now*?"

We're off the scale, Scatty thought, but all she said was "We've gone beyond twelve, heading to thirteen." She saw the Frenchwoman's narrow eyebrows rise disbelievingly. "Okay, maybe fourteen," Scatty amended.

"Well then, we are lucky that there's not a prison in the world that can hold you," Joan said, without a trace of sarcasm in her voice.

Except maybe this one, Scathach thought.

CHAPTER TWENTY-FOUR

*J*osh eased the motorboat up against the wooden dock on Alcatraz, trying to get as close as possible to the gangplank where tourists used to disembark. The engine coughed, then died with a sputter. He turned the key in the ignition and attempted to restart the motor. There was a click, but nothing happened. Leaning forward, he tapped the circular gas gauge. "We're out of gas," he called back over his shoulder, to where Dee was once again slumped over the side of the scarred boat. As soon as the danger of the Nereids had passed, his seasickness had returned. "Did you hear me?" Josh raised his voice to get the Magician's attention. He took a certain amount of pleasure in the English immortal's discomfort.

"I heard you," Dee mumbled. "What do you want me to do about it?"

"It means we're trapped here," Josh said. "How are we going to get off the island if . . . ," he began, and then stopped.

Virginia Dare was sitting on the gangplank, leaning back on one arm, dirty bare feet stretched straight out in front of her. Her wooden flute was in her left hand. She had it pressed lightly against her lips, but if she was making any sounds, Josh didn't hear them over the slapping of the waves against the wooden pilings. The immortal was soaked through and had strands of seaweed wrapped around her waist. And with her long damp hair swept back off her face, she appeared extraordinarily young. She looked down at Josh and smiled. Then she pointed out across the bay with the wooden flute. "Nicely done, by the way. Very nicely done."

"How do you know I did it?" Josh asked, the compliment bringing a touch of color to his cheeks.

"Too subtle for the English doctor." Dare grinned. "Dee would have called down lightning, or drained the entire bay. He does not know the meaning of the word *restraint*."

"You could have helped us," Dee grumbled, sitting up in the back of the boat.

"I could have," Dare said. "I chose not to."

"I wasn't sure I was going to see you again," Josh said. "And I never thought you'd ever see your flute again," he added, nodding to the instrument.

Virginia spun her flute lightly in her left hand. "Oh, we are old friends, this flute and I. We are . . . *bonded*. I will always be able to find her. And she will always come back to me." Dare smiled again. "The Nereid made the mistake of trying to play it—and no one will ever use this flute but me." The immortal's face turned masklike and the smile that

158

curled her lips was suddenly cruel. "Let us say that Nereus now has forty-nine daughters rather than fifty."

"You killed her?" Josh asked. He found it difficult to imagine the young-looking woman sitting on the edge of the dock as a killer.

Virginia spun her flute again, and for a moment Josh thought he heard a ghost of the same music he'd heard the Nereids sing. "We stole her songs, her voice. She is dumb now; she will never sing again . . . and Nereus will have no further use for her," Dare finished, almost gleefully. Then she laughed, and her flute echoed the sound, even though it was nowhere near her lips.

"But you didn't use your aura?" Dee asked urgently as he climbed shakily out of the boat. He reached down and Josh handed him the stone swords Excalibur and Joyeuse.

Dare smoothly climbed to her feet and tapped Dee on the shoulder with her wooden flute. For a single instant the afternoon air trembled with fragments of discordant music. "No, Doctor. I had no need to use my aura. My flute is akin to your swords—ancient, eternal and elemental—but unlike yours, which can only be used to destroy and kill, mine is a subtle instrument. It can even create new life." She turned and walked up the gangplank, heading toward a stone wall inlaid with a clock and a sign with the words ALCATRAZ ISLAND spelled out in white on a brown background. She stopped beside the clock, turned and closed her eyes, lifting her face to the sun. "That feels good."

Josh strapped the other two stone swords—Clarent and

Durendal—to his back and climbed out of the boat. "The boat is out of gas," he repeated, following them. "We're trapped here."

"Not while we have the swords," Dee called back over his shoulder, his voice echoing slightly on the empty dock. "If we were prepared to reveal our location, we could fire them with our auras and use them to create gates to anywhere . . . to any place . . ." His voice suddenly trailed away to a whisper. ". . . to any time on this planet." He stopped as if he'd been struck.

Virginia's eyes snapped open. "Doctor?"

Both Josh and Dare watched as the color disappeared from the immortal's face, leaving it sickly and pale, his lips outlined in blue. The shadows under his eyes turned the color of old bruises. Josh and Dare looked at one another in alarm.

"Doctor?" Virginia asked again. She reached out to lay a gentle hand on his forearm. "John, are you all right?"

Dee blinked, and then blinked again, but although he was looking directly at Virginia Dare, it was clear that he didn't see her.

"John," Virginia said, a hint of alarm in her voice. Drawing back her arm, she quickly cracked him across the face with the palm of her hand.

Dee staggered back, then pressed his hand to his cheek, where the imprint of Dare's fingers was outlined in red. When he looked at Virginia, his eyes were quite, quite mad—pupils huge and black, and against his ashen face, they looked like holes burned into paper. "Yes," he said, his voice thick with emotion. "Yes, I'm fine. Really. I'm fine."

Before Josh could piece together what had happened, footsteps echoed from an archway to their right and the threesome spun around, hands falling to weapons. Two figures appeared, hurrying toward them.

"Now, here's an odd couple," Dee murmured.

Niccolò Machiavelli, still managing to look elegant in a soiled black suit, stopped before the English Magician. The Italian looked over the trio, nodding briefly at Josh, before he turned his attention to Dee. "Did I hear you correctly, or did my ears deceive me? No, you are not *fine,* Dr. Dee," the Italian said in his precise and accentless English. "You have *that* look in your eyes."

"What look?" Dee challenged.

"The look you always get when you're about to do something incredibly stupid and unnaturally destructive."

"I have no idea what you are talking about," Dee said. "I've had a touch of seasickness."

"Oh, he *was* seasick," Virginia Dare said with a quick grin. Striding forward, she stretched out her hand to the Italian. "Since the doctor has completely forgotten his manners and is too rude to do the introductions, I'll do them myself. I am Virginia Dare."

Machiavelli took her hand in his, then leaned over it, almost, but not quite, pressing his lips to the back of her fingers. "An honor to meet you, Miss Dare. Your reputation precedes you."

161

Virginia turned to Billy and her smile widened. "Good to see you again, old friend. How are you doing?"

"Just fine, Miss Dare," Billy said. He stepped forward to give her a friendly hug. "And all the better for seeing you."

"You two know one another?" Dee said in surprise, asking the question Josh was thinking. Then Dee realized that of course, it made sense—the American immortals would have met one another at some stage over the centuries.

"Oh, the Kid and I have had some adventures together," Virginia said, winking at the young man. "Isn't that right, Billy?"

"Not sure I'd call them adventures," Billy said with an almost shy smile. "They usually ended up with me getting shot or stuck with something sharp."

"And me rescuing you," Virginia reminded him.

"Funny, I always thought it was the other way around," Billy said.

Machiavelli turned his attention back to Josh and stretched out his hand. Josh took it, feeling the strength of the Italian's grip. "I am pleased to see you again," Machiavelli said softly, and it took Josh a moment before he realized that the man had spoken to him in Italian and that he had fully understood it. "I'm surprised to find that you remain with our English friend."

"I heard that," Dee snapped. "I do speak Italian!"

"I know." Machiavelli smiled. "I was just reminding young Mr. Newman that he still has choices."

Josh bit the inside of his cheek and struggled to keep

162

a straight face. "It's good to see you, too," Josh replied in English. He genuinely liked the Italian, much more than he liked Dee. Machiavelli possessed the humanity that Dee lacked. "How did you get here?" he asked. "Leygate or . . ."

"Airplane." Machiavelli turned to Billy and beckoned him closer. "This," he said, "is Josh Newman. A Gold," he added significantly. "And one of the prophesied twins."

Billy shook Josh's hand, and Josh was surprised by how cold and rough the Kid's hands were. Josh also discovered that he was slightly taller than the Kid.

"Never thought I'd meet a Gold," Billy said.

"Never thought I'd get to meet a legend," Josh said. He suddenly found himself grinning like a fool, and he made a desperate attempt to keep calm. He'd only vaguely known about Dare and Machiavelli before he met them, and had never heard of Dee, but Billy the Kid was different. This was a genuine American legend. Someone he'd grown up hearing stories about.

The Kid looked almost embarrassed. "I'm not that much of a legend, really. Now, Wild Bill, Jesse James, Geronimo or Cochise, on the other hand—they were legends."

"Well, I think you're a legend," Josh insisted.

Billy grinned. "Well, you're a bit of a legend yourself, aren't you. One of the legendary twins—one to save the world, one to destroy it," he drawled. "Which one are you?"

"I have no idea," Josh said seriously. Although he'd been hearing about the prophecy for the past week, he'd never really stopped to consider the words. *One to save the world, one to destroy it.* He hoped he was the one to save it . . . but that would mean that his sister destroyed the world. The thought left him stunned.

"Come," Machiavelli interrupted, "we should hurry." The Italian turned and motioned to the group to follow him. He strode back toward an archway over a path that led to the water tower. "Nereus is about to awaken the Lotan," he said, the brickwork echoing and reechoing his voice. "I want to be there to see it happen."

Josh fell into step alongside Billy the Kid. "What's a Lotan?" he asked.

Billy grinned. "A seven-headed sea monster."

Josh turned to look back across the bay. A seven-headed sea monster would destroy the city. And then the pieces clicked together in his head. Was he the twin destined to destroy the world? "Seven heads?" he mumbled. "That I gotta see."

"Me too," Billy said. "I wanted him to awaken a kraken, but apparently they're too small."

Virginia Dare waited behind the two young men for Dr. John Dee to catch up. "You're plotting," she said, her voice little more than a whisper. "John, I too saw what Machiavelli observed."

"I was thinking." Dee smiled with genuine good humor, and for a moment he looked almost youthful. *"Fortis Fortuna adiuvat,"* he said.

"You'll have to say that again in English. I didn't get much of a classical education living wild in the woods of North Carolina."

"Fortune favors the brave." He absently rubbed his cheek, which was still red from her blow. "An idea is bubbling. Something truly daring and audacious."

"Your last daring and audacious idea did not end too well," Virginia reminded him.

"This time it will be different."

"The last time you said that, you almost burned London to the ground."

Dee ignored her. He rubbed his cheek again. "Did you have to hit me so hard? I think I lost a filling."

"Trust me," Virginia laughed, "that was not hard."

CHAPTER TWENTY-FIVE

*A*ten, the Lord of Danu Talis, stood on the roof of the Palace of the Sun and watched the vimanas rise out of the mouth of Huracan, the volcano prison.

"And none escaped?" he asked, raising his head slightly.

"None, brother. My anpu captured them easily."

"And the hook-handed man?"

"Separated from the others, as you ordered."

Aten turned to face his companion. Once, it would have been impossible to tell them apart, but recently the Change that overtook all the Elders had started to work on Aten, elongating his skull, nose and jaw, thickening his lips and pulling his eyes back into his head, giving them a pronounced slant. He now wore a heavy metal robe with a deep hood and long sleeves to hide his deformities.

"We should kill them now and be done with it," Anubis said. The Change was also beginning to claim his body. Like

166

his brother, Anubis had once been extraordinarily handsome, but now his teeth had lengthened to resemble those of the creatures he created in his underground laboratories, and the texture and hue of his copper-colored skin was coal black in places, etched through with tiny red veins. Speaking was becoming difficult, and both brothers knew that soon it would become impossible. Unlike Aten, who attempted to conceal the Change, Anubis—like so many of the Elders—exhibited his as a badge of honor.

"Kill them?" Aten said in surprise.

"Kill them. Always, the quickest solution to a problem is to remove it."

"But if we kill them, brother," Aten said, "then we lose the most extraordinary opportunity of our lives. Abraham says they are from the future."

Anubis attempted to spit but failed and ended up hissing between his teeth. "We should kill him, too." He joined his brother and they looked across the circular city toward the volcano.

"Where is your scientific curiosity?" Aten asked lightly. "I remember when you were little, you were endlessly curious."

Anubis spread his hands. His fingers were curling into claws, the nails long and black. "And look where it got me. I am becoming a monster. I am convinced my experiments have somehow poisoned me and affected my Change. Surely we should look alike, brother?"

"Abraham claims that the Change is simply a revelation of our true selves," Aten said mildly.

"So what does that make me?" Anubis growled.

Aten turned away from the low wall that ran around the edge of the roof and stepped onto the first level of the huge hanging garden of the royal palace. He did not want to tell Anubis that he was indeed becoming like the dog-headed monsters he had first created a thousand years previously. "Walk with me," he commanded.

The roof garden—the Garden of the Moon—was divided into seven distinct circular areas, each one a different color and filled with different species of flora. Aten stepped into the first circle, pulled his heavy cloak tighter around his body, closed his eyes and breathed deeply. Within this circle, which completely encompassed the entire roof of the palace, were the lotuses—over one thousand different kinds collected from across the earth—and he could identify each one by its own distinctive scent.

"Little brother, nothing must happen to our visitors," he said, allowing some of his authority to seep into his voice. He knew Anubis was quite capable of acting behind his back. "They will be fed and watered. They will not be questioned— I will do that myself."

"Aten, is that wise?"

Without turning around, the Lord of Danu Talis said quietly, "Do not challenge me again, little brother. Remember what happened to our other brother. You will do as I say, without question. If anything happens to the visitors, I will hold you personally responsible." He turned quickly and caught the arrogant mocking expression on his brother's face. "You think I've become weak, don't you?" Aten asked mildly.

Anubis strode forward. He was wearing a long sleeveless chain-mail robe that came to just above his knees. It swirled around him when he walked, and the edges of the woven metal sliced into the delicate lotus blossoms in the beds surrounding him, destroying them. He dropped to one knee before Aten and bowed his head. "I've seen you fight the Ancients and the Archons. I've hunted Earthlords with you. You rule an empire that stretches from horizon to horizon, from pole to pole. Only a fool would think you a coward or weak."

"Then don't be a fool!" Aten leaned down to catch his brother's muscular shoulder and draw him to his feet. The pupils in his flat yellow eyes narrowed from circles to horizontal lines. "What you didn't add, however, was that all of those deeds were done a long time ago. I have not ridden to battle in eight hundred years."

"Why should we fight, now that we have the anpu to battle for us?" Anubis asked shakily, struggling to keep his voice even, though his eyes had flared in fear.

"You think living here has softened me," Aten continued as if he hadn't heard him. "You think the Change has weakened me," he added, and then his fingers tightened on his brother's shoulder, pinching the nerves, driving him back to his knees on the quartz crystal path. "And a soft, weak ruler could easily be removed and replaced by a stronger man. Someone such as yourself. But you forget, brother, that I have as many spies in the city as there are flowers on this roof. I know what you've been saying, I know what you've been plotting." Wrapping his fist in the chain mail, Aten dragged

169

Anubis back over to the low wall and pushed him up against it. "Look down," he snarled. "What do you see?"

"Nothing . . ."

"Nothing? Then you are blind. Look again."

"I see the people, made tiny with distance. Insignificant people."

"Insignificant people, yes, but they are *my* people, *my* subjects. Not yours. Never yours." Aten dragged his brother closer to the edge. "If you question me again, I will kill you. If I find you are plotting against me, I will kill you. If you speak about me or my queen in public again, I will kill you. Do I make myself clear?"

Anubis nodded. "You will kill me," he mumbled.

Aten flung Anubis aside, sending him sprawling into a pool of pure white lotus blossoms. Their perfume was sickening. "You are my brother, and surprising as this may sound, I love you. And that is the only thing that has kept you alive today. Now bring me the hook-handed man."

CHAPTER TWENTY-SIX

The two greasy-haired youths leaning against the wall of the Esmiol Building in San Francisco watched the large bulky man lurch from the narrow street opposite and steady himself, before turning left and heading down Broadway. Normally, they avoided big men or obviously fit and healthy young men, preferring to rob women, old men or children, but they made an exception for someone who looked like he might be drunk. Drunks were easy. Without looking at one another, they pushed away from the wall and kept pace with the man from across the street.

"See how he's walking? He's had a hip operation," said Larry, an unnaturally skinny teenager with a spiderweb tattooed across his ear. "My granny walks like that."

"Or a knee replacement," his friend Mo said. Mo was stocky and muscular, with a bodybuilder's broad chest and narrow waist. He wore a gold-plated razor blade in his right ear as an earring. "He can't straighten his legs. Look at the size of him; I bet he used to play football. Probably busted his knees." He grinned, showing a mouthful of bad teeth. "Which means he can't run, either."

Larry and Mo hurried up the road, taking pleasure from the way people looked away or moved aside to allow them to pass. Most of the pedestrians in this part of town knew the youths' reputation.

The two teens hurried ahead of their mark and then stopped outside a small beauty salon and looked back across the road to assess the value of their quarry. They had been doing this a long time, and they only mugged people who had something worth stealing. Anyone else was an unnecessary risk and a waste of time.

"He's big," Larry said.

Mo nodded. "Very big," he agreed. "But old . . ."

"Nice leather jacket for an old man," Larry continued. "Retro, biker style."

"Very nice. Worth some money."

"Good boots, too. They look new."

"Nice leather belt, great belt buckle," Mo said. "Looks like some sort of helmet design. I'm keeping that," he added.

"Hey, that's not fair, you kept the last guy's watch."

"And you gave the woman's leather purse to your grandma as a birthday present. We're even."

Suddenly the big man turned and lurched across the road, ignoring the oncoming cars, heading directly for Larry and Mo. The two young men spun around and stared into the window of the beauty salon, watching the drunk's reflection

172

in the glass. Now that he was closer, they got a clearer impression of his size. He was huge, and looked even bigger because of his overlarge clothes: blue jeans and a loose T-shirt that might once have been white but was now an indefinable shade of gray, worn under an enormous metal-studded black leather motorcycle jacket. A black and white bandana was tied tightly across his head and knotted at the back of his skull, and his eyes were hidden behind aviator-style sunglasses.

"Are those Ray-Bans?" Larry asked, trying to see if the man's sunglasses had the distinctive signature logo on the right lens.

"Knockoffs, I bet. But we'll take them anyway. Might get a couple of bucks from some tourist."

They turned as the man staggered past with his stiff-legged gait. The silver metal studs on the back of his jacket picked out a war helmet similar in design to his belt buckle. One red and one blue stud made eyes peering out from either side of the long nose guard.

"He's a biker," Larry said, starting to shake his head. "And bikers are trouble. I think we should let him go."

"So where's his bike?" Mo asked. "I don't think he's anything more than a fat old man who likes to dress tough."

"Could still be a biker, and even old bikers are tough."

"Yeah, but we're tougher." Mo reached under his T-shirt and touched the length of lead pipe tucked into the top of his jeans. "And no one's tougher than our little metal friend here."

Larry nodded dubiously. "We'll follow, but we'll only take him if we get a chance to come at him from behind. Agreed?"

"Agreed."

They watched as the man suddenly jerked to the right onto Turk Murphy Lane, a narrow laneway connecting Broadway with Vallejo Street.

"Aw, man, some people are just asking for it." Mo grinned. "This is our lucky day." He high-fived Larry and they hurried down Broadway after the man in the leather jacket. They didn't even have to discuss a plan. They would mug the old man on the quiet street, grab his coat, boots, belt and money if he had any, and then run the length of the lane. They'd slow to a casual walk before they turned onto Vallejo Street, though—Turk Murphy Lane came out directly facing the central police station. Larry and Mo knew the streets in and around Chinatown like the backs of their hands, and they'd be a couple of blocks away before anyone even spotted the crumpled body and raised the alarm.

"Remember," Mo said, "the belt buckle is mine."

"Okay—I get first pick next time, though. . . ."

But when they rounded the corner, they found the big man waiting for them, standing squarely in the middle of the sidewalk.

A giant fist shot out and grabbed Larry by the front of his filthy T-shirt. The man lifted him straight up in the air and then flung him twenty feet to land in a sprawling heap on the hood of a parked car. The windshield spiderwebbed and the alarm started to sound.

None of the passersby even glanced down the side street.

Mo reached under his T-shirt for the lead pipe, but suddenly an enormous hand closed on the top of his head. And squeezed. The pain was extraordinary. Black spots instantly danced before his eyes and his legs buckled beneath him. He would have fallen, but the man continued to hold him up by the head. Mo watched as the old man—who suddenly didn't look quite so old—lifted the lead pipe, looked at it, smelled it, licked it with a coal-black tongue and then crushed it like a tin can and tossed it aside. The man spoke, but whatever he said was incomprehensible. He tried again and again, using several different languages, until . . . "Can you understand me now?"

Mo managed a strangled squawk.

"You should be happy that I'm in a good humor today," the man said. "I'm looking for directions."

"Directions?" Mo whispered.

"Directions." The man released his grip and Mo staggered and fell back against a wall. He pressed both hands against his skull, convinced that he'd find the impressions of enormous fingers in his flesh.

"Directions," the man repeated. "I have the address written down somewhere," he mumbled, and then reached into his leather jacket. Mo instantly attacked, trying for a karate blow to the stranger's throat. Lightning fast, the man caught Mo's arm, squeezed and then slapped the heel of his hand into the youth's chest. The force of the blow propelled Mo back into the wall, his head smacking off the brickwork. "Don't be stupid," the big man rumbled. He produced a scrap of paper and turned it toward the teenager. "Do you know where this place is?"

It took Mo a few seconds to focus, but finally the address

printed in childish block letters on the lined notepaper swam into view. "Yes." His voice was a terrified whisper. "Yes."

"Tell me."

"Walking or driving?"

"Do I look like I'm driving?" the man growled. "Did you see a chariot anywhere around here?"

Mo swallowed hard. His chest was aching, he was finding it difficult to breathe and his head was still ringing from the blow against the wall. He could have sworn the man had just said "chariot."

"Directions."

"You follow this street, Broadway, until it comes to Scott Street—it'll be on your left. This address is down there somewhere."

"Is it far?"

"It's not close," Mo said, attempting to smile. "You're going to let me go, mister, aren't you? I haven't done anything to you."

The big man folded the scrap with the address and shoved it into the back pocket of his baggy jeans. "Not to me you haven't, but you and your partner have robbed others. You have terrorized this neighborhood."

The youth opened his mouth to lie, but the man took off his Ray-Bans and folded them into an inside pocket. Astonishingly blue eyes locked onto the teen's face. "You tell your friends—or those others like you, because I am sure you have no friends—that I have returned, and that I will not tolerate these attacks."

"Returned? Who are you? You're crazy. . . ."

"Not anymore." The man smiled, and Mo discovered that his mouth was filled with huge incisors that curled like savage vampire fangs. A black forked tongue slid out between the fangs. "Tell your friends that Mars Ultor has returned." Then he grabbed Mo by the front of his shirt, lifted him off the ground and tossed him the length of the alleyway to land on top of his friend. The car alarm died with a squawk.

And Mars Ultor shuffled back onto Broadway, in search of Scott Street and Tsagaglalal.

CHAPTER TWENTY-SEVEN

Sophie knew instinctively that what Perenelle was asking of her was wrong, though she was not entirely sure why. The vaguest of thoughts and memories flickered and danced in her mind, but with the Sorceress's bright green eyes focused on hers, it was hard to concentrate. "You want me to give you my aura?"

"Yes, just a little. . . ."

"How . . . why?" Sophie made no move to take the Sorceress's outstretched hand.

"You are Silver, Sophie, and immensely powerful," Perenelle explained. "You will put your hand in mine and I will draw upon the strength of your aura to supplement mine while I transfer some of my life force into my husband. I could probably do it on my own, but there are some dangers that my aura could overwhelm me and I would spontaneously combust. With you and Tsagaglalal by my side, supporting me, I will be safe."

"Sophie," Tsagaglalal said very softly, "do it. It is for the best."

"What will you do?" the young woman asked, still wary.

"Wrap Nicholas in my aura."

Sophie struggled to focus. She was reminded of how the Witch of Endor had wrapped her in air. Although she'd never thought of it before, she realized now that it must have been more than air—Zephaniah had blanketed Sophie in her aura and had transferred not just a portion of her powers, but her knowledge and memories as well.

"Sophie, we do not have much time," Perenelle said, a hint of annoyance in her voice. "I cannot do this alone."

"Sophie," Tsagaglalal said evenly. "Nicholas is dying."

Still uncomfortable with the idea, Sophie stretched out her right hand and Perenelle took it in hers. Her grip was strong, and there were calluses on her fingertips and palm.

Instantly Sophie experienced a rush of memories she knew were not hers, and it hit her that this was why she'd been reluctant to allow Perenelle to tap into her aura. After the events of the past few days, Sophie did not completely trust the Sorceress. And while there was a lot she wanted to know about Perenelle, there were certain memories, thoughts and ideas that the Witch of Endor had shared with her that she didn't want the immortal to have access to. There was no reason not to tell her. But if the events of the last few days had taught her anything, they had taught her to trust her instincts.

"The scarab, Tsagaglalal," Perenelle said.

Sophie turned to watched Aunt Agnes lift the incredibly detailed carved scarab beetle from the wooden shelf and cup it in both hands. The moment she touched it, the object started to glow with a warm green light and Tsagaglalal's white aura shimmered, streaked with threads of luminescent jade. The beetle throbbed emerald-green and suddenly all traces of age fell away from the old woman and she was once more young and extraordinarily beautiful. It pulsed again and Tsagaglalal reverted to the person Sophie knew as Aunt Agnes.

Sophie looked at the woman, and remembered . . .

. . . *Tsagaglalal sitting across a checkered table from a man wearing a golden mask over half of his face . . . except this was no mask. His flesh was hardening to metal. Cupped in his hands—one of flesh, the other gold—was the scarab. He placed it gently into Tsagaglalal's hands, folding her fingers over it. "You are Tsagaglalal," he said, his voice a deep rumble, "She Who Watches. Now and forevermore. The future of the humani is here in your hands. Guard it well."*

Sophie blinked and saw . . .

. . . *Tsagaglalal standing before two almost identical red-haired and green-eyed teenage girls: Aoife and Scathach. The girls were dressed as warriors, in the decorated buckskin of the Great Plains. Behind them, smoke rose over a huge battlefield, which was littered with the bodies of creatures that were nei-ther man nor beast but something caught in between. One of the girls, smaller than her sister, with a sprinkling of freckles across her nose, stepped forward to accept the jade scarab from the woman known to the tribe as She Who Watches. Then the girl turned and raised the scarab high, and the gathered army screamed her name: "Scathach!"*

Sophie watched the images shift and swirl as . . .

. . . Aoife, clad in black and gray, leapt out of a tower window and fell into an icy moat. Just before she disappeared under the slate-gray water, she held aloft the jade carving she'd just stolen.

Sophie was aware that time was racing by, months and years flickering past in seconds. Now the freckle-faced red-haired girl had become a young woman and . . .

. . . Scathach, dressed in furs and leather, raced through a bamboo forest, huge black arrows raining down around her. She held a thickly curved sword in one hand and the scarab in the other. Behind her, Aoife crashed through the bamboo at the head of an army of blue-skinned monsters.

The memories were flooding in, images crowding fast one after the other, of . . .

. . . Scathach kneeling before a boy wearing the royal robes of Egypt, her arms outstretched to present him with the green jade.

. . . and Scathach again, standing over the unmoving body of the same boy. His arms were crossed on his chest, and she gently extricated the scarab from stiff fingers. She brought it to her lips and kissed it and shed bloodred tears for her friend, the boy-king Tutankhamen. There were shouts and the Shadow turned and then leapt out the window even as the king's Nubian guards burst into the room. They pursued her across the desert for three days before she escaped.

More images, impossibly fast, fragments of faces and places—and then, abruptly, there was . . .

. . . Perenelle, in the elegant costume of the nineteenth century, with Nicholas by her side, accepting a striped ribbon-bound box from Scathach, who was wearing a man's military costume, a sword on her hip. "Why, you have given me a dung beetle," the Frenchwoman said with a laugh when she opened the box.

Sophie blinked and saw . . .

. . . Perenelle, now in the costume of the early twentieth century, wearing a cloche hat, presenting the same ribbon-bound box to Tsagaglalal, She Who Watches. Behind them, the ruins of San Francisco smoldered and smoked in the aftermath of a terrible earthquake.

The memories faded and Sophie opened her eyes and watched as the old woman handed the scarab to Perenelle. "I have known this object for ten thousand years," Tsagaglalal said, "and although it was often out of my possession, it always returned to me, sooner or later. I've often wondered why. Was I—and were all the other Guardians—keeping it safe for just this very moment?"

Perenelle looked up. "I thought you, of all people, would know."

Tsagaglalal shook her head. "When he gave it to me, he said I was holding the future of the human race in my hands. But he often said things like that. He could be very dramatic at times."

The Sorceress looked at the carving, turning it to the light to admire the details. "When Scathach gave this to me for my five-hundredth birthday, I teased her that she had given me a dung beetle. The Warrior answered, 'Dung is more valuable than any precious metal. You cannot grow food in gold.'"

Perenelle looked over at Tsagaglalal. "I did not realize then just how valuable and ancient it was."

Tsagaglalal shook her head. "Neither did I, though he gave it to me on the day before he presented me with the Book."

Sophie frowned. "Who gave you the scarab and the Book?" A name flickered in her mind. "Was it Abraham the Mage?"

Tsagaglalal nodded sadly, then smiled. "Yes, it was Abraham, though I never called him Mage. It was a title he hated."

"What did you call him?" Sophie asked. Her heart was suddenly beating so fast, it left her breathless.

"I called him husband."

CHAPTER TWENTY-EIGHT

$\mathcal{B}$illy the Kid darted from one side of the hall to the other, looking into the cells at the menagerie of sleeping creatures. "I mean, I've lived on this earth for a very long time, and I've never seen anything like that." He was looking at a muscular blue-skinned man with a mass of wiry black hair and two curled horns growing out of his head. "Have you?" he asked Niccolò Machiavelli.

Machiavelli glanced quickly into the cell. "It's an oni," he said. "A Japanese demon," he added, before Billy could ask. "The blue-skinned ones are very unpleasant, but the red-skinned ones are even worse." The Italian continued down the grim prison corridors, hands clasped behind his back, cold gray eyes fixed directly ahead of him.

"You're having those deep thoughts, those dark thoughts again," Billy said, lowering his voice as he fell into step alongside the dark-suited immortal.

"So you're a mind reader now."

"A body reader. Staying alive in the Old West meant watching how people stood and moved, interpreting their little twitches and looks, knowing who was likely to pull a gun and who'd back down. I was very good at it," the American said proudly. "And I always knew when someone was going to do something stupid," he added very softly.

"I'm not going to do anything stupid," Machiavelli said quietly. "I have given my master my word, and I will stick to that: I will awaken the beasts and loose them on the city."

"But you're not happy about it, are you?"

Machiavelli flashed a quick look at Billy.

"I mean, seeing what's in these cells, I'm not sure I want them wandering free in any city," the Kid said, his voice little more than a whisper. "These are all carnivores and blood drinkers, aren't they?"

"Never met a vegetarian monster," Machiavelli said. "But yes, most of these are flesh eaters. Some of the most human-looking, however, feed off the dark energy of dreams and nightmares."

"Do you want them free in San Francisco?" Billy asked quietly.

Machiavelli remained silent, but he shook his head slightly, and his lips formed a word he did not speak aloud. *No.*

"You're cooking up something, though, I can tell," Billy added.

"How can you tell?" Machiavelli asked with a faint smile.

"Easy." The American immortal's blue eyes sparkled in

the gloom. "You're just a bit too obvious. You'd never have survived in the West."

Machiavelli blinked in surprise. "I have survived more dangerous places than your nineteenth-century America, and I've done it by keeping my face expressionless and my opinions to myself."

"Ah, but that's where you're making your mistake, Mr. Machiavelli."

"Call me Niccolò. Educate me, young man."

Billy grinned delightedly, showing his prominent teeth. "Never thought I'd have something to teach you."

"The day we stop learning is the day we die."

Billy rubbed his hands together briskly. "So I think I'd be right in saying that you're a curious man—correct, Mr. Machiavelli?"

"Always have been. It is one of the many traits that Dee and I share. We are both intensely curious. I have always believed that curiosity is one of man's greatest strengths."

Billy nodded. "I've always been curious too. Got me into a lot of trouble," he added. "Now, if you take a quick look behind you . . ."

Machiavelli glanced over his shoulder, where Josh, Dee and Dare followed.

"The boy is obviously astonished and scared . . ." Billy was still staring straight ahead.

Josh Newman was following the two immortals in a daze, his eyes and mouth opening wider as they passed cell after cell and each new creature was revealed. He was frightened—

that was clear. Tendrils of gold smoke curled off his hair and seeped from his ears and nostrils, and both hands were locked into golden-gloved fists.

"Dee's not interested in the creatures, because he gathered them and knows what's here," Billy continued, "and Virginia is not interested either, because she's either fought them in the past or knows that her Elder flute will protect her." He cocked his head to one side, considering. "Or maybe because she knows that she's more dangerous than they are."

"I only know her by reputation," Machiavelli said. "Is she as bad as they say she is?"

"Worse," Billy said, nodding eagerly, "much, much worse. Don't ever make the mistake of trusting her."

Dee and Dare took up the rear. Machiavelli noted that Dee was deep in conversation with the woman. Her face was an inscrutable mask, her gray eyes the same color as the stones making up the floor and walls. She spotted Niccolò looking at her and raised a hand in acknowledgment. Dee looked up and glared, the odor of rotten eggs briefly filling the cellblock, stronger even than the stench of the sleeping beasts. Machiavelli looked away before Dee could see his smile. It amused him to know that he still frightened the English Magician.

"So, given your curiosity, you *should* be looking into the cells," Billy finished. "But you're not. Therefore, you're thinking of something much more important."

"Impressive," Machiavelli agreed. "And your logic is impeccable . . . except for one thing."

"Which is?"

"Oddly shaped creatures and monstrous beasts long ago lost their ability to frighten me. In truth, it was really only mankind—and their close relatives, the Elders and Next Generation—that always had the capacity to terrify me." He nodded at the cells. "These poor beasts are driven solely by their need to survive and to feed. It is their nature, and their nature has made them predictable. But man, on the other hand, has the capacity to change his nature. Man is the only animal that can destroy the world. Beasts live only in the present, but humans have the capacity to live for the future, to lay down plans for their children and grandchildren, plans that can take years, decades, even centuries, to mature."

"I've heard that sort of planning is your specialty," Billy said.

"It is." Machiavelli waved a hand toward a cell holding a trio of sleeping hairy domovoi, each one more hideous than the other. "So these do not frighten or even interest me."

"You sound as arrogant as Dee," Billy snapped, a touch of steel edging his voice. "And I'm sure the people living in San Francisco are not going to agree with you."

"True," Machiavelli conceded.

Billy drew in a deep breath. "If these creatures reach the shores, there will be . . ." He paused, hunting for a word. "Chaos. Mayhem."

"Now who is having deep dark thoughts?" Machiavelli asked lightly. "Who would have thought it—an outlaw with a conscience."

"Probably the same deep dark thoughts you were having," Billy murmured. "I'll admit I'm not comfortable releasing these monsters on my people."

"*Your* people?" Machiavelli teased.

"My people. I know they're not yours, they're not Italians . . . ," Billy began.

"They're humans," Machiavelli said, "and that makes them my people too."

Billy the Kid looked quickly at Niccolò. "When I first met you, I thought you were just like Dee . . . now I'm not so sure."

Machiavelli's lips moved in the tiniest of smiles. "Dee and I are similar in many ways—don't tell him that, though. He'd be insulted. Where we differ is that Dee will do whatever is necessary to achieve his ends. I have watched him follow his master's orders even when it meant the destruction of entire cities and tens of thousands of lives. I have never done that. The price of my immortality was my service, but not my soul. I am now, and I have always been, human."

"I hear you," Billy the Kid murmured.

The corridor ended at a metal door. Machiavelli pushed it open, blinked in the afternoon sunlight and hurried down the concrete steps that led to the exercise yard. The Italian breathed deeply, drawing in the rich salt air, dispelling the musky, fetid animal odor that permeated the cellblocks. He waited for Billy to join him. He turned while the Kid was still on the last step, so that their faces were level. "I gave my word to my master and to Quetzalcoatl that I would unleash the creatures on the city. I cannot go back on my word."

"Cannot or will not?"

"Cannot," Machiavelli said firmly. "I will not become *waerloga*—an oath breaker."

Billy nodded. "I respect a man who keeps his word. Just make sure you're keeping it for the right reason."

Machiavelli leaned forward, and his iron-hard fingers bit into Billy's shoulder. The Italian fixed his eyes on Billy's. "No, you must make sure you're *breaking* it for the right reason!"

CHAPTER TWENTY-NINE

*P*erenelle gently placed the green jade scarab on the center of Nicholas's chest, then moved it slightly to the left until it was resting over his heart.

Tsagaglalal reached out and took the Alchemyst's hands, left, then right, and arranged them on top of the jade beetle, almost completely covering it. Then she looked at the Sorceress. "Are you sure?" she asked.

"I am sure."

"It is not always successful. It is dangerous."

"Dangerous? What do you mean, dangerous?" Sophie asked in alarm. She was still holding the Sorceress's hand, and she picked up a ghostly trickle of fear through their connection. It frightened her to know that the Sorceress was afraid. Although Perenelle's head did not move, her eyes shifted to fix on Sophie's face.

"If this process does not work, then Nicholas will die and

I will have wasted an entire day of my life," she said. "But I have to do this. I have no choice." The Sorceress's grip tightened on Sophie's fingers. "And if it is successful, then we will have Nicholas for one more day." A question flickered through Sophie's mind . . . and Perenelle answered it. "Yes, it would make a huge difference."

Tsagaglalal placed her left hand in Perenelle's and then reached her right across the bed toward the young woman. "Perenelle will draw a little of our auras and channel them into the scarab, which in turn will release them into Nicholas. Think of it as a battery. So long as there is power in the scarab, then Nicholas will remain alive."

Sophie placed her left hand in the old woman's bony clawlike grip.

"It is painless," Tsagaglalal continued. "And you are young; at least your aura will soon replenish."

"And what about yours?" Sophie asked quickly.

"Even if it could, there is no need for mine to regenerate. My purpose in this Shadowrealm is almost done." Her flint-gray eyes turned distant. "My tasks were to watch for you, and then to watch over you. Soon I will be able to rest in peace."

Suddenly the temperature in the room plummeted to a bone-freezing chill. Sophie gasped with the shock. "Whatever you do," Perenelle said, her breath puffing whitely with each word, "you must not break the circle until the scarab is charged with the power of our auras. Do you understand?"

Sophie nodded.

"Do you understand?" Perenelle asked again, more firmly.

192

"If the process is incomplete, then Nicholas dies here now, and I will die tomorrow."

"I understand," Sophie said, her teeth starting to chatter. She looked down on the still body of Nicholas Flamel. His flesh was ashen, and a thin layer of frost crystals had formed around his nostrils and lips.

Perenelle's ice-white aura swirled and billowed around her, and Sophie was abruptly aware of the threads of silver— *her* silver—woven through it. She looked down to find that her aura had formed into protective gauntlets over her hands where she clutched Tsagaglalal and the immortal woman's fingers.

The Sorceress closed her eyes. "And so it begins," Perenelle said.

Sophie felt her silver aura bloom, and the wash of heat took her by surprise. It blossomed in the center of her chest, then radiated outward, flowing down into her legs, tingling in her toes. The heat shivered along her arms, burning through the palms of her hands, setting pins and needles dancing in her fingertips. The wash of warmth rose through her neck and burned in her cheeks, drying her eyes. She squeezed them shut and shuddered as a confusing jumble of memories overwhelmed her. She knew that some were Perenelle's. . . .

. . . a hooded man sitting in the center of a cave, bright blue eyes sparkling with the reflections of the huge crystals embedded in the walls. He was holding a small metal-bound book in his right hand. He rested the curved metal hook that took the place of his left hand on the cover. . . .

. . . Nicholas Flamel—slender and dark-haired, young and

handsome—standing behind a wooden stall that held only three thick vellum-bound books. He turned to look at her, colorless eyes crinkling in a smile. . . .

. . . and Nicholas again, older now, gray-haired and bearded, in a small dark room, a dozen shelves holding twice that many books and manuscripts.

. . . a table that held just one book, the metal-bound Codex, the pages flipping open of their own accord before finally stopping on a page that crawled with sticklike text and flowed with color that formed into the shape of a scarab beetle, then re-formed into what might have been a half-moon . . . or a hook.

. . . and a city burning, burning, burning . . .

A burst of heat almost took Sophie's breath away and the images changed, becoming dark, violent, becoming Tsagaglalal's memories. . . .

. . . a pyramid rent asunder . . .

. . . a circular roof garden blazing, exotic plants exploding into balls of fire, sap boiling, erupting into streaks of flame . . .

. . . a huge metal door melting, carvings of faces elongating in the heat, dissolving, dripping in long sticky globules, gold and silver flowing across a polished marble floor, curling together . . .

. . . hundreds of circular flying craft falling from the sky like burning comets to detonate across a mazelike city . . .

. . . and Scathach and Joan of Arc, bloodied and filthy, standing back to back on the steps of a pyramid surrounded by huge dog-headed monsters . . .

. . . while Palamedes stood over a fallen Shakespeare, protecting him, holding a lion-headed eagle at arm's length, its barbed

flapping wings tearing at him, its savage fangs inches from his head . . .

. . . and Saint-Germain raining fire down from the skies, while behind him the sea rose in a wall of black water . . .

. . . and Sophie . . . or a girl who looked so much like her that she might have been her identical twin . . .

Suddenly Sophie was five years old, standing in this very house, hand in hand with her brother, being introduced to an old woman she had never seen before.

"And this is your aunt Agnes," her mother was saying. "She will watch over you when we're not here. . . ."

Something cold slithered at the corner of Sophie's mind, not a memory but a thought, something sour and bitter. If Aunt Agnes wasn't her real aunt, then what about their other aunt, the mysterious Aunt Christine, who lived on Montauk Point and whom they visited every Christmas? Christine was not related to them either. Who was she? Was she like Agnes, and were the two women related? Sophie desperately wanted to talk to her mother and father; she needed to ask them how they knew Agnes and Christine and how long they had known the two women. She found herself wondering how the two old women had insinuated themselves into the Newmans' lives. She'd heard her father talk about Aunt Agnes, and her mother had spent all her childhood summers with Aunt Christine. The implications were terrifying. How long had the Newman family been under observation? And why? Was it because she and Josh were twins? But why then would Agnes and Christine have been watching her mother and

195

father? Unless they had known, all those years ago, that Richard and Sara would meet, fall in love, marry and give birth to a pair of gold and silver twins. Had they known it would happen naturally, or had they somehow manipulated it to make it happen? A shudder ran through Sophie: even the idea was terrifying.

She needed to talk to Josh about this; she wished he were here.

. . . And suddenly there was Josh. . . .

She felt the connection with her twin and it was as if she had been made physically whole again. For the past fifteen years, she didn't think they'd ever been apart for more than a couple of days at a time, and even then they'd always kept in touch via phone, text and email. Earlier, when Josh had turned his back on her and left with Dee and Dare, she'd felt as if she'd been bodily wounded, as if part of her was missing. But at least she knew now that he was alive.

He was . . . he was . . .

Sophie focused, concentrating on her brother, desperately trying to remember everything she had been taught so far about using her Awakened senses. She just needed to know that he was safe and unharmed. And if she could somehow find out where he was right now, then she could go and get him. She was sure that if it had been just herself and Josh earlier—with no one else around to interfere—then she would have been able to talk sense to him.

She saw him clearly in her head. Shaggy blond hair now turning greasy and in need of a wash, deep black circles under his blue eyes, streaks of black soot across his face . . .

Suddenly she smelled salt and iodine, mingled with the odors of a zoo, musky and meaty, and then the images started to form. One was clearer than the others: the distinctive outline of an island topped by a blocky white building with a lighthouse at one end.

Josh was on Alcatraz.

He was walking down a prison corridor. There were cells on both sides, and each one held a different creature. He couldn't name the creatures, but the Witch of Endor could identify all of them, and Sophie found that she knew them too—here were Celtic cluricauns and Japanese oni, English boggarts and Scandinavian trolls, Norwegian huldu alongside a Greek minotaur, and a Native American Windigo in a cell next to an Indian vetala. She could feel her brother's breath coming in short quick gasps, and she felt his stomach lurch as he passed a cell holding a nue, a Japanese monkey-headed, snake-tailed doglike creature.

He seemed to be unharmed, and no one was paying him any particular attention. Directly in front of him, the man who had chased them in Paris—Niccolò Machiavelli—was talking to a young-looking man in scuffed jeans and beat-up cowboy boots. Josh turned his head and Sophie saw John Dee and Virginia Dare whispering urgently together. They both stopped and simultaneously looked straight at Josh, at Sophie.

Instantly she broke the connection with her brother and forced herself back into the present, concentrating on feeling the heat surge through her body. The room was freezing. She forced herself to be aware of the two women's hands in hers

197

and fully conscious of the flow of aura through her fingertips into Perenelle's hand.

Nicholas Flamel twitched.

Sophie almost dropped Perenelle's and Tsagaglalal's hands in shock. She looked down at the Alchemyst. Strands of her silver aura and Tsagaglalal's white aura were curling around their outstretched arms into Perenelle's hands. Silver sparks and cloudy white filaments crackled from the Sorceress's body and connected with the scarab beetle, which was now pulsing gently, throbbing, pale green turning dark, then pale again. Sophie was abruptly aware of the beating of her own heart . . . and then realized that the scarab was pulsing in time to it. The Alchemyst's skin had taken on a pink tinge, and some of the deep lines around his eyes and forehead had faded. He looked younger.

He twitched again, fingers tightening, loosening, then tightening once more over the carved beetle.

"A little more," Perenelle whispered, voice thick with exhaustion.

"I cannot give you much more," Tsagaglalal mumbled. Blue-white sparks crawled through her hair.

"Then it comes down to you, Sophie," Perenelle said urgently. "I need a little more of your aura."

The girl shook her head. "I can't." She was swaying with exhaustion and she felt as if she were burning up with fever. Her head was pounding, her throat felt raw and her stomach was churning as if she'd just eaten a raw chili pepper. She remembered Scatty's warning about the dangers of using too much of one's aura: if a person used all their natural auric energy, the aura started to feed on that person's flesh for fuel. There was a very real danger that they could then spontaneously burst into flames.

"You must!"

"No!"

Sophie attempted to pull her hand free, but the immortal held it in a viselike grip. "Yes!" Perenelle said savagely, and for a single heartbeat her aura shivered from white to gray, then black, before burning smoke-white again.

Sophie tugged at her fingers but couldn't free them from the woman's grasp. "Let me go!"

"I need a little more. Nicholas needs a little more."

The Sorceress's aura was darkening, thickening, and suddenly the chill air was touched with the odors of green tea and anise. Sophie recognized the scents of Niten and Prometheus a heartbeat before colored strands of their auras began to seep up through the floor, royal blue wrapped around a thick column of bright bloodred. Their auras shifted across the floor before curling up around the Sorceress, darkening her aura briefly to black again.

"Enough, Sorceress," Tsagaglalal croaked. "Enough. You have done all you can."

The door to the room slammed open and Prometheus and Niten burst in. The Elder's and the Japanese immortal's auras had flared into armor around their bodies, but Prometheus's ornate red metal armor was paling, turning crystalline and transparent as all the color was leached from it, and Niten's wood and lacquer samurai armor was ragged and frayed.

"Sorceress," Prometheus roared, "what are you doing?"

"Enough," Niten said icily. "You will destroy us all."

"Never enough," Perenelle snarled. Her aura swirled with tendrils and streaks from all the auras in the room. The colors ran together, becoming cloudy, turning dark, then muddy, before finally changing to a pulsing black aura. A foul musty stink gathered in the air. When the Sorceress turned her head to look at Prometheus and Niten, her green eyes were solid black marble. "I need more . . . Nicholas needs more."

Sophie wrenched her hand free of the Sorceress's grasp. The sudden release sent her spinning across the room, into Niten's arms, where her silver aura turned his samurai armor solid and metallic.

"No!" Perenelle screamed, reaching for Sophie. "We're not done!" A shivering thread of white ran through her black aura, turning it gray, leaching the darkness from it.

Prometheus stepped in front of Sophie and Niten. "You are done, Sorceress." He looked at the old woman and nodded. Tsagaglalal dropped Perenelle's hand and stepped back.

"But Nicholas . . . ," Perenelle whispered. Her aura flicked white again, and her eyes slowly turned green.

"You have done all that you can do for him," the Elder said.

Abruptly Nicholas Flamel sighed, a long hissing breath that curled white smoke from his blue lips into the air. His colorless eyes flicked open and he sat bolt upright and looked around. "Have I missed anything exciting?"

CHAPTER THIRTY

*F*ive huge anpu escorted the hook-handed man through the gold and marble halls of the Palace of the Sun. The normally bustling corridors had been emptied, and armed anpu, some of them holding smaller four-legged anpu-like dogs, guarded every door. Scented candles and aromatic reeds burned in tall holders set at regular intervals along the brightly lit hallway, but their sweet smells were completely overwhelmed by the heavy musky stink of the anpu.

Marethyu was wrapped in unbreakable stone chains, one around each wrist, another encircling his waist and two more around his ankles. The guards each held one chain, keeping him at the center of a circle. He had been stripped of his enveloping cloak, which one of the guards now carried draped over his arm, leaving him wearing a long-sleeved shirt of linked chain mail, which covered him from neck to waist,

201

over a pair of dirty and frayed jeans. Metal caps glinted on the toes of his scuffed and battered work boots. Overlong greasy blond hair fell to his shoulders, and badly cut bangs tumbled over his startlingly blue eyes. A three-day growth of gray-white stubble covered his cheeks and chin. His head was darting to and fro as they moved deeper into the palace, lips moving as he translated glyphs on the ancient wall panels or deciphered the crude Ogham writing decorating the plinths below glass and metal statues that were set at regular intervals along the hall.

The anpu guards pulled him halfway to a tall narrow double door. They made no move to knock or enter.

The hook-handed man leaned forward against his chains to examine the door. Two huge slabs of metal, gold and silver, bracketed the opening, polished to a mirror sheen. Above, a solid gold lintel as tall as a man was carved with thousands of square glyphs, each containing either a human, animal or beast face. Several of the glyphs were empty, or half completed. But in the center of the lintel was one square, larger than the others, which showed a detailed carving of a half-moon . . . or a hook.

Marethyu jerked his left hand, almost pulling the anpu holding that chain off its feet as he raised his arm to compare his hook with the carving. They were almost identical. Squinting, he painstakingly translated the glyphs surrounding the image of the hook.

"Curious, is it not?" A powerful voice echoed through the hallway.

The double doors cracked open and scented white smoke

202

curled out and writhed across the floor. The smoke was rich with the cloying scent of frankincense. The speaker remained hidden until the doors opened fully and harsh white light blazed from within. Framed in the opening stood an unnaturally tall figure, white light running off its long, hooded metal robe like liquid. "I found this doorway in the ruins of an Earthlord city in the middle of a wretched swampland far to the south of here. The swamp had claimed most of the city; the doorway was pristine and untouched. It is ten thousand—perhaps ten times ten thousand—years old."

Marethyu jerked again, and the anpu holding the chain struggled to remain on its feet. He raised his arm and the flat half-moon of metal set into his wrist turned silver, then gold with the reflected light. "It is curious," he agreed, "and yet it does not surprise me. Not much surprises me anymore." He raised his chin, nodded at the line of square glyphs. "Nice to see that they remembered me in their histories."

"The Earthlords knew about you."

"We had a brief encounter."

"More than brief, surely? They carved your symbol up there with their list of kings and rulers." The tall figure in the metal robe stepped forward, pushing back his hood, revealing his elongated eyes and sharp features. "I am Aten of Danu Talis."

"I know who you are. And I am . . . Marethyu."

"I've been expecting you," Aten said.

"Did Abraham tell you I was coming?"

"No," Aten answered. "I've known about you for a long time . . . a very long time." He looked at the anpu guards and then at the stone chains around Marethyu. "Are these bonds necessary?" he asked.

"Your brother seemed to think so," Marethyu said with a smile that revealed small white teeth. "In fact, he was most insistent."

Aten's long teeth pressed against his lower lips. "I assume they are useless?"

"Completely." The air crackled and soured and a shadow flickered around the one-handed man. The stone bonds cracked and then crumbled to dust around him. The shock sent the anpu guards staggering back, scrabbling to draw their kopesh. Marethyu rubbed his left wrist with his right hand.

Aten looked at the jackal-headed guards. "Leave us," he commanded, and then turned and stepped back into the room.

Confused, the anpu looked at one another and then at Marethyu, who grinned and waved them away. "Off you go now, like good doggies." He turned and followed the Elder into the room, then turned to close the doors behind them. Although they were as thick as his body, they fell into place silently and without any effort. "Your brother will not be happy," Marethyu said.

"Anubis is rarely happy these days," Aten said. "He tells me I should kill you."

"Even trying would be a mistake," Marethyu said, smiling as he turned to face the Lord of Danu Talis. "You have no idea how many have tried." Folding his arms across his chest, he looked around. He was standing in an enormous circular room that was lit by a tiny artificial sun that floated

204

just below the high ceiling. He nodded in approval. "I love Archon technology. How long has it burned?"

Aten waved a long-fingered hand. "This is a replacement. It has lit this room for a thousand years and more. However, it is the last of its type. When it burns out, we will have to revert to something a little more primitive."

The round room was empty of all furniture, the solid gold walls and silver ceiling bare of decoration or writing. However, a circular mazelike pattern picked out in gold and silver tiles took up the entire floor: the map of Danu Talis. Silver tiles had been used to represent the water, and the shimmering light gave the impression that it was moving.

Aten took up a position at the center of the maze and then turned back to Marethyu. His huge yellow eyes glowed golden with reflected light. "I found this floor in an isolated Ancient ruin in the middle of the Great Desert. I believe it was once the ceiling of a cathedral." His fingers traced the design. "I modeled this city in its image. I rather liked the idea that an Ancient pattern should become the map of a modern city."

"I've seen the design before," Marethyu said, walking around the edge of the circle. "It turns up across the humani world and into the Shadowrealms and beyond." He unfolded his arms and clasped them behind his back, his head tilted to one side as he admired the pattern. "It is complete."

"Every piece."

"Our ancestors were astonishing," he said, then looked at the Elder. "Don't you agree?"

"You do not fear me?" Aten asked, not answering the question.

"I have no reason to fear you." Marethyu shook his head. "But you fear me, don't you," he said quietly.

"I fear what you represent."

"And what is that?"

"The death of my world."

Marethyu shook his head. "On the contrary. I am here to ensure that your world—this extraordinary and amazing world that you created—lives on."

Aten strode across the maze. He towered over the hook-handed man, but Marethyu remained still, regarding him impassively.

The Elder's yellow eyes narrowed to horizontal slits. "Do you mock me?"

"No," Marethyu said seriously. He held up his left arm and light dripped off the curved hook. Aten took a step back. "You have no idea what it has cost me to come here," the one-handed man continued. "I have endured millennia of suffering and have traveled through countless strands of time to be here in this place, at this particular time. I sacrificed *everything*—every single thing I loved—to stand before you."

"Why?"

"Because between us, we can decide the fate of Danu Talis and the untold generations that will come after it." Marethyu's dark aura flickered, briefly taking on the reflected gold in the room. He gestured, and suddenly the huge map beneath the Elder's feet dissolved, then shattered into ragged pieces. The silver flowed out, across and then over the gold tiles. "If Danu Talis does not fall, then the world to come will never exist. . . ." The silver tiles tarnished to a dull brown, then cracked and split apart. Marethyu gestured again; a chill breeze blew across the floor and the pieces of the ancient map scattered, leaving nothing but bare stone beneath. "Your empire, the vast De Danann empire, will destroy not only itself, but this entire planet within a single generation."

"I was rather fond of that floor," Aten murmured.

"Trust me, Elder, you are doomed to witness far worse destruction than that!"

Aten pushed his hands into his sleeves and turned away. The Elder strode across the bare floor, the edges of his metal robe striking sparks off the stones. He stepped out onto a flower-and-vine-draped balcony that overlooked the city of Danu Talis. Aten breathed deeply, drawing in the sweet scents of life and growth, dispelling the bitter, slightly sour taste of Marethyu's aura.

The light was beginning to dip in the west, the buildings burning gold, the canals winking silver. In the lower levels of some of the taller buildings, lights were burning. From far below came the sound of distant laughter and the faintest hint of music.

Marethyu appeared alongside Aten. Leaning his forearms on the balcony, he looked across the island-city.

"Behold the greatest city this planet has ever known," Aten said proudly.

Marethyu nodded. He raised his head, blue eyes darkening to match the color of the sky as he watched how the dipping sun painted the low-flying vimanas in burnished gold, making them look like streaks of light across the heavens. "It is a wonder."

"There have been great cities on the earth before this," Aten continued. "The Ancients had the city-colleges, their great centers of learning, and the Archons and Earthlords built huge cities in glass and metal in the distant past. But there has never been anything like Danu Talis."

"Its legend will endure for millennia," Marethyu agreed.

"Danu Talis is a city, a state, a country, and I have ruled it for close to two thousand years. My father, Amenhotep, ruled the town that was here before me, and my grandfather Thoth was one of the Great Elders who had wrested the original island from the seabed, ten thousand years previously."

"Yes, I know, I saw him do it," Marethyu said quietly.

"You were there?"

"Yes."

The Lord of Danu Talis looked at the hook-handed man for a long time. Finally he nodded. "I believe you," he said firmly. "And perhaps we will have time to discuss some of the things you have seen in your long life and extraordinary travels."

"We will not," Marethyu said. "I have very little time left in this place in this time."

Aten nodded. "Once, Danu Talis was little more than an island state, surrounded by enemies. When I came to the throne we were besieged on every side. Anubis and I changed all that. Now, Danu Talis is at the heart of a sprawling empire that stretches across the globe with outposts on every continent, including the distant icy Northlands. And all who once stood against us—Ancients, Archons and Earthlords—have been defeated or driven to the very edges of the known world."

"You are a student of history," Marethyu said. "My father—or rather, the man I believed to be my father—taught me that every empire is ultimately doomed. As I traveled through time and history, I found that he was correct. All great empires are destined to collapse."

Aten nodded. "I have studied the histories of the world back to the Time Before Time, and the lesson is clear: empires rise and fall." He turned to face the huge pyramid that dominated the center of the island. One half was lit up by the setting sun, the other dipped in shadow. Tiny fires burned on each of the hundreds of steps that led to the flat top of the structure, which was festooned with colorful flags beginning to flap in the evening breeze.

"Danu Talis is doomed," Marethyu said. "You don't need seers or prophecies to predict its future."

Aten looked at Marethyu. "What are you?" he asked suddenly. "You're neither Elder nor Ancient, and you're definitely not Archon or Earthlord."

"I am none of those things," Marethyu said seriously. "I am your future. You have ruled this city for millennia," he continued. "This has truly been the Golden Age of Danu Talis, but the city is destined to crumble into ruin and despair. And if that happens, then everything you have worked for, every sacrifice you have ever made, will have been for nothing. But it does not have to be this way. You can protect the reputation of your city; indeed, you can ensure that it forms the basis for not just one, but scores of civilizations for millennia to come."

"You know this to be true?"

"I have seen it," Marethyu said quietly, the evening sunlight now turning his eyes gold. "I swear this to be true."

"I believe you," Aten whispered again. "What do you want me to do?"

"I need you to become *waerloga*—an oath breaker. A warlock. I need you to betray your city."

"To whom?"

"To me."

CHAPTER THIRTY-ONE

Somehow, Josh Newman suddenly knew the names of the creatures in the cells: Cluricauns. Oni. Boggarts. Trolls. Huldu. Minotaur. Windigo. Vetala. Before he could wonder how the words had come to him, a coiling movement caught his attention and he stopped to look into a blackened room. He leaned closer and squinted into the darkness. The smell made his stomach lurch, and sour acid filled the back of his throat. He thought he was looking at a monkey, but as his eyes adjusted to the dim light, he realized that while the creature had the head of an ape, it had the striped body of a raccoon, and the legs of a tiger, and in place of a tail, a long black snake twitched on the floor. It was a nue, a creature from the darkest edges of Japanese lore. And one of the most famous nue had been killed by Niten.

Josh's hands froze on the bars of the cell.

How had he known that?

When he'd walked in, only a few minutes ago, the cells had been full of nameless monsters. Some he'd vaguely recognized from stories his parents had told him—like the bull-headed minotaur—but most of the others looked like they'd crawled out of a nightmare.

Now, not only did he know their names, he also knew that Niten had killed one of the Japanese nue.

Sophie.

A sudden image of his sister popped into his head. He wondered why he'd thought of her . . . and then he remembered that the last time he'd seen her, she'd been with Niten. Where she was now? Was she still with the Swordsman? Was she safe?

"Come along, Josh," Dee ordered as he and Virginia walked past.

"Be right there," Josh mumbled. He waited until Dee and Dare had moved on and then turned suddenly, almost expecting to find his sister behind him.

Sophie.

He breathed deeply, searching for the smell of her vanilla aura over the tang of salt and iodine and the heavy zoolike stink of the cellblock.

Sophie.

He felt a sudden wash of heat and rubbed his tingling fingers together. Was she here, now, watching him? She'd done it earlier, spied for Flamel and Perenelle when he'd been in Dee's office about to call Coatlicue.

Sophie. His lips formed her name . . . but there was noth-

212

ing, and for the first time in his life, he realized that he could not *sense* her. For Josh's entire life, his twin had been his one constant. When his parents were away, when the family drifted from country to country and he and Sophie moved from school to school, the one person he could depend on was his sister. And now she was gone.

"Josh?" Virginia said. "What's wrong?"

He shook his head. "I don't know. I'm not sure."

"Tell me what's troubling you," Virginia said quietly. She slipped her arm into his and gently eased him away from the cell, maneuvering him toward the open door at the end of the corridor, where Dee was waiting. When the Magician saw that they were coming, he turned and disappeared into the blinding light outside.

"It's nothing, really . . . ," Josh began, becoming uncomfortably aware of the woman walking beside him.

"Tell me," she urged again.

He took a deep breath. "It's strange. . . ."

Virginia laughed. "Strange?" She waved a hand toward the cells. "And what could be stranger than this? Tell me," she insisted.

Josh nodded. "When I came in here I didn't know what any of these things were . . . and then I did. Not only did I know all their names, I knew that Niten had killed one of them." He shook his head. "But I don't know *how* I knew that."

"Why, it's very simple: you connected with someone. Your sister, probably."

Josh nodded miserably. "That's what I thought." He lowered his voice and looked around again. "I think they might be spying on us."

Virginia shook her head, strands of her long hair blowing across Josh's face. "Not on us. On you. I would know instantly if anyone was watching me. And I can assure you, nothing could spy on Dee or Machiavelli without their knowledge. It might be nothing more than your sister checking up on you." They walked past a cell that contained a goat-headed monster, and Virginia nodded at it. "What is that?" she asked.

Josh took a step closer to get a better look, then shook his head. "I don't know," he admitted. "What is it?"

"A pooka." Virginia smiled. "And the fact that you did not know tells us that whoever was watching you is gone. My guess is that your sister connected with you, and that enabled you to access her knowledge. It is," she added, "a remarkable skill." Virginia reached around and twisted her long hair into a thick knot at the nape of her neck. "Were you very close, you and your sister?"

Josh nodded sadly. "Very."

"You must miss her," Virginia said.

Josh stared straight ahead at the rectangle of light. His eyes watered and he pretended that they were reacting to the harsh light streaming in the door. Finally he said, "Yes, I miss her. And I don't understand what happened to her."

"No doubt she is saying exactly the same thing about you. Do you love her?" Dare asked quickly.

He opened his mouth to respond but closed it again without saying anything. He was suddenly conscious of the beating of his heart. It was hammering in his chest, as if he'd just run the length of a football field. He discovered he was almost afraid to answer, almost afraid to even consider the question.

"Do you love her?" Virginia persisted.

Josh looked at the immortal. There was a time he would have been able to answer in a second . . . but things had changed. Sophie had changed, and his feelings for her were . . . confused.

"Well?" Virginia asked.

"Yes . . . no . . . I don't know. I mean, she's my sister, my twin, my family. . . ."

"Ah. In my experience, when people say they don't know whether they love someone, they usually mean no. But in your case I'm not so sure. You still have feelings for her." She moved slightly ahead of Josh, and half turned so that she could watch his face. "If you had a chance, would you rescue her?"

"Of course."

"What would you do to rescue her?"

"Anything," he said quickly. "Everything."

"Then you still love her," Dare said triumphantly.

"I guess I still do," he admitted. "I just wish I knew what changed her."

"Oh, that's simple: the Flamels changed her." The immortal tapped a finger in the center of Josh's chest. "Just as they—and then Dee—changed you. Though whether he changed you for better or worse . . . well, only you can say." Then she leaned forward and added, "Or only time will tell."

"Are the Flamels really that bad?" he asked, lowering his

215

voice even though Dee had stepped out of the cellblock. "I still don't know if I can believe the doctor or not. I mean, I know you're a friend of Dee's and all that, but I just wondered . . ."

"I may be a friend to Dee—and even by his own admission, he is not a good friend—but my friendship does not blind me to what he is."

"And what is that?"

"Driven." She smiled again. "Driven by the same needs and desires that control both Machiavelli and Flamel. In another time and in different circumstances, I think they would have made wonderful friends."

"Can I trust him?" Josh asked.

"What do you think?" Virginia asked.

"I don't know what to think anymore. But Sophie *was* whipping at Coatlicue. And I still don't know how she could do that. My sister would never hurt anything. She'd even make me scoop up spiders she found in the bathtub and drop them out the window. And she really doesn't like spiders."

"Perhaps she thought she was protecting you," Virginia said gently. "When those we love are threatened, we find we can do the unthinkable."

"You didn't answer me," Josh said. "Are the Flamels really as bad as Dee says they are?"

Virginia Dare stopped at the door and turned to look back at Josh. Her face was in shadow, but her gray eyes blazed with an unearthly light. "Yes, they are as bad as he says. Worse, probably."

"Do you believe that the Elders should return to this earth?"

"They would bring many benefits," Virginia said slowly.

"That doesn't answer my question," he snapped, a touch of genuine anger in his voice. "You're really good at not giving straight answers."

"Your question is irrelevant," Dare said. "The Elders are coming back, whether we like it or not. Shortly, Nereus will release the Lotan, and then Machiavelli will awaken the sleeping menagerie in the cells and unleash them on San Francisco. They will tear the city apart. The police, army, air force and navy of the most powerful nation on earth will find themselves powerless. All their sophisticated weapons will be useless. And when the city is on the point of collapse, when the leaders of this country come to the conclusion that the only way to contain the monsters is to seal off the city and then utterly destroy it, then a representative of the Elders will appear with an extraordinary offer. The Elders will vanquish the monsters and save not only the city but the entire continent and ultimately the world. It is an offer the government of the United States cannot refuse. The Elders will save the day and end up being worshipped as heroes and gods. That's how it was in the past. That is how it will be in the future. Originally this was to be done around the Time of Litha, the summer solstice . . ." Virginia Dare's lips curled in a quick smile. "But the good Dr. Dee forced the Elders to change their plans. Now they are moving far more quickly than they had planned."

"So what Dee is doing is for good," Josh said eagerly. "When the Elders come back, they will bring all the benefits of their ancient technology."

"That is a possibility."

"And what will they do to Dee? He's betrayed them, hasn't he? Are they scared of him?"

"Terrified," Virginia said with a laugh. "The Elders fear a servant they cannot control. And the doctor is, at this moment, completely out of control."

Virginia turned away, and Josh reached out to touch her shoulder. Gold and pale green sparks cracked across his fingertips. The immortal turned her head, narrow eyebrows raised in a question. "The last person who touched me without permission died a miserable death."

Josh jerked his hand back. "You said the Elders are returning—what happens to Dee when they do?"

Virginia Dare looked at him carefully, her pupils turning huge and mesmerizing, but she remained silent, forcing Josh to continue.

"If the Elders are after Dee, then he can't let them return. I mean . . ." Josh hesitated a moment. ". . . they'd kill him."

Virginia continued to stare at him, and in his discomfort, Josh stumbled on.

"Unless he thinks that by giving them the city, he'll get back on their good side," he finally finished.

Dare blinked and shook her head, easing the tension between them. Josh exhaled a breath he hadn't realized he'd been holding.

"An interesting question," Virginia Dare murmured, then

smiled lightly again. "But I'm sure the doctor has thought of that. He'll have a plan. He always has a plan." She stepped out into the light, leaving Josh alone in the dark block. "And it usually goes wrong," she added very quietly to herself. But the sound bounced off the walls and drifted back up to Josh.

CHAPTER THIRTY-TWO

*A*nubis touched the vimana's control and the circular craft rocked gently to one side, keeping in the shadows of the gathering evening clouds. Below, far below, on the rooftop garden of the Palace of the Sun, he saw his brother Aten walking with the one-handed man. "I would give a small fortune to know what they are talking about," he said to the cloaked figure sitting beside him.

"They should not be talking at all," a voice growled from within the folds of fabric.

"What should I do, Mother?"

The figure shifted and leaned forward, and the reflected light from the city below brought yellow eyes to blazing life. The light ran off a furred snout and high triangular ears, quivering off long pointed whiskers. The Change had been particularly cruel to Bastet, mother of Aten and Anubis; while her body had remained that of a beautiful young woman, her head and hands were those of a huge cat. "I sometimes think your father chose the wrong person to succeed him," she hissed. "It should have been you."

Anubis bowed his head. The changes to the structure of his jaw and chin prevented him from smiling.

A long cat's claw pointed to the hook-handed man. "I cannot understand how your brother can even bear to be in the same room as that foul creature."

"Does Aten know what the hook-handed man is?" Anubis asked.

Bastet hissed. "He must. Aten is a student of history. He knows that every legend—Earthlord, Ancient and Archon—speaks of this one: the hook-handed, the destroyer. The Earthlords called him Moros and the Ancients knew him as Mot, while the Archons called him Oberour Ar Maro. This is how we came by our own name for him: Marethyu."

"Death."

"Death," Bastet acknowledged. "And he has come to destroy us. Of that I have no doubt. Even those meddling fools Abraham and Chronos agree about that."

"What should I do?" Anubis asked again, nudging the vimana lower, following Aten and the hook-handed man as they walked on the balcony that encircled the roof.

Bastet's claws dug into the vimana's smooth wall, leaving deep grooves in the virtually indestructible ceramic. "Your father would be shamed. I am pleased that he did not live to see his son speak to this creature." She shook her huge head. "I helped tear this island off the seabed. Along with your father, I ruled Danu Talis for millennia. I will not see it

221

destroyed because of your brother's stupidity." Ropey curls of saliva dripped from Bastet's fangs. "From this day forth, Aten is no longer my son." Her huge savage head turned to look into Anubis's black eyes. "Take back Danu Talis. I will champion your claim to the throne. I will talk to Isis and Osiris; they have no love for your brother. They will support you."

Anubis growled. "They are never at court. Who knows where my aunt and uncle's loyalty lies?"

"Isis and Osiris's loyalty has never been in question. Unlike your brother, they have always known that their duty was to their family and this island," Bastet snarled. "Individually they are strong, and together they command extraordinary powers. I have seen some of the new Shadowrealms they have begun creating, and they are magnificent. And although your aunt and uncle are my age—in fact, Isis is a little older—they have managed to keep the Change at bay. He is handsome and she is still beautiful." Bastet was unable to keep the bitterness out of her voice.

"If Isis and Osiris support me, then the rest of the Elders and Great Elders will join with them," Anubis said slowly, thinking aloud. "But why would they want to back my claim?"

"They have no children of their own. After Aten, you are their next nephew. And they have never shown an interest in ruling just one continent in one realm. Millennia ago, they announced that one day they would rule a myriad of worlds, even if they had to create those worlds themselves." Bastet pointed over the edge of the craft. "Capture Marethyu. You did it before, you can do it again. You will have to move swiftly to arrest your brother, but the anpu answer only to you. Then send some anpu to Murias to capture Abraham and all who support him."

"Then what should I do, Mother?"

Bastet's huge yellow eyes blinked in surprise. She turned her face to the north, where the volcano prison Huracan rose over the island. "Why, you must feed them—all of them, Aten, Marethyu, Abraham and the foreign prisoners—into the fires of the volcano."

Anubis nodded. "And when should I do this?"

Bastet pointed below to where Aten had taken Marethyu's hand in his, sealing whatever bargain they had just made. "Now would be a good time." Her claws wrapped around her son's pawlike hands, squeezing tightly enough to draw blood. "Kill them, Anubis. Kill them all, and Danu Talis is yours."

"And yours, Mother," Anubis whispered, trying to extricate his torn hands.

"And mine," she agreed. "We will rule for all eternity."

CHAPTER THIRTY-THREE

*M*ars Ultor stopped at the corner of Broadway and Scott Street to catch his breath. Leaning against a redbrick wall, he looked back down Broadway. He hadn't realized it was all uphill, and his legs, long unused to exercise, were two solid pillars of pain, muscles cramping and spasming. When Zephaniah had released him from his bone prison deep beneath Paris, centuries of encrusted and hardened aura had fallen to dust around his feet, stripping him of much of his huge bulk, taking inches off his height. Beneath the shell, he'd been horrified to discover that his once-muscular body was flabby and soft, and his legs in particular felt weak, barely able to support his weight. But at least Mars Ultor could get his strength back; Zephaniah would forever be without her eyes, which she had traded to Chronos in return for the knowledge that would keep her husband safe. Mars Ultor drew in a deep breath. When all of this was over—and presuming that he survived—he thought he would pay a visit to the loathsome Chronos. No doubt the repulsive Elder still had Zephaniah's eyes in a jar somewhere. Maybe he could be persuaded to part with them. Mars laced his fingers together and cracked his knuckles. He could be very persuasive.

Turning left, he started up Scott Street.

The Elder felt the extraordinary wash of power and had already stepped away from the road even before the stripped-down, battered army surplus jeep carrying three people pulled up to the curb, tires squealing on the pavement.

A tall, striking-looking Native American with copper skin and hatchet-sharp features leaned out. "You're Mars." It was a statement, not a question.

"Who wants to know?" Mars Ultor asked, looking up and down the street, wondering if this was an attack.

One of the figures in the back of the jeep sat forward and tilted up the brim of a Stetson cowboy hat to reveal a patch over his right eye. "I do."

Mars Ultor froze. "Odin?"

Then the third person, smaller, wrapped in a heavy duffle coat, pushed back the hood to reveal a narrow canine face, with two thick fangs jutting from beneath her upper lips. It was a woman, wearing dark wraparound sunglasses that covered most of her face but could not conceal the streaks of black liquid running from her eyes.

"Hel?"

"Uncle," she rasped.

225

Blue eyes huge in his pale face, Mars Ultor looked from Odin to Hel and then turned to the driver. "Am I still dreaming?"

"If you are, then this is a nightmare." The driver held out his hand, revealing his muscular forearms. A thick turquoise band encircled his wrist. "I'm Ma-ka-tai-me-she-kia-kiak." He was dressed in worn jeans, old cowboy boots and a faded Grand Canyon T-shirt. "But you can call me Black Hawk. My master is Quetzalcoatl. He sent me to collect this pair"—he jerked his thumb behind him—"and I got a call a little while ago, asking me to pick you up. Oh, and he sends his regards, too." Black Hawk leaned over as Mars climbed into the passenger seat. "But I don't think he was sincere." He revved the engine and turned to look at the mismatched trio. "What is this, some sort of badly dressed Elders convention?"

Still shocked, Mars ignored the driver and swiveled around to look at the two Elders behind him. "The last time I saw you two, you were at one another's throats."

"That was then . . . ," Odin said.

". . . and this is now," Hel lisped. "Now we have a common enemy. An *utlaga* servant who thinks he can become the master."

Black Hawk pulled away from the curb and crawled up the hill, dark eyes darting left and right, checking for an address.

"There is a humani called John Dee," Odin said.

Mars Ultor nodded. "Zephaniah told me about him. She said that he had attempted to raise Coatlicue in order to set her on us."

226

"Dee destroyed the Yggdrasill," Odin said, reverting to a language that predated the arrival of the humani by millennia. "He killed Hekate."

There was the sudden stink of burnt meat and a purplered shimmer darkened the Elder's flesh. "Ah, my dear wife forgot to tell me that. A humani killed Hekate?" Mars Ultor asked, voice trembling with rage. "Your Hekate?" he said to Odin.

The Elder nodded. "My Hekate," he whispered.

"And destroyed the Yggdrasill," Hel repeated. "The Shadowrealms of Asgard, Niflheim and the World of Darkness were destroyed. The gates to another six worlds have collapsed, sealing them off forever, dooming them to stagnation and destruction."

"One man did this?" Mars asked.

"The humani Dee," Hel said. She leaned forward, enfolding Mars in a foul miasma. "Dee's masters want him alive. But while Dee lives, he is a danger to us all. My uncle and I are joined in common purpose: we are here to kill Dee." She rested a clawed hand on Mars Ultor's shoulder. "It would be a mistake to stand against us."

Mars swept the Elder's fingers off his shoulder as if he were brushing away some lint. "Don't even think about threatening me, niece. I know I have been gone a long time. Perhaps you have forgotten who I am. *What* I am."

"We know who you are, cousin," Odin said quietly. "We know what you are—we all lost friends and relatives to your rages. The more important question is: why are you here?"

Mars Ultor smiled. "Well, for once, cousin and niece, we

are on the same side. This very day my wife freed me and tasked me with a single mission: to kill Dr. John Dee."

Black Hawk pulled the jeep over and cut the engine before either of the Elders in the backseat could respond. "We're here," the Native American immortal announced.

"Where?" Mars Ultor asked.

"The home of Tsagaglalal the Watcher."

Mars and Odin were helping Hel out of the jeep when the door opened and Prometheus and Niten, both wrapped in their auric armor, appeared at the top of the steps leading to the house. The air soured with a mixture of scents—burnt meat and green tea, anise, sarsaparilla and rotting fish—and then, with a howl of rage, Mars Ultor produced a short sword from beneath his leather jacket and launched himself at Prometheus, the blade flickering toward his throat.

CHAPTER THIRTY-FOUR

"*I*'ve just been talking to the boy," Virginia Dare said, catching up with John Dee as he strode down the pathway that wound around the island.

Dee glanced sidelong at the woman but did not speak.

Virginia shook her head, loosening the knot of hair tied at her neck and letting it fall down her back once more. "He asked me what happens when all the monsters are released into the city."

"There will be terror," Dee said, waving his hand in the air. "Chaos."

"Ah yes, your specialty, Doctor. But what about the Elders?" She raised one eyebrow. "I thought the plan was that the monsters would ravage the city, and then the Elders would appear and save the day."

"Yes, that was the original plan."

They rounded a corner and the wind coming in low across

the bay whipped at them. San Francisco and the Golden Gate Bridge rose across the water through an early-afternoon haze.

"I take it the plan has changed."

"It changed."

Virginia exhaled a deep breath in frustration. "Do I have to drag every sentence out of you, or are you going to share with me? You got me involved, after all. I was happy in London, content and invisible. Now I have a price on my head because of you."

Dee remained silent.

"You are starting to irritate me," Virginia said very quietly. "And you do not want to make me angry. I don't believe you've ever actually seen me angry."

The Magician glanced over his shoulder. Machiavelli was chatting with Billy, while Josh trailed behind them. The three were far enough away that they wouldn't be able to hear him, but he still lowered his voice to little more than a whisper. "I made you promises."

"You promised me this world."

"I did."

"And I expect you to make good on your promise."

The doctor nodded. "I am—and have always been—a man of my word."

"No, Doctor. You are—and have always been—a consummate liar," Virginia said, "but at least you've always been careful to tell *me* the truth." Her voice turned as chill as the wind gusting across the bay. "It is the only thing that has kept you alive these many centuries."

Dee nodded. "You are right, of course. I have never intentionally lied to you." He sighed. "These last few days have been . . . difficult."

"Difficult?" Virginia Dare smiled. "That would seem to be an understatement." Her smile broadened into a grin. "In the space of a week, you have gone from being an agent—no, more than that, *the* agent—of the greatest of the Dark Elders to being declared *utlaga*. They want you dead. You have slain an Elder and destroyed countless Shadowrealms."

"You don't have to remind me . . . ," Dee began, but Virginia continued.

"In only seven days, everything you have ever worked for, everything you have ever believed in, has been changed and changed utterly."

"You're enjoying this, aren't you!" Dee raised his voice.

"I'm curious to see how you extricate yourself, Doctor."

"Well, as you say: you're in this with me now. You've spent most of your life in the shadows, Virginia. But now the spotlight has been shone on you. The Elders and their Next Generation and humani mercenaries will come for me, but they'll be hunting you, as well."

"Which is precisely my problem with you," Virginia said, fingers closing around her wooden flute. She could feel it grow warm beneath her flesh.

"I have a plan," Dee said.

"I thought you might."

"A dangerous plan."

"I have no doubt about it."

Dee stopped before a jumbled pile of boulders on the narrow beach. He looked back at Josh and the approaching immortals. "These last few days have taught me a lot. They made me realize that I should be the master and not the slave. And the week has not been a complete write-off," he continued.

"May I remind you that your offices have burned to the ground, you have no money and there is nowhere safe for you on this Shadowrealm? Even your plan to release Coatlicue has failed."

"But I do have the four Swords of Power and the Codex. Well, most of the Codex," he amended. "Flamel still has the last two pages."

"Has he?" Virginia Dare thought about that for a moment. "You could trade what you have—the four swords and the Book—to the Elders. That might be worth your freedom and your life."

"That would be selling them far too cheaply. With the swords and the Codex . . . there is little I cannot do."

"As soon as you activate the swords, you will betray your position to the Elders. Sell them the swords in return for banishment to an obscure Shadowrealm."

"I've come up with a much better idea. I promised you this world," Dee said quickly. "But I think I am in a position to offer you more, much, much more."

"Tell me," Dare said, suddenly interested.

"You have always been greedy. You told me you want to rule."

"John . . . ," she said, a note of warning in her voice.

"Stay with me," Dee said urgently, "believe in me, protect

and support me, and I will give you not just one world to rule, and not two or three, but all of them."

"All?" Virginia shook her head in frustration. "John, you're not making sense."

Dee giggled. "How would you like to rule the myriad Shadowrealms?"

"Which ones?"

"Just as I have said—all of them."

"That's not possible. . . ."

"Oh, but it is. And I know how to do it." The Magician laughed again, the sound high-pitched and hysterical.

"And if I get the Shadowrealms, what do you get, Dr. Dee?"

"One world—just one. I want the first world. The original."

"You want Danu Talis?" Virginia Dare breathed.

He nodded. "Danu Talis." His eyes glittered madly. "I want Danu Talis, but not to rule—you could rule it for me if you wished. I've spent my entire life in search of knowledge. But in one location, I would have the entire knowledge of four great races—Elder, Archon, Ancient and Earthlord— gathered together."

Virginia stared at him blankly.

"I will make you the new Isis. I will make you the empress of the Shadowrealms." He moved ahead of Dare and then swung around so that he was facing her. He walked backward, his eyes fixed on hers. "I have never lied to you, Virginia. You have said so yourself. Think about it—Virginia Dare: Empress of the Shadowrealms."

"I like the sound of that," Virginia said quietly. "What do you want me to do?"

"*Video et taceo,*" he said.

"What's that supposed to mean?" she said, impatient.

"It is the motto of someone I once loved. It means 'I see and say nothing.' So why don't you take that advice—shut up, watch closely and say nothing."

CHAPTER THIRTY-FIVE

"That laugh is starting to freak me out," Billy murmured.

Machiavelli nodded. "I fear the pressure is beginning to get to the doctor."

"They're up to something," Billy said, looking ahead to where Dee and Dare were deep in conversation.

"You know Virginia Dare better than I do," the Italian said. "Do you trust her?"

Billy stuck his hands in the back pockets of his jeans. "The last person I trusted shot me in the back."

"I'll take that as a no, then."

"Niccolò, I like her. We've had some great adventures together. She's saved my life on a couple of occasions, and I've saved hers." He started to smile and then his face creased in pain. "But Virginia is . . . well, she's . . . she's just a little strange."

"Billy," Machiavelli said with a laugh, "we're all a little strange." He shivered in the breeze and pulled his ruined suit jacket closed.

"But Virginia's stranger than most." The American shook his head. "She is an immortal humani, but she is different—dangerously different. She grew up alone, running wild in the woods of Virginia. The local Native American tribes looked out for her, left her food and clothes. I think they believed she was a forest spirit or something like that. They feared her and called her a Windigo: a monster. When villagers went missing in the forest, it was said that they had been taken by the Windigo. And eaten."

Machiavelli sucked in a breath. "Are you implying . . ."

Billy shook his head quickly. "I'm just telling you the story. As far as I know, she's a vegetarian," he added. "She's always been vague with the dates, but she didn't learn to speak until she was ten or eleven. At that point she could already communicate fluently with animals and her forest craft was second to none, but I don't know how she survived, I have no idea what she had to do. And I'm not going to ask, either. What I *do* know is that those years damaged her. She doesn't really care too much for people, though she's never met an animal she couldn't tame. She told me once that she was happiest when she ruled over the woods of Virginia, where all the creatures knew her, and the natives honored and feared her."

"I had no idea," Machiavelli said. "There isn't much information in her file."

"Do you know she killed her master?"

Machiavelli nodded. "I know that. And I know that she

236

and Dee were close. I believe they may even have been betrothed, though I am sure it was not a love match."

"I also know this," Billy continued, "she wants to rule. In a couple of the nearby Shadowrealms, she is revered as a goddess. She wants people to worship her and to fear her, just like the natives in Virginia did."

"Yes. It makes her feel needed," Machiavelli said. "Hardly surprising for a girl who was abandoned as a baby. So she is dangerous?"

"Oh, she is that. In most of those Shadowrealms, she's worshipped as a goddess of death," Billy said grimly. "The last mistake you will ever make is to underestimate her. The second-to-last would be to trust her."

At that moment the Magician's maniacal laughter was carried back on the wind. "I wonder, does Dee know that?" Machiavelli asked. "Would she be loyal to him . . . if anything were to happen?"

Billy looked at the Italian carefully. "And what might happen?" he said softly.

Machiavelli gazed across the bay to the city and frowned, deep lines appearing on his high forehead. "I've been thinking a lot about my wife, Marietta, recently. Were you ever married, Billy?"

The American shook his head. "Never had time before I became immortal; never wanted to afterward. Didn't think it would be fair to my wife."

"Very wise. I wish I'd been as considerate. I've come to the conclusion that immortals should only marry other immortals. Nicholas and Perenelle are very lucky to have lived so long with one another." He laughed. "Maybe Dee should have married Dare. What a couple they would have made."

Billy grinned. "She'd have killed him within the first year. Virginia has a terrible temper."

"My wife, Marietta, had a temper. But she had every reason to. I was not a particularly good husband. I was away at court too often and for too long, and the politics of the time meant that I lived with the constant threat of assassination. My poor Marietta put up with a lot. She once accused me of being an inhuman monster. She told me I'd stopped thinking of people as individuals. They were masses—faceless and anonymous—either enemies or friends."

"And was she right?"

"Yes, she was," the Italian said sadly. "And then she held up my baby son, Guido, and asked me if he was an individual."

Billy followed the direction of Machiavelli's stare. "So is that a city of faceless masses, or is it filled with individuals?"

"Why do you ask?"

"Because I'm thinking that you would have no problem keeping your word to your Elder master and Quetzalcoatl and unleashing creatures on the faceless masses in the city."

"You're right. I've done it before."

"But if you see it as a city of individuals . . ."

"That would be different," Machiavelli agreed.

"Who was it who said, 'The promise given was a necessity of the past: the word broken is a necessity of the present'?"

The Italian looked quickly at the American immortal and then he dipped his head in a bow. "I do believe I said that once . . . a long, long time ago."

"You also wrote that a prince never lacks legitimate reasons to break his promise," Billy said with a grin.

"Yes, I did say that. You're full of surprises, Billy."

Billy looked from the city to the Italian. "So what do you see—faceless masses or individuals?"

"Individuals," Machiavelli whispered.

"Reason enough to break your promise to your Elder master and a bird-tailed monster?"

Machiavelli nodded. "Reason enough," he said.

"I knew you were going to say that." The American immortal reached out and squeezed the Italian's arm. "You're a good man, Niccolò Machiavelli."

"I don't think so. Right now, my thoughts make me *waerloga*—an oath breaker. A warlock."

"Warlock." Billy the Kid tilted his head. "I like it. Got a nice ring to it. I'm thinking I might become a warlock too."

CHAPTER THIRTY-SIX

*E*very problem had a solution, Scathach knew.

The only catch was that she'd never been particularly good at problem solving. That had always been her sister's specialty. Aoife was the strategist; Scathach preferred the direct approach. Sometimes riding straight into the heart of the enemy worked. She'd rescued Joan that way. But some problems required a subtler approach. And Scatty had never been subtle.

The Warrior sat in the mouth of her cell, her feet dangling over the edge, and looked down into the bubbling lava far below. She wished her sister were with her now. Aoife would know what to do. The Shadow swung her legs back and forth, drumming her heels against the wall, and turned her face to the circle of sky visible high above her head. Before yesterday she hadn't thought of her sister in a very long time, and now she'd thought of her two days in a row. Obviously, being on the island, only a few miles from where her parents and brother were living, had made her think of family. And though she would admit it to no one, Scathach was intensely lonely. She missed Aoife. Oh, she'd had humani friends, but they always aged and died; she'd had plenty of immortal friends—the Flamels were more parents to her than her birth parents had ever been—but even the oldest immortal had no idea of the things she'd done and the places she'd been. For millennia, she'd had no one to share her life with. Joan was as close as a sister to her, but Joan had been born in 1412—she was only five hundred and ninety-five years old. Scathach had spent two and a half thousand years in the earth Shadow-realm, and more than seven thousand years wandering the various other Shadowrealms. Only her twin sister knew what it was like to live for such a vast stretch of time.

She found herself idly wondering if Aoife ever paused to think of her. Somehow she doubted it; Aoife of the Shadows was interested only in herself.

Where was Aoife? Was she still in the earth Shadow-realm? Closing her eyes, Scathach focused on her sister. On those rare occasions in the past when she'd done this, she'd caught glimpses of places and people and wondered if she was connecting with her twin. But now there was nothing . . . only a blackness, an emptiness. The Warrior frowned. Had she connected with her sister, was this what Aoife was see-ing? Scathach had a strong sense that she was standing in a vast dark space . . . except that she wasn't alone. There was something else here. Something that moved in the empti-ness. Something big, that slithered and hissed and chuckled. Something old and evil.

And even though it was unbearably hot in the volcano, Scathach shivered.

Was her sister in trouble? It was an almost inconceivable thought. Aoife was at least as deadly as the Shadow. She was fast and ruthless, and lacked any feeling for the humani . . . except one: Niten—Miyamoto Musashi. Unconsciously, the Shadow nodded. The Swordsman would know her sister's whereabouts. Maybe, just maybe, when all this was over—and if she survived—she'd go to see Niten and ask him to get a message to Aoife. Maybe, just maybe, it was time to try to make amends.

Scathach leaned back on her elbows and looked up again into the circle of darkening sky. The pale blue had deepened to purple, and the first of the night stars had started to twin-kle. They were in configurations that she almost recognized.

A flash of crimson streaking across the sky startled her.

At first she thought it was a shooting star; then she real-ized it was a vimana moving silently through the heavens, lit up by the red glow of the lava below. It was followed by an-other and then another. Instinct and her finely honed sense of survival brought her to her feet, and on the other side of the volcano she saw Saint-Germain also stand. He too knew that something was wrong. Scathach had watched a single vimana fly in and out of the volcano for the past few hours, deliver-ing prisoners and then, more recently, tossing loaves of stale bread and gourds of sour water into the cell mouths. Some of the bread and water never made it and sailed down into the lava, but the anpu piloting the craft didn't seem to care if the prisoners went hungry or thirsty.

"Joan!" Scathach shouted.

"I see them," Joan of Arc called down. Her face appeared over the edge of a cave mouth high above Scathach's head. "I see ten or twelve. . . ."

Scatty squinted against the night sky. "Eight . . . ten . . . twelve—no, thirteen. Fourteen," she said finally. "I think there are fourteen."

Across the volcano, Palamedes waved at her. When he knew he had her attention, the Saracen Knight opened and closed his right hand three times.

"Fifteen," Scathach shouted up at Joan. "Palamedes has counted fifteen."

"So what's the plan?" Joan shouted.

"That depends. . . ."

"On what?"

"On who they come to first. I'm thinking they'll come to either Palamedes or me."

"Then what?"

Scathach's grin exposed her vampire teeth. "Well, the only way in or out of these cells is by these vimana. So we have to take control of one of them."

"Good plan," Joan said sarcastically. "So let us say you single-handedly manage to overpower two anpu while keeping the vimana in the air. What about the other fourteen craft? Do you think they're just going to float idly by?"

"I said it was a plan. I never said it was a perfect plan."

243

"I think your plan is just about to change," Joan called.

A new vimana had appeared. It was larger than the rest, and from below it looked like a long and sleek flattened triangle. Its surface reflected the night sky on one side and the glowing red lava on the other, making details difficult to distinguish. It hovered above the smaller circular craft, a vague menacing shape in the darkness. Abruptly it lit up, red, green and blue lights blazing to life on the three points of the triangle.

"Rukma vimana," Scathach shouted, reverting to the language of her youth. "Battleship. Get back, back into the cell!"

And then the triangular vimana dropped straight into the mouth of the volcano.

CHAPTER THIRTY-SEVEN

*M*ars Ultor lunged toward Prometheus with the razor-sharp short sword. Faster than the eye could see, Niten's hands moved, catching the underside of Mars's wrist with a stiff-fingered blow. The Elder's hand spasmed and automatically opened, and Niten caught the falling blade and deftly reversed it. And suddenly it was pointed at Mars's throat.

Niten cocked his head to one side. "There was a time when I would not have been able to even get close to you. You're getting old."

Mars bared his teeth in a savage grin. "Fast. As fast as I've ever seen." Then he grunted as a cramp bit at the back of his legs, sending him sprawling on the steps.

Niten tossed the short sword to Prometheus and reached down to offer the Elder his hand. "It is an honor to fight you."

"We didn't fight!" Mars came up quickly, the top of his head catching Niten in the stomach, doubling him over, sending him sprawling backward. The Swordsman rolled to his feet and dropped into a fighting stance.

"Stop that. Right this minute!" Tsagaglalal clipped Niten on the back of the head as she pushed past Prometheus and reached over to catch Mars Ultor by the ear. She twisted and he yelped. "And as for you—what have I told you about fighting?"

Mars Ultor turned as red as his aura. "Sorry, Mistress Tsagaglalal," he muttered.

The old woman looked at Niten and then pointed indoors. "Get inside now."

"He started it," he began.

"I don't care who started it. Get inside and wash your hands. They're filthy. You too," she snapped at Prometheus. "And you can give that to me," she said, reaching out her hand for the sword.

Struggling to keep a straight face, Prometheus flipped over the sword and presented it to her, hilt first. "Yes, ma'am," he said, bowing his head.

"And lay the table in the garden. We've got guests for tea." She turned and smiled at Odin, Hel and Black Hawk, who were standing at the bottom of the steps. "You will stay for tea."

No one said a word.

"It was not a request," she added, sudden steel in her voice.

CHAPTER THIRTY-EIGHT

*P*erenelle Flamel turned away from the bedroom window and looked at her husband. "You wouldn't believe me if I told you what I just witnessed," she said in archaic French.

Nicholas Flamel was standing by the mirror, carefully shaving a three-day growth of stubble off his cheeks. He looked at his wife in the glass. "You've just brought me back from the dead. I'll believe anything you tell me."

Perenelle sat on the end of a bed that was so high that her feet dangled above the floor. "Three Elders and an immortal have just turned up. One of them had an eye patch," she added significantly.

Nicholas grinned. "Odin. Come hunting Dee. Who else?"

"An odd-looking girl. It was hard to see her face, but it looked diseased, with black and white blotches. . . ."

"That sounds like Hel," Nicholas breathed. "Odin and Hel together. Dee is in so much trouble. Who else?"

"A big Elder in a leather jacket. I've never seen him before in my life. But the moment he saw Prometheus, he lunged at him with a short sword."

Nicholas smiled. "That could be anyone—Prometheus has many enemies, though very few of them are still alive," he added. "And the immortal?"

"I'm not sure, but his face was vaguely familiar to me." Perenelle frowned, trying to remember. "Native American. Not your friend Geronimo, though," she said quickly.

"Didn't think so," Nicholas said, wiping shaving foam off his chin. "He would never turn up in the company of Dark Elders." He turned to his wife and spread his arms wide. "How do I look?"

"Old." Perenelle jumped off the bed and wrapped her arms around her husband, holding him tightly. Her fingers traced the lines on his forehead. "Even your wrinkles have wrinkles."

"Well, I *am* six hundred and seventy-seven years old . . ."

"Six hundred and seventy-six," she corrected him. "It's still three months till your birth—" she started to say, and then stopped. They both knew they would not live to see his next birthday. Perenelle turned away quickly so that Nicholas would not see the tears in her eyes and pointed to a pile of clothes on the end of the bed. "This room is used by the twins' parents when they're in town. These clothes belong to their father. They might be a bit big on you, but at least they're clean."

"What happened to my jeans and T-shirt?" Nicholas asked.

"Beyond saving." Perenelle sat on the edge of the bed

and watched her husband dress. "A day, Nicholas, I have you for a single day."

"A lot can happen in a day," he said softly. He pulled on a khaki button-down shirt. The neck was too big and the sleeves came to the end of his hands. Perenelle rolled up the sleeves while he buttoned the shirt, and then she picked up the jade scarab from the bedside table. She'd woven a leather cord around it, and Nicholas ducked his head as she placed it around his neck. Resting her hand on the scarab, she pressed it to Nicholas's flesh. He placed his hand on top of hers. Their auras crackled green and white, and the room filled with the sharp odor of mint.

"Thank you," he said simply.

"For what?" she asked.

"For giving me the extra day."

"I didn't do it for you," she said with a smile. "I did it for purely selfish reasons."

He raised his eyebrows in a silent question.

"I did it for me. I did not want to live a day without you."

"We're not dead yet," he reminded her. Then he slipped his hands into hers. "Come, let's go see what the Elders are up to. It is suspiciously quiet downstairs."

"That's because they're all terrified of Tsagaglalal. They all know who she is." Perenelle paused a moment, then corrected herself. "*What* she is."

CHAPTER THIRTY-NINE

"*Showtime*," Billy the Kid muttered. He tapped Josh on the shoulder and pointed toward the Golden Gate Bridge.

Josh crouched on a low rock on the west shore of Alcatraz and watched a long V on the surface of the water sweeping in toward the island. The bow wave broke against the rocks on the beach and white spume flew high into the air. A greenish-black snakelike tentacle burst through the surface of the water and waved about for a moment before it dropped onto the rocks. It twitched, moving delicately across the sand and stone, and then the hundreds of little suckers on the pale underside of the tentacle attached themselves to a boulder. A second tentacle appeared, then a third and a fourth. Josh swallowed hard and shivered. "Snakes."

"You're looking a little green," Billy the Kid said, dropping into a crouch alongside Josh.

The young man nodded toward the tentacles. "They look like snakes. And I really hate snakes."

"Never been partial to snakes myself," Billy admitted. "Got myself bit by a rattler when I was younger. Swelled up, I did, and would have died if Black Hawk hadn't tended to me."

"If it was up to me," Josh said quickly, "I'd have no snakes in the world."

"I hear you."

Josh shivered. Although it was June, the wind coming in off the bay was brisk and the water droplets splashing up onto his face felt icy, but he knew that it was more than the weather that had him feeling cold. There was an almost palpable evil in the air. Ancient evil. "Have you ever met this Ner . . . Nere . . ."

"Nereus," Billy pronounced.

"Have you ever met him before?"

"I've heard of him, but I never met him before today. I've really never had a whole lot to do with any of the Elders or the Next Generation in the West. Dee and Machiavelli are the first of the truly old European immortals I've met." He pushed strands of his long hair back off his face. "I keep myself to myself and do odd jobs for my master, Quetzalcoatl. I run some errands, that sort of thing, act as bodyguard on his rare trips into the city. I've gone adventuring with Virginia into some of the nearby Shadowrealms, but most of them were close copies of this Shadowrealm, and we rarely came across monsters." He jerked his thumb back toward the cellblock above and behind them. "I never saw anything like those things before."

"Here he comes," Josh breathed. The surface of the water rippled and he braced himself, expecting some sort of tentacled serpentine monster. Instead, a surprisingly normal-looking man's head appeared above the waves, a mop of thickly curled hair plastered to his skull. His face was broad, with prominent cheekbones and a strong jaw covered with a thick beard that had been twisted into two tight curls, woven through with strips of seaweed.

"The Old Man of the Sea," Billy whispered. "An Elder."

"He looks normal to me," Josh began, and then Nereus heaved himself upward and the young man could see that the lower half of the Elder's body had been replaced with eight octopus legs. Only, something didn't look right. Three of the enormous legs ended as ragged stumps, and there was an ugly burnt patch of blistered skin in the center of the creature's forehead. The Elder was wearing a sleeveless jerkin of over-lapping kelp leaves stitched together with strands of seaweed, and there was a spiked stone trident strapped to his back. Josh coughed and Billy wiped his watering eyes—the clean salt air had been tainted with the stench of long-dead rotting fish and rancid blubber.

"Nereus," Dee called, marching down to the water's edge. "About time. We've been waiting."

The Old Man of the Sea leaned his human arms on the boulder and smiled at Dee, exposing a mouthful of tiny pointed teeth. "You forget yourself, humani. I do not answer to you." His voice was sticky and liquid. "And I'm hungry," he added.

"That is an idle threat and you know it," Dee snapped.

Nereus ignored him. "So what have we here. . . ." The Elder looked up at Machiavelli and Billy, then Virginia and finally Josh. "Immortals and a Gold, come to end the world. As it was foretold in the Time Before Time." He looked at Josh and the young man's aura flared protectively into golden chain-mail armor around his body. "And you . . . you are as I remember you," he said.

Josh attempted a laugh. "I've never met you before in my life, sir."

"Are you sure?" Nereus demanded.

"Oh, I'm sure I'd remember," Josh said, pleased that his voice didn't tremble too much.

"I was told that you would do my bidding," Dee interrupted.

Nereus ignored Dee and turned to Machiavelli. "Is it time?"

The Italian nodded. "It is time. Did you bring it?"

"I brought it." The Old Man of the Sea looked from Machiavelli to Dee and then back to the Italian. "Who wants to control the Lotan?"

"I do," Dee said immediately, stepping forward.

"Of course you do," Nereus bubbled. A tentacle unpeeled from a boulder and shot out to wrap around Dee's wrist, jerking him forward. The immortal didn't even have time to cry out. Virginia Dare started forward, her flute in her hand, but a look from Nereus stopped her. "Don't be stupid. If I wanted him dead, I could have plucked him off this rock and fed him to my daughters." Behind him, a dozen green-haired Nereids broke the surface of the bay, mouths open to reveal their piranha teeth. "And you and I will have a reckoning for what you did earlier. My family is very dear to me."

"You're not the first Elder to threaten me." Virginia Dare's cruel smile turned her face ugly. "And you know what happened to him."

The stink of rotting fish grew stronger, and both Billy and Josh gagged and inched away. Virginia threw her head back and breathed deeply. "Oh, I do so love the smell of fear."

Nereus turned back to Dee. "A little present for you," he said, pressing what looked like a small blue-veined egg into Dee's hands and closing the doctor's fingers over it. A tentacle wrapped around the English doctor's fist, locking it closed. "Whatever you do," Nereus said, "you must not open your hand." Then he squeezed tightly and the distinctive sound of a shell cracking could be heard.

"Why not?" Dee asked. And then he gasped, his eyes bulging in pain.

"Ah yes," Nereus bubbled once again, showing his teeth in a ferocious grin, "that would be the Lotan biting you."

Dee shuddered but remained silent, gray eyes fixed on the Elder's face.

"You're brave, I'll give you that," Nereus said, his mouth widening in an even more savage smile. "It is said that the bite of the Lotan is more painful than the sting of a scorpion."

The doctor had turned a ghastly white, and his eyes were

huge in his head. Beads of yellow sweat gathered on his fore-head, and the air stank of sulfur. "I thought . . . ," he said through gritted teeth, "I thought it would be bigger."

Billy looked at Josh and winked. "I thought that too."

"It will be," Nereus laughed. "It just needs to feed off a little blood first." Dee's entire body was jerking violently now. He attempted to pull his left arm free, but another of Nereus's tentacles had encircled the doctor's forearm. "Once it tastes your blood, it will be bonded to you. Then it is yours to control. But you must act swiftly. The Lotan are like may-flies; they have a very short lifespan. You have three or four hours at most before it dies." The Elder's tentacles fell away from Dee's arms and he added, "But that should be time enough to begin the destruction of the humani city."

Josh watched as the Old Man of the Sea crawled back over the rocky edge of the island and slid into the chill green waters of the bay. Women's heads popped up around him, green hair spreading like seaweed across the water. The Elder turned to look back and fixed his eyes on Josh. He frowned, as if trying to remember something, but then shook his head and sank beneath the surface. One by one, the Nereids disap-peared as well.

Virginia Dare rushed forward and caught Dee as he swayed on his feet. The Magician's skin was ashen; his left hand was still tightly shut, but blood was seeping from be-tween his fingers, which had turned a bruised purple. "Help me!" Virginia shouted.

Billy clambered over the rocks and wrapped an arm around Dee's waist, holding him upright. "I've got him."

"Let's move him up onto the rocks," Virginia said.

"No!" Machiavelli yelled. "Wait." He picked his way over the slippery boulders and stood in front of Dee. "Josh, help me here."

Without thinking, Josh climbed down over the stones to stand alongside the Italian.

"Observe me," Machiavelli said. He held up his arms and two ornate metal gloves formed over his hands. "Can you copy that?"

"Easy." Josh stretched out his hands, and the salty air was infused with the smell of citrus as golden metal gloves appeared over his fingers.

"Hold his arm," Machiavelli commanded, "and, whatever happens, do not let go." He looked at Virginia and Billy, who were standing on either side of the swaying Magician. "Are you ready?"

The two immortals looked at one another and nodded.

"Josh?"

The young man nodded and took hold of Dee's arm, stretching it out. The Magician's sulfurous aura fizzled and crackled where the golden gloves touched his flesh, but the scent of oranges was stronger than the stink of rotten eggs. Machiavelli reached for Dee's left hand, turning it palm upward, and then carefully opened his fingers. Nestled in the Magician's palm were the remains of the crushed shell. And in the midst of the fragments was the Lotan.

"It's kind of like a skink," Josh said, leaning forward for a closer look. The creature was tiny, not much more than one inch in length, four-legged, green-skinned, with long horizontal lines running down the length of its body. "Except for the heads," he added. Seven identical heads grew out of its body on short necks. Each head was attached to the flesh of Dee's palm, tiny round mouths sucking noisily as they drank his blood.

"If I didn't know any better," Billy the Kid said quietly, "I'd reckon the Old Man of the Sea was playing some sort of joke on us." He nodded at the tiny lizardlike creature. "Not much terrorizing to be done with that."

"Oh, Billy," Virginia said simply. "What do you do when you want to make something grow?"

The American looked at her blankly and shrugged.

Virginia shook her head, clearly disappointed that he didn't know the answer. "Just add water."

The creature raised its seven tiny heads as Machiavelli carefully plucked it off Dee's bloody flesh. It thrashed about violently, squeaking like a newborn kitten, each of the seven heads striking out at the Italian's hands, tiny needlelike teeth squealing and scraping on the immortal's hardened auric gloves. "Filthy thing," he muttered. Holding the Lotan at arm's length, Machiavelli dropped it into a pool of water collected in the rocks by his feet.

"Now what?" Billy asked.

"Now we run," Machiavelli said.

CHAPTER FORTY

$\mathcal{M}$arethyu and Aten raced down a narrow tunnel. The walls were polished black glass, etched with the scripts of a thousand dead languages that twisted and coiled in ever-moving lines and columns. Marethyu's glowing hook sent shadows dancing across the words.

"Tell me something," Aten said. His voice echoed slightly, bouncing off the tunnel walls.

Marethyu held up his hook and pale golden light washed over Aten's narrow features. "What do you want to know?"

"Why are you doing this?" Aten asked.

Marethyu's bright blue eyes widened in surprise. "Do I have a choice?"

"Everyone has a choice."

The hook-handed man shook his head. "I'm not sure I believe that. My life was shaped millennia before I was born. I sometimes think I am just an actor, playing a role."

The tunnel ended in a vast underground cavern. Water trickled in the darkness and the air smelled fresh and clean. Aten turned to face Marethyu. "Perhaps you are an actor, but you have accepted your role. You could just as easily have said no and walked away."

Marethyu shook his head. "If you knew the whole story, you'd see that that was impossible. If I did not fulfill my role, then the world would be a very different place."

The Elder reached out and touched the hook that took the place of Marethyu's left hand. It sparkled and crackled, blazing brighter. "You were not born with this."

"I was not."

"How did you lose your hand?"

"By choice," Marethyu said, his voice hardening. "It was a price I had to pay, and I paid it gladly."

Aten nodded. "Everything has a price. I understand that."

"Do you understand the price you will have to pay for allowing me to escape?"

Aten's lips curled in a smile. "Anubis and Bastet will use it as the excuse they need to move against me. Isis and Osiris will gather the Council of Elders to declare me unfit to rule and probably feed me to the volcano." He clapped his hands sharply together and a ripple of light shivered through the cave. Then he clapped again and the cave slowly lit up in a warm milk-white light. "The fungus on the walls is sensitive to sound," he explained.

There was a lake in the center of the cave, the black water speckled with white, running with long slow ripples. Sitting on the banks of the lake was a crystal vimana. It was almost

259

completely transparent, visible only because of the coating of white reflected light.

"Take it," Aten said. "I found it preserved in a block of ice on a plateau at the top of the world. It is probably the oldest vimana in existence, and despite its fragile appearance, it is practically indestructible."

Shouts suddenly echoed down the tunnel behind them, and the fungus pulsed and rippled in time with the sounds.

"They're coming. Go now, and do what you have to do."

"You could come with me," Marethyu said suddenly.

"The vimana will hold only one. And besides, didn't you tell me that everything has a price?"

The tramp of footsteps was closer, the clink of metal and armor rattling off the walls.

Marethyu stretched out his right hand and Aten took it in his. "Let me tell you this," the hook-handed man said. "We will meet again, you and I, in a different place and a different time."

"You know this to be true?"

"I do."

"Because you have seen the future?"

"Because I have been there."

Anubis and the anpu burst out of the tunnel just as the crystal vimana took to the air. It hovered silently, the hook-handed man clearly visible inside the craft. He raised his hook in golden salute. Aten raised his hand in acknowledgment, and the craft plummeted beneath the surface of the lake and disappeared.

"What have you done, brother?" Anubis snarled. "You have betrayed us."

"I did what I had to do to save the world."

"Chain him," Anubis commanded. He looked at his brother and his stiff face managed to twist and contort in rage. *"Waerloga,"* he spat.

The Elder nodded in agreement. "Aten the Warlock. It has a ring to it, don't you think?"

CHAPTER FORTY-ONE

Sophie Newman stood in the back garden beside the barbecue and watched Prometheus grill sausages. The big Elder was grinning and whistling tunelessly.

"What's so funny?" she asked.

"You should have seen the look on Mars's face," Prometheus said.

"You were—or you are—enemies?" she asked, and even as she was asking, images started to dance in her head.

. . . *Mars Ultor and Prometheus standing back to back against a horde of snake-headed warriors.*

. . . *Prometheus carrying a wounded Mars on his back as he dived off a bridge into a raging torrent . . .*

. . . *Mars snatching a barbed arrow out of the air, a hairsbreadth from Prometheus's throat . . .*

"Now, perhaps. Once we were friends, closer than brothers."

"What happened?"

"He went mad," he said sadly. "Or rather, the sword he carried drove him mad. The same sword your brother now carries."

Sophie looked across the garden to where the big man in the leather jacket stood drinking pink lemonade through a straw. "He doesn't look crazy, though."

"Not at the moment, he doesn't."

"Why did he attack you?"

"It's complicated," Prometheus said, jumping back as hot grease spat at him.

Sophie glanced at the sausages and sizzling hamburgers, then looked away quickly as her stomach turned. Ever since she'd been Awakened, she'd developed an aversion to meat. "How complicated?"

"Well, Mars married my sister, Zephaniah, which made us brothers-in-law. But when the sword drove him insane, I helped my sister capture him and trap him in a shell of his own hardened aura. She buried him deep underground, and over the centuries the city of Paris grew above his head."

"Sophie?" Aunt Agnes had appeared from the kitchen, carrying a tray.

"Just a minute, Aunt—"

"Now, Sophie," Tsagaglalal insisted.

"Excuse me," Sophie said, and crossed the patio.

Tsagaglalal handed her the tray, which held slices of cut sushi. "Will you help me pass these around? Our guests must be famished."

"Aunt Agnes . . . Tsagaglalal," Sophie said. She was completely confused. "What are we doing?"

"Feeding our guests," the old woman said with a smile.

"But they're mortal enemies."

"They know they must put their enmities aside in my presence," she said. "That is the tradition." The corners of the old woman's gray eyes crinkled in amusement. "Everything is as it should be. Now just help me hand out the food and we'll wait for Nicholas and Perenelle to join us."

Sophie followed Tsagaglalal across the patio to where Mars Ultor leaned against a low stone wall. He straightened when he saw the old woman approach, and put down his lemonade.

"Mistress Tsagaglalal," he said, bowing deeply. Suddenly his blue eyes turned huge behind tears. "I thought I would never see you again."

The old woman reached up to place the palm of her hand flat against his cheek. "Mars, old friend. It is good to see you. And you are looking well, too. You've lost weight. It suits you. How is Zephaniah?"

Mars nodded. "She is well, I think," he said cautiously. "We . . . we didn't talk too much. She spoke and I listened while she told me what to do." Mars paused and smiled to himself. "It was just like old times. Then she sent me here to find Dee, but first she told me I had to come to you. She said you had something for me."

Tsagaglalal nodded. "I do. I'll give it to you in a moment, but first I want you to meet—"

"We've already met," Sophie interrupted coldly. She re-

264

membered the creature in the catacombs beneath Paris. "Mars Ultor, who was also Ares, Nergal and Huitzilopochtli." She looked at Tsagaglalal. "He Awakened Josh in Paris."

Tsagaglalal patted Sophie's arm. "I know. Sophie, do not judge him by the Witch's memories, or by what he was forced to do in Paris. When Danu Talis fell, Mars stayed to the very end and led thousands of humani slaves to safety. He was among the last off the island."

Sophie looked at Mars again. "The Witch remembers you as a monster."

"It is true. I was. But Clarent poisoned me," Mars said. "It changed my nature. And now your twin carries it. Unless you get it away from him, it will change him also."

"I'll take it away from him," Sophie said simply, and then her voice shook. "I know where he is."

"He's on Alcatraz. He and I are linked, remember." He threw his head back and closed his eyes, and his nostrils flared as he inhaled a deep breath. "I can smell him and the others with him: Dee and Machiavelli, an immortal who smells like sage . . ."

"That would be Virginia Dare," Tsagaglalal said.

One by one Odin, Hel and Black Hawk crossed the yard and gathered around Mars as he spoke.

". . . and another, a male, young, smelling of red peppers," he continued.

"That would be my friend Billy the Kid," Black Hawk offered.

"You are sure the Magician is on the island?" Odin asked, his voice hoarse, every word labored.

265

"I'm sure." Mars breathed in again. "And there is another." His face twisted in disgust. "Ah, the stench of Nereus."

Prometheus came away from the barbecue carrying two plates, one piled high with hamburgers, the other filled with small cocktail sausages festooned with toothpicks.

Sophie watched Mars stiffen as Prometheus approached. Then she saw Tsagaglalal reach out to grip Mars's arm. The old woman lowered her voice, but the girl caught her words. "You're a guest in my house. I want you to behave yourself."

"Of course, mistress," Mars murmured. He nodded to Prometheus, who smiled in return. "What happened to your hair?" he asked.

"I got old," Prometheus said. "Unlike you, I see." He held out the two plates of food to the small group and everyone shook their heads except Mars and Hel. Mars lifted one of the small sausages, breathed in its aroma and then nibbled almost delicately at it. "The first real food I've had in millennia," he admitted.

Hel leaned forward and opened her mouth. A long black tongue shot out and wrapped around a thick hamburger. She pulled it whole into her mouth, her jutting fangs ripping it apart. The juices mingled with the black fluids running down her chin as she smiled at Sophie. "I'm not a vegetarian."

"I guessed," Sophie said, looking away quickly and swallowing the bile at the back of her throat.

"I made them rare just for you," Prometheus said.

"You remembered," Hel rasped.

"Well, if you recall, the last time we met, you were planning on eating me."

266

"I was going to cook you first."

Odin picked up a piece of sushi and a napkin. He disassembled the sushi, removing the curl of salmon and wrapping the remains of the rice in the napkin.

Black Hawk nodded his thanks as he looked over the plate. "Is that spicy tuna?"

Sophie nodded. "Looks like it."

"I'll stick with the salmon. Spicy food disagrees with me."

Niten appeared with two more plates of sushi. "Freshly made," he announced. "I cut some sashimi for you," he said to Odin, and pointed to the neat slivers of white and red fish. "Albacore and salmon." He looked at Black Hawk. "And cucumber and tuna rolls for you. No spices."

"You have a good memory." Black Hawk smiled.

"Of course."

Sophie looked at the two immortals. She still found the idea of the Swordsman and the Native American knowing one another astonishing. "How do you know one another?"

"We met just over a hundred and thirty years ago," Niten said.

Black Hawk nodded in agreement. "Just after the Battle of Greasy Grass in 1876."

"What a day that was," Niten murmured. "A day for warriors."

Sophie picked up one of the trays of meat and offered it to Hel. The Elder nodded gratefully and grabbed two burgers, one in each hand, before wrapping her tongue around a third. "We came through several leygates to get here," she explained over a mouthful of barely cooked meat, spraying fragments everywhere. "And you know what that's like—they make you ravenous."

Sophie drifted away from the group, heading into the house with the empty platter. She stopped at the doorway and glanced back and was immediately struck by how completely bizarre the scene was. There was Niten talking to Black Hawk; Mars Ultor and Prometheus were deep in conversation, while Odin and Hel were listening intently to Tsagaglalal. It seemed like any other backyard barbecue, with food and drink and the smells of cooking in the air. And yet some of these beings were more than ten thousand years old and far from human.

"Maybe it's a dream," she said softly, "and I'm about to wake up."

"More like a nightmare," a woman's voice answered quietly. "And you're not even dreaming."

Sophie spun around to find Nicholas and Perry standing in the doorway.

"It is good to see you again, Sophie," Nicholas said. "And Perenelle tells me I owe you a huge debt. You helped bring me back to life."

Sophie nodded, not entirely sure how to respond. "I was . . . glad to be able to help," she said. She tilted her head behind her. "I was just thinking what an odd group this is. Odin and Hel are enemies, Prometheus and Mars haven't spoken in thousands of years, and I had no idea Niten and Black Hawk knew one another."

"And what's really odd," Nicholas continued, "is that they are talking civilly and are not at one another's throats."

"Why is that?" Sophie asked. She noted that Nicholas was wearing one of her father's shirts and a pair of his cargo pants, while Perenelle was dressed in jeans that were just a little too short and a high-necked long-sleeved blouse that looked like her mother's. She felt a vague wave of anger that her aunt—no, not her aunt, Tsagaglalal—had given away her parents' clothes.

Slowly the group became aware that Nicholas and Perenelle were standing at the kitchen door looking at them, and all conversation died away as they turned to face the Alchemyst and his wife. Nicholas accepted a glass of water from Perenelle and raised it in salute.

"I have never believed in coincidences," he said, stepping out into the garden. "So I am forced to think that you are all here for a reason."

Tsagaglalal stepped forward. "You are. And if you would all like to sit down, I will tell you the reason."

"So this extraordinary gathering was not accidental?" Prometheus asked.

"Hardly," Tsagaglalal said. "My husband and Chronos predicted it ten millennia ago. In fact, Abraham gave me something to give to you." She opened a cardboard box that was sitting on the table and removed some straw padding. "I have protected these emerald tablets with my life," she said, and began to take out flat rectangular green stones and hand them around. "Prometheus, this is for you. Niten, this is yours. . . ."

"What are they?" Sophie asked.

"Letters from the past," Tsagaglalal said. "My husband wrote them ten thousand years ago."

"And he knew all these people would be here?" Sophie asked incredulously.

Tsagaglalal turned and nodded. "Indeed he did." Then she pulled one final emerald tablet from the cardboard box and handed it to her. "And he knew that you too would be here, Sophie Newman."

CHAPTER FORTY-TWO

⟨S⟩ophie Newman looked at the emerald tablet. It was about four inches across and eight inches long, and the stone felt cool in her hands. Both sides were covered in thin, narrow writing unlike anything she had ever seen before: triangles, semicircles and slashes, vaguely mathematical-looking symbols and abstract dots. It was completely unintelligible.

She turned the tablet over and ran her fingers across the smooth surface, tracing the horizontal lines of text. Wisps of her silver aura streaked across the tablet and she caught her breath. The writing flowed and shifted on the stone, forming and re-forming. She recognized cuneiform and Egyptian hieroglyphs, Aztec glyphs and Celtic Ogham, Chinese pictograms, Arabic swirls, then Greek and Norse Runes . . . and finally, English.

It was a letter.

✧   ✧   ✧

*I am Abraham of Danu Talis, sometimes called the Mage,
and I send greetings to the Silver.*

*There is much that I know about you. I know your name
and age and I know you are female. I have followed your
ancestors through ten thousand years. You are a remarkable
young woman, the last of a line of equally remarkable women.*

*You exist in a world that is incomprehensible to me, just
as I occupy a time that you could not understand. But we are
linked, you and I, by this tablet, which I have engraved with
my own hands and which I am hoping that my own dear wife
has presented to you.*

*I am writing this sitting in a tower on the edge of the
known world on the Isle of Danu Talis. History will give this
island other names, but this is its first name, its real name.
You should know that your world and my world are one and
the same, though separated by millennia, and furthermore,
you should be confident that at heart I want nothing but the
best for both our worlds. Indeed, I have entrusted my beloved
Tsagaglalal to carry this message to you across the ages. By the
time you read it, she will have stood guardian and watched
over your mother and your grandmother and every female in
your clan since it began. And her brother will have done the
same for the men.*

*This you need to know: your world begins with the death of
mine.*

*But you should also know that there are time lines in which
my world does not fall. And in those time lines, your world*

will never come into being, and other life-forms will rise up to control the planet.

There are time lines in which dark forces take hold and control the Isle of Danu Talis, where the humani remain slaves until they are exterminated and replaced by a new breed.

There are other time lines in which your world—your modern world, with all its shining metal and glass, with your terrifying weapons and wonders—falls to chaos and ancient night.

And there are some threads of time in which your world simply does not exist. There is naught but dust and rocks where your planet and its moon now spin in space.

I have always known that the fate of our worlds—yours and mine—is at the mercy of the actions of individuals. The actions of a single person can change the course of a world and create history.

And you are one of those individuals.

You are powerful. A Silver—as powerful as I have ever seen. And you are brave, too. That much is clear.

You have it within you to change history, but to do that you will have to trust me. That may be difficult, because I know you have never trusted anyone in your life except your twin, and my research has indicated that you and your twin are now separated. If it is any consolation, you will be reunited, albeit briefly. I am asking you to trust someone you have never met, writing to you from ten thousand years ago, living in a world beyond your comprehension. But if you trust me and do what must be done, and if you are successful, you will save the world. Not only my world and your world, but all the unseen Shadowrealms and everyone on them. Billions of sentient beings will owe you their lives.

Fail, and those same billions will die.

But I must tell you now that there will be a price for this success. You will pay dearly. Your heart will break a thousand times and you will learn to curse my name now and forevermore.

So you must choose. A thousand years before I wrote this tablet, I created the prophecy that ends with the words The two that are one must become the one that is all. One to save the world, one to destroy it.

Which one are you, Sophie Newman?

Which one are you?

CHAPTER FORTY-THREE

*J*osh Newman looked at the pool of water at his feet. "Nothing's happen—" he began . . . and then stopped—all the water in the rock pool had suddenly vanished. He could see the tiny green creature wriggling and twisting on the gritty beach like a fish out of water. Josh squinted; did it look a little plumper? The Lotan shuddered, scrabbling in the grit and dirty sand. And then Josh realized that it was growing, doubling and then redoubling in size with each twitch of its ever-elongating body.

From a few inches in length to a foot long took a heartbeat.

From twelve inches to three feet took another heartbeat.

The resemblance to a skink was pronounced, but with each shuddering increase in size, it began to look more like a Komodo dragon. Long yellow forked tongues flickered in each of its seven mouths, and when it raised its heads toward the skies, its breath reeked of rancid meat and long-dead things from the bottom of the sea.

The Lotan convulsed, doubled in size again, becoming six feet long . . .

"We need to get out of here," Billy said urgently. He and Virginia still held Dee between them. "Look at those teeth— a critter like that needs meat. And we're the closest meal."

. . . trembling violently, bones popping, muscles cracking, skin stretching to become twelve feet . . .

All seven heads fixed on the five humans, fourteen solid black eyes watching them unblinkingly. And then it lunged forward, a quick—almost shockingly swift—movement that halved the distance between them.

"Move!" Billy yelled.

"No!" Dee gasped.

Josh watched in horror as the creature spasmed violently, growing to more than twenty-four feet long, almost the same length as one of the cable cars that ran in the city across the bay.

"Just how big does this thing get?" Billy demanded.

"Let's slow this down." Still holding on to the Magician, Virginia pulled out her flute with one hand and pressed it to her lips. The sound was too high for human hearing other than the faintest trembling on the air. A trio of seagulls flying overhead fell out of the sky, tumbling into the sea, but the Lotan was unaffected. It edged closer, and all seven mouths opened to reveal multiple rows of savage teeth. Thick strands of foul-smelling saliva dripped onto the rocks.

Dee coughed out a laugh, and when he spoke his

voice was a ragged whisper. "It is deaf. Your magic flute is useless."

"I gathered that," Virginia muttered.

The Lotan's green skin rippled with colors, red and black waves surging up and down its body. Abruptly, all the colors flowed into the heads, turning each a different shade of crimson, except for the central head, which had grown almost twice as big as the others and was now solid black.

Josh clenched and unclenched his fists and his golden auric gloves formed again and started to work their way up his arms, sheathing them in metal.

The Lotan's seven heads instantly fixed on the young man.

"Josh," Machiavelli said quietly, not taking his eyes off the Lotan. "I suggest you stop whatever you're doing. Right now!"

"I was shielding myself with my aura," Josh began.

Dee shook himself free of Dare and Billy. A little color had returned to the Magician's ash-white face, but his eyes were still ringed with shadows, and he cradled his swollen left hand. He stepped toward the creature, which reared its heads as if it was about to strike, and then all its nostrils opened stickily and seven tongues tasted the air. Dee turned his back on the creature. "The Lotan feeds off more than flesh. It's vampire-like—it will suck the aura from any living creature." He looked at Machiavelli. "Are you brave enough to stretch out your arm?"

"Brave enough, perhaps, but not so foolish," Machiavelli said, eyes still fixed on the creature.

Billy immediately stretched out his left arm and the air was touched with the earthy scent of red pepper. A reddish-purple gauze wrapped around the immortal's hand.

The Lotan shuddered, all the heads transferring their attention to him, tongues flickering. Billy suddenly grunted and staggered forward as his aura started to coil and stream away from his arm toward the creature. The yellow tongues lapped the gossamer red smoke from the air.

"Stop it, Billy!" Machiavelli said.

The American tried to lower his arm. "I can't," he gasped. His aura had deepened in color, the stream clearly visible in the air as it flowed toward the lizard. The veins on the back of Billy's outstretched hand were pronounced, and he hissed in pain as his fingernails turned red, then purple, before changing to black, cracking and falling off.

Josh immediately stepped in front of Billy and cracked the flat of his hand across his face. The immortal grunted in surprise. Josh caught the front of his shirt and used a tae kwan do standing leg sweep to bring Billy to his knees. The immortal hit the stones with bruising force and his aura instantly faded.

"Oh man, that hurt. I think you just busted my kneecap," Billy grumbled. He stretched out his hand and Josh hauled him to his feet. "Never thought I'd thank someone for hurting me, but thanks. I owe you—and I never forget my debts." He flexed his left hand. It was pale, shot through with veins and broken blood vessels and the ovals where his fingernails had fallen off oozed a clear liquid. "That really stings," he muttered.

278

"That was a stupid thing to do," Virginia snapped.

"Stupid is my middle name." Billy grinned.

"This is the beast you're going to unleash on the city?" Machiavelli said quietly. "A flesh eater, an aura drinker?"

"The first of many beasts," Dee said with a laugh that turned into a gurgling cough and doubled him over. "Let it prowl through the streets and feast for a while. You have the spells: awaken the monsters in the cells and send them into the city."

"And then what?" Machiavelli asked.

"Our work here is through." Dee spread his arms wide. "We have done as we were ordered to do by our respective masters. You can return on the next flight to Paris . . . well, maybe not the next flight, I'm not sure the airport will be operating much longer." He pointed back toward the cellblock with his chin. "I saw some wyverns inside. Perhaps you should send them to the airport." He laughed again.

"And what about you, Doctor?" Machiavelli asked. "What happens to you when the Elders return?"

"You let me worry about that."

"I think I would like to know," the Italian said icily. His lips moved in a smile that didn't come close to his eyes. "We are in this together."

Dee folded his arms across his chest and the huge Lotan crept closer to him. The long tongues flickered up and down his back and ruffled his hair. He absently brushed them away. "I am considering my options," he said finally. "But first, let us send this beastie on its way. . . ."

"No," Billy and Machiavelli said simultaneously.

"No?" Dee looked confused. "Ah, I see. You think we should awaken some of the creatures and send them all in together?" He nodded. "We could bring them ashore at a couple of places, a multipronged attack."

Billy the Kid shook his head. "We've been thinking. . . ."

"You shouldn't strain yourself," Dee quipped.

Billy's face turned hard. "Your smart mouth is going to get you into trouble one of these days."

"Perhaps," Dee said, "but not by you."

"Enough," Machiavelli yelled. "What my impulsive young friend is trying to say is that we have decided the monsters should not be released into the city."

Dee blinked in surprise.

"It wouldn't be right," Billy said.

"Not *right*?" The Magician started to laugh. "Is this some sort of joke?" He looked at Virginia. "It's a joke, right?"

Dare shook her head slightly. "I don't think so," she said, moving slowly away from the Italian and American immortals.

Billy shifted his body, half turning so that he could watch both Dee and Dare at once.

"Why are you doing this, John?" Machiavelli asked. "It gains you nothing."

"It buys me time, Niccolò," Dee said. "Our Elder masters expect the creatures to be released into the city, and we must not disappoint them."

"Or they might come to investigate," Machiavelli said slowly. "And find you here . . ."

"Just so," Dee agreed. "Let them watch the city from

280

their Shadowrealms and rub their hands in glee at the destruction."

"So it's a distraction?" Billy the Kid spat. "Just a distraction!"

Dee grinned. "Like a stage magician's card trick. They'll be focused on the city and they'll not bother me here."

"Why? What are you up to, John?" Niccolò demanded.

"That's none of your business."

The Italian patted his jacket pocket. Paper rustled. "I have the spells to awaken the creatures; I won't do it. Moreover, I'll contact the Flamels and warn them what's coming across the bay. We both know just how dangerous Perenelle can be. She'll stop the Lotan."

"I don't think so," Dee whispered. "Remember, this creature drinks auras. I'm sure the Sorceress would taste sweet indeed." He looked from Billy to Machiavelli and then back to Billy. "And you're in this with him?"

The American took a step closer to the Italian immortal. "Sure am."

"Last chance," Dee warned.

"Oh, should I be scared?"

"So you've finally betrayed your masters," Dee said, speaking so softly that the words were barely audible over the breeze. "You have broken your oaths of service to them. Warlocks."

"You're hardly one to talk," Machiavelli said.

"Yes, but now your decision compromises my plans," the Magician said. He looked at Josh. "And where do you stand?" he demanded. "With me or with the Italian?"

Josh looked blankly from Dee to Machiavelli, mouth

opening and closing in confusion. Of course he didn't want the monsters released into San Francisco; that was just wrong. He felt a sudden surge of heat on his shoulder and he reached around to pull Clarent free. As soon as it settled into his hand, warmth bloomed along the length of his arm and something shifted in his mind. The doubts eased, washed away with the certainty that it was absolutely right that the creatures be released in the streets. In fact, it was necessary. He remembered a phrase his father had used during a lecture he had given at Brown University the previous Christmas. He'd quoted Charles Darwin: "It is not the strongest of the species that survive, not the most intelligent, but the one most responsive to change."

A little death and destruction, a little hysteria and fear, would be good for the humani. The thought of the Lotan wandering along the Embarcadero was kind of funny. He started to grin at the image. And the more he thought about it, the more he saw it was *necessary* for the Lotan to be released—that would bring the Elders back, and that was what this was all about.

"Think of the destruction, Josh," Machiavelli said.

Buildings crumbling; people running, screaming . . . The sword throbbed with each image.

"You've lived in San Francisco, Josh," Billy said. "You don't want that to happen there, do you?"

Virginia Dare stepped forward and put her arm around Josh's shoulder. "Josh knows where he stands," she said, her steely gray eyes locking onto his. "He stands with us. Isn't that right?"

Josh turned bright red, blinking as the musky sage scent of Dare's aura caught at the back of his throat. Disappointing Virginia Dare was the last thing he'd ever want to do. "Well, yes, I think so. I'm not sure. . . ." The sword's hilt grew warmer and his fingers were pulled in tightly against it. He was suddenly so hot that he thought he was going to pass out. Images of destruction and chaos danced at the edge of his consciousness. Flames blossomed, and he was entranced by their beauty; he heard screams, but the sounds were almost musical.

"Where do you stand?" the Magician repeated.

"Think a moment before giving an answer," Billy warned.

"Oh, that is rich, coming from you," Dee said. "Josh, are you with me or with the Italian? And if you are with Machiavelli," he added contemptuously, "notice that moments ago he threatened to betray us to the Flamels. Here is someone else who will do everything possible to remain in control, even if it means condemning the world to a long, slow, lingering destruction."

"There are over eight hundred thousand people living in the city of San Francisco," Billy said angrily. "A lot of them—maybe even most of them—will die. You don't want that, Josh, do you?"

"Remember when we talked in Ojai last week?" Dee asked before Josh could answer. "Remember when I showed you the world as it could be, as it *would* be if the Elders returned—with clear air, pure water, unpolluted seas . . ." As the Magician spoke, images flickered before Josh's eyes.

. . . an island set under cloudless azure skies. Endless fields of

283

golden wheat marching into the distance. Trees laden with an assortment of exotic fruit.

. . . huge wind-blown desert dunes turning green with lush grass.

. . . a hospital ward with a long row of empty beds.

Josh nodded, mesmerized by what he saw. "A paradise."

"A paradise," Dee agreed. "But that is not what the Italian and the outlaw want. They want the world as it is: dirty and damaged, so they can work in the shadows."

"Josh," Billy said firmly, "don't listen to him. This is Dee, remember—a prince of liars."

"Flamel lied to you also," Dee quickly reminded him. "And remember what he and his wife did to your sister."

"Turned her against you," Virginia whispered. She reached over and rested her fingertips against the back of Josh's hand as if in sympathy. "And there is one thing I can teach you that neither Machiavelli nor Billy can," she said, lowering her voice and leaning in so that only he could hear her. "I will train you in the Magic of Air. The most useful of all the magics," she added persuasively.

The Magic of Air. The words had gotten his attention. "Sophie knows the Magics of Air, Fire and Water. I only know Water and Fire." As Josh spoke he was suddenly aware of how close Dare stood, of the heat from Clarent burning through his body. He was sweating, but the wind off the sea chilled the moisture on his flesh. He shivered.

"The Magic of Air," Virginia repeated. "It would make you the equal of your sister," she murmured. Then she

284

leaned forward. "And maybe, one day, you will even be more powerful."

Josh turned away from Virginia and looked at Dee. "I'm with you," he said.

Dee grinned. "You've made the right decision, Josh."

"You've made the biggest mistake of your life," Niccolò said quietly, and Josh found that he could no longer look the Italian or Billy the Kid in the eye.

Out of the blue, Billy moved, launching himself at Dee, while Machiavelli turned toward Dare, but the immortal woman already had her flute to her lips. "Too slow," she breathed into the flute, and as the words turned to music, Niccolò Machiavelli and Billy the Kid crashed to the ground, unconscious.

Virginia rolled Machiavelli over with her foot and then stooped to pluck an envelope from his inside pocket. She tossed it to Josh, who handed it over to the Magician. "The instructions for awakening the monsters," Dare said.

The Magician clapped Josh on the shoulder. "Well done," he said sincerely. "Now let's get this pair into cells before they wake up."

"Aren't you forgetting something?" Virginia said, nodding toward the Lotan.

Dee smiled, eyes dancing wildly. He looked at the creature and then waved both hands in front of it. "Go. Shoo." He pointed at the city less than a mile away. "Go and feed."

The Lotan turned, waddled over the rocks and splashed

into the water. The seven heads bobbed above the waves for a moment before dipping below the surface, and then a curled bow wave headed toward the city.

"I wonder what the tourists on the Embarcadero will make of that," Dare said.

"Oh, I would imagine we'll hear the screams from here." The English Magician tapped the envelope against his leg impatiently. "Come, let us awaken some very hungry creatures." He looked down at the unconscious and bruised Machiavelli and Billy. "Hmm, maybe they'd like a little snack first." Then he turned to Josh, who was standing watching the trail of the Lotan as it headed toward San Francisco. "You've made the right decision, Josh," he said again.

Josh nodded. He hoped so. He sincerely hoped so. He looked at Dare and she smiled at him, and the young man felt easier. Even if he didn't entirely trust Dee, he did trust Virginia Dare.

CHAPTER FORTY-FOUR

Sophie raised her gaze from the emerald tablet. Her eyes were swimming and her throat felt raw, as if she'd been screaming. She had a hundred questions, but no answers. Even the Witch of Endor's knowledge was no help: she didn't know how Abraham had foreseen all that he did.

Sophie looked around the group and immediately noticed that no one was speaking. Some had finished reading, while others were still concentrating on their tablets. Judging by their reactions, they had all received deeply personal messages written by a man—no, surely Abraham was more than just a man—who had lived ten thousand years ago.

Hel was crying, black tears dripping onto the emerald block, burning into the stone and sending gray smoke sizzling toward the sky. Sophie watched as she lifted the tablet and pressed her lips to it. For an instant her beastlike features faded, revealing her as she had once been: young and very beautiful.

Perenelle put down her green slab and rested her hands on it. She looked over at Sophie and nodded. Her eyes were huge with tears that reflected the emerald of the stone, and her expression was inexpressibly sad.

Prometheus and Mars simultaneously looked up from reading their own messages. Without speaking, they reached across the table to grasp one another's arms.

Niten's face had settled into an unreadable mask, but Sophie noticed that his index finger kept moving in what looked like a figure eight over the stone.

Odin shoved the tablet into his pocket and then stretched out to pat his niece's hand. He whispered something in her ear that made her smile.

Black Hawk's face was expressionless, but his fingers tapped an irregular beat on the back of the block of emerald.

Nicholas slipped his tablet into a trouser pocket and took his wife's hand, and when he looked at her, Sophie thought she saw something like awe in his eyes, as he if were seeing her for the first time.

"I have no idea what my husband wrote to any of you," Tsagaglalal said suddenly, breaking the deep silence that had fallen over the group. "Each message is unique to you, keyed to your DNA and your aura." The old woman was sitting at the head of the wooden picnic table. She was carefully slicing the skin off a vibrant green apple with a triangular sliver of black stone that resembled an arrowhead.

Sophie noticed that Tsagaglalal had arranged the green skin into shapes not dissimilar to those that had formed the words on her tablet when she'd first looked at it. She frowned: she'd seen someone else do that, though she couldn't remember where or when . . . maybe it was one of the Witch's memories rather than her own.

Tsagaglalal indicated the empty chairs. "Join me," she said, and one by one, the group settled around the table. Nicholas and Perenelle sat side by side, facing Odin and Hel, while Mars and Prometheus sat facing one another, as did Niten and Black Hawk. Sophie sat alone at the end of the table, looking directly at Tsagaglalal.

"Some of you here knew my husband personally," she began. "Some of you," she added, looking at Prometheus and Mars, "he counted among his closest friends." She looked down the table at Odin and Hel. "And while some of you would never have sided with him, I would like to think that you respected him."

All the Elders sitting around the table nodded in agreement.

"Even before the destruction of Danu Talis, our world was beginning to fragment. The Elders were masters of the world. There were no more Earthlords, the Ancients had vanished and the Archons had been defeated. The new races, including the humani, were still looked upon as little more than slaves, and so, with no one else to defeat, the Elders started to fight among themselves."

"It was a terrible time," Odin rumbled.

Tsagaglalal looked up and down the table. "Some of you were with me on the island when it fell. You know what it was like then."

The Elders nodded.

"Well, now Dr. John Dee intends to ensure that it never happened."

Hel looked up. "Is that a bad thing?" she asked, and then the realization of what she was saying seemed to sink in. "Where does that leave us?"

Tsagaglalal nodded. "This world, and the ten thousand years of history that created it, will simply cease to exist. But, more importantly, if Danu Talis does not fall, then the warring Elders will destroy it. And not just the island—the entire planet."

"So Dee must be stopped," Odin said simply. He nodded to his niece. "But that is why we are here. We have come to kill Dee for his crimes."

"It is why I am here too," Mars said.

"And we know he is on Alcatraz," Hel said. "Let us go there and finish this."

"I can take you," Black Hawk offered quickly. "I've got a boat."

"And I'm going too," Sophie added. "Josh is there."

"No, you're not," Tsagaglalal said firmly. "You are staying here."

"No." There was no way the old woman—no matter who she was—would be able to keep Sophie off Alcatraz.

"If you ever want to see your brother again, you will stay with me."

Prometheus leaned forward and tapped the emerald tablet he still held in his hand. "I too was told to remain here."

"And I," Niten added. The Swordsman looked at Tsagaglalal. "Do you know why?"

She shook her head.

"I do," Perenelle whispered. She held up her own tablet. "There was no message to me from the past. When I looked at it, I saw Alcatraz, and I saw the ghost of Juan Manuel de Ayala, the man who named the island and who now stands guardian over it. He helped me escape when Dee held me there. De Ayala spoke to me through the tablet, and I floated high over the island and saw through his eyes."

"And what did you see?" Nicholas asked.

"Dee and Dare, Josh, Machiavelli and Billy the Kid. And the Lotan."

"The Lotan," Odin rumbled uneasily. "Fully grown?"

"Fully grown. But there is dissension among the immortals," Perenelle continued. "I could not hear what was happening, could only see the images, but it seemed to me that Machiavelli and the Kid did not want the Lotan released onto the city. There was an argument, and Dare rendered them both unconscious."

"And the Lotan?" Odin asked. "I have seen its work before. It is a terrifying creature."

"Dee sent it into the water. It is heading toward the city right now." She turned to Prometheus and then to Niten across the table. "This is why both of you were asked to remain here. You must stand against the monster and protect the city. The creature is heading toward the Embarcadero. It will come ashore within the hour."

"Take my car," Tsagaglalal said immediately. "It's parked in the front." She pushed her keys across the table, and Niten snatched them up and was already hurrying away when Nicholas stood.

"We'll come with you," he called after the man, and Perenelle nodded.

Suddenly everyone was moving. Prometheus scrambled to his feet, then leaned over to kiss Tsagaglalal's cheek. "Just like old times, eh?"

She pressed her hand against his face. "Be safe," she whispered.

Mars came around the table and embraced his former enemy. Their auras crackled and fizzed, and for a moment, the image of two warriors in matching exotic red armor appeared. "Fight and live," Mars said. "And when all this is over, there will be time for many adventures. Just like the old days."

"Just like the old days." Prometheus squeezed the Elder's shoulders. "Fight and live."

"I'll get my jeep," Black Hawk said. He left, whistling tunelessly.

"Wait," Sophie said. "Perenelle, what about Josh? What about my brother?"

Everyone turned to look at the Sorceress, and Sophie suddenly knew the meaning of the expression she'd seen earlier in her eyes. "He chose Dee and Dare again. Sophie, your brother is truly lost to us."

CHAPTER FORTY-FIVE

$\mathcal{T}$he triangular vimana was so wide it almost completely filled the mouth of the volcano. It struck two of the smaller craft as it dropped down. One exploded in a ball of fire; the other spun into the side of the sheer cliff face and detonated in a splash of flame and metal that sent red-hot shrapnel in every direction.

All the prisoners ducked back into the safety of the caves as metal ricocheted off the walls. Only Scathach remained in the cave mouth, watching the approaching Rukma vimana. She moved her head to one side as a piece of burning fuselage as long as her arm screamed off the rock over her head. Another vimana was struck a glancing blow by the huge warship and the circular craft spun too close to the volcano wall. It struck an outcropping of rock, ripping open the side of the craft. As it sailed past her cell, Scathach caught a glimpse of the two anpu within desperately attempting to correct the plummeting ship. When it hit the lava, it erupted in a massive fireball that shot a plume of magma high into the air. The molten rock stuck to the cliff face, then slowly dribbled back down.

The wide Rukma vimana dropped slowly, its pointed nose and wing tips barely clearing the walls. The Shadow nodded in approval: a master pilot was at the controls. The craft edged lower and lower, passing Shakespeare's and Palamedes's cells.

The remaining smaller vimana darted in and around the bigger craft, taking care not to get too close. Scathach desperately tried to remember what she knew about the machines, but that was precious little. She didn't think the smaller ships were armed, but she guessed that at least one had headed back to the capital to bring reinforcements. The big vimana was so close now that Scathach could see that, unlike the smaller craft, which were metal, this one was made of polished crystal and gleaming ceramics. It was almost completely transparent, and she could make out a single figure moving within the craft.

The air was buzzing with the hum of the vimana's electromagnetic engine, a high-pitched whine that set her teeth on edge and shot crackling static through her spiked red hair. The vibrations pulsed off the volcano's black walls, and she watched as tiny cracks spiderwebbed along the surface. Suddenly a chunk of rock at her feet fell away and slid down into the lava below. Scathach danced back as the edge of the cave crumbled to dust.

One wing of the vimana swung around until it was almost directly above her, and the red light on the tip of the wing shattered. The edge of the craft scraped along the wall, raining pebbles of black stone onto her head. Scathach knew that if it came any lower it would get stuck. Crouching, she took a deep breath of the sulfur-tainted air, coughed and then propelled herself upward, just as the vibrations dissolved the walls around her cell into chips of dusty stone. Her fingers caught the two sides of the Rukma vimana's wing tip, but her right hand slipped off the slick glassy surface, and she desperately scrabbled to grab hold again before she lost her grip with her left hand as well. Looking down between her legs, she realized that there was nothing between her and the glutinous pool of lava. The Rukma started to rise.

From the corner of her eye, she caught a flicker of movement. A small circular vimana was dipping toward her. It buzzed in as close as it could get, obviously attempting to knock her off the edge of the craft. She kicked out at it, but the effort almost made her lose her grip.

The crystal Rukma vimana rose slowly, with Scathach still dangling beneath. The Warrior attempted again to swing herself up onto the craft, but the surface was too slick, and she realized that she was not going to be able to hold on for very much longer. She abruptly remembered that she'd once been told that she'd die in an exotic location. Well, it didn't get much more exotic than hanging beneath a vimana warship in the mouth of an active volcano.

The smaller vimana swept around again, close enough for Scatty to see the two leering doglike faces beneath its crystal dome. The anpu bared their teeth and swung the craft in again. This time they were going to smash into her.

295

And then Joan of Arc landed directly on its glass dome.

The Frenchwoman had leapt from the mouth of her cell. Clinging to the dome, she smiled down sweetly at the slack-jawed anpu inside. *"Bonjour."* The vimana wobbled, then dipped, bucking left and right as the anpu pilot attempted to throw her off. "You are wasting your time," she said, laughing delightedly. "I'm stronger than I appear! I've carried a sword all my life—I can hang on for hours."

The craft passed directly below Scathach and she released her grip and dropped onto the top of the vimana alongside Joan with enough force to send the larger craft plunging down. The French immortal laughed. "So nice of you—"

"Don't you dare crack any dropping-in jokes," Scathach warned before her friend could finish.

The vimana dipped and spun, but the two women had firm grips on the transparent dome and held on while the pilot tilted the craft, attempting to shake them off.

"So long as he doesn't get too close to the lava," Scatty said, "we should be okay."

At that moment the vimana dropped straight down, zooming dangerously close to the lava's sluggish bubbling surface.

"I think he heard you," Joan said, coughing as the air became almost unbreathable. She was covered in a sheen of sweat, and the ends of her short auburn hair were crisping with the heat. "My hands are getting damp," she admitted. "I don't know how much longer I can keep my grip."

"Hold tight," Scathach muttered. Closing her right hand

into a fist, she folded her thumb over her index finger. Then she drew her arm back. "When you absolutely, positively have to knock a hole through something . . ." The Warrior grunted as she drove her fist into the glass dome with tremendous force. ". . . you cannot beat a Jeet Kune Do punch." The dome cracked. The two anpu looked up, eyes and mouth wide in shock. "Guess it's not as unbreakable as you thought!" Scathach punched it again, and the dome crumbled into fragments beneath her fist. Stinking hot air swirled in around the anpu, stinging their eyes, doubling them over with coughing barks. The pilot sent the craft surging upward, away from the lethal heat and dust.

"Too fast," Scathach called. "We're going to hit something!"

The edge of the vimana brushed against a protruding rock, metal screaming as it crumpled, then tore away. The craft wobbled, almost pitching Scatty and Joan off the dome, but continued to rise. And then it hit the edge of the large Rukma vimana warship, which had remained hovering in place. Metal scraped off glass and a huge chunk of the side of the smaller ship was ripped away. But the force of the blow shook the two women's grips free. Joan screamed and Scathach defiantly howled her war cry . . .

. . . and strong hands grabbed both women and plucked them off the back of the vimana in the last second before it hit the rock face and shattered in two.

Palamedes gently lowered Scatty and Joan down onto the wing of the vimana. The Saracen Knight was standing alongside Saint-Germain on the wing of the Rukma. Saint-Germain wrapped his arms around his wife and hugged her close. Neither of them could speak.

"I thought I usually saved your life," Scathach said lightly, squeezing Palamedes's arm.

"I thought it was about time I returned the favor," the knight said, his deep voice trembling. "A close call, Shadow."

"Maybe today is not my day to die," Scatty said, smiling at him.

Palamedes squeezed her shoulder. "The day's not over yet," he said seriously. "Come, we need to get inside." He turned away, jerking his thumb up toward the mouth of the volcano. "Our dog-faced friends are gathering."

Scathach followed Palamedes across the Rukma's wing toward a long oval opening in the top of the craft. "How did you get onto the ship?"

"When the wing came level with my cave cell, I just stepped out onto it," the Saracen Knight said. "Francis did the same." He swung himself into the opening. The Shadow could see his distorted outline through the craft's crystal skin. She stood and waited while Joan, followed by Saint-Germain, disappeared into the interior of the craft; only then did she catch the top of the opening and swing inside.

"So this was a rescue," Scatty said. "I was sure it had come to kill us."

A shape moved within the crystal interior of the Rukma. "If they just wanted to kill you," a deep voice rumbled, "then why send a warship?"

"I'm guessing they did it because they knew what they

were up against," Scatty said, turning to the sound. "I am Scathach the Warrior Maid, the Shadow, the Daemon Slayer, the King Maker, the—"

"I've never heard of you." A huge red-haired warrior in shimmering crimson armor stepped forward and ran his hand across the edge of the opening. A glass dome whispered into place.

"Uncle!" With a cry of delight, Scathach flung herself at the red-haired man.

But the big man caught her before she could wrap her arms around him and held her at arm's length, feet dangling off the floor. "I am Prometheus, and I do not have a niece. I have no idea who you are. I've never met you before in my life." He placed her carefully on the ground and took a step back.

Joan burst into laughter at the look on Scathach's face. Then she took her by the hand and drew her away. "You must forgive my friend. She forgets where she is . . . and *when* she is," she added significantly, looking at the Shadow.

Scathach nodded, surprise transforming her face. "You remind me of someone," she said to Prometheus, "someone very dear to me."

The red-haired Elder merely nodded, then swung away. The group followed him down a tall corridor into a sunken circular area in the center of the Rukma. He settled himself in a deep form-fitting molded chair and rested his hands on the arms. Instantly the entire crystal wall before him lit up with lights and crawling lines of text and graphs superimposed over the glass. Red dots swarmed on the left side of the wall.

Prometheus pointed. "That's not good. We need to get out of here fast. It looks like the entire vimana fleet is heading our way."

"Where are you taking us?" Saint-Germain asked.

"I'm taking you to—"

A voice, clear and deathly calm, echoed around the circular control room. "Prometheus, my friend, I need you now. The tower is under attack." In the background, a series of dull rattling explosions was clearly audible.

"I'm on my way," Prometheus said into the air.

"And our friends?" The voice echoed around the chamber. "They are safe?"

"Safe. They were exactly where you said they'd be, in the Huracan cells. They're here with me now."

"Good. Now hurry, old friend. Hurry."

"Who was that?" Scathach asked, though, like the others, she had already guessed the answer.

"That was your savior: Abraham the Mage."

CHAPTER FORTY-SIX

Sophie Newman walked around the empty back garden. Everyone had left. The Flamels, Prometheus and Niten were heading for the Embarcadero, while Black Hawk was driving Mars, Odin and Hel to the marina.

Her stomach felt sour from the mixture of auric odors she'd encountered, and her head was beginning to throb. She needed time to think, to make sense of what she had just learned. Everything changed, and continued to change, and it was beginning to get difficult again to distinguish her own thoughts from the Witch of Endor's memories. The Witch had known every single person who had turned up at Aunt Agnes's—Tsagaglalal's—house, and she had an opinion about all of them. She liked none of them . . . and yet Sophie found she disagreed with her.

She felt she was beginning to get to know the Witch

now . . . in fact, with the Witch's memories swirling around inside her head, she thought she might know her better than anyone alive.

And she didn't like her.

The Witch of Endor was petty and vindictive, spiteful and bitter and filled with a terrible rage and jealousy. She envied Prometheus his powers and strength and Mars his courage, she feared Niten and his association with Aoife. She hated Tsagaglalal because she'd been so close to Abraham. The only good thing Sophie could say about the Witch was that she did seem to genuinely care about the humani and had battled tirelessly to keep them safe from the more dangerous of the Dark Elders.

Sophie walked along the irregular paving stones set into the grass. The ground dipped sharply, and when she looked back, she could just make out the top of her aunt's house. She ducked through a wooden archway covered with ivy and climbing roses that led into the uncultivated lower part of the garden, where the grass grew waist-high and was speckled with native wildflowers.

This had always been the twins' favorite spot.

When they were children, they'd discovered a little en-closed secret area at the bottom of the garden, tucked away behind the hedges, and it immediately became their den. It was a completely circular clearing, surrounded by a tangled mess of spiky thornbushes and several ancient apple trees that never bore fruit, despite their many blossoms. A weathered and rock-hard stump of an old oak tree poked out of the ground in the center of the clearing. It was almost three feet across, and one summer Sophie had spent an entire week trying to count its rings to figure out its age. She'd gotten as far as two hundred and thirty before she stopped. The twins called the clearing the secret garden, after the book by Frances Hodgson Burnett, which Sophie had been reading at the time. Every summer when the Newman family came to San Francisco, Sophie would race out into the back garden to check that it was still in place and Aunt Agnes's gardeners hadn't cut it down or tamed it into the neat orderly rows that bisected the rest of the garden. Each year the grass grew taller, the bushes wilder and the pathway more and more lost in the undergrowth.

There was a time when Sophie and Josh had spent their every waking moment during their visits in the secret garden, but as the years went by, Josh had lost interest in it—the clearing was too far from the house to get a wireless signal for his laptop. So the secret garden became Sophie's private place, a place where she could read and daydream, a place to escape and think. And right now, she needed time alone, she needed to be able to think about everything that had happened . . . and about Josh. She needed to think about her twin, how she was going to get him back and what she needed to do. "Anything. Everything," she breathed aloud.

And she needed to think about the future, because the future was starting to terrify her and she needed to make a decision—without any doubt, the biggest decision of her life.

At least here she could be alone; no one knew about the secret garden.

Sophie pushed through the bushes and stopped in surprise. Aunt Agnes—Tsagaglalal—was sitting on the tree stump, eyes closed, face turned up to the afternoon sun.

The old woman opened her gray eyes and smiled. "What? Didn't you think I knew about this place?"

CHAPTER FORTY-SEVEN

"*I* have always known about this place," Tsagaglalal said to Sophie. She waved her hand. "Come, sit, join me."

Sophie started to shake her head.

"Please," Tsagaglalal said gently. "I created this space for you and your brother. Why do you think I never allowed the gardeners to tend to it?"

Sophie moved around the clearing, then sank to the ground with her back against the trunk of a gnarled apple tree, legs stretched straight out in front of her. "I don't know what to think anymore," she said truthfully.

Tsagaglalal remained still, gaze fixed on the girl's face. The only noise was the droning of bees and distant traffic sounds.

"I was just thinking," Sophie said, "a week ago today I was serving coffee at the Coffee Cup and looking forward to the weekend. Josh had come over to the shop for lunch, and we shared a sandwich and a slice of cherry pie. I'd just talked to my friend Elle, in New York, on the phone, and I was excited because there was the possibility that she was going to come out to San Francisco. My biggest worry was that I wouldn't be able to get time off from the coffee shop to spend with her." The girl looked at Tsagaglalal. "Just another day. Just an ordinary Thursday."

"And now?" Tsagaglalal whispered.

"And now, a week later, I've been Awakened, learned magic, been to France and England and back again without flying; my brother is gone; and I'm worrying about the end of the world." She tried a laugh, but it came out high-pitched and a little hysterical.

Tsagaglalal nodded slowly. "A week ago, Sophie, you were a girl. You have lived a lifetime in the past seven days. You have seen so much and done so much more."

"More than I wanted to," Sophie muttered.

"You have grown and matured," Tsagaglalal said, ignoring the interruption. "You are an extraordinary young woman, Sophie Newman. You are strong, knowledgeable and powerful—so very, very powerful."

"I wish I weren't," Sophie said sadly. She looked down at her hands in her lap. They were resting on her legs, palms facing up, right hand on top of left. Unbidden, threads of silver aura gathered in the creases in her palm, then flowed to form a small pool of shining liquid. The liquid aura sank back into her flesh, and silver gloves, at first like delicate smooth silk, then stitched leather, and finally studded metal appeared around her hands, encasing them. She flexed her fingers; the gloves disappeared and her flesh reappeared. Her fingernails briefly remained silver polished mirrors before they too returned to normal.

"You cannot escape what you are, Sophie. You are Silver. And that means you have a responsibility . . . and a destiny. Your fate was decided millennia ago," Tsagaglalal said, almost sympathetically. "I watched my husband, Abraham, work with Chronos. Chronos spent his entire life mastering Time. It was a task that utterly destroyed him, warping and twisting his flesh into a hundred different forms. It made him one of the most repulsive creatures you have ever seen . . . and yet my husband called him friend, and I have no doubt that Chronos had the welfare of the humani and the survival of this Shadowrealm at heart."

"The Witch didn't like him . . . ," Sophie said, shuddering as a hint of Chronos's true form gathered at the edges of her memory.

Tsagaglalal nodded. "And he despised her for what she did."

"What did she do?" Sophie began, but the memories came so quickly that they physically shook her body.

. . . a war hammer crushing a crystal skull to shards of broken glass, and then smashing a second and then a third . . .

. . . metal books running molten liquid off collapsing library shelves as smoking acid ate into them . . .

. . . extraordinary glass and ceramic aircraft, delicate, beautiful and intricate, circular, oblong and triangular, being pitched off cliffs to sink into the sea . . .

Tsagaglalal leaned forward. "The Witch destroyed millennia of Earthlord, Ancient and Archon artifacts: what my husband called the eldritch lore."

"It was too dangerous," Sophie said immediately, parroting the Witch's point of view.

"That was the Witch's opinion." Tsagaglalal's expression turned indescribably sad. "Your friend, the immortal William Shakespeare, once wrote that 'there is nothing either good or bad, but thinking makes it so.'"

"That's from *Hamlet*. We did the play in school last year."

"Zephaniah believed that the eldritch lore was dangerous and that therefore she was justified in destroying it. But what you must remember is that knowledge itself is never dangerous," Tsagaglalal insisted. "It is how that knowledge is used that is dangerous. The Witch's arrogance destroyed incalculable millennia of knowledge, so when she needed a favor, Chronos made her pay dearly. Perhaps he was also trying to prevent her from destroying anything else, although by then it was probably too late. I sometimes wonder whether if we had access to that knowledge now, humani would not be where we are today."

Sophie had brief glimpses of ancient technology, flickering sights of soaring cities of glass, vast fleets of metal boats, crystal craft streaking through the skies. And then the images turned dark and she watched a delicate gemlike city turn to molten liquid as the appalling shape of a deathly mushroom cloud bloomed in its center. She shook her head and sucked in a deep shuddering breath, blinking back to the present, trying to dispel the images. The sounds of an everyday San

Francisco afternoon—a distant ship's horn, a car alarm, the wail of an ambulance siren—came rushing back. "No, we would have destroyed everything," she murmured.

"Perhaps . . . ," Tsagaglalal said quietly. "The destruction of the earth and every living creature on its surface was a possibility that my husband and Chronos considered on a daily basis. I sat and watched them search through the myriad strands of time looking for those lines that kept the humani and this Shadowrealm alive for as long as possible. They called them the Auspicious Threads. Once they had isolated an Auspicious Thread, they did everything in their power to ensure that it was given every opportunity to prosper."

A cool salt-and-exhaust-scented breeze whispered through the trees and surrounding bushes. Leaves hissed softly together, and Sophie suddenly shivered. "And Josh and I were in one of those Auspicious Threads?"

"There were a boy and a girl, yes. Twins. Gold and Silver." Tsagaglalal looked at the girl. "My husband even knew your names."

Sophie touched the emerald tablet tucked into the waistband of her jeans. It was addressed to her by name.

Tsagaglalal nodded. "He knew a lot about you, though not everything. The strands of time are not always precise. But Abraham and Chronos knew without question that the twins were critical to the survival of the humani race and the world. And they knew for certain that they had to protect a perfect set of twins, a Gold and a Silver."

"Josh and I aren't perfect," Sophie said quickly.

"No one is. But your auras are pure. We knew the twins

would need knowledge, so Abraham created the Codex, the Book of the Mage, which held the entire world's knowledge in its few pages." The old woman's face creased in pain. "He was Changing then. Do you know what the Change is?"

Sophie started to shake her head, then nodded as the Witch of Endor's knowledge meshed with hers. "A transformation. Most of the very oldest Elders morph into . . ." She stopped, blinking hard at the images. ". . . into monsters."

"Not all, but most. Some of the transformations are beautiful. My husband thought the Change might be a mutation caused by solar radiation acting upon incredibly aged cells."

"But you haven't Changed. . . ."

"I'm not an Elder," Tsagaglalal said simply. "And when Abraham created the Codex, he manipulated its essence so that only the humani would be able to handle it. Its very touch is poisonous to the Elders. A series of humani guardians were chosen to keep the Book safe through the ages."

"And that was your role?" Sophie asked.

"No," Tsagaglalal said, surprising her. "Others were chosen to guard the Book. My jobs were to protect the emerald tablets and to watch over the Golds and Silvers and be there at the end when they needed me."

"Tsagaglalal," Sophie whispered. "She Who Watches."

The old woman nodded. "I am She Who Watches. Using forbidden Archon lore, Abraham made me immortal. I was to watch over the twins, to guard and protect them. And to watch over me, to guard and protect me, my husband granted my younger brother the same gift of immortality."

"Your brother . . . ," Sophie breathed.

Tsagaglalal nodded. Her eyes were fixed on the sky. "Together, we have lived upon this earth for more than ten thousand years and watched over generations of the Newman family. And what a family tree it has been. My brother and I have guarded princes and paupers, masters and servants. We've lived in just about every country on this planet, waiting, waiting, always waiting. . . ." Her eyes grew large behind sudden tears. "There were occasional Golds in your family line, some Silvers, too, even a couple of sets of twins, but the prophesied twins never materialized, and my brother's mind began to collapse with the weight of years."

"But what about the Flamels? Why have they been looking for twins?"

"A mistake, Sophie. A misinterpretation. Perhaps even a little arrogance. Their role was simply to guard the Book. But at some point the Flamels began to believe that their task was to find the twins of legend."

Sophie felt as if all the breath had been sucked from her body. "So everything they did . . . was worthless."

Tsagaglalal smiled kindly. "No, not worthless. Everything they did brought them closer and closer to this city, in this time, and ultimately, to you. Their role was not to find the twins—it was prophesied that the twins would find them. It was their role to protect the twins and bring them to be Awakened."

Sophie thought her head might explode. It was terrifying to think that everything about her life from the moment of her birth had been foreseen ten thousand years previously. A sudden thought struck her. "Your brother," Sophie said quickly. "Where is he now?"

"We first went to England when we learned that Scathach had helped put a young man named Arthur on the throne. My brother grew close to the boy; Arthur became like a son to him. When the boy died . . . well, my brother was devastated. His mind started to fragment, and he found it hard to tell past from present, reality from fantasy. He believed that Arthur would come again and would need him. He never left England. He said he would die there."

"Gilgamesh," Sophie breathed.

"Gilgamesh the King," Tsagaglalal whispered, "though in England they knew him by a different name." Tears crawled down her lined face and the garden filled with the scent of jasmine. "Lost to me now, long lost."

"We met him," Sophie said urgently, leaning forward to touch Tsagaglalal's arm. Her aura cracked. "He's alive! In London." She blinked away her own tears, remembering the ragged and filthy-looking old homeless man with the shockingly blue eyes whom she had first met in the back of a taxicab.

The jasmine soured. Tsagaglalal's voice was bitter. "Oh, Sophie, I know he is still alive and in London. I have friends there who keep an eye on him for me, who ensure that he is never short of money and he never goes hungry." She was crying now, huge tears that dripped from her chin to spatter onto the grass. Tiny white jasmine flowers unfurled, blossomed and curled up in the space of a single heartbeat. "He does not remember me," Tsagaglalal whispered. "No, that is not true: he does remember me, but as I was, ten thousand years ago, young and beautiful. He does not recognize me now."

"He said he wrote everything down," Sophie said. She brushed silver tears from her face. "He said he would write about me, to remember me." She remembered the old man who had shown her a thick sheaf of paper held together with string. There were scraps from notebooks, covers torn from paperbacks, bits of newspapers, restaurant menus and napkins, thick parchment, even pieces of hide and wafer-thin sheets of copper and bark. They had all been cut and torn to roughly the same size, and they were covered in minuscule scrawl.

"This immortality is a curse," Tsagaglalal said suddenly, angrily. "I loved my husband, but there are times—far too many times—when I hated him for what he did to me and my brother and I cursed his name."

"Abraham wrote that I would curse his name now and forevermore," Sophie said.

"If my husband had a flaw, it was that he always told the truth. And sometimes the truth is hard."

Sophie's breath caught in her chest. Some of the Witch's memories were trickling into her thoughts, and they were about something important. She concentrated to make sense of them. "The process that made Gilgamesh immortal was flawed. But if his immortality is removed—" She stopped.

"What are you remembering, child—something else the Witch knew?"

"No, something Gilgamesh asked Josh to do."

"What was that?"

"He made my brother promise that when this was all over—if we survived—we would return to London with the Codex."

The old woman frowned, creases deepening to line her forehead. "Why?"

"Gilgamesh said that there was a spell on the first page of the Codex." She wracked her brain, trying to remember the King's exact words. "He said . . . he said that he stood by Abraham's shoulder and watched him transcribe it."

Tsagaglalal nodded. "Both my brother and Prometheus were always by my husband's side. I wonder what he saw?"

"The formula of words that confers immortality," Sophie said. "And when Josh and I asked why he wanted it, since he was already immortal—"

"To reverse the formula," Tsagaglalal answered. "It might work. He could become mortal again, he might even regain his memories and remember me," the old woman breathed. "We could become human again and die in peace."

"Human again?" Sophie asked. She was suddenly reminded of something the old woman had said earlier. "You're not an Elder," she said, "and you're not an Archon or an Ancient. What are you?"

"Why, Sophie," Tsagaglalal said with a sad smile, "why do you think the Codex was created so that the Elders could not bear it and only humani could hold it? Gilgamesh and I are humani. We were among the first of the First People brought to life by Prometheus's aura in the Nameless City on the edge of the world. Now the First People are no more.

Only Gilgamesh and I remain. And only one thing is left for me to do," the old woman added.

The girl sat back against the apple tree and folded her arms. She knew what her aunt was about to offer. "Can I refuse?"

"You can," Tsagaglalal said, surprising her. "But if you do, then tens of thousands of people who lived and died through time in order to protect you will have died in vain. All those people who guarded the Codex, the previous generations of twins, the Elders and Next Generation who sided with the humani—all will have died in vain."

"And the world will end," Sophie added.

"That too."

"And did your husband see that?"

"I do not know," Tsagaglalal said. Her eyes were red-rimmed, but she had no tears left to shed. "The Change was surging through his body in those last days, turning it to solid gold. Speech became impossible. I am sure he would have found a way to tell me . . . but then Danu Talis was destroyed in the Final Battle." Tsagaglalal turned away from Sophie and her gaze followed a fat droning bumblebee as it buzzed around the clearing, dropping onto the grass where moments earlier jasmine flowers had blossomed and died. "Abraham and Chronos saw many lines of history, and each of those lines was created by individual decisions. Often it was impossible to tell—except in the very broadest sense—who had done what. That is why the original prophecy is so vague— 'one to save the world, one to destroy it.' I do not know

315

which one you are, Sophie." She pointed back toward the house with her chin. "There is one other tablet in the box, and it is addressed to your brother."

Sophie gasped in shock as the realization struck home.

Tsagaglalal nodded. "Yes, it could just as easily have been Josh I was talking to now, while Sophie Newman stood alongside Dee and Dare on Alcatraz. But there will come a moment—and soon—when you must choose. And the choice you make will dictate the future of the world and the countless Shadowrealms." She saw the stricken look on Sophie's face and reached over to rest her palm against her cheek. "Forget what you know—or think you know—and trust your instincts. Follow your heart. Trust no one."

"But Josh. What about him? I'll be able to trust him, won't I?" Sophie said in alarm.

"Follow your heart," Tsagaglalal repeated. "Now close your eyes and let me teach you about the Magic of Earth."

CHAPTER FORTY-EIGHT

*V*irginia Dare sat on the huge steps in the recreation yard of Alcatraz prison and looked out toward the city over the high wire-topped walls. Josh sat beside her.

"I wonder how close the Lotan is," he said.

Virginia shook her head. "Hard to tell, but trust me, when it arrives we'll know. I imagine we'll hear the screams from here."

"Where do you think it will come ashore?"

"I have no idea. It's big, but I don't think it's that heavy. Currents run fast here. That's another reason this place was chosen as a prison. Even if someone did manage to get out of their cell, they wouldn't survive the water." She pointed to the Bay Bridge. "I imagine the Lotan will be swept toward the bridge before it manages to swim to shore."

"Will it cause much destruction before the Elders arrive?" Josh asked.

Dare shrugged, a movement that sent her hair rippling down her back. "It depends how long they wait before intervening." Then she frowned. "In the old days, people would summon the Elders by praying to them, but no one believes in the Elders anymore, so no one is going to summon them. So yes, there will probably be quite a bit of chaos. The Lotan will eat any meat that comes its way, though I'm not sure how much bigger it could get. It will also drink the aura of any Elder, Next Generation or immortal who gets too close. You saw what happened to Billy."

Josh shivered at the memory and nodded.

"If you hadn't intervened, it would have drained him to a husk. However," she continued, "the Lotan has such a short life span. It had three hours to live when it was set loose—it will have four if it continues to feed—before it starts to shrink back into its shell."

A foul stink suddenly wafted across the yard, blanketing the sea air.

Virginia's hand shot out and gripped Josh's arm as a creature straight out of legend padded across the exercise yard, claws click-clacking on the stones. It was a sphinx, an enormous lion with the wings of an eagle and the head of a beautiful woman. The sphinx turned to look at Virginia and Josh, and a long black tongue flickered out of its mouth, tasting the air.

Josh dropped his hand onto the stone sword he'd placed on the steps and Virginia slowly and deliberately raised her flute to her lips.

The sphinx turned and scuttled away without saying a word.

"Now," Virginia continued, as if nothing had happened. "You wish to learn the Magic of Air?"

"I do."

"I need to tell you," she said, "that I've never done this before. But I've seen it done."

"And how did that go?"

"It went well . . . most of the time."

Josh looked at her quickly.

"I saw an immortal—it might have been Saint-Germain—try to teach another immortal the Magic of Fire." She stopped and shook her head.

"What happened?"

"Well, let us say that there was a bit of a mishap."

"Saint-Germain taught Sophie fire magic," Josh said.

"And she didn't burst into flames?"

"She didn't."

"So he's obviously gotten better at it. And who taught you?"

"Prometheus."

"Impressive," Virginia said. She pushed back her sleeves and picked up her flute. "Now, I know there is a certain formula of words that are used when students are being taught the Elemental Magics, about how each magic is stronger than the other—but I'm afraid I don't know those words, and I don't believe them anyway. What you have to remember is that no matter who taught you, magic is as strong as the will of the user and the strength of their aura. Great emotions—love, hate, terror—intensify any magical working. But be careful. These same emotions raging through your body can also consume your aura. And once your aura is gone, then so are you!" She clapped her hand suddenly, the sound sending seagulls soaring. "Now look up at the skies," she commanded.

Josh leaned back, resting his elbows on the step behind him, and looked up into the afternoon sky.

"What do you see?"

"Clouds. Birds. An airplane contrail."

"Pick a cloud, any cloud . . . ," she said, and her words trembled through her flute with little whistling sounds.

Josh focused on a cloud. He thought it looked like a face . . . or a dog . . . or maybe a dog's face. . . .

"Magic has to do with imagination," Virginia said, her words rising and falling with the notes of the flute. The air filled with the scent of sage. "Did you ever meet Albert Einstein? . . . No, no of course you didn't. You're too young. He was a remarkable man, and we remained good friends throughout his life. He knew what I was; he once said to me that the stories I told him about my immortality and the Shadowrealms inspired his interest in time and relativity."

"He's always been one of my heroes," Josh said.

"Then you will know that he said that imagination is more important than knowledge. For knowledge is limited to all we now know and understand, while imagination embraces the entire world, and all there ever will be to know and understand." She laughed and her flute turned the sound beautiful. "I offered to find someone to make him immortal, but he wasn't interested." Virginia's music changed, becoming wild and dramatic, like a storm over the ocean. "Look at the cloud and tell me what you see."

The cloud had shifted, twisted. "A sailboat," Josh breathed.

The music crashed and swelled.

"With waves washing over it . . ."

And the music stopped.

"It's gone." Josh blinked in surprise. He'd watched the cloud twist and roil in the air, then disappear.

"But I didn't make it disappear," Virginia said. "You did. The music planted the images in your brain and you saw the boat in the storm, and then your imagination filled in everything else and when the music stopped, you imagined the boat had sunk." She pointed with the wooden flute. "See that cloud?"

Josh nodded.

"Watch it," Virginia Dare said. Pressing her flute to her lips, she played a long, slow, gentle lullaby.

"Nothing's happened to it."

"Not yet," the immortal said. "But that's not my fault. It's yours." The flute echoed and reechoed in his head, the notes striking memories, bringing up fragments of songs he'd heard in the past, snatches of dialogue from movies and TV programs he'd seen. The sounds wrapped around him like a blanket, and he felt his eyes grow heavy and gritty with sleep. "Look at the cloud again."

"Sleepy," Josh mumbled.

"Look," Virginia commanded.

The cloud was curling and squirming, and Josh realized that it was forming pictures of the images he was seeing in his head, faces of movie stars and singers, characters from games he'd played.

"You are doing that," Virginia breathed. "Now focus. Think of something you hate. . . ."

The cloud suddenly grew larger, darker, and abruptly it fell from the sky, a long wriggling python.

Josh shouted, and the cloud dissolved.

"Again," Virginia directed. "Something you love." The music swirled and howled.

Josh tried to form his sister's face in the cloud, but couldn't see it clearly enough and the cloud ended up looking like a blob. He refocused and the blob turned into an orange, which transformed into a golden ball, which flattened to become a page covered in tiny shifting sticklike writing. . . .

"Very good," Virginia said. "Now look across the yard."

Josh sat up straight and looked to the wall at the far side of the recreation yard.

"It is covered in dirt," Virginia said. She took a deep breath and a gust of wind whistled across the open space, curling the dust in the air. "Imagine something," she commanded.

"Like?"

"A snake," she suggested.

"I hate snakes."

"So you should be able to see them clearly in your imagination. We always find it easier to visualize what we fear; it's what keeps us afraid of the dark."

Josh looked at the swirling twist of dust, and instantly it changed, gathering into a thick rope of grit that curled into a red-and-black-patterned garter snake. Josh remembered seeing it in the San Francisco Zoo. Instantly the snake dissolved into the distinctive animal and tree logo of the zoo.

"You need to concentrate," Virginia said firmly. "You created the snake, then you remembered where you saw it; that's why the image changed."

Josh nodded. Focus. He needed to focus. Instantly the logo twisted back into the shape of the snake. He visualized it curling to swallow its own tail, and across the yard the coil of dust formed a perfect circle.

"Impressive," Virginia said. "But now let me tell you the greatest secret of air magic, which, I'll wager, the Witch of Endor did not teach your sister." She smiled. "And don't tell the doctor that you know this."

"Why not?" he asked.

Virginia reached out and poked Josh in the chest. Paper cracked. "We all have our secrets, Josh."

Josh pressed his hand against his T-shirt, startled. Beneath it, in a cloth bag around his neck, he carried the last two pages from the Codex. He started to panic, wondering if Dee knew but instantly guessing that Dare must not have told him yet. "How long have you known?" he asked.

"For a while."

"And you haven't told Dee?"

"I am sure you have good reasons for not telling him. And I am equally sure you will tell him when the time is right."

Josh nodded again. He still wasn't entirely sure why he hadn't told Dee that he had the missing pages. He just knew he wasn't ready yet. And now he wondered why Virginia hadn't told Dee either.

"Close your eyes again," Dare commanded.

Josh squeezed his eyes tightly shut. The music had changed, becoming soft, gentle, the sound of the wind rustling through trees on a summer's day.

"You know how powerful the air can be," Dare continued. "Strong enough to knock down buildings. You've seen hurricanes devastate cities and tornados rip apart entire towns. That is the power of the wind. You've seen skydivers fall from the sky and ride the thermal waves like surfers. No doubt you've used cans of compressed air to clean your computer keyboard."

With his eyes still squeezed tightly shut, Josh nodded.

"We're talking about air pressure." The woman's voice suddenly grew distant, as if she'd moved away from him. "And if you can shape and control the pressure . . . why then, Josh, you can do anything. Open your eyes."

Josh turned to Virginia, but she was gone. And then he scrambled to his feet and looked up into the air, mouth wide with shock. Virginia Dare was floating ten feet off the ground over the recreation yard. Her long hair was spread out behind her like a fan and her arms were flung wide. "Air pressure, Josh. I visualized a pocket of air pressure beneath me."

"Can I do that? Can I fly?"

"It will take practice. Lots of practice," she said, slowly drifting back down to the ground. "Floating first, then flying.

But yes, you will be able to do it. Now, there is one final thing I can do for you: you need a trigger."

"I know what that is—Flamel and Sophie have them tattooed on their wrists." He held up his left hand and spread his fingers wide. Burned into the flesh of his palm was the perfect imprint of an Aztec sunstone with a face in the center. "Prometheus gave this to me."

"We need not do anything so commonplace." She tapped her flute against her chin. "Did you see the movie *Close Encounters of the Third Kind*?"

"Sure—it's on TV every Christmas. And my dad has it on DVD."

"I guessed you did. You know the tune that's played at the end?"

"To communicate with the spacecraft?" He pressed his lips together and whistled the five distinctive notes.

"Exactly," Virginia said, mimicking the sounds on her flute, and Josh shuddered as a rush of cool sage-scented air washed over his body. "There is your trigger. Now whenever you need to call upon the Magic of Air, just give a little whistle!"

Josh looked across the recreation yard and whistled the five notes. A discarded soda can suddenly spun up into the air and smashed against the stone wall. "That is so . . . cool!"

"And remember, floating before flying."

Josh grinned. He'd been on the verge of trying to create a cushion of air beneath his feet at that very moment.

"And a tip—try it sitting down first. If you sit on a small carpet or rug you can create the cushion of air beneath that, just like a hovercraft." She smiled. "Where do you think the stories of flying carpets came from?"

Suddenly, from within the prison block came a blood-curdling high-pitched scream.

"Dee," Virginia said. Her easy grin disappeared, and before Josh could react she was already racing to the stairs.

Josh grabbed Clarent and ran after her, the sword flickering to blazing light in his hand.

CHAPTER FORTY-NINE

$\mathcal{T}$he Rukma vimana hummed across a landscape of extraordinary beauty. A vast forest stretched as far as the eye could see. Twisting rivers meandered through trees and opened out into enormous lakes that were so clear it was possible to see deep below the surface.

They flew over enormous herds of mammoth and watched saber-toothed tigers stalking them in the long grass. Huge black and brown bears reared up on their hind legs as the vimana droned overhead, and flocks of pterosaurs scattered as the craft appeared.

"Truly a magical landscape," William Shakespeare said to Palamedes. "I think I might have to rewrite *A Midsummer Night's Dream*."

The Saracen Knight nodded but then turned his friend toward one of the rear-facing portholes. "Though this world is not without its flaws," he murmured, pointing into the skies behind them.

"We have company," Scathach announced, pulling away from a window. "Lots and lots of company."

"I know," Prometheus said. The huge red-haired warrior pointed to a glass screen set into the floor almost directly in front of him. It was covered with racing red dots.

Palamedes looked around the craft. "This is a warcraft. Are there weapons?"

The big Elder grinned from the controls, teeth white against his red beard. "Oh, there are weapons, lots of weapons."

"I fear we are about to hear a 'but,'" William Shakespeare murmured.

"But they do not work," Prometheus continued. "These craft are old. No one—not even Abraham—knows how to repair them. Most of them barely fly, and usually one or two drop out of the air every day." He jerked a thumb toward a cloth-wrapped bundle in the seat beside him. "You might want to arm yourselves. I took the liberty of retrieving your weapons from the anpu."

"Ah, now I'm happy," Scathach said, slipping her swords into the empty sheaths on her shoulders.

Saint-Germain and Joan were sitting together, heads touching, both staring out of one of the circular portholes. "They're gaining fast," the Frenchwoman said. "There are too many to count."

"The only consolation we have is that few of those will have active weapons either," Prometheus told them.

Palamedes looked over at Scathach. "When you say 'few . . . ,'" she began.

"Some will be armed," Prometheus clarified.

"Incoming!" Saint-Germain yelled. "Two of them have launched missiles."

"Sit down and strap yourselves in," Prometheus commanded. The group scrambled to get into the seats behind him, and he added, "We're too slow to outrun them, and the smaller ones are infinitely more maneuverable."

"Is there good news?" Scathach demanded.

"I am the finest flier in Danu Talis," the Elder said.

Scathach smiled. "If anyone else said that I would think they were boasting. But not you, Uncle."

Prometheus glanced quickly at the Warrior. "How many times do I have to tell you—I'm not your uncle."

"Not yet, anyway," she muttered under her breath.

"Everyone strapped in?" Prometheus asked. Without waiting for an answer, he brought the triangular vimana straight up into the air, then flipped it back, so that the ground was directly overhead and the sky below them, before he leveled it off and the earth and sky resumed their normal positions.

"I'm going to throw up," Scatty muttered.

"That would be very unfortunate," Shakespeare said. "Especially since I am sitting directly behind you."

Joan reached over and caught her friend's hand. "You just need to focus on other things," she said in French.

"Like what?" Scathach pressed a hand against her mouth and swallowed hard.

Joan pointed.

Scatty looked directly ahead and instantly all her nausea vanished. They were facing at least a hundred vimanas. Most of them were the small circular craft they had seen earlier, but others were large oblong shapes, and Scatty could spot two Rukma vimanas.

And Prometheus was flying directly toward them.

William Shakespeare shifted uncomfortably in his seat. "Now, I've never been a warrior, and I know little about tactics, but shouldn't we be flying in the other direction?" They were close enough now to see the wide-eyed anpu in the nearest craft.

"We will," Prometheus said. "Just as soon as the missiles explode."

"Which missiles?" Shakespeare asked.

"The two just behind us." Prometheus hauled back on the vimana's controls and it once again reared straight up into the air and back in the other direction, earth and sky flipping. Scathach groaned.

And the two missiles, which had been on their tail, shot past the craft, straight into the two nearest vimana. They exploded in balls of fire. Streamers of flame washed over another three craft, while two more crashed into one another.

"Seven down," Palamedes announced, instantly becoming a warrior again, reporting the fallen enemy to his commander.

"Ninety-three to go," Saint-Germain finished, winking at his wife. Joan reached out and caught his hand in hers. She turned it over and tapped the back of his wrist, where a

330

dozen tiny butterflies were tattooed onto his flesh. She raised a pencil-thin eyebrow in a silent question.

"I have a proposal," Saint-Germain called up to Prometheus. "I am a Master of Fire. Why don't we just open the door and I'll draw down a little lightning?"

Prometheus grunted a laugh. "Try it," he said. "Try to call up your aura."

Saint-Germain snapped his fingers. His party trick was to bring his index finger alight. But nothing happened. He brushed at the butterfly trigger on the back of his wrist and tried again. A wisp of black smoke curled out from under his fingernail.

"Whatever process keeps the vimanas in the air negates your aura," Prometheus said. "In fact, Abraham believes they fly because they draw a trickle of their power from the pilot's aura."

"So we can't use our auras," Saint-Germain said, "we have no weapons and we cannot outrun them. What *can* we do?"

"We can outfly them."

The Rukma vimana dropped out of the sky. Palamedes and Saint-Germain whooped, while Shakespeare and Scathach screamed. Only Joan remained calm and composed.

Ten vimanas peeled off the larger fleet and followed it down.

Prometheus took the Rukma low, humming over the ground close enough to behead flowers and flatten grass. One vimana closed in and they could see the anpu within readying a weapon. Prometheus sent the craft over a stand of trees. He deliberately drove it into one young sapling, but tilted the nose up at the last moment so that the tree didn't break but bent—and then snapped back, straight into the trailing vimana. Startled, the pilot lost control. The craft wobbled and plowed into the ground.

"Another one down," Palamedes said.

"A neat trick," Saint-Germain agreed, "but I'm not sure you can repeat it."

The nine remaining vimanas closed in fast.

"The tops have opened," Saint-Germain reported. "They're fixing what look like rifles to the roofs."

"Tonbogiri," Prometheus said, shifting the craft left, then right as two of the rifles fired. "They're also called cutters." Metal screamed off the Rukma, and then there was a solid bang as something punched a hole in the side of the craft close to Scathach. A misshapen ball rolled to her feet. "Don't touch it," Prometheus warned as the Warrior bent over. "The balls are razor sharp. If you dropped it in your hand, it would sink in one side of your flesh and be out the other side before you even felt it."

The Elder brought the Rukma down over a lake and then deliberately dipped it in the water. An ice-cold spume fountained up behind the craft and washed into the open top of the closest vimana. Shocked, the pilot jerked away from the controls. The craft wobbled directly in front of the one behind it, just as the anpu sniper fired. The tonbogiri ball sliced straight through the vimana's control box and the craft dipped and plunged into the lake.

"Only about ninety-two to go," the Saracen Knight said.

Prometheus carved a perfect circle in the lake, churn-

332

ing up the water. A vimana drew up alongside them and the anpu leveled its tonbogiri. Prometheus cut the power and the Rukma dropped like a stone. It hit the water in an explosion of foam and sank in a cloud of bubbles. Instantly water started to seep in around the window and door seals, and rushed through the hole left by the tonbogiri. The Elder hissed in frustration. "Never done that before. Used to be you could fly these into space," he muttered.

Metal clinked off the roof and they looked up through the water. They could see the shadow of the circular vimana overhead. It was joined by a second and then a third. Tonbogiri balls started to fall into the lake, trailing streams of bubbles, only to lose velocity in the water's drag. They slowly spiraled downward, some landing with a light thud on the vehicle's roof, others drifting past to the bottom of the lake.

Suddenly there was a pop and a panel rose from the floor. Icy water flooded in around Joan's feet. "We are leaking!"

"Up!" the Saracen Knight yelled. "We need to go up before we become too heavy to rise."

"In a minute," Prometheus said. He nodded to the screen at his feet. Two red dots were approaching fast.

"How did they get behind us?" Saint-Germain asked.

"Below us," Prometheus corrected him. "And they didn't. We've awakened something from the depths."

"You did that deliberately," Scathach accused the Elder, "that's why you churned up the water."

"Whatever it is, it's closing fast . . . very fast. . . ." Palamedes pointed to the screen. "And more coming."

"I can see something outside—moving in the water,"

Saint-Germain said urgently. "Something . . ." He stopped, temporarily speechless. "Big . . . with teeth . . . lots of teeth."

Prometheus hit the controls and the Rukma surged upward. It exploded out of the water, followed by two enormous sharklike creatures. The first smashed into two of the circling vimanas, sending them spinning into the lake, while the second actually bit into the third craft, almost snapping it in two, and dragged it down.

Three more of the monstrous creatures broke the surface, teeth gnashing. "Sharks," Scathach said.

"Megalodons," Prometheus announced, pulling the Rukma higher and higher, little fountains of water spilling from the leaks in its sides.

"They were at least thirty feet long!" Scathach said.

"I know," replied the Elder. "They must have been babies."

CHAPTER FIFTY

"There are those who will tell you," Tsagaglalal began, "that the Magic of Fire or Water or even Air is the most powerful magic of all. Some would disagree—would say that the Magic of Earth surpasses all others. They are wrong."

Sophie was still sitting with her back to the apple tree, the palms of her hands flat against the grass.

Tsagaglalal sighed. "In truth," the old woman continued, "I think all magics are equal and identical. A lifetime of study has led me to believe that they are all the same."

"But the elements," Sophie pressed, "air, water, fire and earth are different."

Tsagaglalal nodded. "But the same forces control those elements. The energy you use to control fire is the same energy you use to shape water and mold air." She patted the ground. "And the earth, too. That energy comes from within: it is the power of your aura."

The garden filled with the odor of jasmine, and Tsagaglalal rubbed the palm of her hand across the earth. A speckling of brightly colored daisies appeared. "Now, was that earth magic?" she asked.

Sophie was a bit unsure, but she nodded. "Yes . . ."

Tsagaglalal smiled. "Are you sure? Why not water magic? These plants need water to survive. Or maybe it was air magic—they need oxygen, too, don't they?"

"And fire?" Sophie asked with a little smile.

"They do need warmth to grow," Tsagaglalal said.

"I'm confused. What's the Magic of Earth, then? Are you saying that there's no such thing?"

"No. I'm saying that there is no such thing as the individual magics. There should be no differentiation between earth, air, fire and water. And why stop at those four classifications? Why isn't there wood magic or silk magic, or fish magic?"

Sophie looked at her blankly.

"Let me tell you the secret that was revealed to me by my husband." The old woman leaned closer, enveloping Sophie in the sweet aroma of her aura. "There is no such thing as magic. It is a word. A silly, foolish, overused word. There is only your aura . . . or the Chinese have a better word for it: qi. A life force. An energy. This is the energy that flows within you. It can be shaped, molded, directed." She plucked a single blade of grass and held it up between thumb and forefinger. "What do you see?" she asked.

"A blade of grass."

"What else?"

336

"It's . . . green," Sophie said hesitantly.

"Look again. Look deeper. Deeper," Tsagaglalal commanded.

Sophie stared at the waving blade of grass, noting the faint pattern that ran along the underside, the pointed tip turning brown. . . .

"Use your aura, Sophie. Look at the grass."

Sophie allowed her aura to wrap around one forefinger like the finger of a silver glove.

"Look into it," Tsagaglalal urged. "See it."

Sophie touched the blade of grass . . . and instantly she saw . . .

. . . the structure of the grass, growing huge, unfolding like an entire garden . . . the outer layer peeling back to reveal veins and threads beneath . . . and then these dissolved to reveal the cells . . . and within them the molecules . . . and beyond those the atoms . . .

Suddenly she felt as if she was falling, but was it up or down? Was she flying into space, or dropping deeper . . .

. . . into planet-sized protons . . . and neutrons and electrons like whirling moons . . . and even smaller still, the quarks and leptons surging like comets . . .

"I cannot teach you earth magic," Tsagaglalal said. Her voice sounded distant, but suddenly Sophie was surging back toward the sound, seeing everything in reverse, minuscule becoming tiny, tiny growing to small . . . until she was looking at the blade of grass again. For a moment it seemed as big as a skyscraper, and then Tsagaglalal pulled it away from the girl's face and it returned to its normal size.

337

"You have seen what shapes us, one and all. Even I, who was created out of dust and animated by Prometheus's aura, have the same structure deep within me."

Sophie's head was spinning and she pressed her hands to her temples. Just when she thought she'd seen everything, she was hit with something new, and it was too much to take in.

"If you want to do water magic, you shape the hydrogen and oxygen atoms with your imagination and then impose your will on it." Tsagaglalal leaned forward and caught Sophie's hands in hers. "Magic is nothing more than imagination. Look down," she commanded.

Sophie looked at the ground between her outstretched legs.

"Visualize the earth covered in blue flowers. . . ."

Sophie started to shake her head, but Tsagaglalal squeezed her fingers painfully. "Do it."

The girl struggled to create the image of the blue flowers in her head.

Two tiny bluebells appeared.

"Excellent," Tsagaglalal said. "Now do it again. See them clearly. Visualize them. Imagine them into existence."

Sophie focused. She knew what bluebells looked like. She could see them clearly in her mind's eye.

"Now imagine the grass turning to bluebells. Change it in your head . . . force it to change . . . *believe* it will change. You have to believe, Sophie Newman. You will need to believe, to survive."

Sophie nodded. She firmly believed the grass was now covered with bluebells.

338

And when she opened her eyes, it was.

Tsagaglalal clapped her hands in delight. "See. All you had to do was have faith."

"But is it earth magic?" Sophie asked.

"That is the secret of *all* magic. If you can imagine it, if you can see it clearly, and if your aura, your qi, is strong enough, then you will achieve it."

Tsagaglalal attempted to stand. Sophie got easily to her feet and helped the old woman up. "Now why don't you run on up to the house and get changed. Put on heavy jeans and hiking boots and wear something warm."

"Where am I going?"

"To see your brother," Tsagaglalal said.

Nothing sounded better to Sophie at that moment. She kissed her aunt quickly on the cheek before darting off through the garden.

"And I don't think it is going to be a happy reunion," Tsagaglalal murmured.

CHAPTER FIFTY-ONE

*P*rometheus pointed directly ahead to a shining crystal tower rising out of the sea. "That's where we're headed."

Palamedes twisted to look at the vimana fleet trailing behind them. The enemy ships had grown more cautious since they'd lost the three craft to the megalodons and had hung back, obviously content to trail the Rukma to its destination.

"The tower is under attack," Scathach said, leaning forward in her seat to get a better view.

A larger triangular Rukma vimana hovered over the tower. Long ropes trailed from the Rukma down to a platform close to the top of the tower, where a single armored warrior with a sword and battle-ax guarded an open door against a dozen howling anpu, which slashed at him with serrated spears and deadly kopesh. At least ten anpu lay sprawled around him, and in a flurry of steel, he sent another staggering off the platform into the crashing waters below. And while his weapons were dark with anpu blood, his own gray armor was cracked and broken, bright with red blood. An anpu appeared in the Rukma vimana's door and fired a tonbogiri down at the warrior. He ducked and the metal balls struck blue sparks where they hit the crystal wall, and the ground around the warrior was streaked with pitted white scars.

"Now, *there* is a warrior," Palamedes said in admiration.

"None finer," Prometheus agreed. "Hang on, old friend," he said softly, "we're coming."

A huge anpu with an enormous curved sword slashed at the warrior in gray, catching him on the side of the head, knocking his helmet off and sending it spinning into the air.

It took a moment for the immortal humans in the Rukma to recognize him. They had only ever known him as old and ragged, lost and crazed, but here he was in all his glory—it was Gilgamesh the King, howling with laughter, teeth bared and bloody as he fought against impossible odds. More anpu rappelled out of the hovering Rukma.

Scathach pulled herself out of her chair. "Get us down there!"

"I'm doing my best," Prometheus muttered.

Behind him the vimana fleet closed in.

"Get us close and I'll jump," the Shadow said. She pulled her two short swords from the sheaths on her back.

"No," the Saracen Knight said. He pointed to the hovering Rukma. "Get on top of it. We'll go down by the same ropes."

Shakespeare unclipped his restraints. "I am no warrior," he said to Prometheus. "But you are. Show me what to do, and I will attempt to hold this carriage in place."

341

Prometheus brought their Rukma in almost directly on top of the one hovering over the tower. Even before he had it properly positioned, Scathach had popped open the door and dropped the ten feet onto the second craft. She hit it hard and rolled to her feet. The anpu sniper poked its head out of the opening, wondering what the noise was, and Scathach caught it by the throat, lifted it bodily out of the craft and flung it into the air. It shrieked as it fell into the sea.

"I guess not all of them are mute," she muttered.

She caught hold of the dangling ropes, wrapped an arm and leg around one and slid to the platform below, landing in the middle of the startled anpu.

"I am Scathach!" she howled, her swords a blur, driving the anpu before her. "I have been called the Daemon Slayer and the King Maker." Three anpu attacked simultaneously. She ducked, chopping at one, driving another into its companion's weapon, forcing a third to the edge of the platform. It staggered and then, arms windmilling, fell over the edge. "I have been called the Warrior Maid and the Shadow." She fought with feet and fists, her swords screaming extensions of her arms. "Today, I am adding the Anpu Killer to my list of titles."

The shocked anpu fell back, leaving Scathach alone with Gilgamesh. "It is good to meet you again, old friend. You were magnificent."

The warrior looked at her with puzzled blue eyes. "Do I know you?"

A wave of anpu attacked, howling their terrifying war cry.

"They must not get inside," Gilgamesh said. He grunted as a kopesh shattered against his breastplate. "Abraham is finishing the Book."

Scathach's swords slashed another kopesh in half, then chopped at the warrior holding it. The anpu shrieked and spun away.

"Did you come alone?" Gilgamesh asked.

And at that moment four figures rappelled down the ropes into the melee.

The Warrior smiled. "I brought some friends."

Prometheus caught two anpu—one in either hand—and tossed them off the platform, while Joan's blindingly fast sword work sent another staggering over the edge. Saint-Germain fought with two long daggers, and his speed and agility meant that there was no way to defend against his attack. Prometheus used his hammerlike fists to punch his way through to stand alongside Gilgamesh.

"My friend," Prometheus said, "are you hurt?"

"Merely scratches."

Scathach drove the last of the anpu over the edge. "Let's get out of here and—" she began, but Prometheus caught her and flung her to the ground—just as a trio of tonbogiri balls spat into the crystal wall above her head. "—go inside," she finished.

With tonbogiri balls ringing and screeching off the platform around them, they scrambled into the tower.

A beautiful young woman in white ceramic armor holding two metal kopesh faced them. She flowed into a fighting

343

stance when she saw the strangers passing through the doorway, only relaxing when Prometheus and Gilgamesh ducked inside.

"Let me introduce you to my sister, Tsagaglalal," Gilgamesh said proudly. "If the anpu had gotten past me, she would have stood as the last line of defense for Abraham."

"I knew you would come, Prometheus," the young woman with the huge gray eyes said. She pressed her hand against his cheek. "I'm glad you're safe," she whispered.

"I am sorry I got delayed." He jerked his head to a side door. "Is he nearly finished?"

"He is on the last few lines," Tsagaglalal said.

Scathach risked a quick look outside. "Shakespeare is a sitting duck."

While they had been fighting the anpu, the vimana fleet had closed in. The Rukma, with Shakespeare at the controls, was coming under sustained fire. They could see puncture marks all across the craft, and as they were watching, there was a sudden bang, and black smoke started to pour from the left wing tip, tilting the craft at a sharp angle.

Palamedes turned to dart outside. "We've got to get—" he began, but Prometheus and Saint-Germain dragged him back as tonbogiri balls peppered the doorframe where he had stood only moments earlier, ripping it to pieces.

There was sudden movement on the Rukma and Shakespeare appeared, pulling himself up out of the domed roof. With tonbogiri balls cutting chunks out of the craft around him, he crawled out on the tilting triangular wing, then spread his arms and allowed himself to slide off the craft and drop onto the Rukma directly below. He slipped into the opening of the second vimana and reappeared outside a moment later, holding the anpu sniper's tonbogiri.

"He's never fired a gun in his life," Palamedes said. "He abhors weapons."

As Palamedes spoke, the group could see Shakespeare put the tonbogiri to his shoulder, then jerk three times.

Two of the attacking vimanas spun out of control, both of them crashing into two more. The four flaming craft spiraled into the sea.

"But then he's always been full of surprises," Palamedes added.

Shakespeare fired again and again and destroyed another two craft. One of them flew into the side of the crystal tower, and the entire building rang like a bell.

But more and more of the vimana had arrived, with the bigger Rukma warships and the oblong vimana moving up to the front.

"They will be armed," Prometheus said. "They'll shoot him out of the skies and then turn their weapons on us."

"We could make a run for the ropes—get into the vimana and leave . . . ," Scathach said.

"They'd pick us off as we climbed up. Besides," he added, "Abraham cannot climb."

Saint-Germain risked a quick look outside. Shakespeare had driven off the snipers. "I think we've got more trouble coming."

They crowded around the door and peered up into the darkening skies. Another vimana had arrived, a slender crystal

345

craft that looked shining and new. The setting sun painted one side of it a warm gold, leaving the other almost completely transparent.

"So who is this newcomer? The fleet commander?" Scathach asked.

Prometheus frowned. "I've never seen anything like it—only a member of one of the Ruling Clans would have something like that—Aten, maybe, or Isis. Aten would not do this—he would not move against Abraham. But the anpu are Anubis's creatures, and that dog-headed monster is very much under his mother's thumb. He'll do as she tells him. Whoever it is, though"—he shook his head—"it cannot be good news."

A series of tiny dots winked around the rim of the crystal ship, and a dozen vimanas, including one of the Rukmas, exploded into flame.

"Or I could be wrong," Prometheus conceded.

The crystal vimana swept past, and for an instant, they all saw who was piloting the craft. Marethyu waved his hook in greeting before racing into the heart of the vimana fleet. Almost immediately a dozen craft blossomed into flame and the fleet dissolved into chaos. Vimana crashed into vimana as they attempted to escape. Those few craft with weapons tried to bring them to bear on the crystal vimana, but it was too fast, and they only succeeded in firing on their own ships.

Marethyu swept through the fleet again and again, targeting the Rukma vimana and the oblong craft, sending them, flaming, into the sea below.

When the vimana fleet finally scattered, less than half remained. None of the bigger craft were still in the air, and the seas and rocks around the crystal tower were scattered with bright metal and dark debris.

Marethyu brought the crystal vimana in and landed it on the platform. He sat inside, not moving.

Scathach was the first out the door. She picked her way across the platform around chunks of metal and ceramic from the downed Rukma. When she reached the crystal craft, she looked inside, and then she nodded and turned away. She had seen Marethyu sitting with his right hand covering his eyes, his shoulders shaking, and she knew he was weeping for the death and destruction he had caused. It had been necessary, she knew, and she had no doubt that he had saved their lives. But in that moment, seeing him weep for what he had done, she trusted him more than she had at any time in the past. She knew then that whatever he was—whoever he was—he had not lost his humanity.

CHAPTER FIFTY-TWO

*B*lack Hawk brought the boat in close to the dock and expertly flung a loop of rope around a wooden piling. He nodded to the expensive motorboat Dee and Josh had used to get to the island. It had slipped free of its moorings and was in danger of drifting out to sea. "Well, at least we know they're still here."

Mars hopped off the boat and turned to hold out his hand to Hel. She hesitated, as if surprised, and then took it. "Thank you," she mumbled.

Odin stepped out onto the dock and then looked back at the immortal. "Are you coming with us?"

Black Hawk laughed. "Are you insane, or do you think I am? One immortal and three Elders, heading onto an island of monsters. I know who's not coming back from that trip."

Mars worked his head from side to side, easing the stiffness. "He's probably right—he'd slow us down."

"I'll be right here," Black Hawk said, "so that when you all come screaming back here, I'll be able to get you off the island."

Even Hel laughed. "We'll not come screaming to you."

"Have it your way. I'll be here, though. For a while, anyway," he added with a grin.

"I thought you would want to rescue your friend Billy," Mars said.

Black Hawk laughed again. "Trust me, Billy never needs rescuing. Usually people need to be rescued from him."

CHAPTER FIFTY-THREE

*D*r. John Dee stood in the middle of the cellblock and howled his rage. Behind him, a ragged and filthy sphinx regarded him with an expression of distaste on her face.

Virginia and Josh came racing into the building and Dee spun around to greet them, his face contorted with anger. "Useless!" he shouted. "Useless, useless, useless!" He flung a pile of paper into the air and it rained down like confetti.

"What's useless?" Virginia said, keeping her voice calm, eyes trained on the sphinx. The creature flickered her tongue at Dare, who touched her flute. The tongue disappeared.

Josh picked up two pieces of a torn page and held them together. "These look like they're from an Egyptian tomb." He turned the page sideways. "They sort of look familiar. I think my dad may have had photos of something like this on the wall of his study."

"It is from the pyramid of Unas, who reigned in Egypt

over four thousand years ago," Machiavelli said from the cell directly behind Dee. "They used to be called Pyramid Texts, but nowadays we call them . . ."

". . . the Book of the Dead," Josh finished. "My dad *does* have these pictures. Was this how you were going to awaken the creatures?"

Machiavelli, clutching the bars of his cell, smiled but said nothing.

Virginia stood in front of Dee and stared into his eyes, using her will to calm him down. "So you tried to use the pages to awaken the creatures. Tell me what happened."

Dee jabbed a finger into the nearest cell. It was empty. Virginia stepped closer and discovered the pile of white dust in the corner.

"I don't even know what was in the cell—some winged monstrosity. Giant vampire bat, I think. I said the words, and the creature opened its eyes and immediately crumbled to dust."

"Maybe you said a word wrong?" Virginia suggested. She plucked a scrap of paper from Josh's hands. "I mean, it looks difficult."

"I am fluent," Dee snapped.

"He is," Machiavelli said, "I will give him that. And his accent is very good too, though not quite as good as mine."

Dee spun back to the cell holding Machiavelli. "Tell me what went wrong."

Machiavelli seemed to be considering it; then he shook his head. "I don't think so."

Dee jerked his thumb at the sphinx. "Right now she's

351

absorbing your aura, ensuring that you cannot use any spells against me. But she'll be just as happy eating your flesh. Isn't that true?" he said, looking up into the creature's female face.

"Oh, I love Italian," she rumbled. She stepped away from Dee and dipped her head to look into the opposite cell. "Give me this one," she said, nodding at Billy the Kid. "He'll make a tasty snack." Her long black forked tongue flickered in the air before the outlaw, who immediately grabbed it, jerked it forward and allowed it to snap back like an elastic band. She screamed, coughed, and squawked all at the same time.

Billy grinned. "I'll make sure I'll choke you on the way down."

"It might be difficult to do that if you have no arms," the sphinx said thickly, working her tongue back and forth.

"I'll still give you indigestion."

Dee looked at Machiavelli. "Tell me," he said again, "or I will feed your young American friend to the beast."

"Tell him nothing," Billy yelled.

"This is one of those occasions when I am in agreement with Billy. I am going to tell you nothing."

The Magician looked from one side of the cell to the other. Then he looked at Machiavelli. "What happened to you? You were one of the Dark Elders' finest agents in this Shadowrealm. There were times you even made me look like an amateur."

"John, you were always an amateur." Machiavelli smiled. "Why, look at the mess you're in now."

"Mess? What mess? I'm not in a mess." Dee's eyes started

to dance wildly, and a giggle bubbled up from his chest. "You have no idea what I've planned. It is, not to put too fine a point on it, masterful."

"Your arrogance will be your downfall, John," Machiavelli said. He turned away from the cell door and lay down on the narrow cot.

"I will kill the outlaw," Dee said suddenly. "I will feed him to the sphinx."

Machiavelli remained lying on the bed, staring at the ceiling.

"Do you want me to do it?" Dee screamed at Machiavelli. Do you want me to kill Billy the Kid?" He leaned against the cell and looked in on Machiavelli. "What! No last-minute attempt to save your new friend?"

"I can save Billy and condemn thousands to death, or I can condemn Billy and save thousands," the Italian said quietly. "What do you think I should do, Billy?" he called out.

The outlaw stepped up to the bars of the cell. "When I went to school—which I did for a bit—we were taught a saying that really stuck with me. 'It is better that one man die for the people than that the whole nation perish.'"

Niccolò Machiavelli nodded. "I like that. Yes, I like that very much." Then he turned his head away from Dee. "You have your answer."

Dee spun back to the sphinx. "He's yours."

The creature's long black tongue snapped out and wrapped around Billy's throat, pulling him in hard against the bars. "Lunch," the sphinx rasped.

A single pure note rang out in the cellblock, and the sphinx collapsed into an ungainly heap on the floor. "No," Virginia breathed.

Billy crashed back into his cell, both hands holding his neck, which now had a solid red stripe around it. He was gasping for air.

Dee was speechless with rage. His mouth kept opening and closing, but no sound came out other than a hissing breath.

"John, be reasonable," Virginia said. "I've known Billy a very long time, and we have had some great adventures together. He's as close as I have to a friend. When he dies, which he will, sooner or later, because he can be so stupid," she added, glaring at the American immortal, "it should be with a degree of dignity, rather than being fed to this . . . this *thing*."

"Thanks," Billy wheezed.

"You're welcome. And you owe me."

"I'll remember."

Virginia turned back to Dee. "I'll make a deal."

"For what?" he demanded.

"For Billy's life," she said evenly.

"Do you forget who you're dealing with?" Dee snarled.

"Do *you*?" she asked softly.

Dr. John Dee drew in a deep shuddering breath. He took a step backward, hit the heavy bulk of the sphinx and sat down hard on the ground at her feet. A strong musky miasma swirled around him. "A deal . . . ," he coughed.

"A deal."

"What can you offer me?"

Virginia twirled her flute in her fingers, the sudden movement sending a quartet of notes rushing through it. They hung heavy on the air.

And then movement rustled through every cell.

Dee shot to his feet. He darted from one side of the cellblock to the other. All the creatures were stirring. "You can do this? You can awaken them?"

Virginia twirled her flute. "Of course. Usually I put things to sleep, but the same song, reversed, brings them awake again. This is obviously nothing more than a simple Somnus spell."

Josh stepped away from Virginia and peered into the nearest cell. Something with fur, feathers and scales lay curled in a heap. But even as he watched, a shudder ran through it.

"Virginia," Billy said urgently. "Don't do this."

"Shut up, Billy."

"Think of the people in San Francisco."

"I don't know any of the people in San Francisco," Virginia answered, then paused. "Well, actually I do, and I don't like them. But I do like you, Billy, and I'm not going to allow you to end up as lunch for some raggedy lion-monster-thingy."

"A sphinx," Machiavelli corrected her. He was standing at the bars again. "Mistress Dare," the Italian said carefully. "I absolutely applaud you for what you want to do for your friend. But I urge you to think of the bigger picture."

"Oh, but you are mistaken, Italian," Dee said quickly. "Virginia *is* thinking of the bigger picture. Aren't you, dear?"

Virginia smiled. "The doctor has promised me the world," she said quietly. "In fact, he has promised me *all* the worlds."

And then she put the flute to her mouth and the scent of sage wafted through the cellblock as a beautiful, delicate and ethereal melody bounced off its walls.

Josh felt Clarent tremble in time to the music, vibrating and pulsing to the ancient rhythm. And then Durendal, still strapped to his back, started to throb against his flesh like a heart.

And Josh felt a terrible hunger, accompanied by a ferocious rage, burn through him. It washed through his body, until a red mist actually drifted across his eyes, and he was looking at the world through a film of crimson. His aura blazed, the gold touched with streaks of bloodred. Sparks crackled off the cell bars, spitting, hissing off the metal, crackling in time to Virginia's eldritch music.

And then all the creatures in the cells came awake.

CHAPTER FIFTY-FOUR

$\mathcal{T}$he wind whipping around the crystal tower was icy and tainted with the stink of battle and broken metal, but none of the group standing on the battle-scarred and blood-streaked platform seemed to feel the chill.

Abraham the Mage, a being more gold than flesh, stood in the chipped doorway, a copper-bound book held to his chest with his right hand. His left was frozen into solid gold by his side. Tsagaglalal stood next to him, supporting him. When he smiled, only half of his face moved, and a pale gold liquid leaked from his single gray eye.

"My friends," he said, obviously in pain. "I feel I can call you that. Even though this is the first time I am seeing some of you in the flesh, I have seen you all lo these many centuries. I have followed you through the present and into your futures. I know what tricks of fate and quirks of circumstance brought you here. And in truth, I was responsible for some of them." He drew in a deep ragged breath and his chest moved slowly.

"Prometheus—my oldest friend: you brought so many great gifts into my life, including my dear wife, Tsagaglalal, and her irrepressible brother, Gilgamesh. I count both of you as my own brothers, the family I never had. Both of you know what must be done."

The two men bowed, unashamed of the tears on their faces.

Half of Abraham's face moved in a smile. "I am now and will eternally be grateful." Although his neck remained stiff, his eye moved. "Joan of Arc . . . what a history you have. What a life you have led."

The Frenchwoman bowed her head slightly, eyes still fixed on Abraham's face.

"Soon you will fight for all you hold dear, and you will be forced to make a choice that will threaten to tear you apart. Follow your heart, Joan. Be as strong as you have always been."

Joan reached for her husband's hand and squeezed.

"And what of you, Saint-Germain? I recall when I first discovered that your life intersected with Joan's, I thought it was a mistake. I spent a month checking and rechecking my data, looking for the error. But there was none. You are, in your heart, a simple man, Saint-Germain. You are a rogue and you know it. But this I know for a certainty—you have always loved Joan with all of your being."

Saint-Germain nodded and Joan glanced sidelong at him and squeezed his hand again.

"You will know what to do when the time comes. Do not hesitate.

"Palamedes the Saracen Knight and William Shakespeare. Another unlikely pairing, and again I thought my research was incorrect. But when I checked and discovered that you were both in search of the same thing—family—I knew I was not wrong. You are here today because soon we will need your special skills: your imagination, Bard, and Palamedes, he will need you to protect him. I know you would give your life for him." Abraham raised his head slightly to where the Rukma still hovered in the air. "Just as he was prepared to give his life for all of you."

Shakespeare dipped his head, then pulled off his glasses and furiously polished them, so that no one would see the flush of color on his cheeks.

"And Scathach. The Shadow. For ten thousand years I have watched you. I could fill a library with your adventures and another with your mistakes. You are, without doubt, the most infuriating, irresponsible, dangerous, loyal and courageous person I have ever encountered. The world would be a poorer place without you. You have given much to the humani, and they have not given you back as much as you deserve. But I have a gift for you. It is in two parts, and the first part I will share with you now. The second part . . . well, it may have to wait for another place and another time. Here is my gift: your sister lives. She is trapped now in a Shadowrealm with Coatlicue the Archon. You should know that she went there willingly, sacrificing herself to keep you safe."

The Shadow swallowed hard, fists opening and closing

tightly. Her skin was the color of chalk and her eyes blazed green.

"You are her only hope of rescue. Remember that. Hold on to it, even when all seems lost. You must live."

Scathach nodded.

"Now you must go," Abraham finished. "Go back to Danu Talis and destroy this world." Then, as quietly as he had appeared, he turned and, flanked by Tsagaglalal and Gilgamesh, disappeared back into the tower.

Without a word, Prometheus pulled himself up the dangling rope into the Rukma vimana. The craft shuddered, then slowly dipped until it was level with the edge of the platform. One by one, the four human immortals walked out onto the wing and climbed into the craft.

Only Scathach remained. She had turned to face south, to where the lights of the distant city of Danu Talis lit up the clouds. Her clan, the Clan Vampire, were supposedly incapable of any real emotion and were certainly incapable of tears, so why, then, was there liquid on her cheeks? It could only be spray from the sea far below, she decided. Brushing it away, she turned, climbed onto the wing and swung herself into the craft.

"Let's go," she said, strapping herself in. "Let's get this over and done with. I've got a sister to rescue."

CHAPTER FIFTY-FIVE

"I've never been here before," Nicholas Flamel admitted. He stopped and looked up at the sign above his head.

PIER 14

"Oh, Nicholas, I told you, you need to get out of the shop more often." Perenelle slipped her arm through her husband's as they walked beneath the blocky gray entrance to the new pier. "It's been open about a year now. And it is one of my favorite places in the city."

"You never told me," he said, sounding surprised.

"So even after all these years, we can still surprise one another," she teased.

He leaned over and kissed her quickly on the cheek. "Even after all these years," he said. "So enlighten me—how often do you come to this place?"

"Five, maybe six times a week."

"Oh?"

"Every morning when I'd leave the shop, I'd usually walk down to the Embarcadero, amble along the promenade and end up walking the length of this pier. Where did you think I was for that hour?"

"I thought you'd popped across the road for coffee."

"Tea, Nicholas," Perenelle said in French. "I drink tea. You know I hate coffee."

"You hate coffee?" Nicholas said. "Since when?"

"Only for the last eighty years or so."

Nicholas blinked, pale eyes reflecting the blue of the sea. "I knew that. I think."

"You're teasing me."

"Maybe," he admitted. He looked down the pier. "This is nice. Long, too."

"Fifteen feet wide and six hundred and thirty-seven feet from the shore," she said significantly.

"Ah," Flamel nodded in understanding. "The trick will be to stop the Lotan from even coming ashore."

"If it gets onto dry land, we've lost," Perenelle said. She pointed off to the left, to where Alcatraz was hidden by the curve of the bay. "The currents run very fast around the island. Anything going into the water will be swept down here, into the bay. I cannot imagine it coming ashore farther up the coast."

"If it does . . . ," Nicholas began.

"If it does, we'll deal with it," Perenelle finished. Then she smiled to take the sting from her words. "If the current pushes it beyond the bridge, then there's a good chance it will end up on the other side of the bay, in Alameda, per-

362

haps. Getting there at this time of the afternoon, in traffic, is going to take a while. It could do immense damage before we reached it."

"So we have to make sure we stop it here," he said.

"Exactly. Well, you asked me to get you as close to the water as possible. I presume you have a plan?"

"My love, I always have a plan."

They heard footsteps rattling behind them and turned as Prometheus and Niten came hurrying up. They were both carrying fishing rods over their shoulders. The slender Japanese man grinned. "Do not ask him how much it cost to hire these," he said.

"How much?" Nicholas asked.

"Too much," Prometheus answered furiously. "I could have bought an entire fishing boat, or at least a very good fish dinner, for what it cost to rent them for a couple of hours," he grumbled. "Plus a deposit in case we don't bring them back."

"What's the plan?" Niten asked. He held out an empty bucket. "We can't really go fishing. We don't have bait."

"Oh, but we do." Nicholas smiled. "You are our bait."

Niten and Prometheus stood side by side, leaning over the rail of the semicircular viewing point at the end of Pier 14. With their fishing rods arced out over the water, they looked like any other fishermen, chatting quietly together, ignoring the views of the city, the bridge, Treasure Island and the Embarcadero.

Nicholas and Perenelle sat on seats behind them. The

Alchemyst had discovered that the seats revolved and had been amusing himself by swinging back and forth. His chair squeaked with each turn. Finally Prometheus turned and glared at the immortal. "If you do that one more time, I'm going to feed you to the Lotan myself."

"And I will help," Niten added.

Perenelle suddenly stood. "Something's coming," she said quietly.

"I don't see anything . . . ," the Alchemyst said, and then he spotted it. A curling wave, a dark irregularity in the waters of the bay. He turned back to the Elder and the Swordsman. "You know what you have to do."

They nodded and returned to their fishing rods.

"Perenelle," Nicholas said.

The Sorceress nodded. Leaning on the rail, she glanced at the people walking along the pier. Some were obviously tourists—the cameras were always a dead giveaway—while the mother with a toddler in a stroller was probably a local. There were a couple of elderly fishermen who seemed fixed to the rail and a trio of young men who were practicing their juggling skills with oranges and apples.

Perenelle focused and her hair crackled with static sparks.

Immediately the two fishermen packed up their rods and buckets and ambled away, still not speaking. The tourists suddenly lost interest in the views of the city and the bay, and the child in the stroller started wailing, deciding it was time to go home. Only the three jugglers remained.

"They are concentrating on their juggling," Nicholas muttered. "That is why you cannot influence them."

"Of course." Perenelle laughed. "I'm getting slow in my old age."

A seagull swooped in and snatched an apple from one of the jugglers as he tossed it into the air. A second seagull speared an orange, and suddenly four of the huge birds dived in around the boys, pecking at them, speckling them with stinking bird droppings. The youths tossed the remainder of the fruit into the sea and hurried back down the pier.

"Nicely done," Nicholas said. "Now make sure no one gets close."

Perenelle nodded.

The Alchemyst looked at the Elder and the immortal. "Prometheus, Niten. It's time."

The air suddenly filled with the sweet odor of green tea, and then the sharper smell of anise. A faint red glow formed around Prometheus's hands and spiraled out along the length of his fishing rod. It crackled and sizzled and then dipped down along the fishing line and hissed into the water.

Niten's royal blue aura crept over his hands like a tattoo. It flowed up the length of the carbon-fiber fishing rod, discoloring it, and then dripped like ink down the fishing line to stain the water under the pier a deep navy.

And the dark shape in the water suddenly changed direction.

"The Lotan will be drawn to your auras," Nicholas said. "It will taste them in the water the same way a shark smells blood. We need to get it close, as close as possible, but you will both have to be careful. We don't want it consuming you."

"Here it comes," Niten said. The whites of his eyes, his teeth and his tongue had turned blue.

"Ready," Prometheus said.

Nicholas Flamel touched the green scarab he now wore around his neck and felt it grow warm in his hand. The spell was a simple one, something he had performed a thousand times before, though never on such a large scale.

A red-skinned head broke the surface of the water . . . followed by a second . . . and a third . . . and then a fourth head, black and twice as large as the others appeared. Suddenly there were seven heads streaking toward them.

"Let's hope no one is filming this," Niten murmured.

"No one would believe it anyway." Prometheus grinned. "Seven-headed monsters simply do not exist. If anyone saw it, they'd say it was Photoshopped."

"I can feel it," Niten said. "It's sucking the aura from me."

"Me too," Prometheus agreed.

"Let it come a little closer," Nicholas muttered. He placed a hand on each of their shoulders, and their auras were tinged with his green.

"Alchemyst." Niten's voice was strained.

"Another few feet. Closer is better."

"Nicholas," Perenelle said in alarm.

The red and blue stains in the water were now flowing toward the creature like iron-filings pulled to a magnet. They watched as the Lotan's long thick body rose higher in the water.

"It's going to jump!" Prometheus shouted.

Niten gritted his teeth and said nothing.

The Lotan sucked one last taste of their auras and then erupted straight up out of the water, rising on its tail, seven mouths gaping wide, hundreds of savage teeth ready to . . .

Mint flooded the air, heavy, thick and cloying.

There was a pop . . . followed by an explosion of green, red and blue that covered the three men in a mist of scented colors.

Nicholas shot out his fist and caught a small blue-veined egg that dropped into the palm of his hand.

Prometheus and Niten staggered back and slumped against the metal rails. They were both breathing heavily, and there were new lines on their faces. Strands of gray hair had sprouted in Niten's dark eyebrows. Nicholas Flamel held up the small egg between thumb and forefinger. "Behold the Lotan," he said.

Prometheus gasped. "Impressive. What did you do?"

"When your auras had drawn it in to the pier, I allowed it to ingest a little of my own aura. Once that was within its body, I used a simple Transmutation spell, converting one element into another. It is one of the basic principles of alchemy." He grinned. "I returned the Lotan to its original form."

"An egg." Prometheus looked surprised.

"Where we all begin," Flamel said. He tossed the blue-veined egg into the air . . . where a seagull snatched it, threw back its head and swallowed it whole.

CHAPTER FIFTY-SIX

*J*ust as she was told, Sophie changed into jeans, hiking boots and a red hooded fleece and then returned downstairs. She found Tsagaglalal in the kitchen, putting dishes into the dishwasher.

"Is this okay?"

Tsagaglalal looked her up and down. "Perfect for where you're going."

"Is someone coming to pick me up?" Sophie asked.

The old woman ignored the question. "There is a possibility," Tsagaglalal said, "that I will never see you again."

Sophie looked at the old woman in shock. She opened her mouth to protest, but Tsagaglalal raised her hand and Sophie noticed that each of the woman's fingertips was smooth—she had no fingerprints.

"But I want you to know how proud I am of you. And

your brother, too," she added, "though I always guessed that he would choose a difficult path." Tsagaglalal slipped her arm through Sophie's and led her out into the garden. "I have watched over you from the day you were born. I held you in my arms when you were barely an hour old, and I looked into your eyes and I knew that with you—finally—the prophecy was about to come true."

"Why didn't you say anything?"

"Say what, and to whom?" Tsagaglalal cackled. "Would you have believed me if even one week ago I had suggested any of this?"

Sophie shook her head.

"I had waited ten thousand years for you to appear. I was prepared to bide my time. Another decade or so was not going to make that much difference. Now, you might think that your journey is coming to an end, but Sophie, I am afraid it is only just beginning. All you have learned, all you have experienced, was simply to prepare you for this next stage."

"Will I get to talk to Josh?"

"Yes, I can guarantee that."

"When do I leave?"

"Do you have the emerald tablet with you?"

Sophie unzipped the fleece jacket's pocket and pulled it out. She moved to hand it to Tsagaglalal, but the old woman shook her head. "It is solely for you. Were I to look upon it, I would find it indecipherable."

Sophie ran her hand over the smooth tablet once more.

The words, pictograms and hieroglyphs she had read earlier had vanished and the surface was a smooth, cool mirror.

"What do you see?" Tsagaglalal asked.

"I see my reflection."

"Look deeper."

Smiling, Sophie stared into the glass. She saw her own reflection, the trees in the background, the roof of the house. . . .

She saw Dee.

She saw Virginia Dare, her flute to her lips, fingers working.

The world shifted, twisted, turned, and Sophie realized she was looking through Josh's eyes.

She saw creatures stirring in their cells, stretching, awakening, claws appearing through bars. . . .

The world spun again.

And here was Mars, magnificent in his red armor, and Odin in gray and black, followed by Hel in bulky chain mail that made her even more beastlike, racing toward the creatures, weapons in their hands. . . .

Shifting, moving.

A cell door opened and a huge, hulking, bearlike beast appeared. Mars hammered it to the ground with a single blow.

Josh was moving fast now, the jerking of his perspective upsetting Sophie's stomach.

. . . pulling open door after door, allowing monsters to surge out into the corridors, some of them so appalling to look upon it made her feel even sicker.

A sphinx appeared, and instantly Mars, Odin and Hel backed away. One by one, all the monstrous creatures in the corridors fixed their attention on the three Elders.

The monsters charged. And the Elders turned and fled down the corridor, pursued by an extraordinary collection of beasts.

The world shifted and twisted uncomfortably. Looking through Josh's eyes, Sophie saw something fall from Mars's pocket. She recognized it as his jade tablet and she watched her brother . . .

. . . *darting forward, dodging the piles of animal droppings to retrieve it.*

And when he picked it up and stared into it, turning it over and over in his hands, his face was inches from hers. She saw the changes then, saw the hard lines around his eyes, the cruel twist of his lips. The Josh she had known had never looked like this.

"Oh, Josh," Sophie gasped. "What have you done?"

Josh Newman raced out into the recreation yard, breathing in great gulps of cold fresh air. "Everything is free on this floor. . . ."

Dee and Dare were standing in the middle of the yard. The Magician had arranged two of the four Swords of Power in a reverse L shape on the ground. "Give me your swords," he demanded.

Josh immediately tossed him Durendal, but held on to Clarent, reluctant to hand over the blade.

The Magician added the third sword to the pattern on the ground. Now only the left side of the square was open. Dee stretched out his hand.

Josh felt Clarent throb in his fist.

"Quickly!" Dee shrieked, and Josh realized that the immortal was terrified. "That was Mars and Odin and Hel. Sworn enemies one and all."

"They've obviously put aside their differences to hunt you down." Virginia grinned.

"You're safe," Josh said. "The last I saw, they were being chased down the corridor by the sphinx and the other beasts."

The door behind them burst open and Mars appeared. When he spotted Dee, he howled his terrifying war cry and raced toward him. He was carrying a broadsword as long as he was, and its tip dragged along the ground, striking sparks from the stones.

"Sword, Josh!"

The young man jerked Clarent free and tossed it to Dee, who deftly caught it and placed it at the open end of the long rectangle.

The sudden movement knocked the emerald tablet out from Josh's pocket and it fell to the ground.

And then Dee poured his considerable aura into the four swords, bringing them, one by one, to blazing life.

"Go, Sophie," Tsagaglalal said.

"Go? Go where?"

"The tablet acts like a leygate mirror." She tapped the image on the tablet. "Go there. Go to your brother."

"How?"

"What did I tell you?" Tsagaglalal demanded.

"Imagination and will."

"Do you want to be with your brother?"

"Yes."

"More than anything else in the world?"

"Yes."

"Then go."

And Sophie Newman gripped the edges of the tablet and the surface flooded silver, turning it into a perfect mirror . . .

. . . and on Alcatraz, the emerald tablet on the ground became silver, and the air filled with the unmistakable odor of vanilla.

"Soph?" Josh spun around in time to see his sister wink into existence behind him. He stared at her, dumbfounded.

A hole appeared in the ground, a long rectangle, bounded on four sides by the burning swords, filled with nothing but shifting blackness, like thick bubbling tar.

"Josh!" Dee yelled, and then leapt into the hole.

Josh immediately turned toward Dee.

"Don't go!" Sophie pleaded.

"Josh," Virginia Dare called. She stepped, almost delicately, into the blackness after Dee and was instantly swallowed up.

"I've got to go," Josh said, turning to the hole in the ground. Already the fires blazing off the stone swords were beginning to die down.

"No!"

Josh put one foot into the inky blackness and Sophie caught his hand and attempted to pull him back. His face turned to an ugly mask as he struggled to wrench himself free. "I'm not coming back. I saw what they did to you."

"Josh, they tricked you. They're using you."

"I'm not the one being used," he snapped. "You need to open your eyes. The Flamels are using you. And they will use you up—just like they've done with everyone else." He shook his head. "I'm going. Dee and Virginia need me. You don't."

"I do," she said. "I'm coming with you." And instead of pulling away, she pushed, and they both tumbled into emptiness.

There was no sensation of movement.

There was nothing.

The only fixed point in the emptiness was the warmth of her brother's hand in hers.

Sophie was blind, even though her eyes were wide open. There was nothing to hear, and when she screamed, no sound came out.

And though it seemed to go on forever, she thought it might have lasted no more than a single heartbeat.

There was a spot of light.

Tiny.

A pinprick directly ahead of them. Were they falling into it, or was it rushing toward them?

She could see now.

She saw Josh's terrified face and knew it was the mirror of her own. He looked at her, and for an instant, he was her brother again, until his features hardened and he looked away. But he didn't let go of her hand.

The light swallowed them.

Sensation returned, painful sight and agonizing sound, the feel of gravel and stones beneath their feet, the musky scents of animals, the taste of exotic perfumes in their mouths.

Sophie opened her eyes. On the grass, crushed beneath her face, were flowers that had never grown on the earth she knew, tiny creations of spun glass and hardened resin.

When she rolled over, she discovered that they had company. She nudged her twin. "You better wake up."

He cracked open one eye, groaned, and then, when the realization of what he'd just seen sank in, he jumped awake and sat bolt upright. "That's a . . ."

". . . a flying saucer," she said.

"A vimana," Dee breathed. "I never thought I'd see one in my lifetime." He was kneeling on the grass, staring in awe at the object. Virginia Dare sat cross-legged beside him, her wooden flute held loosely in her hand.

The vimana descended, filling the air with a subsonic buzzing, and then the top opened and a couple appeared. They were wearing white ceramic armor, etched with patterns and hieroglyphs that almost resembled Roman letters. They were tall and slender, with deeply tanned skin that stood out in stark contrast against their armor. The woman's hair was close cropped, whereas the man's skull was smooth shaven, and their eyes were a brilliant blue.

Dee crouched on the ground, trying to make himself as small as possible. "Masters," he said. "Forgive me."

The couple ignored him. They were staring at the twins.

"Sophie," the man said.

"Josh," the woman added.

"Mom . . . Dad," the twins said simultaneously.

The couple bowed. "In this place we are called Isis and Osiris. Welcome to Danu Talis, children. Welcome home."

End of Book Five

AUTHOR'S NOTE ON VIMANAS AND FLIGHT

Like everything else in this series, the vimanas have their roots in mythology, specifically in the ancient mythological texts of India. In the epic Sanskrit poem *The Mahabharata,* which is at least twenty-five hundred years old, there is a detailed description of a vimana that was twelve cubits in circumference, with four strong wheels. (A cubit was a unit of measurement from the tip of the elbow to the tip of the middle finger.) The most famous vimana in Indian lore is the Pushpaka vimana—the flying chariot of the god Kubera. It was described as looking like a "bright cloud."

Although flying chariots, wheels and carpets are described in myths and legends from across the world, the details in Indian epic poems are both specific and extraordinary. In another epic Sanskrit poem, *The Ramayana* (also first written down around twenty-five hundred years ago), vimanas are common. The poem contains accounts of gods and heroes fighting aerial battles with other vimana and attacking cities. Lengths, heights and weights of the craft are even given.

There were many variations of the four basic types of vimana—Rukma, Sundara, Tripura and Sakuna—and descriptions of the craft differ. Some are wooden, and some are made from a mysterious red and white metal; some are triangular, with three wheels, while others are circular or oval; some are described as three stories tall.

Of course, none of this is proof that there were aircraft

in the ancient past, but it is an indication that from the very beginning, mankind has always looked to the skies.

The dream of flight is woven through history and goes back much further than one might think. It is generally accepted that the Wright brothers took to the air in December 1903 in the first controlled and powered heavier-than-air craft. But the latest research suggests that this could be wrong. Hiram Maxim got off the ground briefly in 1894 with a craft weighing 7,000 pounds, and Samuel Langley sent an unmanned craft airborne for 3,300 feet in 1896.

Throughout the nineteenth century, gliders and balloons rose into the skies over America, Europe, India and South Africa. There are reports from 1895, for example, that a craft designed by Shivkar Bapuji Talpade flew in Bombay, and the wonderfully named Goodman Household flew a glider for just under three hundred feet in Natal, South Africa, in 1871. But the first recorded heavier-than-air powered flight took place in England in 1848, when John Stringfellow managed to get a ten-foot monoplane off the ground. It was steam powered.

If the nineteenth century was the era of the glider, then the eighteenth century belonged to the balloon. Experiments in flight culminated when Etienne Montgolfier took to the air in the winter of 1783 in a spectacularly decorated 75-foot-tall, 50-foot-diameter hot-air balloon.

Back further in history, Leonardo da Vinci famously created designs for what is clearly a prototype helicopter. His notebooks are also full of designs for flying machines, gliders and artificial wings. In his diary for the year 1483, he drew up the design for the first parachute. (On June 26, 2000, a replica of this parachute, made using only the tools, fabrics and materials that would have been available to da Vinci, successfully brought a man to earth from a height of ten thousand feet.)

Back further still, in the ninth century, there is an account of the great Berber inventor and poet Abbas Ibn Firnas strapping wings on his back and gliding. And five hundred years before that, the Chinese were describing flying craft made of bamboo and leather.

As we move back in time, into that space where history and mythology blend, we find many mentions of flying vehicles. Flying is commonplace in mythology. Most of the gods can fly, usually without any additional help. But in some ancient traditions, the gods fly with the aid of wings, and these images appear on rock carvings and temple paintings all across the world. However, in myth and legend, there are also accounts of artificial means of flight and flying craft.

The Persian king Kai Kawus tied four tall poles to the corners of his throne, and eagles were chained to the top of each pole. When the birds flew, they carried the throne into the air with them. The term *flying chariot* appears throughout Chinese lore, and there are many stories of the first Chinese emperor, Shun, taking to the air—he once even escaped a burning building by using his huge hat as a parachute.

Perhaps the most famous story of flight is the tale of Icarus, whose father, Daedalus, made him a pair of artificial wings. Daedalus was a great inventor of many wonders, including the Labyrinth, created for King Minos of Knossos.

379

The details in the story of Daedalus's quest for flight are interesting: we see Daedalus rejecting silk because it was too light, and the canvas used for sails because it was too heavy. Finally, he settled upon a wooden frame covered with bird feathers held on with beeswax. Like any good inventor or scientist, Daedalus did his research: he gave his son clear instructions not to fly too high, and not to swoop low over the sea, or the salt spray would dampen and ruin the wings. Icarus soared into the sky but flew too high, and the hot Mediterranean sun melted the beeswax holding the feathers together. Unfortunately, Daedalus had not created a parachute.

Given the level of detail, one cannot help wondering whether, as in many myths, there might be more than a grain of truth in the story. It is also worthwhile to remember that today we accept as commonplace something that was once considered truly magical.

THE ENCHANTRESS

The sixth and final book of

Available Summer 2012

I am legend.

There was a time when I said that death had no claim over me, that illness could not touch me. That is no longer true. Now I know the date of my death, and that of my wife, too: and it is today.

I was born in the Year of Our Lord 1330, more than six hundred and seventy years ago. I have had a good life, a long life, and I have been many things in my time: a physician and a cook, a bookseller and a soldier, a teacher of languages and chemistry, both an officer of the law and a thief.

And I was *the* Alchemyst.

Gifted—or was it cursed?—with immortality, Perenelle and I fought the evil of the Dark Elders and kept them at bay while we searched for the twins of legend, the Gold and Silver. We always thought they would help us defend this planet.

We were wrong.

Now the end is upon us and the twins have vanished, gone back in time to the Isle of Danu Talis, back ten thousand years, back to where it all begins. . . .

Today the world ends.

Today, Perenelle and I will die.

But I will not go down without a fight.

For I am the immortal Nicholas Flamel.

From the Day Booke of Nicholas Flamel, Alchemyst
Writ this day, Thursday, 7th June,
in San Francisco, my adopted city

ACKNOWLEDGMENTS

No writing is ever done in a vacuum. Surrounding the writer is a network of people who, in so many ways, help make it happen. I especially need to acknowledge:

Beverly Horowitz, Krista Marino and Colleen Fellingham, and all of the extraordinary team at Delacorte Press.

A special thanks, as always, must go to Barry Krost and Richard Thompson.

I need to thank Alfred Molina and Jill Gascoine for the home-away-from-home.

A sincere thank-you to Michael Carroll, Patrick Kavanagh, Colette Freedman, Julie Blewett Grant and Jeffrey Smith, Brooks Almy and Maurizio Papalia, Sonia Schormann and especially Vincent Perfitt.

With special thanks to Melanie Rose and Claudette Sutherland, of course.

ABOUT THE AUTHOR

An authority on mythology and folklore, Michael Scott is one of Ireland's most successful authors. A master of fantasy, science fiction, horror, and folklore, he has been hailed by the *Irish Times* as "the King of Fantasy in these isles." *The Warlock* is the fifth book in the *New York Times* bestselling series The Secrets of the Immortal Nicholas Flamel. Look for book one, *The Alchemyst;* book two, *The Magician;* book three, *The Sorceress;* and book four, *The Necromancer,* all available from Delacorte Press.

You can follow Michael Scott on Twitter @flameauthor and visit him online at DillonScott.com.

He holds the secret that can end the world . . .

*N*icholas Flamel was born in Paris in 1330. Legend has it that the Alchemyst discovered the secret of eternal life – and that his tomb lies empty.

The legend is true . . .

Nicholas and his wife Perenelle have survived for almost seven centuries, thanks to the elixir of life. Their secret lies within the pages of a powerful book, the book of Abraham the Mage – a secret that they must protect at all costs. In the wrong hands, the book would destroy the world.

As Dr John Dee well knows. Desperate for ultimate power, Dee and the Dark Elders will hunt for the book at all costs – and humanity won't know what has hit it until it's too late.

Only the mythical twins of legend have the power to stop Dr John Dee. Now, Nicholas and Perenelle must find them before Dee does. Suddenly, the lives of fifteen-year-old Josh and Sophie Newman are thrown into a whirlwind of dark magic and danger.

ASHES TO ASHES...

The battle in Ojai is over. Dr John Dee and the Dark Elders
have captured the legendary book of Abraham the Mage,
but two pages are missing. Without these pages,
they are powerless. With them, they would possess
the key to ultimate, terrifying domination.
The hunt resumes . . .

Sophie and Josh have fled to Paris. But with Dee and his
immortal ally Machiavelli in hot pursuit, they are far from safety.
And time is running out for Nicholas Flamel – for every day
he spends without the book, his body grows frailer,
his magic weaker.

*Their only chance is for Sophie to learn the second elemental magic:
fire magic. Can they save the world? Or will they destroy
one another first?*

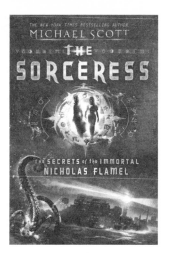

Darkness approaches...

*D*r. John Dee has destroyed Paris in his mission to find
Nicholas Flamel and Josh and Sophie Newman. The twins still
have the missing pages of the book of Abraham the Mage and
the Dark Elders need these for the Final Summoning which
will herald the destruction of the human race.

Nicholas Flamel knows he must protect Josh and Sophie but he
grows older and weaker every day. His only hope is the power
of Clarent – twin sword to Excalibur. But Clarent's power comes
at great cost – it is almost impossible to wield the blade
without its evil seeping into the soul . . .

What price must be paid to protect the twins
and defeat the Dark Elders?

TRUST NO ONE . . .

*J*osh and Sophie Newman have finally made it home – but
San Francisco is no longer a safe haven for the twins.
They have not yet mastered the magics they desperately
need for protection against the Dark Elders, and
Dr John Dee is still hunting them down. Worse still,
the twins are no longer sure if they can trust
Nicholas Flamel – or anyone.

Having failed to retrieve the missing pages of the Codex
for the Elders, Dee is now an outlaw – and the new prey
of all the creatures sent to hunt down Nicholas Flamel.
But Dee has a plan – to raise the Mother of the Gods from
the dead. For that, he must train a necromancer. And the
twins of legend will make the perfect pupils . . .